THE GHOST LOVERS DANCE

THE GHOST LOVERS DANCE

By

ARTEMUS ROOT

Dedicated to the memory of my mum Brenda.

She would have disapproved of the humour and bad language in this book. I can hear her voice clearly in my head—

"You were brought up better than that!"

1

Return to sender

Dating from the fifteenth century, Saint Mary's church lies at the heart of the sleepy English village of Little Takeham, where it has played a pivotal role in the residents' lives for hundreds of years. Unfortunately, over the last few decades, the newer generations had found no need for religion in their lives, so the ageing congregation was slowly drifting out of the pews and under the grass of the churchyard.

The vicar of Saint Mary's, fifty-four-year-old Nancy Dickens, had been assigned to the parish after an incident that ended with the previous incumbent having a full-size altar candle surgically removed from his rear orifice, requiring rather more than the power of prayer – in fact dozens of stitches – to return it to anything like its previous state. It was not so much what he did with the altar candle that upset the heads of the church; the problem was that he had been doing it in the vestry. Two elderly spinsters who had gone to arrange the church flowers found him there, bent over his desk with his trousers and pants around his ankles, screaming in agony and raving at the devil for leading him into temptation yet again.

Before being given her own parish, Nancy Dickens had come close to quitting her life as a preacher. Twenty years earlier, she had been full of religious zeal to help improve people's lives, but after years of being passed over for promotion by men, she was stuck in a rut of being a locum vicar for parish priests who were on holiday or on retreat. Her appointment at Saint Mary's changed all that. The truth was that no man wanted the job there because of the candle episode, so the bishop, who secretly thought women in the church should either be nuns or cleaning it, made her an offer she could not refuse, and she arrived in the parish of Saint Mary's, with its dwindling congregation.

On this particular July afternoon, Reverend Nancy Dickens was standing outside the large oak doors of the church in her 'God clothes', as she called them, a white surplice over a black cassock with the obligatory clerical collar. With her worn Bible in her hands, she waited impatiently for the elaborate horse-drawn hearse to crunch its way up the newly laid shingle on the church drive. The sheer weight of the coffin had driven the narrow wheels of the hearse deep into the gravel, and the power of the two feather-plumed horses was now augmented by the six black-suited pall-bearers pushing the hearse with all their might. The problem was not just the size of occupant, who was no lightweight, but the coffin itself, which was a replica of the one Elvis Presley had been buried in. The occupier had been obsessed with Elvis and had bought the *Return to Sender* coffin on eBay, convinced by its certificate of authenticity, which read, *The Elvis coffin, as recommended by the late King of Rock'n'Roll!*

Reverend Nancy glanced at her watch and muttered, 'Bollocks.' The horse she was really interested in was the hot racing tip she had been given in the pub at lunchtime by somebody who knew someone who had a brother who part-owned the dead cert that was running later that day. Despite it being a sure thing, she was told to expect odds of twenty to one. As her credit card was maxed out, a short-term loan from this year's collection-plate takings was necessary to furnish her with the fifty pounds burning a hole in her pocket. But before Reverend Nancy could dash down to the local bookmaker's to put her wager on, there was this women's funeral to get through.

The female funeral director, whose name was Mary, hurried towards her. She was short, in her mid-forties and with a waistline that had seen too many wake buffets. Dressed in black Edwardian clothes, accessorised with a veiled top hat and an ebony cane, she gasped, 'Sorry, vicar, the bloody thing's just not budging.'

'Jesus Christ!' sighed Reverend Nancy under her breath, checking her watch again. 'Well, you'll have to trolley the coffin in from there!'

When a coffin was too big or heavy for pall-bearers to lift, it was slipped on to a discreet trolley. Mary rushed back to her sweating colleagues, still heaving at the hearse, and informed them that the vicar had said the trolley was to be deployed.

The disgruntled pall-bearers managed to slide the weighty Elvis coffin out of the hearse on to the hastily positioned trolley. Now free of its burden, the empty hearse was pulled clear by the grateful horses. The bearers soon found they had another problem, though, as the trolley's wheels immediately sank into the shingle, and the coffin remained impossible to move up the drive.

Mary hurried back to the vicar. 'The bloody trolley's stuck now.'

'Christ on a tree trunk!' moaned Reverend Nancy. She checked her watch yet again; the funeral was ten minutes behind time already. 'You'll have to carry the coffin in from there. I do have an important appointment to keep, so please hurry up.'

Mary rushed back to the bearers and relayed what the vicar had said. The pall-bearers expressed their dismay, with mutterings along the lines of, 'You must be fucking joking, it's far too heavy!'

The pall-bearers had already strained every sinew in the brief time it had taken to lift the coffin out of the hearse. Now, with an effort so great that their buttocks clenched more tightly than a male ballroom dancer's, they took the huge coffin by its handles while Mary folded down the wheels beneath it.

'My handle's coming loose,' warned one of the pall-bearers. The most experienced of their number, known as coffin carrier number one, said, 'Get it on our shoulders before it's too late!'

With hernias popping out like champagne corks and sciatica spreading like a virus, they managed to shoulder the coffin. Whimpering in pain, they staggered faster and faster towards the church, propelled by the momentum of the heavy weight. Reverend Nancy had to leap out of the way as coffin carrier number one shouted, 'We can't stop! Get the trestles ready!'

Mary rushed into the church and hurriedly set up the wooden supports stored beside the pipe organ. She began to panic as the grimacing bearers tottered towards her, with coffin carrier number one begging her to, 'Hurry up!'

'All set up!' shouted Mary, and within seconds, the weighty Elvis coffin was dropped on to the wooden trestles. They groaned under the stress, but did not collapse, unlike the coffin bearers who crumpled to the stone floor, still whimpering and grimacing in pain.

4

To Reverend Nancy's increasing annoyance, there was a further five-minute delay before she could start while the mourners took their seats. There where twenty or so people, mainly elderly, spread out over the hundred available seats. She knew from experience that swivelling her head from one side to the other to address them all would give her neck ache. Why couldn't the bastards sit near each other? In the front pews sat Beryl's sons, Elvis and Aaron. The twin brothers were mid-fifties in years, with waistlines in the mid-fifties in inches to match. Sitting alongside them were their equally rotund wives and teenage children.

Reverend Nancy did a quick mental time check. Five minutes for the introduction, six minutes for the hymns, say some nice things about the dead person – call that another five minutes, a eulogy, sum up and mention God, job done. Twenty-five minutes should do it, plus another ten for shoving the coffin in the ground. Once that was all done, she could nip down to the bookmaker's.

Happy that she would still have time to spare, Reverend Nancy climbed into the pulpit and began the funeral proceedings for the late Beryl Buckler, only to be distracted by a latecomer who crept in and sat at the back. 'Who arrives late at a funeral?' she wondered, giving the person a disapproving stare.

After briefly welcoming the mourners, Reverend Nancy began to recite the same funeral script she had been using for years. All she had to do was change the name. Once she had done the welcome and reminded herself who was dead, she invited one of Beryl's chubby teenage grandsons to read a verse from the Bible. 'Is he dyslexic or just thick as shit?' thought Reverend Nancy as he struggled with the word *resurrection*, eventually saying, 'I am the re-erection.'. After the torture of the reading, she glanced at her notes and saw that the first hymn was *Abide With Me*. She hated that bloody dreary old tune and wondered why people even bothered choosing hymns for their loved ones' funerals when the bastards never made an effort to sing them. Any attempt at singing was usually left to her and whichever funeral director happened to be on duty. Once she and Mary had given up on the dirge, Reverend Nancy went back to her memorised script.

'I never knew…' Reverend Nancy had forgotten the dead person's name already and checked her notes. 'I never knew Beryl,' she said, faking a touch of emotion. 'But if I had, she would most certainly have been my best friend.' That always won the family over. 'When you lose a would-have-been best friend like Beryl, you ask, "Why, God? Why did you let my would-have-been best friend die so young?"' Spotting some confused faces, Reverend Nancy checked her notes again. 'I mean "let her die in the prime of her later years".' She paused to show she was almost overwhelmed with emotion and blew her nose for added effect. 'But my would-have-been best friend Meryl – I mean Beryl – is not dead. She is in God's special place for special people… heaven.'

Reverend Nancy felt pleased with her stirring words; Beryl's twin sons were already sobbing and being consoled by their partners. It always gave her job satisfaction to see people crying their eyes out.

The eulogy was to be read by Beryl's 80-year-old brother Jethro, who tottered towards the pulpit on his walking frame at a top speed of one step every five seconds. Losing patience, Reverend Nancy rushed over, gently said, 'Let me help you' and basically dragged him up to the front. When Jethro began slowly reading the eulogy from a piece of paper, Reverend Nancy's verdict was decisive: 'This yokel's not dyslexic, he is just thick as shit.' He painstakingly read

6

out a series of dates from Beryl's life in a monotone. He gave the date of her birth, the day she started school, the date of her first job, the date of her engagement, her marriage and every other major date, right through to the day she died.

'What lovely words, Jethro,' lied Reverend Nancy when he finally finished. 'Very informative.' Jethro started his slow trek back to his seat. By now, Reverend Nancy had concluded that Beryl would not have been her best friend. In fact, she hated Beryl and her bloody family. Her hopes of getting the funeral finished reasonably quickly took another blow when a grief-stricken Elvis began wailing, 'Mummy, please don't die!'

His twin brother, Aaron, soon joined in. 'Don't go, Mummy,' he sobbed, in an effort to out-blub his brother.

Reverend Nancy had met the twin brothers briefly to discuss the funeral a week earlier and decided there and then that they were both first-degree idiots. A glance at her watch confirmed that, thanks to the stupid coffin, Beryl's thick-as-shit brother and the dopey grandson, she was now a good twenty minutes behind schedule. She rushed through the commendation, but as soon as she said, 'Amen', Elvis decided to throw himself on top of Beryl's coffin and started knocking on the lid like it was a door. 'Wake up, Mummy, wake up!'

Reverend Nancy spotted Mary running up the aisle, screaming, 'It won't take the weight! It won't take the weight!' just as Aaron chose to throw himself on the Elvis coffin as well.

The sound of wood cracking echoed off the church walls. One trestle had broken, leaving Beryl's coffin at a forty-five-degree angle. Elvis and Aaron had been dumped face down on the ancient flagstones with several wreaths on top of them. The loud noise alerted the pall-bearers, who were outside nursing their injuries. Coffin carrier number one limped in first, took in what had happened and muttered, 'Shit, shit, shit!' before rushing to help Mary. He was promptly followed by his pall-bearing colleagues, all muttering similar expletives as they too rushed to put Beryl's Elvis coffin upright. While Mary's team strained to bring Beryl level, the vicar hurried to find another trestle. Coffin carrier number one exclaimed, 'No, no, no!' as two of Elvis's podgy sons and Aaron's similarly obese son and daughter were so overcome with grief that they decided it was their turn to throw themselves on Beryl's coffin, with much sobbing and cries of, 'Nana, don't die!'

'I don't get paid enough for this!' screamed one of the pall-bearers, as he and his colleagues lost the battle to keep Beryl level under the mass of blubbering blubbery bodies.

With half the pall-bearers now trapped under the coffin, Reverend Nancy had no choice but to call the local fire service and beg them to bring heavy lifting equipment. Ten minutes later, ten firefighters freed the pall-bearers. An ambulance had also been called, which was just as well, because coffin carrier number one needed urgent treatment for a crushed left leg.

With the help of all ten firefighters, the pall-bearers who could walk took the coffin out into the churchyard and heaved it over to a section for newly dead arrivals. Reverend Nancy rushed through the committal. The Elvis coffin looked like it would just manage to squeeze into the standard-width hole, but halfway down, it became stuck. Fortunately, a grief-stricken, sobbing Elvis decided to prostrate himself on his mother's coffin again, which helped it to drop several inches.

'I want to be buried with Mummy!' he pleaded.

Distraught, Aaron climbed down to join his brother, which pushed the coffin a bit further down. 'Bury me as well,' he sobbed.

Elvis Buckley's wife could not bear to live without her loving husband, so she clambered down, begging to be buried alongside him. Aaron's wife was fucked if she was going to be outdone by her sister-in-law, so she not only declared that she wanted to be buried alive, but insisted that her kids wanted to be buried alive as well, so they all jumped down into the grave. With all the extra weight, the coffin finally dropped to the bottom.

The firefighters dragged Beryl's family out of her grave one by one, but it was another twenty minutes before Reverend Nancy could do her *ashes to ashes* reading, throw dirt on to the coffin and finally bring the funeral service from hell to an end. She checked her watch: she had missed the horse race by minutes.

Forty-five minutes later, Reverend Nancy was in the church hall kitchen, cracking open another bottle of red wine, when the part-time gravediggers Stan and Cynthia joined her.

'All filled in and six feet under, vicar,' said Cynthia.

'Thank God for that.'

'You're hitting the vino an hour earlier than normal,' said Stan, picking up a chipped mug from the sink and holding it out to be filled.

Nancy topped up the communion chalice she was drinking from before filling Stan's mug. 'Twenty-five to one! That's what price that horse came in at.' She took a long swig of wine. 'God, it's so unfair. I could have done with that money.'

'Didn't you preach about the sin of gambling recently?' said Cynthia, searching for a spare mug.

'When you get tipped off about a dead certainty, it's not gambling, so it's not a sin.'

Cynthia found a mug, rinsed it under the cold tap and held it out for the vicar to fill up. 'Never mind, there's always a next time.'

Reverend Nancy filled Cynthia's mug, knocked back the wine left in her chalice and said, 'God, I need a cigarette.' Unsure whether Stan had heard her, she said it again. 'God, I could do with a cigarette.'

Stan had heard her the first time. The vicar was always cadging cigarettes off him, and she had not bought a packet in months. But under her gaze, Stan's resolve wilted, and he offered her his cigarette packet.

'Oh, go on then, Stan, just the one. Thank you.' She took one and waited for Stan to light it. 'I'll be outside if you need me.' Staggering slightly as the wine took effect, she headed out of the side door that overlooked the churchyard. She sucked cigarette smoke deep into her lungs and let it out slowly, muttering, 'Twenty-five to one.'

Reverend Nancy took another lungful of smoke and peered out over the churchyard. Low black clouds had dimmed the afternoon light considerably. A thick ground mist had begun to appear, which was not that unusual because there was a stream babbling not far away. What was unusual was the misty shape between the two large yew trees. It was floating above the rest of the mist that covered the ground. Reverend Nancy wondered if it was the effect of the wine and cigarette smoke or maybe the fresh air, but to her astonishment, the strange misty shape morphed into two misty shapes.

10

Stan and Cynthia joined the vicar outside, hoping to persuade her to open another bottle of wine. Reverend Nancy shushed them with one finger on her lips and pointed with her other hand towards the strange misty shapes that were now spinning around each other. The local crows fell silent, as if they sensed something, and a faint hum that sounded like a waltz was the only sound to be heard.

Cynthia had lived in the village her whole life and knew all the local tales and folklore. As a child, she had been told that the churchyard was haunted by the ghost lovers: a couple who had tragically died in a stagecoach accident close by. It was a rite of passage for the local children to run through the churchyard at night to prove their bravery.

'The ghost lovers!' exclaimed Cynthia, more loudly than she had intended.

The misty shapes stopped moving and promptly disappeared, leaving the three onlookers open-mouthed.

'Wait till I tell the village about this!' said Cynthia, with a beaming smile.

2

Tuppence

Tuppence Crow had known from a very early age that she was special. Her multimillionaire father had told her so, as had her nanny, the servants and anyone else employed by Daddy. Tuppence believed wholeheartedly that she had been put on God's earth to brighten ordinary people's lives with her specialness. She knew it must be true because ever since she had first been able to walk and talk, ordinary people, or 'scum' as her father called them, had told her she was special and had pandered to her every whim. The fact that they were being paid to do so had never occurred to her at all.

Being the only child of a successful businessman had given Tuppence a lifestyle that others could only dream of, and if that was not enough, she had also been blessed with extraordinary natural beauty. Her timeless, classic attractiveness was of the kind that had been depicted in works of art for centuries. Through attending the best private schools in Europe, she had easily become friends with the sons and daughters of politicians, the even-more-extremely wealthy and royalty.

Tuppence's had her belief that she was special confirmed when she appeared in a TV documentary series about the English tradition of debutantes being introduced into London society. Out of all of the young women featured in the series, it was Tuppence who received the most attention, at least partly because of her willingness to share her belief that she was better than anyone else.

The programme's producers and director then asked her to star in a new reality TV show called *Young, Rich and Beautiful*. The premise was simple: Tuppence just went about her normal life for six months with a camera crew following her around. It became apparent very quickly that Tuppence was incredibly vain and dull. Despite her expensive education, Tuppence was, in the words of the director in an unguarded moment, 'as dumb as a waxwork dummy' when it came to having any idea about what went on in the real world. It soon became clear that endless trips to buy designer clothes or order salad in expensive restaurants were going to make for a boring show. Tuppence had no personality and no sense of humour. The producers' answer was to give her a hidden earpiece, so a team of scriptwriters could tell her what to say. The contrast between Tuppence's blank expression and the witty comments coming out of her mouth made the show a surprise hit.

Her meteoric rise to TV celebrity stardom was brought to a sudden halt after an aggrieved ex-employee of the reality TV production company leaked the revelation that every clever word coming out of Tuppence's mouth was scripted. To respond to the accusations, she appeared on a popular daytime TV show and dismissed the allegations as vile and bogus, with the help of a team of scriptwriters talking to her through her concealed earpiece of course. Unfortunately, Tuppence had a habit of demanding that employees of the production company should be dismissed if she felt they sullied her field of vision by being ugly. Consequently, another aggrieved ex-employee revealed that, throughout her daytime TV denial, Tuppence had again been wearing an earpiece. The ratings for *Young, Rich and Beautiful* plummeted and she became a laughing stock.

Despite having the security of knowing that she need not work a day in her life, just being wealthy was tedious for Tuppence. After all, she had been rich her whole life, so it meant nothing to her. But having briefly tasted fame, she wanted more. Being recognised and talked about in whispers when she walked into a room delighted her. It confirmed what she had always been told: she was indeed very special. When the excited whispers of recognition turned to mocking smirks and giggles, Tuppence did what she always did when she wanted something. She went to Daddy to fix it for her and told him in no uncertain terms that she wanted to be a famous celebrity no matter what it took, and if he didn't make it happen, she would hate him forever.

3

Gus

Forty-three-year-old American Gus Shaver had a reputation for not just thinking outside the box, but thinking outside the outside of the box and with blue-sky thinking to boot. Over the last decade, he had worked with the great and the good. In fact, the reason they were the great and the good was because he had made them the great and the good. Gus was not just one of America's top media manipulators, he was without doubt the best. Gus could take the most corrupt politician and make them look generous and saintly in the public's eyes. Over the years, he had built a reputation for manipulating the facts, and especially the media, that was unsurpassed; if you were fortunate enough, or in truth rich enough, to be able to use his services, you could pretty much get away with anything.

However, several months ago, Gus's illustrious career had hit a brick wall when he had been caught with his pants around his ankles in a park's public toilet cubicle. In that setting, having his pants around his ankles was not unusual in itself, but Gus had inserted his penis into a glory hole that had just been drilled out by a keen DIY pervert in the next cubicle. The holes that Gus had stuck his knob in during earlier visits had been filled by the park's maintenance team, who likened the job of filling the holes to painting the Golden Gate Bridge: never-ending. Unfortunately for Gus, on this occasion, the freshly drilled glory hole was slightly smaller than the girth of his erection, and once he had squeezed his knob into the hole right up to the hilt, there was no way of pulling it back out again without causing serious damage. Gus's whispered pleas for help from the keen DIY pervert in the next cubicle, who was enjoying the fruits of his labours, had fallen on deaf ears, because the keen DIY pervert was actually deaf. The more Gus had pulled at his throbbing member, the more swollen and thus more wedged it had become.

An elderly cleaning lady had found him four hours later. By that time, his knob had been three times its usual size, and he had begged for help, promising the woman vast sums of money if she would rescue him. Being a devout Christian, the cleaner had called him a sodomite and a servant of the devil before swinging her bucket at his bloated member and calling the police to arrest the sinner. The police had arrived, fallen about laughing and called the local fire station. Word had rapidly spread around the emergency services that a man was wedged in a glory hole, and within twenty minutes, numerous ambulances, fire engines and police cars had turned up to take a look. The press had followed not long after, having heard the gossip on the emergency services radio wavelengths. Gus had then been caught on video being stretchered out of the public toilet with a large cut-out section of cubicle wall on top of him. A firefighter had placed his helmet over the swelling to prevent public offence, but when offered a sum of money by the press, who had recognised the media manipulator, he had happily removed it. The pictures had gone viral on social media, and no matter how hard Gus had tried to spin a story about losing his balance when trying to pull his pants up and accidentally finding his penis in the hole, he was now known by everyone in every state as Glory-Hole Gus.

With his career in tatters, Gus had had no choice but to leave the country. His destination had been decided when he received a request for his services from the United Kingdom. A middle-aged politician in England had been caught using the services of a rent-boy delivery service while staying at a top London hotel. He had paid for two young Thai men to come to his room at two in the morning. One of the young men had shot a video on his phone that showed the naked politician sniffing coke from the other young man's buttocks, which was damning. Gus had spotted an opportunity to get away from all the gossip about himself, and within days, he was in London, coming up with a plan to manipulate the evidence in the politician's case.

The politician's name was Giles Mayfair. He was married with two grown-up children and had been elected because of his views on immigration (which he said was ruining the country he loved), and same-sex marriage (which he bitterly opposed as an abomination in the eyes of God).

Gus had an idea after reading an article in an in-flight magazine about sumo wrestling. He instructed Giles to buy as many books on Japan as he could, and to have his photograph taken with his wife and children wearing kimonos. Two days later, Gus arranged, by way of a well-placed bribe, for a journalist to do an exclusive interview with Giles Mayfair at the MP's north London home. Giles was accompanied by his kimono-wearing wife, numerous coffee-table books about Japan were scattered around the room, and photographs of him and his family wearing kimonos filled the walls.

Giles explained to the journalist that he was investigating illegal immigration and wanted to find out first-hand about the trials young men faced when they fell victim to sex traffickers. The young men he had contacted voluntarily removed their clothes to show him the scars they had from beatings by their evil pimps. When asked to explain why he was naked and snorting cocaine from the buttocks of one of the young men, Giles stuck to the story he had rehearsed with Gus.

'Video footage can be deceiving. The young men were incredibly grateful for my concern about their well-being, and said to me, "Please, sir, you are so unselfish and willing to help us, we no longer feel alone and vulnerable. How can we poor mature Thai men, not boys, repay your kindness?" Of course, I said to them that thanks are not needed for common decency, and that I have a soft spot for the Asian community because of my love of Japan. The young men, who in fact were a lot older than they looked, had studied Japanese culture back in Thailand and were themselves admirers of the country. We spoke for some time, and they both complimented me on my vast knowledge of Japan. It was at that moment… With hindsight, I should have stopped enthusing about that ancient culture and mentioned that I did not fully understand the rules of sumo wrestling. Before I knew it, their little faces lit up. They asked if I had salt in the room, which the hotel did have in sachets, and sprinkled it on the carpet to ward off evil spirits like they do in Japan. They then demonstrated the noble art of sumo by taking all their clothes off and grappling on the carpet. I was still not one hundred percent sure of a move they called *Yori-Kiri*, so they said the best way to learn was to actually do the move and out of respect for the ancient sport, I must remove all my clothes, which, in seeking knowledge, I did in all innocence. The incident you refer to as "snorting" was in fact me helping the young man by blowing salt away from the lesions he'd received from the cruel sex traffickers. The poor little chap had fallen badly on the carpet which was covered in ceremonial salt. It was all very innocent.'

'Is it true the that the young men have been deported?' asked the journalist, earning his bribe by following the script Gus had given him.

'Alas, it is true. The mature men were unfortunately sent back, which is a shame because they would have backed up my story one hundred percent.'

'What is your opinion of the newspaper that printed the original story?'

'Gutter journalism and fake news!' declared Giles. 'It's outrageous that I, a democratically elected Member of Parliament, have to take time away from my public duties to deny these ludicrous accusations.'

Despite the sizeable incentive he had received, the journalist rolled his eyes when he saw what he had to say next. 'Giles Mayfair, please accept my sincere apologies on behalf of the British press for printing lies about you.'

Giles's bottom lip trembled with feigned emotion. 'I can't say I'm not tempted to sue that slanderous newspaper for printing the story, but your apology on behalf of the great British press and my desire to get back to work and faithfully serve my constituents have stopped me from wasting any more of my valuable time. Thank you for letting me tell the true story.' Giles posed for photographs with his kimono-clad wife, who smiled through gritted teeth and blinked back any threat of tears.

After the interview was printed, a number of prominent newspapers ran the headline *Innocent!* and attacked the undercover investigation as deplorable. Coincidentally, all of these papers were owned by Richard Crow, also known as Daddy. He was so impressed by the way Gus Shaver had twisted a story that was true and backed up by evidence that he offered the American spinmeister the job of helping his daughter Tuppence become a famous celebrity.

Gus viewed the Tuppence task as a tough challenge, but if he could succeed, he would become indispensable to one of the wealthiest men in the country, so within a day of receiving the details, he sat and watched the reality series that had made Tuppence Crow a minor celebrity. Why the public would take to such an arrogant and vain young woman was beyond him, but then again, the British were a strange bunch. As far as Gus was concerned, *Young, Rich and Beautiful* was obviously scripted, and he easily spotted her eyes going blank every time lines were given to her through her hidden earpiece. She was definitely not a natural actor, but she was pretty, and that was always a plus. Before meeting Tuppence, Gus warned Richard that she would have to do exactly as he told her, and if that was going to be a problem then he would rather not accept the assignment. Richard Crow assured him that he would make it clear to his daughter that she must do as she was told or lose her monthly allowance.

Gus's first meeting with Tuppence was to take place at Crow Tower, a luxury hotel and apartment building in a prime position beside the River Thames, where Tuppence had a penthouse suite. Gus found himself sitting around for two hours in the reception area before she made an appearance. When she did amble into the building, laden with designer shopping bags, Gus informed her that he been waiting and that they had had an appointment.

Tuppence beckoned one of the hotel staff over and handed them the bags. She glanced coldly at Gus. 'You'll wait as long it takes because you work for my father. And that means you work for me.'

Gus shook his head in despair and walked out.

Tuppence was straight on the phone, demanding her father sack Gus for disrespecting her. Richard reminded his daughter that unless she listened to Gus's advice, he would not be funding her any longer. Another meeting was arranged. Once more, Gus waited at reception. When Tuppence turned up fifteen minutes late, Gus quietly informed her, 'You're late,' then walked out on her again.

Tuppence shouted after him, 'Your fired! No one walks out on Tuppence Crow!'

One week later, with her bank account overdrawn and not even a mention on social media or in the tabloid news, Tuppence pleaded with her father for another meeting with Gus. This time, she was waiting in her apartment for him.

'I'm only going along with this because I have no money,' she informed him as soon as he strolled in.

'It makes no difference to me,' said Gus. 'Your father asked if I could help make you a famous celebrity and I said I could, but if you don't need my help, I'll go.' Gus hoped that his bluff would work.

'I'm already famous,' sneered Tuppence. 'I was voted the most popular reality TV celebrity in two magazines, so fuck you!'

Gus had some figures prepared on a notepad. He referred to them. 'The two magazines in question have a combined readership of thirty thousand, mainly young single women. They are hardly big numbers. Do as I say, and in a few months, I'll make you the most talked-about celebrity in the country.'

This piqued Tuppence's curiosity. 'How would you do that?'

'The first part of my plan is to get you a role in a TV commercial for a perfume house.'

Tuppence scoffed, 'A TV commercial for a perfume?! This is what my father pays you, for is it? Well, it's not good enough.'

'It's not just any old perfume, it's for *Femme Crédule*.'

Tuppence was well aware of the brand *Femme Crédule*. It was the most expensive perfume in the world. Even her father commented on the price when she demanded it for her birthday and at Christmas. 'That would be a good idea!' enthused Tuppence. She was wise and vain enough to know that being in a TV advert for such a brand was an amazing opportunity.

Gus smiled inwardly. He had known that would appeal to her vanity. It had taken a combination of blackmail and bribery to get her the part, but fortunately Richard Crow was happy to pay whatever was needed. 'The director is the BAFTA nominee Sheena Grunt.'

Tuppence had no idea who Sheena Grunt was, but if she had been nominated for a BAFTA, that was good enough. 'Okay,' conceded Tuppence, 'I'll follow your advice.'

4

Tolly

It was fitting that Tolly Pipkin had been born under the water sign Pisces, because on the day he arrived in the world, clouds as black as night had been sending down torrents of rain for several hours with no sign of stopping. According to the Met Office weather report, it had officially been the area's wettest day on record, and as time passed, the local people referred to it as the *wet-wet day*.

The ambulance that had carried Tolly's mother, Mia, in the early hours of the *wet-wet day* had tried three different routes to the hospital, but had had to divert each time because flooding had made the roads impassable. Anika, the paramedic who had been driving, knew the area well, but she was quickly running out of options. The screams of pain from the young woman in the rear had not helped, nor had her colleague's shouts of, 'We're losing her!'

Taking a gamble, she had headed the wrong way up a narrow one-way street that was a foot deep in water and prayed nothing was coming the other way or, even worse, had broken down. It had been a nail-biting slow drive, but luckily the road had been clear.

Gabrielle, the paramedic in the rear, had done all she could to help Mia, but the pregnant woman had still been in considerable pain and distress. The baby had not been due for another two weeks and something had clearly been wrong. By the time the ambulance had finally screeched to a halt outside the hospital, Mia's waters had broken, and she had fallen silent and lifeless.

The paramedics, who were hardened and cynical from dealing with death and pain on a daily basis, had shed tears as the doctors took over and whisked the young woman away. They had cried because they were near the end of their shift, and if the patient had died in transit, the paperwork was going to take hours. When the news had reached them twenty minutes later that the young woman had actually died in the hospital while giving birth to a boy, they had cried tears of relief.

It had been a *wet-wet day* in all kinds of ways when Tolly Pipkin had been born.

Now, at the age of twenty-four, Tolly was struggling to get his foot in the door of the theatre world despite having a performing arts degree. For two years, he had been auditioning for parts along with all his equally desperate peers, and had met with nothing but rejection. He had been told from the very start that this was part of the business, but he still found it hard to take and had begun to give up hope of finding any acting work. One day, he was wondering again whether he was really suited to such an uncertain lifestyle when his agent, Suzanne, called him out of the blue with some good news. There was a non-speaking part in a TV advert if he wanted it. Suzanne knew the casting director who just needed someone of his age. Tolly grabbed the chance of work with both hands. After years of rejection, he did not really care if it was not proper acting work, or that it was with a minor reality TV celebrity.

A few days later, he was one of six extras in the costume department of a TV studio, wearing tight white skimpy shorts and a tee shirt. No matter what strings Suzanne had had to pull to get him the job as an extra in the *Femme Crédule* advert, and even after two years of constant rejection, he would have thought twice about doing it if he had known what he would have to wear.

The director and the perfume house's artistic director made the extras stand in a row, so they could decide in which order they would appear in front of the camera. Each young man was given a number to indicate his place in the line-up. It was no surprise to Tolly that he found himself one from the end at number five.

Tolly and the five other young men were to throw themselves down at the feet of reality TV celebrity Tuppence Crow, so she could use them as stepping stones. They would save her from getting her shoes wet in a gold puddle, which would be magically computer generated and added later.

Tolly had only ever seen one episode of the show Tuppence Crow starred in and vowed never to watch another. It was so badly scripted that, at first, he had thought it was a comedy. In spite of hating the show and all the rich twats in it, he was surprised by how naturally pretty Tuppence was in the flesh, despite the ton of make-up she was wearing. Though she looked beautiful and swanlike when she was still, her walk, with stupidly high eight inch platform heels, was undeniably more ducklike. In fact, she struggled to keep her balance whenever she had to do something as simple as putting two steps together. It was now day three, and Tolly's face ached from smiling. His knees hurt like hell from throwing himself on the floor, only for Tuppence's awkwardness to ruin take after take.

On yet another take, Tuppence lost her footing and trod on Tolly's knee, causing him extreme pain. Rather than apologise, she stared down at him accusingly, as if it were his own fault. 'No apology necessary,' winced Tolly with a touch of sarcasm. Bafta-nominated director Sheena Grunt was not quite as generous as Tuppence, and told Tolly that if he got trodden on again, he would be sacked for not lying on the floor properly. Luckily for him, Tuppence managed to stomp on the other five young men, who must have been lying awkwardly as well.

During the shoot, Tuppence kept to her dressing room and had meals brought to her from an upmarket restaurant rather than eat from the catering vans that supplied the crew and extras with endless drinks and snacks. However, by day three of the shoot, she was bored of looking at the same four walls of her RV and opted to eat her restaurant salad outside at one of the bench tables beside the catering van.

Tolly was sitting at a table with the other five young men who threw themselves under Tuppence. The rest of the group were unworried about how long the filming was taking because their agents had arranged a generous day rate. Tolly was the only one who was slightly pissed off because Suzanne had negotiated a one-off fee that meant he was getting poorer by the day.

'If she treads on my face and smudges my make-up once more,' declared young man number two, 'I'm going to say something. I will, I mean it.'

Young man number four nodded. 'I felt grit go into my pores, it wouldn't surprise me if I came out in spots. If you do say something, I'm right behind you.'

Tolly had heard nothing but whingeing from most of his fellow actors. They were all slightly camp apart from number six, whose name was Barry. He came from Sheffield and was determined to keep his northern accent and stay true to his heritage.

Barry shook his head at his fellow extras. 'My granddad was lucky to get a job down the pit, and you're moaning about smudged make-up. Ha, you don't know how tough life can be.' Barry never mentioned that his father drove a taxi for a living because he was afraid of hard physical work.

'Oh, listen to Sean Bean,' jeered young man number one. 'It's all right for him and number five, they don't have good looks to lose. My face will be my fortune.'

Tolly was a bit put out by that comment. True, the first four had looks that would really wow people, but he was hardly ugly, only normal-looking. Still, that would explain why he was at the back.

Young man number three had sussed out that the numbering order had been based on looks and was convinced that he should be at the front in the number one spot. 'Some people aren't as photogenic as they think,' he snidely remarked, staring at number one. 'And when you have a big nose, they shouldn't put you close to the camera. You might knock it over.' Three and one had history, having been to the same performing arts college and developed mutual contempt over the years.

Number one had a complex about the size of his nose and had confided in number three when they had first started college. 'Well, they probably don't want someone with a lazy eye staring at the camera.'

Number three had confessed to being born with a lazy eye and was paranoid that it would come back. Not to be outdone, number three said, 'If some people were as good-looking as they think they are, they wouldn't have to suck off the artistic director to be at the front.'

Before number one could deny this vile allegation, even if it was true, Tuppence strolled over in search of a compliment to boost her ego, and said, 'It's hard to keep my balance in these shoes. Did I hurt any of you?'

'No, no, no,' giggled number two.

'You can tread on me as much as you like,' joked number four.

'You're doing very well,' number three assured her. 'You've done well not to step on anyone's nose, considering the size of some.'

'You must have good eyesight, Tuppence,' said number one, staring down number three. 'Someone with a lazy eye would have stamped all over us.'

Tuppence turned to Barry. 'I stepped on your neck earlier. Did it hurt?'

Barry put his shoulders back and in his broad northern accent said, 'I come from a family that had police kicking them in the head on a picket line. So, no, it didn't hurt.'

Tuppence looked baffled. 'Sorry, I didn't catch a word of that.' She looked around at the other young men for help. They shrugged.

'He said it didn't hurt,' translated Tolly.

'What about you?' asked Tuppence, looking down her nose at Tolly. 'I always seem to end up treading on your knees. Did it hurt?'

'Yes, it did,' snapped Tolly. 'It felt like you were stamping on them with hobnailed boots on.'

Tuppence's smile froze on her face at this unexpected answer.

When Tolly did not get the laugh he had been anticipating, he said, 'I'm joking. It didn't hurt that much.'

Tuppence suddenly screamed with laughter. The young men immediately joined in, hoping to get in her good books.

Tolly did not think it was that funny, but he shrugged and smiled.

Tuppence kept giggling for a lot longer than Tolly thought was necessary.

'That is so, so amusing,' tittered Tuppence. 'What did you say it felt like… What number are you again?'

'I'm number five,' replied Tolly with a smile. 'I said it felt like you were stamping on my knees with hobnailed boots on.'

Tuppence screamed with laughter again, then ambled back to her table, still giggling.

'That was odd,' said Barry.

'That was odd,' repeated number three, who had not understand a word Barry had just said.

'She's probably so used to sycophants,' guessed Tolly, 'she thought it was a refreshing change to have some jokey banter with someone.'

'She's having a joke with the director now,' remarked number one, who had a good view from his seat. 'You lucky bastard, the director's looking over at you.'

Tolly wondered if this could give him the break he wanted. Having a BAFTA-nominated director knowing who you were must be priceless.

'She's coming over,' whispered number one. 'She's laughing.'

Sheena Grunt was still chuckling when she reached the extras' table. 'Which one of you is number five?'

Tolly slowly raised his hand. 'I'm young man number five, Tolly Pipkin.'

'Well, Tolly Pipkin,' chuckled Sheena, and her face suddenly turned deadly serious, 'you're sacked. Get your things and get off my set.'

Tolly was lost for words for a few seconds, then managed to say, 'What for?'

'For insulting the star. Now, get out.'

Tolly felt numb at the injustice. This feeling quickly turned to rage, and he limped over to Tuppence, who was now standing outside her giant RV.

'You bitch! I needed this job, and just because you're a spoiled brat and can't take a joke, I've been sacked. Oh, and another thing, I've seen wooden puppets walk with more grace than you!' Tolly started to limp away but could not stop himself from aiming one more outburst at Tuppence. 'You're clumsy as fuck and your feet smell.'

The next day in his agent's office, Tolly explained what had happened, concluding by saying, 'I told her straight. She's a bitch and her feet are smelly.'

Tolly's agent, Suzanne Fisher, had been in the business for forty years. Her early dreams of having A-list movie stars or leading theatre actors as clients had slipped away over the decades like sand through an hourglass. Now in her mid-sixties with two ex-husbands to support, she was disillusioned and broke, and more parts of her body seemed to ache on a weekly basis. She now represented only bit-part actors whose huge egos were out of kilter with their meagre talent. Suzanne had seen Tolly in a play while he was still at college and had always hoped that, with a bit of luck, he would make it all the way to the top. He was a natural actor who could play any part, and she had secretly thought that if any of her clients had what it took to be a great, Tolly was the one, and when he did, she would use him as her pension. Now, his career was in tatters and so was her potential future income.

'You'll never work again,' sighed Suzanne, searching her desk drawer for an indigestion tablet to chew on.

Tolly was confused. 'Sorry, what do you mean by that?'

'You fucked up, Tolly. You are now unofficially blacklisted.'

'I don't understand. What does that mean?'

'It means your name is top of a list that's been circulated to every director and casting director in the business. You… are… fucked!'

Tolly was dumbstruck. 'Is it that easy to get blacklisted?'

'I've never had a client blacklisted in forty years, but you've managed it after a few days' work. Sorry, kid, no one will touch you now. I'll have to let you go. This is a ruthless business.'

Tolly stood in front of Suzanne's desk in shock. Could his career be over before it had even started? His eyes began to redden.

Suzanne's laptop beeped to indicate an email arriving. She read it while Tolly digested the devastating news. The email was from one of her ex-clients who had left acting due to a lack of talent and was now going to direct a play. She had managed to raise the finances for a theatre production that was to go on a month-long tour. Her requirements were extremely specific. She was after a male actor in his early twenties, willing to play the lead role as and when required. The actor would not receive any billing or credits, but would nevertheless be amply rewarded. Suzanne took a couple of minutes to get her head around all this. Then the penny dropped. 'Hold on, Tolly. There might just be a glimmer of light for you. Have you heard the movie term *body double*?'

'Of course, it's quite common to use someone else in shots where you can't see a face.'

'Give this some thought while you contemplate never working in this business again: would you like to take the lead role in a play under someone else's name?'

'No,' said Tolly immediately.

'Okay then,' declared Suzanne, 'you are no longer my client. Goodbye, have a great life, and shut the door on the way out.'

'Wait one sec,' begged Tolly. 'Explain to me properly what the role is.'

Suzanne reached for the phone on her desk. 'Because it's you, I'll get some clarification.' She pointed towards a worn armchair by the window. 'Grab a seat.'

Tolly slumped down in the armchair and stared down at the bustling street below. It was ten minutes before Suzanne put the phone down and turned to him.

'It seems my ex-client has raised all the money for the play with a small arts grant and backing from her stinking rich sister. Apparently, the funding is subject to the proviso that her sister's son plays the lead role.'

Tolly shrugged. 'Nepotism's common enough in this business. Why does he need a double?'

Suzanne smiled. 'You'll love this. He can't act. He's one of these spoiled little bastards who gets what he wants. All you need to do is play the part until he's ready to take over. After the rehearsals, just look it at it as a four-week, very well-paid holiday. It's a tour of small theatres, so no one will have a clue that you're acting under a different name. Hopefully, by the time the tour's over, your name will have fallen off the bottom of the unofficial blacklist.'

'In a way, it would be poetic justice,' mused Tolly. 'I got sacked because of one spoiled little bastard, so getting work because of another one feels right.'

'Good,' said Suzanne, printing off an address and some other important details. 'You still have to audition, but with a bit of luck, you'll get the part. Try not to fuck it up; this might just be your last chance.'

'You just ditched me a minute ago. Can I renegotiate a new contract?'

'Do you want the fucking audition or not?'

Tolly smiled. 'I was joking.'

Suzanne handed him the printout. 'No wonder you were blacklisted, your jokes are shit. Oh, by the way, make sure you're wearing a paisley silk scarf. It's become an essential part of the look for auditions recently.'

5

Zibby

Twenty-two-year-old Zibby had only been four weeks into the six-month run of her first professional engagement after leaving dance school when she had found herself out of work, along with the rest of the dance company, after the show she had been performing in, *East Side Story*, had been cancelled. This show had been, according to the copyright holders of *West Side Story*, a blatant rip off! The *East Side Story* producers had fervently protested their innocence. That their show had happened to be based on *Romeo and Juliet* and set in a city with gangs had been purely coincidental. Besides, the two lovers in *East Side Story*, Mary and Alan, did not die at the end; they were left in a coma, and the country was Canada. They denied that the songs from their show, which included, *Mary*, *You Look Pretty* and *I Love to Live in Canada*, had been anything like *West Side Story*'s songs. If some of the notes in the songs had happened to be in the same order, that had been, again, just pure coincidence, and they would fight their case in the highest court in the land! After a one-minute consultation with a copyright lawyer, the producers had promptly pulled the plug and cancelled the tour.

For Zibby, finding employment as a dancer had become difficult. The entire company had now been applying for the same few jobs available, and many of the dancers had had more experience than her. She had begun to feel disheartened by all the constant rejection at auditions. If it had not been for her friend Michelle's upbeat positivity, Zibby would probably have packed it all in.

Three weeks after losing her job in *East Side Story*, she was sharing a small apartment with Michelle, knowing that if they could not find any work, they would soon be homeless.

Zibby knew her parents had made sacrifices to help her career, and the thought of having to go home and live with them again made her determined to try every avenue to make a living from dance. But when Michelle found out about a Soho shop that wanted exotic dancers to perform in its small vintage theatre, Zibby at first dismissed this opportunity with mild amusement. However, the pay was good, the hours were short, and Michelle was even more keen to give any dance job a try because she was also broke, so Zibby reluctantly went along to give her moral support at the open auditions.

The Soho shop turned out to be a sex shop with the theatre adjoining. A billboard outside the shopfront advertised its world-famous erotic dance revue, which had been running since 1957 in Soho's oldest private theatre.

Inside the shop, Michelle and Zibby giggled as they ducked under the hundreds of dildos hanging from the ceiling, so they could follow the large luminous arrows pointing to *Babs' dance auditions*, which led them through to the small theatre. Despite it being attached to a sex shop, the luxurious theatre was a Victorian jewel that seated over a hundred people. Standing on the small stage holding a clipboard in one hand and a cigarette in the other was Babs, a slim, blonde-wigged woman in her fifties, who waved for Michelle and Zibby to join several other girls looking bored and apathetic as they waited in the front row.

'There's not that many girls here for the audition,' noted Michelle. 'My odds of getting a job are pretty good.'

Zibby cast her eye over some of the other women. They did not look that young, nor did they have the build of fit dancers. Michelle stepped up to the stage and gave the woman with the clipboard her name.

Babs peered at the young black woman in front of her, feeling envious of Michelle's youthful natural beauty. She added her name to the list. Babs turned to Michelle's friend, who was as pale as a vampire, but with freckles. 'What's your name, love?'

'I'm not auditioning, I'm just here to support my friend,' said Zibby.

Babs shrugged and turned to the rest of the auditionees. 'Listen up, ladies.' She took a drag on her cigarette. 'I want you to warm up, and when I call your name, step up here and give me an idea of what you can do. The number one priority is it has to be sexy as fuck. If you hear me say "next", then get your things and go.' Babs stepped off the stage and made her way to a seat on the back row.

Zibby watched Michelle warm up with stretches and some standard ballet moves. A few of the other girls did not even attempt to warm up, and just fiddled with their phones.

It was ten minutes before Babs called out from the back of the theatre. 'First up, Debs. Be as sexy as fuck.'

Debs, a hard-faced woman in her thirties, took out her chewing gum, stuck it on her phone, which she left on a seat, and stepped up on to the stage. A fast disco beat began to play. She started to gyrate her hips and dance in the sexiest way she could. Twenty seconds into her performance, Babs shouted, 'Next!'

Debs shook her head and stepped off the stage. She grabbed her things, peeled the chewing gum off her phone, put it in her mouth and strutted off with a one-finger salute.

'Cindy! You're up!' shouted Babs. 'Be as sexy as fuck.'

Cindy was in her twenties, bottle blonde and curvaceous. She bounced on to the stage, and as soon as the disco beat started, she began to thrust, pout and twerk while maintaining a seductive smile. After thirty seconds, Babs called out, 'Yes!' and told her to sit and wait till the end of the auditions.

Cindy stepped off the stage and glanced over to the other girls with a smirk, as if to say, 'That's how you do it.'

Over the next twenty minutes, Zibby and Michelle watched the other girls get up and take their turn at thrusting, twerking and pouting. Babs only called out, 'Yes!' to one other girl. The last one left to dance was Michelle.

'Next up, Michelle. Be as sexy as fuck.'

Michelle froze. 'Zibby, I don't think I'm a sexy enough dancer.' She felt anything but sexy when she danced.

'Go on,' Zibby encouraged her. 'You're a better dancer and sexier than any of them.'

'I haven't got all fucking day!' screamed Babs, setting off her smoker's cough.

Zibby grabbed Michelle's hand and led her on to the stage as the disco track began to play once more. 'Come on, we'll dance together.'

Zibby began to use some of the dance moves from *East Side Story*. She danced the male role, grabbed Michelle's hand and spinning her into a whole sequence. Michelle could have done the steps in her sleep, so she quickly followed Zibby's lead. They started laughing at the ridiculous situation and exaggerated the passion of the moves.

Babs had cut short every other dance routine, but she let Zibby and Michelle carry on until the music ended. They were both breathing heavily and giggling.

'Okay, you two,' coughed Babs, 'you're in. Sit with the others.'

'No, no,' gasped Zibby, 'it's just Michelle who's auditioning.'

Babs stood up and headed back to the stage. 'Well, you can both go then.' She lit up another cigarette. 'Look, I've got more exotic dancers than a pervert can shake his dick at, but two girls dancing like I just saw is sexy as fuck, and in this business, sexy as fuck is the key. It's both of you or nothing.'

Michelle gave Zibby a pleading look; she desperately needed the work. Zibby was desperate too, but the thought of gyrating in front of a lecherous crowd made her feel uncomfortable.

'I'll give you top billing,' offered Babs, 'and a three-month contract.'

'It's just a dance job,' whispered Michelle, 'and it's only for three months. We can still go for auditions while we earn some money.'

'Okay,' said Zibby, turning to Babs. 'When do we start?'

6

The waiting room

Tolly had been told that the Method Hall, as it was now called, had been a Methodist chapel before being converted into a rehearsal space thirty years ago to cater for London's numerous theatres. Most of the shows in the West End had been rehearsed at the Method Hall, and Tolly felt a slight thrill at the thought of visiting a space where some of the greatest stage actors had also set foot.

It was a ten-minute walk from Victoria tube station to the rehearsal hall. Tolly guessed it must be a listed building because it was the oldest structure on the narrow street. To his dismay, he saw several people already queuing to get in. He took his place in the line behind a short, middle-aged woman wearing a paisley silk scarf. He cursed himself for forgetting to buy one, especially after what Suzanne had told him. He glanced over the short woman's head; sure enough, everyone else was wearing a paisley silk scarf. He blamed the thespian luvvies for this latest trend. When he had first started doing amateur dramatics, the in thing had been to wear a beret. Tolly had tried one on, but it had made him look like a village idiot, so he had given it a miss. He checked his phone. It was twenty past; he should still be on time.

The short woman turned round and looked Tolly up and down. 'Are you in the right queue? This is for actors' auditions,' she informed him haughtily.

'I am an actor,' he answered, matching her haughty tone. He thought she looked familiar but could not place her.

'You're not wearing a paisley silk scarf.'

'You must be an actor then, because you are wearing one.'

'I'm not just an actor, I'm a renowned thespian!' she said brusquely. 'Anyway, what part are you auditioning for?'

'I haven't a clue. I don't even know what the play is. Do you know?'

'Of course I know,' snapped the short woman. 'It's one of the finest plays ever written by the country's finest playwright.'

Tolly smiled. A chance to play a role in a Shakespeare production would be great experience. 'Which Shakespeare play is it?'

'*The Waiting Room*,' she whispered reverentially, and because she believed Tolly to be an idiot, she added, 'By Shaftesbury? It's critically acclaimed!'

Tolly sighed. 'Oh, not that all-out-shit play.'

The woman gasped in shock and wobbled as if she were about to faint. 'It's a critically acclaimed piece of work!' She was so shocked that she touched the arm of the young man in front of her, who happened to be loosening the paisley silk scarf round his neck, and informed him, 'This so-called actor behind me has just said that *The Waiting Room* is an all-out-shit play!'

The actor looked shocked. However, this was not because of what he had just heard, but rather the recent Botox injections he had had in an attempt to stay looking young. 'It's by Shaftesbury! So it's a work of genius,' he explained.

'It's been critically acclaimed!' repeated the short woman.

'So you keep saying, but I still think it's an all-out-shit play,' said Tolly stubbornly. 'It makes no sense.' He remembered the quote from the one renowned critic who had originally called it the worst play ever written but had changed his mind after everyone else raved about it. He had ended up pretentiously calling it *an allegory of an allegorical tale about an allegory.*

'But it's Shaftesbury!' said the short woman and Botox face simultaneously.

Tolly sighed. He had had the same response when he first moaned about the play when he had been in a production at college. His tutors had said in no uncertain terms that if he was hoping to be an actor of any merit then he had better learn to like it. His request for them to explain the plot or what it was trying to say were met with gasps of despair. 'It doesn't matter. It's fucking Shaftesbury!'

Tolly was relieved when the audition queue began to move quickly, so the pair in front had to turn round and stop looking daggers at him. He waited behind the short woman as she remonstrated with a man in yet another paisley silk scarf behind the reception desk. 'It's outrageous that I, a renowned TV star and acclaimed locum thespian, should have to queue!'

The receptionist nervously fiddled with his scarf. 'There's not much we can do about that, seeing as this is an open audition.'

The woman pointed to her face. 'Don't you know who I am? I am Choco Chocs Doreen!'

Tolly remembered where he had seen her face now. She was the woman in the TV advert who selfishly stuffed her face with Choco Chocs chocolates rather than share them.

'My face puts bums on seats,' said Choco Chocs Doreen. 'I'm a name!' In fact, she had changed her name from Doreen Smith to Choco Chocs Doreen, so she could cash in on her TV role. Her smiling, chocolate-smeared face had been appearing on billboards and posters everywhere for several years now.

The receptionist laughed nervously. 'As I said, it is an open audition. If you would just take a seat in the waiting area, someone will call you.'

'When I auditioned for Choco Chocs chocolates, I was not told to sit and wait!'

The male receptionist, whose name badge said *Hugo*, had volunteered to swap his day off with a colleague, and now wished he hadn't offered. 'Like I said a moment ago, it is an open audition and I'm afraid everyone has to wait. The waiting room, excuse the pun, is just over there. Help yourself to tea and coffee from the machine.'

Before walking away, Choco Chocs Doreen turned to Tolly and sneered, 'Yes, I am a somebody, and I'll make sure you never get a part in this play.' She then headed for the waiting area.

'Never get a part in this all-out-shit play!' Tolly corrected her.

Receptionist Hugo gasped. 'I can't believe my ears! Did you just say "all-out-shit play"? You do realise it's by Shaftesbury!'

Tolly gave another sigh; he could not face another argument about the stupid play. 'The new word on the street for very good is "all-out shit",' he bluffed. 'I thought everyone knew that.' He handed over the printout Suzanne had given him.

Despite being middle-aged and middle class, Hugo desperately wanted to be in touch with youth culture, and pretended to have misheard him. 'Oh, I thought you said "all-out-ship play". My mistake. Yes, you're right, it is an all-out-shit play.' He suddenly did a double take when he

42

noticed Tolly's outfit. 'Are you really in the business? Where's your paisley silk scarf?'

Tolly looked around: everyone was wearing a paisley silk scarf. 'I lost it on the way here,' he said, deciding not to bother moaning about them.

Hugo stepped out from behind the desk and gave him a hug. 'You're so brave to audition without one. I'll make sure I write it down in the appointment book.'

'Thanks,' said Tolly, slightly confused by the hug.

Hugo gave Tolly's hand a squeeze, as if to say, 'I feel your pain.' He called out to an elderly woman wearing a paisley silk scarf who was standing beside the double doors into the main auditorium. 'Celia! Tolly is next.' To avoid any awkward questions, he quickly added, 'He's lost his scarf!'

Celia was a retired actress who had spent the majority of her professional acting career fighting depression caused by the constant rejection. When she heard Hugo say Tolly had lost his scarf, she clutched both hands to her heart in sympathy, close to breaking down in tears.

Choco Chocs Doreen had overheard the receptionist calling out that Tolly was next and angrily stomped back to the desk. 'I demand to know why I, a renowned TV star and acclaimed locum thespian with a profile that puts bums on seats, has to wait, while a… a nobody goes before me!'

'Tolly has been invited to audition,' explained Hugo. 'I believe you just read about an open audition in the *Theatre News* and came along like everyone else.'

Choco Chocs Doreen's face began to turn red with rage. 'He called *The Waiting Room* by Shaftesbury an all-out-shit play, and he doesn't even have a paisley silk scarf!'

'For your information,' said Hugo, with a new-found confidence inspired by Tolly's courage, 'Tolly lost his scarf on the way here, but bravely wants to carry on without it.'

He then rolled his eyes at Choco Chocs Doreen, and shook his head with pity for her. 'And everyone on the street knows that "all-out shit" means very good. So he's right. It is an all-out-shit play.'

Celia had joined them at the reception desk and smugly nodded her head in agreement, not wanting to appear ignorant of youth culture.

Tolly raised an eyebrow at Choco Chocs Doreen and chuckled. 'I told you it was an all-out-shit play.'

Humiliated, she muttered, 'Shit,' and reluctantly went back to the waiting area.

Celia said to Tolly, 'I'll take you in to see the director. We'll have to be quiet because an audition is still in progress.' She led him down a wide corridor to a large rehearsal room. There was a small stage at the far end where a gormless-looking man in his late twenties, wearing the obligatory paisley silk scarf, was coming to the end of Hamlet's *To be or not to be* soliloquy. Tolly had seen a lot of bad auditions before, but this moron was just reading words from a piece of paper. He briefly wondered if it was a comedy routine. It was something of a surprise when the director and her assistant began applauding.

'Splendid, Archie, darling, absolutely splendid,' enthused the director, Esmeralda Sykes. She was a full-figured woman in her fifties with dreadlocks tied in a ponytail. She wore denim dungarees over a baggy tee shirt. Her paisley silk scarf hung loosely over this ensemble.

'Archie, darling,' pleaded Esmeralda, 'next time you introduce your monologue, make sure you say it's by William Shakespeare, not Liam.'

Esmeralda's nephew, Archie Billings, was an only child and had been a spoiled little bastard for as long as she could remember. Her sister Isabella had divorced his father, Ralph

Billings, when Archie was just a toddler. Ralph had inherited a vast property empire that leased twenty percent of the ancient buildings in the City of London, so with a multimillion-pound divorce settlement, Isabella had devoted her life to raising her precious Archie, making sure her darling boy wanted for nothing. Isabella had decided that even the most elite private schools in London were too rough for her delicate Archie, so he was schooled at home. Whenever any teacher suggested, in the most tactful way possible, that Archie might be naturally gormless, they were immediately fired. Consequently, while growing up, Archie had been told constantly how wonderful he was. Archie was bright enough to know that, as the only child of Ralph Billings, he would eventually inherit his father's business empire, so when he hit his twenties, he chose to do whatever he fancied for a while. By chance, he had overheard his aunt Esmeralda begging his mother for help with financing a play she was planning to direct. At that moment, he had decided that it was his lifelong ambition to be an actor.

'Well, darling,' said Esmeralda, 'you did very well, and I'm sure you'll be perfect for the lead. Of course, we'll have another actor playing the role until you're one hundred percent happy that you can do it, so you can be the understudy to start with.'

Archie did not seem to be at all grateful. 'I should be the only actor playing the lead role! I'm brilliant!'

Esmeralda spoke to him as if he were a toddler. 'Archie, darling, you will be the lead once you learn all the lines. I promise.'

'I am the lead actor; otherwise I'll tell mother not to bother to sign any more money over.'

The director's assistant, Pippa, fiddled nervously with her paisley silk scarf. 'Shall I put Archie down as the lead actor?'

'Yes', sighed Esmeralda, 'put Archie down as the lead actor.'

Pippa nodded and jotted this down.

'That's better,' said Archie, with a smirk. He stomped towards the exit, pushing Celia and Tolly out of the way.

'Esmeralda,' called out Celia, 'Tolly Pipkin is here for his audition. He lost his scarf.'

Esmeralda had been in the theatre business for thirty years. For twenty-five of those years, she had not worked at all, but because she came from a well-off family, this did not matter too much. She never had to wait tables or do low-paid jobs between auditions; she just went on exotic holidays in the summer and skiing in the winter. She loved being an actor and loved telling anyone who did not know all about her profession. But even for an actor who had no need of an income, it started to become embarrassing when her peers who had dragged themselves to the top through hard work and diligence were getting parts based on their huge amounts of experience. When she had found herself reminiscing about her last play to a group of working actors at a dinner party, she had had to embarrassingly confess that it had been over twenty years ago. The very next day, she had decided to become a theatre director. After all, how hard could it be? Even though her parents were wealthy, they were now selfishly eating into her inheritance by both having major health problems and needing round-the-clock care. Fortunately, her sister Isabella had been willing to fund her project, providing Archie could star in her first play. Esmeralda knew that she could make a name for herself by touring a production of *The Waiting Room* around the country. Shaftesbury's work was the holy grail in her profession. Esmeralda had covered for the fact that she did not have a clue what the play was about by employing an assistant who had worked on a West End production of it many years ago.

Esmeralda took one look at the man Celia had introduced and decided she was not overly impressed with his presence. She thought Suzanne might have sent someone a bit more dynamic, but then maybe it was just down to his lack of a paisley silk scarf. 'Have you prepared anything to read?' she asked Tolly.

'I have a John Osborne monologue,' he said, as he walked over to the stage.

Esmeralda took Pippa to one side and asked her who John Osborne was. After being assured that Osborne was highly thought of in the theatre, Esmeralda made a mental note to drop the name at her next social gathering. 'In your own time, Tolly!' instructed Esmeralda, indicating the stage.

Tolly performed a monologue by Jimmy, from *Look Back in Anger*, about witnessing the death of his father at the age of ten.

After the climax, Celia burst into tears. 'You poor thing.'

Esmeralda could feel tears welling up in her eyes too. 'Darling', she said, stifling a sob, 'you're obviously still upset about losing your father. Just take ten minutes and then try again.'

Tolly was puzzled. 'Sorry?'

'You should try not to let your personal life intrude into your professional life.'

Tolly began to suspect that he was being set up. 'That was my monologue.'

Esmeralda was confused. 'So what you just said wasn't true?'

'It's the monologue from *Look Back in Anger*, the play,' explained Tolly.

'So your father's not dead?' asked Celia.

Tolly was now completely baffled. 'No, he's dead, but it wasn't about my father, it was the character Jimmy's father.'

'Are you saying that was all pretend?' asked Esmeralda.

Tolly was now quite sure he was being set up and was wasting his time. 'It's an all-out-shit play anyway,' he said, heading for the door.

'That means it's good!' explained Celia, who was keen to show off her street knowledge.

'Hold on, Tolly!' called Esmeralda before he reached the door.

Tolly stopped and turned.

'I have the shared part of Sid,' said Esmeralda. 'Our financiers do have their own choice of lead, but it's a good opportunity for you.' She was now convinced he was the person she wanted. Even Pippa, who had seen some household-name actors play the part of Sid, nodded her approval.

Even though he was not a fan of the play, Tolly knew that the role of Sid was a major one and he would be on stage for most of the time. It was too good a chance to miss, even if he had to act it under a different name, so he shrugged and said, 'Okay.'

Esmeralda, who was quick to pick up new street words, assured Tolly that, 'You'll be all-out shit in the part.'

One week later, Tolly attended the first day of rehearsals at the Method Hall. He had been sent a copy of the play the day after the audition and had spent twelve hours a day memorising his part, so he felt well prepared to hold his own from the start. Seeing Hugo the receptionist and his paisley silk scarf again, Tolly smiled to himself as he recalled how Hugo had accepted his claim that 'all-out shit' meant good on the streets. Hugo was speaking on his phone.

'We look forward to seeing you tomorrow… No problems… And I hope you have an all-out-shit day as well. Bye.' He hung up and turned towards Tolly, recognising him as the young man who had bravely auditioned without a paisley silk scarf. 'No luck in finding your scarf?' he asked.

Tolly had meant to get himself a stupid scarf just to stop the other actors staring at him with suspicion, but he had forgotten all about it. 'I'm hoping it will turn up,' he lied. 'It had sentimental value.' He hoped that would end the conversation, but just to amuse himself, he could not resist adding, 'But until it turns up, I'm wearing an environmentally friendly invisible paisley silk scarf. The kids on the street say invisible paisley silk scarves that save the planet are the real all-out shit.'

Hugo nodded sagely, mentally adding to his middle-class street-knowledge bank the fact that environmentally friendly invisible paisley silk scarves were the real all-out shit.

'What colour is your environmentally friendly invisible scarf?' he asked curiously.

Tolly thought he must have gone too far with the invisible scarf bit and that Hugo was about to laugh or make a joke, but to his surprise, the receptionist looked serious. So, with a shrug, he said, 'Reddish?'

Hugo held a forefinger to his lips, as though deep in thought. 'What a coincidence; that's also my favourite colour of environmentally friendly invisible paisley silk scarf. In fact, I might just put mine on as well.' He took off his scarf, opened a drawer in the reception desk, pulled out an invisible one and went through the motions of putting it on.

Tolly was now convinced that Hugo was just going along with the joke. 'That is a real all-out-shit environmentally friendly invisible paisley silk scarf,' he said.

Hugo had been so pleased with his new street-slang knowledge that he had called everyone he knew just to call things all-out shit and then explain to them all about the phrase. Perhaps surprisingly, this had made him very popular for the first time in his life. All his acquaintances were either actors or involved in the arts, and living in their protective bubble of privilege and affluence made them totally ignorant of terms used by street-smart youth. He was delighted to find that he was now asked to parties where he could take centre stage and casually drop the phrase 'all-out shit' as if he had been saying it his whole life. Now, knowing that no one else in his circle of friends had an environmentally friendly invisible paisley silk scarf made him smile with glee. 'Thank you for the compliment,' he said to Tolly, as he slightly rearranged his invisible scarf.

Tolly was now one hundred percent sure that Hugo was going along with the joke. 'I like the way you wear it. Some people just have natural style, and some people don't, but I can honestly say, you wear an environmentally friendly invisible paisley silk scarf better than anyone else I've seen.'

Hugo could feel his heart beating fast at the thought of his street cred among his friends absolutely soaring.

Tolly asked Hugo for a demonstration of how he had tied his invisible scarf, but the director's assistant, Pippa, interrupted them, informing Tolly that they would be starting the day with a read-through and that he should follow her to their rehearsal room.

A sheet of paper was pinned to the door with the words *The Waiting Room cast only* written on it in black felt-tip pen. The room had a dozen chairs positioned around a large rectangular table. Pippa led him in and went over to a drinks machine and small refrigerator in the corner. 'Help yourself to tea or coffee. There's also bottled water in the fridge.'

'Thanks. Where's Esmeralda?'

'I'm sorry to say she's having a bit of a crisis to deal with this morning,' said Pippa sadly.

'I'm sorry to hear that,' said Tolly, trying to fathom out how the coffee machine worked. 'I hope it's nothing too serious.'

'It is for Esmeralda,' said Pippa in a serious tone. 'Her Zen and karma are clashing, so she's having to have an emergency yoga session to put them right.'

Tolly was not sure if he had heard correctly. 'Emergency yoga session? How does that work?'

'You call the emergency yoga doctor. The yogi arrives and fast-tracks you through an appropriate session.'

Tolly had questions about the emergency yoga doctor, but he had to put them on hold due to the arrival of his first fellow cast member. This slim man in his sixties was called Stan. He was to play the part of Grandad and would die at the end of the second act. He had been given this part because he had played a corpse in several TV police dramas.

Twenty-seven-year-old Tasmin arrived next. She had snagged the part of Jenny the granddaughter for two particularly good reasons: she had been in a TV advert for washing-up liquid when she was three years old, and she was Esmeralda's husband's niece.

Next to come in was a young man in his mid-twenties, Sinclair. He was to play the part of young man waiting. He was good-looking, and by God did he know it. Every few minutes, he would take a small mirror out of his jacket pocket and look at himself in admiration. His appearance in the country's longest-running TV soap opera had been record-breaking. Unfortunately, the record was for newly introduced character killed off in the shortest amount of time. He had been cast in the soap purely for his looks, in an attempt to attract a younger female fanbase to the show. However, on his first day, Sinclair had managed to piss off all the actors who had been in the show for years by giving them acting tips. He also pissed off the crew by telling them how he wanted the set to be lit and how the sound could be improved. He then pissed off the director by questioning her instructions. Finally, he managed to piss off the writers by suggesting that their dialogue was too on the nose and explaining, wrongly, the difference between plot and storyline. His next episode had been written months before, but it was changed overnight, and Sinclair's character was killed off by being shot. And stabbed. And dismembered. And set on fire. Esmeralda had given him the part in the play because she owed his mother a favour.

Thirty minutes after the arranged start time, Choco Chocs Doreen turned up. She had actually been hanging around in a coffee shop down the road for the last forty minutes, so she could make her grand entrance. She was slightly pissed off to discover that Esmeralda had not yet turned up, but went into full apology mode, blaming her agent and the persistent marketing people from Choco Chocs incessantly begging her to make a fresh TV advertisement.

Once everyone was seated, Pippa explained that she would make a start rather than waiting for Esmeralda to arrive. She then asked the cast to stand up in turn, introduce themselves and give a brief résumé of their experience. Tolly went first and truthfully said that his parts in college plays had received good reviews. This was met with audible scoffing and mockery from his fellow cast members.

Despite having not worked since the age of three, Tasmin managed to name-drop Steven Spielberg and Kenneth Branagh. Supposedly, they both used the brand of washing-up liquid she had advertised, having been convinced by her star turn.

Stan was next to stand up. He listed the cop shows he had appeared in very slowly, with a dramatic pause after mentioning each one. He saved the best till last. 'I was the corpse Miss Marple found in last year's Agatha Christie Christmas special.' Feeling superior thanks to this professional coup, he sat down with a smug grin on his face.

Not to be outdone, Sinclair spun his single soap-opera episode as a positive. 'It had the highest ever number of viewers for a Tuesday morning repeat.'

Choco Chocs Doreen stood up and waited for applause that never came. Undeterred, she went on, 'My name is, of course, Choco Chocs Doreen. Apart from being the face of Choco Chocs chocolates, and solely responsible for the seven percent increase in sales…' She waited once more for applause that never came. 'I have played numerous stage roles.'

'What have you done?' asked Tolly, who was genuinely keen to know.

'Too numerous,' boasted Choco Chocs Doreen.

'Just name a few,' said Stan, who could not bear to think someone might have more experience than him.

'I would love to talk about some of the amazing stage productions I've been in,' gushed Choco Chocs Doreen, 'but, alas, as a locum thespian, my first duty is confidentiality.'

In truth, Choco Chocs Doreen had only worked on the Choco Chocs advert and had become increasingly frustrated that she was not inundated with roles because of it. So, just for the benefit of friends and neighbours, she had invented for herself the role of locum thespian: an understudy on call to rush in at the last moment to save a production whenever a leading female thespian was needed. As a locum thespian, she insisted she was sworn to secrecy and was unable to give any details of the shows she had saved.

'I can only humbly say,' boasted Choco Chocs Doreen, 'that after I've saved a play, the cast and director always cry when I leave.' She dabbed her eye, wiping away an imaginary tear.

Esmeralda rushed in just as Choco Chocs Doreen had finally sat down, grudgingly accepting that, no matter how long she waited, applause was never going to come.

'Sorry for the delay, everyone. My yogi doctor pulled both hamstrings this morning while he was doing an emergency yoga session for me. Thankfully, my Zen and karma had stopped clashing before that happened.' Esmeralda slung her satchel over the back of a chair next to her assistant and sat down. 'How's it going, Pippa?'

'Archie hasn't turned up yet.'

'He'll turn up later. His mother likes to make sure he's eaten all his breakfast before she'll let him out of the house. Have we done the introductions?'

'Just finished,' said Pippa.

'Fabulous, darling, well done. What would I do without you? Now, if everyone has their scripts in front of them, let's just have a little read-through, shall we, just to get a feel for the flow? Pippa, darling, if you could read the stage directions, that would be wonderful.'

The door opened, and a yawning Archie entered and sat down next to Tasmin.

'Ah! Archie, our leading man. Just in time to introduce yourself,' said Esmeralda.

Archie stood up. 'I'm Archie Billings, and I'm a better actor than all of you and can get you sacked if I want.'

'Not quite what I meant,' said Esmeralda, 'but let's get on with the read-through.'

Pippa cleared her throat, picked up the script and read, 'The pitch-black stage gradually brightens to reveal a large waiting area. An old man enters left, holding a newspaper and a large parcel—'

At the sound of a loud cough, Pippa looked up to see Choco Chocs Doreen had her hand in the air.

'Do you mind if I whisper my lines?' she asked. 'It's just that I like to save my vocal cords for the actual performances.'

Esmeralda reluctantly said, 'Of course, darling.'

Archie's hand shot up. 'I want to whisper my lines. Because I'm brilliant, I should save my voice as well.'

'Archie, you just concentrate on learning the lines,' said Esmeralda. 'You've had the script for weeks, and you still haven't remembered the first page.'

Archie stood up. 'I'm a better actor than everyone here. Wait till I tell mother what you said!'

Esmeralda forced herself to smile, and repeated in her head the words, 'We need him for the money, we need him for the money.' Out loud, she said, 'Okay, my darling, what if I let you whisper the lines that you're not going to say while you're learning them? Would that be all right?'

Feeling happy that he had won the battle, Archie grunted, 'That's more like it,' and sat back down.

This had given the other cast members pause for thought, and one by one, all of them except Tolly declared that they too wanted to whisper their lines for the very same reason as Choco Chocs Doreen.

After Esmeralda had reluctantly agreed that they could all whisper their lines, Pippa resumed reading the opening scene. Only Tolly delivered his lines in his normal voice, but they were sixty percent of the script. Things began to go wrong when the other actors became competitive about who could whisper most quietly. The last thirty minutes were silent apart from Tolly and Pippa as the others resorted to just moving their lips.

At the end of the read-through, the cast sat in silence, looking at Esmeralda. It took her twenty seconds to realise they had reached the end. 'Oh, have we finished? Well, I must say, for a first read, that was fabulous. We'll take five for a comfort break, then do one more read-through with a bit more emphasis on pronunciation.'

Tolly's mood had gone from optimistic to despairing in just two hours. He felt he had been imprisoned with a bunch of egomaniacs who were all just out for themselves.

After another twenty-minute wait for Choco Chocs Doreen to sit back down, Esmeralda gave her first piece of direction. 'This time, I want you all to deliver the lines in character.'

After the first read, Tolly was in no mood to lip-read the others again. 'Would it be possible for people not to whisper so softly? I couldn't hear my cues.'

Choco Chocs Doreen jumped in quickly. 'I can hear my cues perfectly well,' she assured Esmeralda. 'When you're a locum thespian, you learn very quickly to listen.'

Tolly was not greatly surprised when the others agreed that they had had no trouble hearing their cues either.

Esmeralda turned to Tolly. 'Try listening, darling. Learn from the others.'

'Okay,' thought Tolly, 'she wants me to learn from the others.'

'Maybe I should whisper my lines as well. Then I'll be able to hear theirs better,' he suggested.

'Good idea, darling. Okay, Pippa, let's go again, and remember, everyone, I want to hear some characterisation.'

Pippa once more began to describe the action, and after ten minutes of ever-quieter whispers, it was another read-through for lip-readers only.

'Stop, stop, stop,' demanded Esmeralda after ten minutes of lips moving in silence. 'The whispering isn't working.'

'Can I suggest we speak in low voices?' proposed Choco Chocs Doreen. 'I can still save my voice if I speak in a low voice.'

It was unanimously agreed that they would speak in low voices instead of whispering. Pippa started once again from the beginning. But as the actors competed to see who could speak most quietly, the low voices soon turned to whispers, and after fifteen minutes, they were all back to just moving their lips again.

'This whispering and speaking in low voices just isn't working,' declared Esmeralda. 'Whose idea was it to whisper in the first place?'

'I believe it was Tolly,' said Choco Chocs Doreen. 'He wanted us to whisper because he couldn't hear his cues.'

The others nodded in agreement.

'I only started whispering because they were all whispering,' protested Tolly.

'We've wasted a whole morning because of your demands,' Esmeralda told Tolly accusingly. 'From now on, use your normal voice.'

Tolly began to protest. 'It wasn't me—'

'If it's okay with you, Esmeralda,' interrupted Choco Chocs Doreen, 'I'm going to read in character. We locum thespians don't have the time to massage our egos like some people.'

'See, Tolly?' said Esmeralda, pointing to Choco Chocs Doreen. 'Professionals just get on with the work without making a big fuss.'

The next read-through started reasonably well, with no whispers or low voices. Then Choco Chocs Doreen began to raise her voice, which encouraged the others to raise theirs. Soon, with the exception of Tolly, they were all competing to see who could speak loudest.

'Stop, stop, stop!' said Esmeralda. 'You're whispering again, Tolly.'

'I'm not whispering, I'm talking normally. It's the others, they've raised their voices.' Tolly thought this had been obvious, but the look he was getting from Esmeralda told a different story.

'It's known in the business as projecting,' she explained. 'Don't they teach that in college any more?'

'Yes, but—'

'As a locum thespian, you have to master the art of projection,' explained Choco Chocs Doreen condescendingly. 'It's so important.'

'Unless you're a corpse,' added Stan. 'Then you have to learn not to project, because the last thing the public wants to see is a corpse projecting.'

'I'm brilliant at projecting,' said Archie, who felt he needed to say something.

'I learnt to project when I was three years old,' chipped in Tasmin.

Sinclair was too busy admiring himself in his hand mirror to say anything.

If Tolly thought the first day of rehearsal had been as bad as it could get for him, he was in for a shock. Having pretty much memorised his part in week one, he found the next few weeks unremittingly frustrating. Even though he had the biggest part in the play, with the most lines, Esmeralda spent most of her time trying to get Archie and the others to say their lines without needing to be prompted every time.

With Archie still struggling to remember any lines from even the first page, Tolly had to perform the first run-through rehearsal. It turned out to be a complete shambles, just as he had expected. No one knew their lines apart from him. Later that day, he rushed to see his agent and begged Suzanne to find a get-out clause in his contract.

'You're getting paid,' said Suzanne unsympathetically. 'Who cares if it turns out to be the worst production ever?'

'I'm being mentally scarred by it,' protested Tolly. 'I can feel myself getting panic attacks.'

Suzanne laughed. 'Relax, it's just first-performance nerves, most actors get them. It's probably not as bad as you think it is.'

'It is that bad. It's so bad I haven't had a full night's sleep in days. I keep having these nightmares where I'm being lynched by the audience.'

'Tolly, I think you're getting a bit carried away,' sighed Suzanne, who was now fed up to the back teeth of his whingeing. 'I'm sure it will be a triumph, just wait and see. I'm looking forward to the first-night party. You get fuck-all perks as an agent, apart from the occasional first night.'

7

A meeting in Soho

It was day twenty of rehearsals for *The Waiting Room*. Tolly was having another frustrating day, delivering his lines to his fellow actors who had still not memorised the twenty or thirty words they had in the play, when Esmeralda excitedly made an announcement to the whole company.

'I have some fabulous news for you all. The previews of *The Waiting Room* will start in two weeks in the West End where, I am delighted to say, you will perform in front of the media's theatre critics before we start our tour of the country. We'll be in a small theatre called the Aphrodite. An old friend is letting us use it from now on for rehearsals and then our two previews.'

'Is it wise to preview the play so soon?' asked Tolly. 'We can't get through the first act without everyone needing prompts. It'll get savaged.'

'I have faith in this company of acting talent,' said Esmeralda. 'I see actors who are perfectionists.'

'They haven't perfected learning their lines,' replied Tolly. Having discovered they were all self-absorbed idiots, he did not care if he offended them.

'Knowing one's lines is not the mark of a great thespian,' said Choco Chocs Doreen, who was still struggling to remember any of her sixty words. 'It's the ability to absorb and project the play's intentions.'

The rest of the actors had no clue as to what Choco Chocs Doreen was on about, but they agreed wholeheartedly because none of them could remember all their lines off by heart either.

'You might remember lines,' sneered Choco Chocs Doreen, 'but if you don't project intentions, don't expect the rest of us to absorb!'

Stan was also still struggling to remember his one line – 'I don't feel well' just before he dropped dead – and was grateful to have a good excuse for this. 'When I was the corpse in the Christmas Miss Marple, I was flooded with intentions. It was so easy to absorb, but Tolly doesn't project anything. There's nothing for me to… to absorb.'

The other actors gratefully jumped on the absorbing bandwagon, and agreed it was all going wrong because Tolly was not projecting enough intentions for them to absorb.

'I hope you've learnt a lesson!' said Esmeralda, glaring at Tolly. 'Before you go around accusing others of not remembering lines, make sure you're… you're…'

'Projecting intentions!' said Choco Chocs Doreen with a smug smile at Tolly.

'Exactly,' said Esmeralda. 'Give your fellow actors something to absorb and they might just remember.'

'That is crazy!' protested Tolly.

'As a renowned TV star and acclaimed locum thespian with vast experience, I can assure our temporary leading man that he should spend more time learning to project intentions rather than learning lines that his supporting thespians cannot absorb!'

Tolly searched the scornful faces in the hope of finding at least one sympathetic expression, but even Pippa turned her head away.

'So, tomorrow,' said Esmeralda excitedly, 'we will meet up at the theatre. Pippa will give everyone the address at the end of today's rehearsal.'

'I've probably played there,' said Choco Chocs Doreen. 'As a locum thespian, I have played most of the West End theatres. Alas, the locum thespian's Hippocratic oath prevents me from saying which ones.'

Tolly's afternoon went on in the same exasperating vein. It still took three hours to stagger through the ninety-minute play as he delivered his dialogue then waited for his co-stars to ask Pippa for a prompt on every single line. They all had a good excuse now. They blamed forgetting their lines on Tolly's delivery and inability to project intentions.

The next day, Tolly popped in to see Suzanne on his way to the theatre. He told her about the play being previewed in two weeks despite his fellow actors still needing a script and their accusation that this was his fault. Suzanne told him that it was good news because the play would get savaged and close early, but he would still get paid. Now certain that he only had to put up with it for a while longer, he felt quite happy and even left her office with a skip in his step.

The Aphrodite theatre was in a side street in Soho, surrounded by the area's specialities of sex shops, strip shows and prostitutes. Tolly checked the time on his phone. He was twenty minutes early and, taking into account Choco Chocs Doreen's habit of making a late entrance, he figured he had time for a cup of coffee and a croissant. He spotted a small café at the end of the road. According to the sign above the door, it was *The Proper Kaff.* Tolly had some vague memory about the name but could not remember why.

The café had mismatched tables and chairs up each side of the room with a small counter at the far end that fronted a busy kitchen. Most of the builders, tradespeople and office workers seated at the tables were tucking into fried food with chips. Tolly attracted a few curious glances as he made his way to the counter. A large, unshaven man in his fifties with chunky gold rings on every finger and a gold chain around his neck that was thick enough to tow a cruise liner stepped out from behind the counter. He took two plates of eggs and bacon to a nearby table and flung them down in front of a man and a woman in their forties, wearing paint-splattered overalls. 'Get that down yer neck,' he said.

The woman, who had a splash of green paint on her nose, said, 'Oi! Where's me sauce?!'

'Sauce?!' said the large man. 'You've got bleedin' sauce, asking me about sauce.'

The decorator woman was not intimidated by the bull of a man. 'Are you getting me sauce or what?!'

'You got fucking legs, get your own sauce.' He pointed to a table with sauce bottles and condiments by the counter.

'You're the bleedin' waiter! You get it,' protested the lady decorator.

The large man grabbed a bottle of tomato sauce, marched back to her table and slammed it down. 'There's yer fucking sauce. 'Appy now?!'

'I wanted brown sauce,' she said.

The large man stared down at her. 'Are you pulling my fucking plonker?'

The woman gave a coarse, raspy laugh. 'I fucking had you going, didn't I, Deano?'

The large man gave a hearty laugh and put the woman in a gentle headlock. 'You fucking cheeky mare.'

63

Deano marched back to the counter with a chuckle. He glanced over at Tolly. 'What can I do you for?'

'Could I have a cappuccino and a croissant, please?' asked Tolly.

'A what and a what?' said Deano, looking mystified.

'A cappuccino and a croissant,' repeated Tolly.

Deano peered past Tolly at the diners. 'Oi, you lot! Can anybody here speak foreign? 'Cause what this bloke is saying don't make sense. Here,' he said to Tolly, 'say what it was you wanted again.' Deano nodded for him to tell the other customers.

'A cappuccino and a croissant,' said Tolly, bemused.

The other patrons all shook their heads in bafflement.

Deano tapped Tolly on the shoulder. He turned back to face him.

'See, the problem is that this place is called the Proper Kaff, so we only do proper caff food. If you want poncey fucking cakes and la-di-da coffee—'

'I like la-di-da coffee,' said a builder at a nearby table. He had been engrossed in looking at his phone up till this point and had missed exactly what was going on.

'I bet you fucking do,' said Deano, staring at the builder. 'Because you, Danny, are a fucking tart!'

'I'm only just saying,' grumbled Danny.

Tolly was beginning to feel distinctly uncomfortable until he noticed two young women sitting at a window table. They were trying to keep straight faces, and there on the table in front of them were two croissants and two coffees.

Deano spotted Tolly looking over at the young women's table and burst out laughing. The rest of the diners joined in as Deano put Tolly in a gentle headlock and said, 'I fucking 'ad you going, didn't I?!'

Tolly laughed with relief as Deano let him go and produced from behind the counter a tray with a croissant and a cappuccino. Tolly recalled now why he had heard about the Proper Kaff: the owner was notorious for making fun of his customers. He took out his wallet to pay.

'Have that on me,' said Deano. 'You were a good sport. I had you fucking going, didn't I?'

Tolly laughed. 'You really had me going.'

'Sit there,' said Deano, pointing to the only two empty seats, which happened to be at the table where the two young women were sitting. Both were in their early twenties, slim and beautiful.

'Here, dancer girls!' shouted Deano. 'Let the man take his weight off.'

'We're just going, Deano,' said one of the young women, who Tolly thought could have earned a living as Beyonce's double.

Her friend stood up. Her light red hair was cut in a French bob like the character from the film *Amélie*. She gave Tolly a big smile. 'He did that to us when we first came here.'

'It's an experience I won't forget in a hurry.' Tolly waited for them to shuffle out of their seats before sitting down at the table.

'He's lovely when you get to know him,' said the Beyonce lookalike.

Two office workers had shouted their goodbyes to Deano, only for him to tell them to, 'Fuck off, and don't come back!'

The one with the *Amélie* hair said, 'Deano always says that. Enjoy your croissant.'

'I will, thanks.' He watched them walk to the exit, along with most of the male customers.

As they opened the door to leave, the young women called out, 'Bye, Deano!'

'Fuck off, and don't come back!' shouted Deano in response. He gave them a big grin and a wave.

Tolly watched them walk down the street, wishing that he were better-looking because beautiful woman like that would never look at him twice.

The day's rehearsal in the Aphrodite theatre went as Tolly had expected. He was happy that he was line perfect, but the others were still struggling. To make matters worse, Isabella Billings, the money behind the production, was present and insisted that her son Archie should be included in the stage rehearsal in the afternoon. Archie could not even put two words together without a prompt, so Tolly had a torturous three hours of watching Archie read from a script with the other actors constantly fluffing their lines. At the end of the day, Esmeralda declared the rehearsal to have been a complete success.

Choco Chocs Doreen was now Isabella Billings' constant companion. She was clever enough to know that the real power in the company was Isabella and her extreme wealth, not her poorer sister Esmeralda, even if she was the director. 'Your Archie is a natural,' Choco Chocs Doreen gushed to Isabella, who remained blind to her son's faults. 'If he were to be guided by a qualified thespian with, say, TV and locum acting experience, he could be a giant in the acting world.'

The next day, Tolly arrived in Soho early and headed for the Proper Kaff again in the hope of bumping into the two women from the day before. Deano spotted Tolly as he came in and said, 'Fuck off, La-di-da, we don't serve your kind.'

'Good morning, Deano. Could I have a tea and a bacon sandwich, please?'

'Coming right up, La-di-da. I'll bring it over.'

Tolly paid and sat at the table where the two young women had been. After a few minutes, Deano waddled over with his tea and sandwich.'

'Those two women at this table yesterday, do they come in here often?' Tolly asked Deano.

'The dancer girls? Yeah, they come in here a lot. Why? You got the hots for them?'

'No, no, no,' said Tolly, blushing, 'I was just asking.'

'Which one do you fancy?' asked Deano.

'I don't fancy either of them,' said Tolly defensively. 'I was just asking.'

The door opened and the young woman with the *Amélie* haircut strolled in. Deano's face lit up. 'Hey, dancer girl. La-di-da was just asking about you and your mate, but don't worry because he doesn't fancy either of you. The usual?'

'Yes, please, Deano; to take out.'

Tolly felt her eyes on him. 'I was just making conversation with Deano,' he explained. 'I was just making small talk.'

'I don't believe a word of it,' she said, 'You have a creepy look about you.'

'I swear it was just innocent small talk.'

She laughed. 'As Deano would say, I had you fucking going, didn't I?'

Tolly smiled with relief. 'Yes, you certainly did.'

Deano appeared with two coffees and a brown takeaway bag. The woman paid and said, 'Bye, Deano.'

'Fuck off, and don't come back,' he shouted in reply as the young woman left with a farewell wave.

Through the window, Tolly watched her step out on to the pavement. She turned and smiled at him before walking away.

Over the next few days, he popped into the café whenever he had the chance, but never saw the dancer girls in there again. Two days before the first preview, Tolly was on his way back from lunch at the Proper Kaff when he spotted the dancer girls staring at the poster for *The Waiting Room* pasted up outside the Aphrodite.

'Hello,' he said. 'We meet again.' He knew it sounded corny and clichéd, but he could not think of anything else to say. 'We met in the Proper Kaff. Deano calls me La-di-da, after the coffee episode.'

'The one who was asking about us,' said the Beyonce lookalike.

'I was only making conversation…' Tolly noticed their giggles. 'You had me fucking going, didn't you?'

The dancer girls laughed.

'My name's Zibby,' said the redhead.

'And I'm Michelle.'

'So, you're an actor,' said Zibby pointing to the row of cast photographs, one of which showed Tolly's unsmiling face. 'What part do you play?'

Tolly told himself he was not vain, but he sounded it when he said, 'Actually, I'm playing the lead role.'

'You're Archie Billings? You're not what I expected,' said Zibby.

Tolly cursed his vanity. He had forgotten that he was filling in for that idiot until he took over. 'Yes,' he said sadly. He hated telling lies, but his vanity had got the better of him.

'Maybe we should come and see you in it,' said Michelle.

'Please don't,' said Tolly. 'It's a terrible production.'

'You're not selling it, Archie,' said Zibby playfully.

The thought of the dancer girls seeing him in a play that was going to be savaged by critics while he pretended to be someone else added up to too much embarrassment. 'I'd better go. Please don't waste your money, it's terrible.' He gave a half smile and rushed into the theatre, feeling sad and cursing his own stupidity.

Tolly decided to avoid the Proper Kaff the next day in case he bumped into the dancer girls. He felt like a fraud, and that did not sit comfortably with him. Turning the corner to head towards the theatre, he saw the two young women walking down the street and then disappearing into a building. Curious, he looked at the premises they had entered: it was a large-fronted sex shop called Erotic Vibes. The window display promised the largest range of dildos in the country. In addition to the breathtaking array of sex aids, a section of the shopfront was dedicated to advertising its world-famous erotic dance revue in Soho's oldest private theatre. This show had been performed since 1957. Old black and white photographs were displayed alongside more recent images of scantily clad young women in various dance poses, and there in the last photograph were the two dancer girls in full erotic flight.

8

The first night

After weeks of rehearsal, the curtain finally came down in the Aphrodite theatre on the first of the two preview performances of Esmeralda's production of *The Waiting Room*. The theatregoers were baffled, but because it was a Shaftesbury play, they gave the cast a standing ovation, with Esmeralda proudly taking centre stage as director.

Befitting her self-awarded status as star of the show, Choco Chocs Doreen pushed to the front to take the applause alongside Archie, who had slept through most of the play in the wings. Tolly was happy to let the others get in front of him, eager to distance himself from the mess the play had turned out to be.

It was usual for first-night parties to go on until the reviews appeared in the first editions of the papers. Suzanne had joined the party to take advantage of the free food and champagne.

'It was a load of all-out shit!' moaned Tolly, as he watched Suzanne swig back another glass of fizz. 'They all needed prompts and overacted! It's fucking embarrassing.'

'All-out shit means good,' said Suzanne, stuffing a canapé into her mouth. 'I heard it the other day. Anyway, it pays,' she said with a shrug.

'What if someone finds out I was in it?! It will be terrible because everyone will know how all-out shit it was. When I say all-out shit, I mean all-out-shit bad.'

'Look on the bright side,' said Suzanne, still munching. 'Remember I told you that the reviews will be bad, the play will be pulled, and you'll still get paid. Because I'm a good agent, I made sure you get paid either way. I recognise a train wreck coming when I see one.'

The reminder that the play would be pulled because of bad reviews and he would still get paid cheered Tolly up immensely.

'Even though it was an all-out-shit-bad play,' added Suzanne, 'you were the best thing in it.'

It was past midnight when Esmeralda spotted the first online review on her tablet. News spread among the cast that she had it, and a jostling group surrounded her. Esmeralda let out a wail.

Tolly smiled. The review must be really bad. 'Thank God for critics,' he said to himself.

Choco Chocs Doreen had wrestled the tablet out of Esmeralda's shaking hands and began to read. 'A triumph!' she shouted. 'It says this new production takes the unfathomable play in a new unfathomable direction with unfathomable performances by the majority of the cast.'

'What else does it say?' asked Tasmin.

Choco Chocs Doreen continued, 'Under the superb direction of Esmeralda Sykes, the larger-than-life performances of the cast revitalise this classic piece of British theatre.'

'There must be a mistake,' gasped Tolly. 'The play is all-out shit!'

Suzanne reached for her phone and searched online. 'It's just one review, don't panic.' She saw that more reviews were now coming in. 'The other reviews are all-out shit.'

Tolly breathed a sigh of relief. 'Thank God for that.'

'When I say all-out shit, I mean very good. All the reviews are raving about the play.'

Tolly's vanity meant he could not resist asking, 'Do they say anything about my performance?'

'All all-out shit,' said Suzanne with her eyes fixed on her phone screen.

Tolly perked up. 'What did they like about me?'

'Not that all-out shit, the other all-out shit,' said Suzanne with a shake of her head. 'The consensus seems to be that you underplayed your part too much. Look on the bright side, you're now performing in a critically acclaimed play, and as soon as the real Archie Billings remembers his lines, you're basically on holiday.'

'The cast are selfish and they're rubbish actors. The next few weeks are going to be torture. I don't think I can do it. I'll end up nuts! Suzanne, I'm begging you, get me out of this nightmare.'

Suzanne looked him in the eye and slapped his face.

'Jesus! What did you do that for?' demanded Tolly, rubbing his reddening cheek.

'You're an ungrateful little bastard. Your career was pretty much dead and buried, but you got a break, so stop being a prima donna. In a few months, your little spat with Tuppence Crow will be forgotten, and your name will no longer be top of the blacklist.'

'You don't know what it's like being with them every day,' moaned Tolly. 'I don't like any of them.'

Suzanne slapped him again. 'For Christ's sake! Most people do jobs they hate, with people they hate, for eight hours a day, and they do that for years. Is it so hard to work for a few more weeks with all your food, travel and accommodation paid for? I get it that you hate the play, and hate the others because they're terrible, but guess what. It's called fucking life. Now, do what all the great actors do, and soak up all this experience, smile and just get on with it, because believe you me, parts do not grow on trees, and it could be a very long time until you work again, unofficial blacklist or no unofficial blacklist.'

'You didn't have to hit me. You could have just said all that,' grumbled Tolly.

'I know,' confessed Suzanne, 'but I regret never slapping my two-timing ex-husbands, so I like to dish a few out now and again. It's a kind of therapy.'

'I'm sorry I whinged. You're right,' admitted Tolly. 'If you want to slap my face again, go ahead. I deserve it.'

Suzanne smiled and slapped him clean across the face with her left hand.

'Bloody hell, Suzanne, that hurt!' gasped Tolly. 'I was making a gesture when I said that.'

'And what a lovely gesture it was too.' Suzanne managed to grab another glass of champagne from a passing waitress and took a swig. 'But doing it feels so nice, I couldn't resist the offer.'

Elated by the overwhelmingly good reviews, Tolly's fellow cast members were all busy trying to take individual credit for the success, including Archie because his name was in the programme. Esmeralda called for a promotional cast photograph of them all holding celebratory glasses of champagne. A tussle broke out among the cast as they jostled to be in the middle. No one seemed to notice that Tolly was not even in the group, and he was quite glad of that.

'Thank God I've got a day off tomorrow,' said Tolly. 'Two performances on the trot with those morons would have scarred me for life.'

'With any luck, your colleagues might soon start managing to remember their lines. What are you going to do, sleep all day and whinge like you normally do?'

'Do I whinge that much?'

'Yes.'

'I won't be whingeing tomorrow because I'm going to a surprise birthday party back in my home town. It should be fun.'

'Good for you. Oh, I was going to come and see you on the last night here, but after sitting through that once, I don't think my sanity could take it.'

'What about my sanity?!'

'You worry too much,' remarked Suzanne as she finished off her champagne. 'Get the last London show out of the way and you're on holiday.'

'And then I'm sure the weeks will fly by,' sighed Tolly.

'In a flash,' said Suzanne. 'And don't fret, the worst is over.'

9

The surprise birthday party

'Charlie! Charlie… CHARLIE!' screamed Ruby Jenkinson, as she stuck her head out of the bungalow back door. 'We have to go in five minutes, do you hear me, Charlie?! Answer me!' yelled Ruby. She began to suspect that he had turned his hearing aid off again. Eighty-three-year-old Ruby had been married to Charlie for fifty-two years, and since Charlie had retired nine years ago, she had spent most of her days shouting at him out of the back door. Ruby had stopped walking down the long back garden after knee surgery several years ago meant there were now too many steps to negotiate. Ruby thought about calling Charlie on his phone, but then she spotted it on the windowsill by the door. With one more deep breath, Ruby hollered out of the back door, 'CHARLIE!'

Eighty-four-year-old Charlie appeared from the end of the garden wearing light brown overalls and clutching a hoe. Despite his age, his silver grey hair was thick and in need of a haircut. His dark-rimmed glasses were held together by masking tape and sat wonkily on the bridge of his nose, 'Did you call me?'

'Have you switched off your ear thing again?!' demanded Ruby. She often wondered why they had stayed together so long. They were complete opposites. Ruby took pride in how she looked and was never seen without make-up. Even when she had had a heart attack in the early hours of the morning, she had made Charlie get her make-up bag, so she could put some slap on before the ambulance turned up. Ruby was proud of the comments that she received from her peers about her hair and her choice of clothes. In contrast, Charlie had been mistaken for a down and out more than once over the years.

'Hold on, said Charlie, 'I'll switch me hearing aid on.' After several attempts, he said, 'There… What was you saying?'

Ruby shook her head in frustration. 'Don't keep switching the ear thing off! What's the point of having an ear thing if you keep switching it off?'

'Saving the batteries,' declared Charlie proudly. 'There's no point in wasting battery power.'

Ruby had this conversation with him at least once a day. She stifled her urge to moan at him more because they needed to keep an appointment. 'We have to pick up Tolly from the station at four o'clock. It's twenty to now, so let's go.'

Charlie hesitated. 'Have I got time to leave some music on for my tomato plants?'

'No! We're going to be late.' Ruby caught the flash of distress that crossed Charlie's face. 'Okay, but hurry up.'

Charlie smiled and hurriedly tottered off to his greenhouse. Ruby had come to the conclusion that her husband had gone completely nuts over the last few years. He thought more of his vegetables and fruit crops than he did of his own children and grandchildren. In spring and summer, she hardly saw him, and in winter, he spent hours planning his vegetable beds and swooning over seed catalogues.

By the time Ruby had carefully made her way along the driveway, leaning on her walking stick, and settled herself behind the wheel of their fifteen-year-old Ford Fiesta, Charlie was shutting the front door of the bungalow and double locking it. He checked the handle, took two steps away then went back to check the handle again, before finally climbing into the passenger seat.

'In your own time,' grumbled Ruby.

Charlie was oblivious to Ruby's glare. 'Guess what. I'm trialling Louis Armstrong on my tomato plants,' he said excitedly. 'Dolly Parton didn't seem to make any difference last year.'

'You've still got your dirty overalls and old broken glasses on,' sighed Ruby. 'What will Tolly think when he sees you looking like a destitute repairman?'

Charlie reluctantly clambered out of the car, shrugged off his overalls and hung them on the garage door handle. 'I can't find my other glasses. Anyway, there's nothing wrong with these ones.'

'Oh, just hurry up!' moaned Ruby.

Charlie climbed back into the passenger seat. 'I don't see why we have to pick him up. Why can't our Gary do it?'

'I told you all this at breakfast. You never had your ear thing on, did you?' said Ruby.

'I was saving the batteries,' admitted Charlie. He had found that he could read the newspaper in peace and quiet by just nodding every now and again and adding the occasional, 'Yes, dear' whenever he thought it might be appropriate.

Ruby started the engine, put the car into gear and sped off in the direction of the railway station. 'Well, if you'd put your ear thing on, you would have heard me say that our

Gary is taking Sam on a track day for his birthday. You know, they drive fast cars around a racetrack.'

'I know what a track day is, I'm not stupid. Why can't Jenny go and pick him up?' Charlie worried that he was losing precious time with his vegetables.

Ruby sped through a red light at a pedestrian crossing, forcing several high-school lads to jump out of her path. 'They should teach these kids how to cross the road. Anyway, where was I? Jenny can't pick him up. Who do you think is doing all the organising at the house?' Ruby tailgated a learner driver who was going at the appropriate speed for the built-up area. 'Here we go, another idiot on the road holding the traffic up. They don't teach 'em properly any more.'

'Why can't Sam's pal pick him up? That Anton.'

'That Anton? You mean Sam's husband, is that who you mean?' Ruby slammed on the brakes to avoid hitting a bus after she had strayed on to the wrong side of the road. 'Bus drivers are a law unto themselves. Unbelievable.'

'He's not his husband, they're just mates.'

'So why did they have a wedding and rent a flat together?'

Charlie shrugged. 'They was just mucking about like mates do.'

'OK, have it your way. But that Anton cannot keep a secret. He would have told Sam all about it.'

'Who is this other mate we have to pick up then?' asked Charlie, wondering how his tomato plants were doing.

'Tolly, the one who worked with that celebrity.'

Charlie was bewildered. 'Celebrity?'

'I pointed her out to you the other night on the TV! You know the one, Tuppence Crow… She's very glamorous.' Ruby took a moment to beep at a Lycra-clad, overweight, middle-aged cyclist for no other reason than he made her feel sick.

'I don't know her,' said Charlie adamantly. 'And why has she got a stupid name?'

'Tuppence is not a stupid name, it's posh and classy!'

'Only rich people have stupid names like that,' moaned Charlie.

'It's a nice name and you do know her,' insisted Ruby. 'She was in that advert for the posh perfume.'

Charlie shook his head. 'I don't remember her or the advert.'

'You do know who I mean,' said Ruby. 'You even said she was pretty because she had tomato-coloured lips.'

'Oh, yes! She was pretty. So, this friend of Sam's worked with her.'

Ruby cut up a black cab to nip into a parking space outside Brenford railway station, prompting angry beeps from the irate cabbie. 'These Uber drivers should have some sort of eyesight test before they let them loose on the roads.'

The railway station was small. People were being dropped off in time to catch the next through train.

'What does he look like?' asked Charlie.

'You'll know him when you see him,' said Ruby. 'He and Sam were close friends before he moved away.'

Before Charlie could deny knowing what the young man looked like, a train approached and pulled into the station. They waited until it had set off again before getting out of the car and heading over to the station exit. Several people walked briskly past them and jumped into waiting cars or taxis.

'Where is he?' asked Charlie.

'Oh, it's a shame if he couldn't make it,' sighed Ruby. 'It would have been a nice surprise for Sam.'

'Give him a call,' suggested Charlie.

'I don't have his number.'

'Oh, well, let's get back, so I can check on my tomatoes,' said Charlie.

Charlie's hopes of rushing back to his precious tomatoes were dashed when a young man appeared at the station exit, glanced around, then gave them a wave and headed in their direction.

'Is that him?' asked Charlie.

Ruby stared at the young man walking towards her. 'I'm not sure.'

It had been years since she had last seen him. The young man in front of her bore no resemblance to the small twelve-year old boy she remembered. 'Tolly?!'

'Hello, Mrs Jenkinson. I swear you haven't changed since I last saw you.'

This was more or less true. One advantage of Ruby plastering make-up on her face with a trowel for donkey's years was that she still looked the same.

Ruby opened her arms and hugged him, more for the compliment than any pleasure at seeing him again.

'Thank you for picking me up. I could have easily taken a taxi.'

'It's no trouble at all, and call me Ruby. Mrs Jenkinson makes me sound old.'

Charlie shook his hand. 'Hello, young Tolly.'

'Hello, Mr Jenkinson.'

'Call me Charlie. Everyone calls me Charlie.'

'It's a shame you're not staying the night,' said Ruby. 'You could have stayed in our spare room.'

'I have to get back tonight,' explained Tolly. 'I have a play to do tomorrow.'

'That sounds exciting,' exclaimed Ruby. 'A play, you say. Do you have a good part?'

Tolly put his hands together as if in prayer and looked to the heavens. 'I do, but thankfully it's just temporary. It's a terrible production.'

Ruby made Charlie sit in the back of the car, so Tolly could sit beside her. 'Sam will be so pleased to see you. Have you met his husband, Anton?' Ruby crunched the car into gear and set straight off, making a couple in their forties run for their lives. 'People just don't look where they're going,' shouted Ruby in the direction of the shaken pair.

'Yes, several times,' said Tolly. 'I couldn't make the wedding, but I met them for dinner when they got back from their honeymoon and stayed with them a couple of times.'

'Anton is just Sam's mate,' piped up Charlie from the back seat. 'They're just mates.'

'Ignore my homophobic husband,' said Ruby, who was now driving so slowly that a queue of traffic was building up in her wake. 'He's an idiot.'

'Is it still OK for me to stay with you until the party starts?' asked Tolly, beginning to wonder if the car had a third gear.

'What party?' asked Charlie, his head appearing between the two of them.

Ruby shook her head in despair. 'Sam's surprise twenty-fifth birthday party! If you didn't keep switching your ear thing off, you'd know about it!'

Tolly spotted a mobility scooter undertaking them on the pavement, but Ruby was oblivious as she launched into the story of the hysterectomy she had had several years ago and how the surgeon had been impressed to see she was the only woman wearing full make-up thirty minutes after coming round from the anaesthetic.

The slow journey back ended with Ruby driving over part of the front lawn before pulling up on the driveway outside the bungalow. 'That was a nice clear run,' she said with a smile, 'not a car in sight.'

'Not such a clear run for the traffic jam behind us,' thought Tolly, who had noticed the long line of cars in the wing mirror on his side.

'Do you like tomatoes?' asked Charlie, as he struggled to get out of the back seat.

'I suppose I do,' answered Tolly. He climbed out of the car and stood looking at Ruby and Charlie's bungalow. It had not changed at all; it was just as he remembered.

'Let the man come in and have a cup of tea before you bore him half to death about tomatoes,' groaned Ruby. She took a bunch of keys out of her coat pocket and unlocked the front door.

Ten minutes later, Tolly was sitting in their kitchen, drinking tea and eating a piece of sponge cake that Ruby had made especially for her guest, while Charlie talked him through two hundred pictures of his tomato and vegetable crop from last year.

'…and my beefsteak tomatoes were very poor. I'm not sure if it was Dolly Parton's fault or not,' sighed Charlie.

'Leave poor Tolly alone,' said Ruby, topping up Tolly's cup and giving him another slice of cake. 'He doesn't want to look at photographs of veg.'

'Ah!' said Charlie, holding up one finger to emphasise the importance of his point. 'Botanically speaking, tomatoes are fruits—'

'We don't bleedin' care!' screamed Ruby.

'I don't mind,' said Tolly out of politeness.

Charlie beamed. 'Well, Tolly, if you liked those photos, just wait till you see the crop I had with Bing Crosby! I'll get them.'

Ruby rolled her eyes as Charlie hurried off to find the relevant photo album. 'He's mad, Tolly, mad as a hatter. This is what I have to put up with. I blame the paint factory he worked in for forty years. All those fumes have done something to his brain.'

Charlie was chuckling with enthusiasm when he rushed back in carrying a large photograph album. He placed it in front of Tolly and flicked through the pages until he came to a picture of tomatoes on a vine. 'There you go, Tolly. Tell me if you've ever seen a better crop of Fandangoes in your life.'

Tolly decided that Ruby was right, and that Charlie was as mad as a hatter.

Sam's surprise birthday party had been planned for months and would start at seven o'clock that evening. The plan was for his father, Gary, to take him out for the day while his mother and Anton arranged catering and decorating at the family home. At seven p.m., Gary would bring him back to the house, and when Sam entered, the hiding guests would jump out to surprise him.

The grandparents' bungalow was only two streets away, so at the designated time, Ruby, Charlie and Tolly were supposed to make their way to the house. The strict timetable started to crumble when Ruby refused to let Charlie leave the house unless he put his nice glasses on. It took twenty minutes of searching before Charlie found them in his greenhouse. There was another delay after going into the greenhouse reminded Charlie that he needed to set the plug timer up for his CD player. His plants needed to be asleep by half past nine, and too much Louis Armstrong on the first day might be a strain.

By the time they reached the house, it was already seven o'clock. As soon as they stepped inside, a female voice whispered loudly, 'Gary's car's just pulled up! You lot hide, and everyone be quiet.'

Ruby tapped Tolly on the shoulder and pointed to a door, and they quickly darted through into the kitchen. It had been over twelve years since Tolly had been inside the house, and he remembered it being slightly bigger than it actually was.

The excited giggling of those in hiding died down until there was near silence. This was broken by Charlie opening the fridge door and pulling out a shop-bought tomato. 'Look at this, Tolly, they call that a tomato! It's been forced, forced, I tell you!'

'Shut up, you silly old fool!' snapped Ruby as quietly as she could under the circumstances. She whispered to Tolly, 'He's turned his bloody ear thing off again!'

A key turned in the lock, and Gary Jenkinson led his unsuspecting son through the front door into the house. 'Why are the curtains drawn?' asked Sam when they stepped into the living room.

The lights came on and the collective shout of 'SURPRISE!' had Sam clutching his chest and laughing nervously. 'Oh, my God!'

Sam was soon surrounded by friends and family. Anton gave Sam a big kiss on the cheek.

'They're just mates,' Charlie assured Tolly.

Lively music began to play, and drinks were passed around as Sam went from person to person. When he saw Tolly standing beside his grandfather, he was overjoyed. The friend who had been at his sixth birthday was here on his twenty-fifth. He hugged him and kissed him on the cheek.

'That's just a mate's kiss,' said Charlie before ambling away to see if he could get a bloody Mary to drink.

Tolly had known Sam Jenkinson since his first day at Brenford Primary School when he was six years old. At the time, Tolly was small, nervous, and through no fault of his own, a year behind all the other kids. He was given the seat next to Sam, and from that day onwards, they had been close friends.

Sam introduced Tolly to some of the others at the party. There was a mixture of neighbours, workmates and friends. Word soon got around that Tolly had been in the *Femme Crédule* advert. He did try to explain that he had been sacked before it was completed, but that did not seem to matter. The younger women asked questions about Tuppence Crow's diet and the make-up she used. He was tempted to tell them that she was a bitch, but decided it was not his job to shatter their illusions.

Despite limiting his alcohol intake because of his need to get back to London, Tolly enjoyed the party and the chance to catch up with his old friend from school.

The large back garden had been decorated with bunting and birthday balloons. There was a makeshift bar that seemed to be stocked with more beer than the pub down the road, and under three large gazebos, tables had been laid out, straining under the amount of party food.

Sam's dad, Gary, was in control of the barbecue in the back garden. He rated himself highly as a barbecue chef despite never lifting a finger in his own kitchen. 'It's man's work,' he told his wife, Jenny. 'There's a lot of heat!' The aforementioned heat went on to burn most of the food, but

Gary insisted this was an essential part of the barbecue experience.

In between answering questions about Tuppence, Tolly managed to chat with Jenny in the garden. She seemed not to have aged at all, though maybe she was wider by a few inches.

'Who'd have thought, Tolly, that you'd be appearing in a TV advert? It must have been exciting.'

'I wasn't in the final cut,' Tolly explained. 'I got sacked.'

'Still,' said Jenny, 'it must have given you a bit of experience. What did your aunt Wendy say when you told her?'

Tolly had been bought up by Wendy and the last thing he wanted was to give her something to worry about. Besides she was now living on the other side of the world.

'I didn't see the point in telling her I was sacked from my first paid job. How are you and the family, Jenny?' he asked, changing the subject.

'We're all okay. My father-in-law is mad, but apart from that, we're fine. It's such a shame Liza couldn't make it tonight,' sighed Jenny. 'She would have loved to have seen you.'

Tolly had forgotten about Liza, Sam's younger sister. She must have been about eight or nine when he had left the area. Back then, she was a tubby, spiteful little red-haired girl, who would scream her head off to get her own way. He and Sam jokingly used to call her the chubby monster, and he dreaded to think what she was like now. 'I would have loved to have seen her too,' he lied. Before he could ask where she was, the sky lit up and a thunderclap boomed in the near distance.

Charlie appeared from the house and ambled to the bottom of the garden. With his hands on his hips, he confidently informed everyone, 'That storm's miles away. It's nowhere near us, take my word for it.'

Hearing his father's prediction and knowing his track record at forecasting the weather, Gary shouted out, 'Quickly, get everything undercover! It's going to pour down any minute.' Seconds later, a flash of forked lightning lit the dark sky, and another almighty thunderclap rolled through the air.

'It will miss us!' insisted Charlie, bemused by his son's overreaction. 'You mark my words.'

Minutes later, torrential rain was pouring down as the lightning flashes and ear-splitting booms of thunder continued.

The house lights, which had been switched on to compensate for the sudden darkness, began to flicker.

Charlie stared out of the window. 'I think it must have turned a corner.'

Another monstrous boom caused several people in the house to scream, and also set off numerous car and house alarms in the area. The lights went out, and the music that had been competing with the storm fell silent.

'It won't last long,' sniffed Charlie, confidently. 'It's just a noisy shower.'

Gary and Jenny rushed around for candles and torches, while Sam had the idea of getting his old battery-powered radio to play music. Switching it on and twiddling the dial, he tuned in a local news report. '…the Met Office has said that the thunderstorms in part of the county have caused flash floods. There are reports of extensive power failures, major roads are reported to be flooded, and all trains have been temporarily cancelled. Stay tuned for further information.'

Tolly checked the app on his phone for train times. His plan to take a late train back to London was scuppered when he saw that all departures from Brenford were being reported as cancelled. As much as he hated having to do another performance of *The Waiting Room*, he was contracted to do just that, even if it meant he had to go to the expense of taking a taxi back. He decided to wait a couple of hours to see if there might be any change to the train timetable.

The party continued in the light from candles and people's phone torches until the electricity came back on at eleven thirty. The house lights then flickered intermittently until midnight when they went off again. The candles were relit, and the battery-powered radio was switched back on.

Tolly was hoping that by now all possible questions about Tuppence Crow had been asked, but he found himself being interrogated in the candlelit kitchen by two drunken young women about what shade of lipstick she wore. Above the noise of chatter and music, he heard Sam's mother, Jenny, scream with delight from the sitting room, 'It's Liza!' Tolly's interrogators were obviously friends of hers because they pushed him out of the way and rushed into the next room to meet her. Just twenty minutes later, Tolly was asked once again how nice Tuppence Crow was. His usual diplomatic reply of, 'She's very nice' was interrupted by Jenny.

'Tolly, do you remember Liza?'

Liza's face was hard to make out in the shadows thrown by the one flickering candle in the kitchen.

'Hello, Liza,' he said. 'I think you'd be too young to remember me.'

'She was still in her tubby phase when you knew her, Tolly,' said Jenny.

'Mum! Don't keep going on about me being tubby.'

'I don't remember her being tubby, just a nice kid,' lied Tolly.

The power came back on to a big cheer from the partygoers. To Tolly's sheer amazement, Zibby's equally shocked face stared back at him.

Jenny proudly gave Liza a hug. 'Would you have recognised her, Tolly?'

'No, I would not have known her in a million years. I can guarantee it.'

Zibby's wide eyes pleaded with Tolly not to let on that they knew each other.

'I see you've been reacquainted with my baby sister,' said Sam, putting an arm around Tolly's shoulder and leaning over to kiss Liza on the cheek.

'I was just saying to your mum I wouldn't have recognised her.'

Sam chuckled. 'Do you remember, Tolly, what you used to call her? The chubby monster.'

'You called me the chubby monster?' asked Zibby angrily.

'Tolly would never have called you that,' said Jenny. 'You never called her that, did you, Tolly?'

'Not that I recall,' said Tolly, recalling just how often he did call her that.

Sam laughed. 'He said it all the time.'

'Hold on,' said Tolly, turning to Sam. 'It was you who called her the chubby monster.' He hoped that would pacify Zibby.

'I did call her the monster,' confessed Sam with a giggle, 'but it was you who added the word chubby.'

With all eyes on him, Tolly felt cornered. 'Kids,' he said, shaking his head, 'they say the funniest things.'

'Chubby,' said Zibby with a scowl.

Tolly thought she had the prettiest glare he had ever seen.

'Hold on, Miss Innocent,' said Jenny. 'I do remember you calling Tolly Concorde nose.'

'Concorde nose?' said Tolly. 'Did I have a big nose back then?'

'Kids say the funniest things,' Zibby reminded him.

The lights went off again, and Sam and Jenny rushed off to find more portable lighting.

'Don't say anything to my family about what I do for a living,' pleaded Zibby in a hushed voice. 'They still think I'm rehearsing with my old company for a new production. Keep pretending this is the first time we've met in years.'

'I won't say anything,' Tolly assured her, 'but I don't see why you should want to keep it a secret.'

'People just assume exotic dancers take all their clothes off. My mum and dad would be embarrassed and ashamed of me.'

'I'm sure that's not true. They would support you.'

'They wouldn't. They didn't pay for my ballet lessons and ferry me around for years to see me end up dancing in a sex shop's theatre. I'm still auditioning for other shows, so with any luck, I'll find something else soon, and they won't be any wiser. So please don't say anything.'

'Okay, if that's what you want.'

'You lied about your name. I've been calling you Archie for the last few weeks.'

'I never meant to lie to you. It's a bit complicated…'

'Go on,' Zibby urged him. 'Tell me.'

'I was unofficially blacklisted, and the only acting job I could get was to fill in for the backer's idiot son until he learns his lines for the play. Archie is his name. I was trying to impress you and forgot his name was on the poster.'

'How long were you going to carry on with that little lie?'

'I just assumed you and Michelle would never see me again once the play goes on tour. Anyway, what about you?' asked Tolly. 'You said your name was Zibby.'

'I had to choose a different name when I applied for my Equity card. They already had a Liza Jenkinson, so I used my nickname, Zibby.'

'Which name do you prefer?'

'Zibby. Ever since I was—'

'A chubby monster?' suggested Tolly.

'No! Ever since I was nine, I've wanted to be called Zibby, and now, thanks to Equity, I am.'

Just then, several of Zibby's friends appeared and whisked her away to the sitting room.

The party began to thin out at midnight. The storm had passed, and the power was restored. Tolly had at last managed to spend some time reminiscing with Sam instead of answering questions about Tuppence Crow.

By one thirty a.m., only friends and family were left. Tolly caught Zibby's eye a couple of times and smiled, but she did not acknowledge him. He kept glancing over at her, but she acted as if he did not exist. By two a.m., the house had been cleared and the furniture put back in position, and the only evidence of the party was a few drunken stragglers.

Tolly checked his phone to find out when the next train to London was due. They were now running again, and one was due to leave at three forty-five a.m. 'You're in luck,' declared Sam, giving him a pat on the shoulder. 'Liza's driving back to London in the next twenty minutes, she can give you a lift.'

'No, it's okay. I can catch a train. I'll just order a cab to the station.'

Sam beckoned his sister over. 'Liza, Tolly can get a lift back to London with you, can't he?'

'If he wants,' muttered Liza, indifferently.

'There you go then! You've got a lift with the chubby monster,' Sam chuckled.

Twenty minutes later, after farewell hugs and promises to keep in touch, Tolly waved goodbye through the passenger window as Zibby put her small hatchback car in gear and sped off.

Before they had even reached the bottom of the road, Zibby said, 'You never said anything to Sam or my parents, did you?'

'You asked me not to say anything, and I did what you asked, even though I felt terrible because Sam's one of my best friends and your mum and dad were good to me in the past.'

'Are you sure you never let on you knew me?'

'How many times do you want me to say no? I never mentioned you once.'

'Do you swear you never said anything?'

'I swear I said nothing! My God, Zibby, you could get a job as an interrogator!'

'Sorry, it's just that I don't want to break their hearts.'

During the two-hour drive back to London, they chatted easily, taking turns to tell the story of their lives so far.

Zibby already knew a lot about Tolly. His mother had died giving birth to him and his father had died five years later while he was in foster care. His Australian auntie Wendy had brought him up in the UK until she had to go back to Sydney to care for her own grown-up daughter, taking twelve-year-old Tolly with her. Tolly filled in the parts she did not know. He had come back when he was eighteen to study for a performing arts degree. He told her of his hunt for work after his training and dealing with the rejection. He made her laugh with his tales of being blacklisted because of

Tuppence Crow treading on his knees and the dreadful play that he was now doing.

It turned out that the flat Zibby shared with Michelle was only three or four miles from the house Tolly shared, so she insisted on dropping him off at the door. It was just after four thirty a.m., with the sun about to break over the distant horizon, when Zibby pulled up outside the semi-detached house. Tolly noticed the house alarm light was on, so he quickly checked his phone.

'Oh, bollocks! I deleted the text.'

'What is it?' asked Zibby.

'I can't get in the house. The couple I share with must be out on an airport run. They have a twelve-seater passenger van and do the odd fare even though they're not licensed.'

'I still don't understand.'

Tolly sighed. 'One of them, Bethan, is paranoid about security after watching a documentary about rising crime. In fact, you could say she's a bit nuts about it. She puts the house alarm on when no one's home and changes the code on a daily basis. She did text me the latest alarm code, but I deleted it by mistake. Hold on, I'll give her a call.'

Tolly pressed Bethan's name and put the call on speakerphone. It rang for five seconds before being answered.

'Is that you, Tolly?' said Bethan's soft Welsh voice.

'Hi, Bethan. What's the code for the house alarm?'

'I texted it to you.'

'I deleted it by mistake.'

'How do I know you're not being held against your will and being coerced into getting the house alarm code by a ruthless gang?'

Tolly put his hand over his phone and whispered to Zibby, 'I said she was nuts.'

'I heard something about nuts,' said Bethan. 'Have the ruthless gang got you by the nuts?'

'Bethan, you'll have to take my word for it that a ruthless gang have not got me by the nuts. Can you just give me the code, please?'

Tolly smiled at Zibby and rolled his eyes.

'If it really is Tolly, what day is my mother's birthday?'

'How the hell would I know that?'

'It's on the calendar in the kitchen, and if you really were Tolly, you'd have seen it.'

'Bethan, I'm tired, please just give me the code.'

'Who's that you're speaking to?' said Malcolm, the other half of the couple, on the phone.

'Someone who may or may not be Tolly, wanting to know the house alarm code,' explained Bethan.

Tolly covered his phone again and turned to Zibby. 'Malcolm's not quite so nuts. It should be okay now.'

'If you are Tolly,' said Malcolm, 'on what part of my body do I have a birthmark?'

'For fuck's sake, Malcolm, I don't know! Just give me the alarm code.'

'It sounds like him,' said Malcolm. 'A bit rude.'

'We believe it is you,' Bethan conceded. 'It's two—'

The signal dropped out. Tolly cursed and called Bethan again. 'Sorry about this,' he said as he waited for a connection that never came. 'Great, I've lost the signal now. I'll give it a few minutes and try again.' He opened the passenger door. 'Thank you for the lift, I owe you one.'

'I can't just leave you on the doorstep; you might have to wait for hours. Look, I know you have a performance to do tonight. Why not just crash on my couch for a few hours? Michelle never gets out of bed before ten, so you'll get at least four hours' sleep.'

The idea of sitting on the doorstep for God knows how many hours did not appeal to him. 'You would be doing me a favour. That will be two I owe you.' He closed the passenger door.

Zibby pulled away into the fresh morning light. 'I'm only doing this because you're a friend of the family.'

'I appreciate it, I really do.'

Ten minutes later, Tolly followed Zibby up two flights of stairs to the flat she shared with Michelle. With exaggerated tiptoeing, she led him into the hallway, pointed out where the bathroom was and beckoned him to follow her into the open-plan living area. 'You crash on the couch,' whispered Zibby. 'I'll just let Michelle know you're here in case you give her a shock, and I'll get you a blanket.' She tiptoed off.

Two minutes later, she crept back and found Tolly was already stretched out on the couch and fast asleep. She placed the blanket over him and stared at his face. It wasn't handsome in the conventional sense, but it was nice to look at.

It was the smell of toast that woke Tolly up later that morning. That and a raging erection which was just taking the edge off his urgent desire to urinate.

He was still wearing his clothes and covered by the blanket that Zibby had given him. He sat up to see her and Michelle sitting at a small table.

'Would you like some toast, Sleeping Beauty?' giggled Michelle.

'Can I just use the bathroom?' asked Tolly. 'I'm desperate for a pee.'

'You know where it is,' said Zibby, pointing to the hallway.

Tolly was conscious of his aroused state and held the blanket in front of him while hunching over in a vain attempt to hide it.

'Morning wood?' laughed Michelle before biting into her slice of toast.

'I can't confirm or deny that,' mumbled Tolly as he dashed towards the hallway.

'Who'd have thought that Archie or whatever his name is—'

'Tolly,' said Zibby.

'—that Tolly would be your brother's best friend, the one boy I've ever known you to have the hots for.'

'I never had the hots for him!' protested Zibby. 'All I said was that I liked him. Anyway, even if I did have the hots for him, as you so elegantly put it, my family treat him like he's one of us, so it would be… weird.'

'Just because the rest of your family treat him that way, you don't have to. Until yesterday, he was a complete stranger to you.'

A few minutes later, Tolly carried the blanket back in, now folded, and placed it on the couch. 'Thank you for letting me stay here last night, or this morning, I should say, but I'd better get going. I have a lot to do today.'

'I'll give you a lift,' offered Zibby.

'No, no, you've done too much for me already. I know the area, and I could do with a walk to wake me up.'

Michelle offered him some buttered toast from a pile on a plate. He took a slice and thanked them once more.

'Break a leg,' shouted Zibby as Tolly headed for the door.

Tolly turned and smiled. 'I wish I could break my leg, then I wouldn't have to do the play with a bunch of idiots.' He waved and was gone.

Zibby watched him from the window as he strolled down the street.

'If you don't want to be incestuous with a family friend,' said Michelle, 'I might just see if he's interested in me. Would it bother you?'

'No, he's just a family friend.' Zibby stood watching Tolly until he was out of sight.

10

Dancing and dildos

When Tolly arrived at the Aphrodite theatre that night, he had the distinct impression that the rest of the cast were looking down on him. The newspaper reviews of the first night had been good, but as Choco Chocs Doreen had mentioned on numerous occasions since then, they would have been even better if Tolly had played the part properly by projecting his intentions. Tolly was baffled to find his efforts at polite small talk with the other cast members being met with cold shoulders and mumbles of, 'Amateur' when his back was turned. Tolly had just figured out that the bitchy Choco Chocs Doreen must be behind it, and was marvelling that she had so much influence, when to his surprise Esmeralda took him aside.

'I don't want you to take this as criticism,' she said, critically, 'but it's about your performance.'

Tolly had a feeling that he was now going to find out why he was being treated badly by the others. 'What was wrong with it?'

'It just wasn't big enough!' explained Esmeralda.

'Not big enough?' said Tolly, not quite believing what he was hearing.

'The only negative from all the reviews was that you underplayed the part, and the rest of the cast are not happy about it.'

'I played it naturally,' said Tolly. 'Everyone else was playing it far too big and over the top!'

'It's called projecting, and you need to project like the others! It sounds like you're mumbling your lines.'

'I'm speaking normally!' protested Tolly. 'Everyone else is shouting. Anyway, before the reviews, you said my portrayal was real and a joy to see.'

'It is a joy to see, it's just not a joy to hear. It needs to be, you know, acted better and projected.'

'Acted better and projected?' said Tolly incredulously. 'I feel like I'm in a butcher's shop with all those hams on stage with me.'

'Try it, darling, try it tonight. Project yourself loudly, roll your eyes and use those hands a lot more. Make it big, make it bold!'

That night, Tolly stubbornly played it like he had for the first performance, letting the others attempt to outact each other, which they did with vigour.

He was flabbergasted when they received another standing ovation. Everyone's acting was way over the top, and Choco Chocs Doreen had built up her part with some extra lines of her own because she thought her character should have more to say.

Esmeralda was not pleased with Tolly when she burst into the dressing room after the play. 'What was that?' she demanded. 'I never saw you project once!'

'It's called acting,' said Tolly defiantly. 'I will not ham up my performance. Anyway, you shouldn't moan at me, you should moan at Choco Chocs Doreen. She's added extra lines; I couldn't get mine out because she wouldn't stop rattling on.'

'Choco Chocs Doreen is convinced that Shaftesbury meant to give her some extra lines; she is the star after all, and she has done TV. Her face is putting bums on seats.'

'Her part is not the leading role. Her character is there solely to portray the perceived reactions of a working-class woman to the abstract and absurd difficulties my character struggles with. She doesn't need extra lines.'

Archie strutted into the dressing room. 'Have you told It yet?'

'I was just about to, darling,' said Esmeralda. 'Just give me a min—'

'I'm playing the lead in Aberdeen, and I'm going to be brilliant, because I'm a brilliant actor,' announced Archie, unable to wait.

Tolly could not quite digest this new piece of information. He didn't know whether to be annoyed or pleased. 'Really?'

Esmeralda stared at Tolly's face reflected in the dressing-room mirror. 'Archie knows how to project, don't you, darling?'

'YES!' bellowed Archie.

'He's learnt ninety pages of dialogue?' said Tolly.

'Not quite,' confessed Esmeralda, 'but after Isabella read the lukewarm reviews of your performance then saw that you didn't even try to project tonight, she feels Archie could do a better job.'

Tolly could see a sliver of light. 'Does this mean I'm sacked?' He crossed his fingers, thinking of the full-payment clause Suzanne had negotiated in his contract.

'Oh, no,' said Esmeralda. 'This means you are the new understudy for Archie.'

Twenty minutes later, Tolly was still going through mixed emotions about the way he had been replaced by an idiot who couldn't remember lines or do anything that might be recognised as acting for that matter. His self-esteem really had hit an all-time low. Trying to look on the bright side, he reminded himself that he was getting paid, and his name would never appear in any of the credits for the play. All he had to do was put up with all this for a few weeks. One of the theatre staff popped into his dressing room and informed him that someone was waiting for him in the bar. He assumed it was Suzanne, hoping for more champagne and canapés. The theatre bar was full, with Choco Chocs Doreen holding court and telling everyone how brilliant she was in her usual subtle way.

'You might well say I was brilliant,' she gushed, in response to a compliment no one had given, 'but because I am a renowned TV star and acclaimed locum thespian, modesty forbids me from confirming it myself.' She spotted Tolly, snorted her disapproval and turned her back on him.

Tolly decided that if he ever snapped and went on a killing spree, Choco Chocs Doreen would find herself very near the top of his list of potential victims. He surveyed the bar area for Suzanne, but it was Zibby and Michelle who waved to him from a corner table. He was pleased to see some friendly faces and went over to sit with them.

'We just watched the play,' said Michelle.

'Oh, please don't tell me you paid to watch that rubbish,' sighed Tolly.

'We thought you were great,' said Zibby. 'But you're right, the rest of it was terrible, thanks to your co-stars.'

Tolly noticed the girls had soft drinks. 'Can I get you a glass of wine or something?'

'We have to work in fifteen minutes, so no booze for us,' explained Zibby.

'But we could go for a drink after our show,' suggested Michelle, who had made it clear to Zibby that she was going to make a play for Tolly.

Tolly smiled and nodded. 'You came to see me, so I'll come and see you. And afterwards, I'll buy you a drink for sitting through this all-out-shit play.'

'Agreed,' laughed Michelle, holding out her hand for Tolly to shake. 'But all-out shit means good.'

Tolly shook her hand, then held his hand out for Zibby to shake. She felt his firm but gentle grip on her hand and was surprised to find the feeling stayed with her for a long time afterwards.

'We better get going,' said Michelle.

'Yes,' agreed Zibby, standing up, 'we need to warm up before we dance.'

'Let's swap phone numbers,' suggested Michelle, 'just in case we miss each other.'

Tolly swapped numbers with her to ensure they would meet up after the show. He watched the two of them leave, thinking about how attractive they were. He might have been sacked from the lead role and now be understudy to a moron, but his ego and vanity received a boost from all the envious male eyes now glaring at him.

Tolly was surprised at how full the theatre was for an exotic dance show that started so late in the evening. It was not just men, but an even mix of both sexes. He took a seat at the end of an aisle. He was surprised to hear at least three different languages from people around him, having not realised this was a tourist attraction. The lights dimmed, and a spotlight shone on the figure of an overly made-up middle-aged woman wearing the most glittery outfit Tolly had ever seen. She welcomed the audience in at least ten different languages, receiving grateful applause. The spotlight briefly went out, and an energetic Eurodisco beat began to play. The stage lit up, the curtains opened, and the first dancer leapt on to the stage in a dominatrix outfit, skilfully wielding a whip while she gyrated to the pounding beat. The dance was less than five minutes, but the dominatrix gave it her all and ended up gasping for breath. The applause was generous, including a standing ovation from a group of Japanese businessmen. To Tolly's surprise, the dancers who followed were sexier and even more energetic. By the time Michelle and Zibby appeared on stage, Tolly doubted there was anything they could do to top what he had seen already, but he was wrong, oh, so wrong. The two girls were artistic, sexy and passionate, and danced with such enthusiasm, it made it seem like the other girls had not been trying. They threw themselves into a dance that was like a tango, but at an accelerated pace. The girls hurled each other across the stage with such violence that the audience gasped in anticipation of a serious injury. At the end of their set, the girls passionately embraced. Tolly could not believe that, after all that physical activity, they were not panting like some of the audience. The girls received a standing ovation that only stopped when the curtain closed. Tolly stayed seated as the other happy spectators made their way out through an exit straight on to the Soho streets.

Once the theatre had emptied completely, he went through into the sex shop, which was still doing a brisk trade well after midnight. He browsed uncomfortably, feeling sexually naive and worried that his libido must be on the low side. He blushed as he ducked under the dildos of every shape, size and colour dangling on wires from the ceiling. He jumped when most of them suddenly began to vibrate and dance around.

103

'They do that once an hour,' said a camp voice in a soft Danish accent. The voice belonged to a stout man in his thirties, standing behind a glass counter showcasing a wide selection of butt plugs. He was wearing a rubber bondage suit. 'It always cheers me up. There's nothing more comforting than the buzz of a dildo, is there?'

'I wouldn't know,' said Tolly quickly.

The assistant noticed Tolly suspiciously eyeing the largest dildo dancing on the ceiling, so he produced a demonstration model from under the counter. 'My name is Sven, and I would like to introduce you to one of our bestsellers, the Pelvic Bone Shaker.' He licked his lips and held it up for Tolly to admire. 'It's got twelve different movements, it's rechargeable, and it will give you forty-eight minutes of bliss on the highest setting.' Sven smiled, leant forward, and added in a hushed voice. 'I speak from experience.'

'I'm sure you do,' said Tolly, hoping this wouldn't encourage Sven to keep talking.

'It feels just like a real penis,' said Sven. 'Do you want to touch it? It's got veins and everything.'

'I'll take your word for it.'

'It comes with a free butt plug!' said Sven, sensing a sale.

'We get a staff discount if you want to buy it,' said Zibby's voice.

Tolly turned to see her and Michelle standing behind him, laughing.

'I wouldn't have put you down as a dildo connoisseur,' Michelle teased him.

'Were you thinking of buying that one?' asked Zibby, innocently.

'No,' said Tolly defensively. 'It just took me by surprise when I saw it.'

'It took me by surprise as well,' said Sven. 'A very pleasant surprise though!'

'Sorry, Sven,' said Michelle. 'He was just waiting for us.'

'Shall we go, Tolly?' said Zibby. 'Or do you want to keep browsing dildos?'

'I wasn't browsing! I was just waiting,' insisted Tolly. He watched the girls head for the door, giggling again.

He hurried after them. 'You had me going then!'

He caught up with them outside. 'You were both amazing tonight. I was blown away by how fantastic you were, it was truly wonderful.'

'Why, thank you,' said Michelle with a flirty smile.

'We're pleased you liked it,' added Zibby.

Michelle put her arm in Tolly's. 'We know a little club round the corner where we can get a late drink. Shall we go?'

'I can only stay for an hour,' warned Tolly. 'I have a lot of things to sort out before I go on this stupid tour.'

The little club was called the Little Club, and it was just a few streets away down a back alley. Michelle held on to Tolly's arm as if they were a couple. Zibby had never been bothered by Michelle's flirty behaviour, it was part of her nature, but seeing her flirt with Tolly made her feel oddly jealous.

A few people were standing outside a Victorian red-brick building, smoking cigarettes and other substances. They glanced at Tolly suspiciously, but as soon as they recognised Zibby and Michelle, they welcomed them with smiles and air kisses. Inside the doorway of the Little Club, a staircase led down a flight of stairs to a pair of heavy doors. As soon as Zibby pulled one open, the smell of alcohol and the noise of people talking and laughing escaped into the night air.

'What sort of club is this?' asked Tolly as they walked into a tiny bar area.

'It's a club for Soho workers,' Michelle informed him. 'It's open twenty-four hours a day, and you can come here and not be judged for your choice of career.'

Tolly had to admit that it seemed friendly and welcoming.

'Because most people here are in the sex business, they want somewhere to get away from it and relax,' added Zibby.

At the bar, a beautiful blonde barmaid in her early thirties gave them a broad and perfect smile, and in a deep, gruff and manly cockney accent said, 'The usual, ladies?' She reached for a bottle of white wine.

'Yes, please, Tabitha,' said Michelle and Zibby.

'What about you, mate?' said Tabitha, filling two wine glasses.

'I'll have the same, thanks, mate,' said Tolly without thinking. 'I meant miss, sorry, I meant miss.'

'You can call me whatever you like,' said Tabitha with a seductive smile, thrusting out the perfect breasts squeezed into her tight-fitting lemon-coloured dress.

'Ignore her,' laughed Michelle. 'She is a real flirt.'

Tolly shyly paid for the drinks with a contactless card, trying to keep his eyes strictly above Tabitha's neckline, before following the girls over to a row of cushioned bench seats upholstered in plush red velvet. One was free, so Zibby sat on one side while Michelle sat on the other and patted the seat next to her, indicating that Tolly should sit there.

'What do you think of the place, Tolly?' asked Zibby, as she noticed Michelle sliding along the seat so her body brushed Tolly's.

His initial apprehension at being in a club for workers in the sex trade had faded, and Tolly now felt safe and relaxed. 'I really like it. It's bohemian.'

Zibby smiled. 'I'm glad you like it.'

Michelle took a sip of wine. 'Zibby's boyfriend, Pepe, hates the place.'

Tolly had not even considered the possibility that Zibby might have a boyfriend. The information brought on an instant melancholy that he could not explain. Why had he thought Zibby was single? She was pretty, funny, the sort of girl who would have numerous admirers. For the next hour, he forced himself to act as if he were carefree and unconcerned about Zibby having a boyfriend. When he finally checked his watch and told them he had to go, Michelle kissed him on the lips and whispered in his ear, 'Call me when you get home.'

Zibby watched Tolly walk away. She noticed that he deliberately went over to Tabitha to say his farewell before heading for the door. She wondered whether he would stop and turn for one last glance back, but he kept on going.

'Why did you have to mention Pepe?' asked Zibby.

'Because you said Tolly was like a brother and you weren't interested,' said Michelle. 'You know what, Zibby? I think I could really fall for him.'

11

Trouble up north

The next day, the cast and crew of *The Waiting Room* headed north. The crew took the props by truck while the company went by train. Isabella Billings had made it known to her sister from the beginning that she would be joining the tour and had bought all the seats in a first-class carriage, so that her precious Archie did not have to mix with ordinary people, or 'plebs' as Archie liked to call them.

Tolly sat alone for the seven-and-a-half-hour journey to Aberdeen. Under the influence of Choco Chocs Doreen, the rest of the cast had ostracised him and now took every opportunity to mention to Isabella, and in earshot of Tolly, how pleased they were that Archie was playing the part of Sid, and how he would do it so much better than his predecessor.

A luxury coach was waiting at Aberdeen station to take the group to the William Wallace Hotel, where they were staying for two nights. The hotel was a large, grey-stone Victorian building that catered primarily to the American tourist market. The carpets were tartan, along with the curtains and anything else covered in fabric. Tolly was handed his room key and was not overly surprised to find his room was at the back of the building with a picturesque view over the tartan-painted waste bins.

Thankfully for Tolly, the crew arrived five hours later. The three-man crew, which was actually two men and one woman, were shocked at first when Tolly told them he was now understudy to Archie. But then it struck them as hysterically funny; so much so that Tolly ended up laughing with them and spent a pleasant evening in their company.

On their first morning in Scotland, Tolly told Esmeralda that he would go with the crew and help set up. Esmeralda was pleased to get rid of him because his presence had been upsetting the rest of the cast.

The small theatre was a delight. It seated six hundred people in the most beautiful ornate building Tolly had ever seen. It dated back to the late eighteen hundreds and was famous for having had Laurel and Hardy perform there in the nineteen fifties.

The following day, Aberdeen's local press would declare that the opening performance of *The Waiting Room* had been memorable – for the wrong reasons. Archie shouted his lines, which he had to read from a script. The rest of the cast decided to ad-lib like Choco Chocs Doreen had in London, and they all competed to be the loudest and project the furthest. Tolly chuckled to himself when members of the audience began to boo after just a few minutes. Choco Chocs Doreen appealed to the crowd from the stage, 'But it's Shaftesbury!' Despite that fact, the punters kept booing all the way to the long queue for refunds.

Back at the hotel bar that evening, the general consensus among the cast was that Scottish people were heathens and would not know culture if it slapped them in the face. Tolly thought there were probably five million highly cultured people in the country who would strongly disagree with that verdict.

'Once we're back in England, the appreciation of culture will resume,' Choco Chocs Doreen reassured the others. Secretly, she thought the play would have gone down better if only the Choco Chocs adverts had been shown on TV north of the border.

Naturally, Isabella thought her son had done a wonderful job. 'I had to pinch myself,' she told Esmeralda. 'My Archie is the best actor in the world. Who knew?'

Esmeralda did not entirely share her sister's blinkered admiration. 'He will need to stop reading the script on stage and try to remember it.'

'My Archie wants to carry on playing the role, and I want to keep on watching him. So, seeing as I are funding the play, he will be the lead. Just make sure the others act as well as he does. My poor Archie found it difficult to give his performance one hundred percent when the other actors were getting booed. Choco Chocs Doreen said my Archie is a dazzling light compared to the rest of the cast, and he proved his greatness by ignoring the boos aimed at the lesser cast members.'

Choco Chocs Doreen was diligently continuing her charm offensive with the real power in the company, still making every effort to sit beside Archie's mother or tell her how wonderful she thought Archie was. 'He's so brilliant at acting,' she informed Isabella after the disastrous first performance, 'that it is a privilege to be on stage with him and bask in his natural talent.' Choco Chocs Doreen pretended to cry. 'He's such a wonderful young man. To have that much talent and be so humble is a gift, and if I might say so, I think those star qualities come from you.'

Isabella smiled with joy. This only confirmed what she had known all along: her Archie was a natural talent, and she would see that he became a star of the theatre. Without hesitation, she approved Choco Chocs Doreen's suggestion that her character should be on stage more because her vast experience as a TV thespian would allow her to highlight Archie's greatness.

The next performance of *The Waiting Room* was in two days' time in the historic town of Berwick-upon-Tweed, just south of the Scottish border. The venue informed Esmeralda that ticket sales were strong. Thankfully, news of the Aberdeen performance had evidently not travelled south.

The following day, an executive coach drove the company to their hotel just outside the border town while Tolly travelled with the crew to help set up the stage.

Weeks before, Esmeralda had secured a promotional interview on the local radio station, Tweed Radio, for the afternoon they arrived. Choco Chocs Doreen had immediately volunteered to be interviewed because she had the highest profile, thanks to her TV adverts. Isabella also insisted that her Archie should be on the show because he was, after all, the main star.

Kenny Humble had the afternoon spot on Tweed Radio and liked to add a bit of culture among the middle-of-the-road pop songs that filled most of the time between the adverts for double glazing and funeral directors. Kenny saw himself as a rare cultural beacon for the Berwick-upon-Tweed area and would have a ten-minute culture segment every afternoon. The previous week he had invited the Three Three-Hundred-Pound Tenors into the studio. They were three tenors who each weighed around three hundred pounds. Their individual singing careers had never taken off, so they had decided to team up, with incredible success. The great British public clearly knew a bargain when they saw one. Three tenors for the price of one was excellent value for money. If it had been a tight squeeze getting them into the tiny radio studio, getting them out had proved even more difficult after two of the Three Three-Hundred-Pound Tenors had got jammed in the narrow doorway. When Kenny and his female producer had failed to free them, an urgent call had gone out to the local fire service. After the firefighters had failed to budge them, another call had gone out to the local volunteer lifeboat crew who had recently rescued a stranded whale. Between them, they had eventually managed to free the large singers without causing any major structural damage to the building.

Kenny Humble had been looking forward to interviewing the director and cast of the Shaftesbury play. He had read about the play online and was pleased to see the critics had used a lot of big words. Big words meant culture, and *The Waiting Room* had had more big words written about it than anything else he had covered in a long time. A pan-pipe version of a song from *Evita* was playing, to set the tone for Kenny's culture section, as the radio show's producer led Esmeralda, Choco Chocs Doreen and Archie into the small studio and introduced them to Kenny.

Esmeralda had been listening to Kenny's voice on the drive over to the studio and expected him to be middle-aged. She was caught off guard when Kenny turned out to be in his seventies and looked as though he had had a hard life. His deeply lined face had a deathly pallor and was framed by long, dyed dark hair that was beginning to thin. He wore round, wire-rimmed glasses with blue-tinted lenses, and his teeth were bright, denture white. He was dressed in the same hippy fashions that had suited him in his twenties because he had never found any reason to change his style.

'Grab a seat, guys,' said a smiling Kenny, indicating three chairs beside his desk.

Choco Chocs Doreen rushed over to the seat nearest Kenny, so he would know that she was the important one.

'The song finishes in forty seconds,' Kenny informed them. 'And after that, I'll talk about the play, and you can introduce yourselves to the culture-hungry Berwick audience.' The pan pipes faded out and Kenny introduced his culture section.

'An allegory of an allegorical tale about an allegory, of course I'm talking about the landmark play *The Waiting Room*. I love an allegory,' said Kenny, now wishing he'd looked up the word in the dictionary beforehand. 'And to have an allegory about an allegory is the best.'

'And it's allegorical,' said Choco Chocs Doreen helpfully.

'The critics have called the play an apologue of asinine juxtapositions,' added Esmeralda. She had read the quote somewhere and liked to use it, even if she did not have a clue what it meant.

Kenny was excited; this was real culture with long words that he did not understand. 'That was my first thought after seeing the play for the first time,' lied Kenny. 'Now, let's have a chat with the cast. Who have we got here?' He pointed to Archie.

'I'm Archie Billings and I'm a brilliant actor,' shouted Archie.

'Tell me, Archie,' said Kenny, 'what part do you play?'

Archie was stumped. He looked over to his aunt Esmeralda.

'He plays Sid Galton, the lead character,' said Esmeralda quickly.

'Now, Esmeralda is the director of the play,' explained Kenny. Esmeralda held her hand up to confirm her identity. 'And I would love to hear how this production of this classic play came about.'

'Like every culture lover in the business—' said Esmeralda.

'Just for my listeners, I'll explain that you mean show business,' said Kenny.

Esmeralda restarted. 'Like every culture lover in the business, I adore the work of Shaftesbury, and just had this inner calling to bring his work to the wider public.'

'Can I just say, in my own appreciative way,' said Kenny with false sincerity, 'thank you for bringing classic culture to our town and theatre? How has the play been received so far?'

'Wonderful reviews in London,' said Esmeralda. 'A triumph, said the London news. We were all overwhelmed by the response.'

'Please do not mention Aberdeen,' thought Esmeralda, behind her fixed smile.

'You just played Aberdeen,' said Kenny, right on cue. 'How did the play go down in Scotland?'

Rather than being ready to pounce on her answer, Kenny was responding to a button flashing on his console, so Esmeralda felt pretty sure that he had not seen the reviews from further north. 'There's always a clash of cultures when you get a very English play being performed in Scotland, but considering how English it is, it did better than expected.'

Kenny turned to Choco Chocs Doreen. 'According to my list, you must be Choco Chocs Doreen.'

Choco Chocs Doreen laughed a little bit too loudly. 'You spotted me straight away, didn't you, Kenny?' She pointed at her own smug face. 'The Choco Chocs TV advert... Yes, it is me in the flesh and not on your television screen.'

'What is it like, performing a classic piece of work like *The Waiting Room*?'

'Oh, very different from my Choco Chocs TV experience. In the play, the character is written, but in my Choco Chocs advertisement, I had to invent the character I portrayed. The director said that I breathed life into a one-dimensional character to produce a two-dimensional one. Praise indeed.'

'The play is on for one performance only at the Berwick Theatre tomorrow night,' Kenny informed his listeners. 'I'll be there, because I love an allegory, and it's not often you get a chance to see a work of genius performed locally. Thank you all for coming in today and being my guests—'

'I will be signing autographs after the play,' interrupted Choco Chocs Doreen.

Kenny pushed a button on his console. 'Now, from one piece of culture, let's go to another.'

The song *Do You Really Want to Hurt Me* by Culture Club, but the pan-pipe version, began to play to radio listeners all around Berwick.

Esmeralda was pleasantly surprised to be informed, later that evening, that ticket sales had increased thanks to their appearance on Kenny Humble's show. After the terrible performance in Aberdeen, Esmeralda had doubts about letting Archie play the lead again, at least until he had memorised some of the script. When she mentioned to her sister in the hotel restaurant that it might be prudent to let Tolly play the part in Berwick, just to give Archie a chance to learn his lines, Isabella was furious.

'My Archie knows all his lines! He just needed to read the script to make sure he was saying them in the right order. Anyway, Choco Chocs Doreen says my Archie could use cue cards like Marlon Brando did, because he has the same star quality.'

Esmeralda sighed. 'Brando was a movie actor. The cue cards were placed out of shot. You can't do that in a play.'

'Choco Chocs Doreen said we can put cue boards up on the side of the stage, so my Archie can check which words he should be projecting.'

'Isabella,' pleaded Esmeralda, 'let's just let the understudy play it tonight. Archie can use the extra time to get word-perfect.'

'This play would not have got off the ground without Billings money bankrolling it,' said Isabella. 'So my Archie will play the lead tonight and every night because he's the star!'

'I couldn't help but overhear you mention dearest Archie,' interrupted Choco Chocs Doreen. As always, as part of her quest to consolidate their friendship, she had been sitting close to Isabella. 'If I could just say, speaking as a humble renowned TV star and acclaimed locum thespian, I thought his performance as Sid the other evening was bewitching. It was so compelling that I forgot completely that he was reading from a script. That is what the great actors do, they bewitch you. I'm sorry, emotion prevents me from saying more, but Archie has the star quality that we jobbing thespians can only dream of.'

'See?' said Isabella. 'My Archie is bewitching and...?'

'Compelling,' said Choco Chocs Doreen. 'Transcendent as well.'

'There you go,' concluded Isabella. 'My Archie is compelling and transcendent, and that is the professional opinion of a renowned TV star!'

Esmeralda had begun to regret giving a role to Choco Chocs Doreen, who was starting to exert too much influence on her sister and the play. 'Okay,' she said. 'Let's see how Archie does tonight with cue boards.'

Esmeralda found Tolly and instructed him to write out Sid's lines on cue boards, which he would have to hold up for Archie to read during the performance. Even with Pippa's help, it took Tolly hours to write the pages and pages of dialogue on to the boards, and he was still scribbling away that evening when the theatre began to fill up with people.

Meanwhile, as Archie gazed into his dressing room mirror with his adoring mother beside him, Esmeralda explained to him that Tolly would hold up the cue boards for him to read from during the play.

'So when I see the cue boards,' said Archie, as his mother combed his dark hair, 'I absorb the lines like Choco Chocs Doreen told me.'

'What do you, mean absorb the lines?' asked Esmeralda.

'Because I'm a brilliant actor,' explained Archie, turning his head to admire himself from another angle in the mirror, 'I just need to know the intention behind the words and I can say what I think my character would. Choco Chocs Doreen said I was brilliant at it.'

'It's a Shaftesbury play, you have to say the words he wrote,' insisted Esmeralda.

Isabella stared at her sister as if she was an idiot. 'No, you do not! According to Choco Chocs Doreen, who is, may I remind you, a renowned TV star, all you have to do is absorb the words and project the intention, and my Archie is a natural at that.'

'As director of the play, I insist that the script should be stuck to,' said Esmeralda firmly.

'As producer of the play,' retorted Isabella, 'I say you're sacked. Choco Chocs Doreen would be better at directing than you.'

'I'm your sister!' exclaimed Esmeralda, briefly reflecting that she had had the same love-hate relationship with her older sister ever since they were children. 'And Archie wouldn't even be acting if I hadn't had the idea to put this play on.'

Isabella enjoyed the feeling of power that marrying into a wealthy family had brought her. As soon as people knew she was rich, she was treated differently, respected and even feared. Knowing that her sister was so dependent on her financial backing gave her a great deal of pleasure. 'Choco Chocs Doreen recognises Archie's genius,' she said earnestly. 'A once-in-a-generation lead actor – that's what she thinks of Archie, and she's right. Have I mentioned that she's a TV star and a renowned locum thespian/director?'

'Locum thespian/director?!'

'Choco Chocs Doreen confessed to taking the directing reins from Noel Coward when he had the flu,' said Isabella.

By now, Esmeralda had stopped believing a word that came out of Choco Chocs Doreen's mouth. 'Isabella, Noel Coward's been dead for years. I'm not even sure she was alive when he died.'

'He can't be dead,' stated Archie, 'because his plays are still being performed, I checked.'

Choco Chocs Doreen had been patiently waiting in the corridor for Isabella to inform her sister of the changes. She now made her entrance into the dressing room. 'I hope I'm not interrupting,' she said, with the intention of interrupting them.

'I've just informed my sister that you will be taking over as director,' declared Isabella.

'This is my production!' shouted Esmeralda. 'I am the director!'

'I believe,' said Choco Chocs Doreen, humbly, 'that dear Isabella is the play's main investor and can change whatever she likes.'

'You're making a big mistake,' Esmeralda warned her sister.

Choco Chocs Doreen shook her head and smiled. 'There is no mistake. Isabella knows that I, a renowned TV star and acclaimed locum thespian/director, appreciate the charisma and star quality which oozes from Archie while he is on the stage. He is a talent that must be nurtured for the sake of show business and the whole nation.'

'Tell her how good I am at absorbing,' said Archie.

'The delightful Archie is like a sponge,' said Choco Chocs Doreen obligingly. 'He absorbs it and projects the intention in a compelling, transcendent way.'

'While being bewitching,' added Archie, who was not afraid to blow his own trumpet.

'Isabella, don't do this,' pleaded Esmeralda. 'You can't mess with a classic play like *The Waiting Room*. The audience could get ugly.'

'As a renowned TV star and acclaimed locum thespian/director, I disagree,' said Choco Chocs Doreen. 'The public appreciate star quality. When they witness Archie projecting the intention of the play they will be captivated, mesmerised, enthralled' – she glanced down at the words she had written on the inside of her wrist – 'and entranced!'

Isabella enjoyed seeing her younger sister's eyes mist over and her bottom lip tremble. 'Tonight, my Archie will give a triumphant performance. Berwick-upon-Tweed will be talking about my Archie's acting ability for years.'

'Tonight, a star will be born,' proclaimed Choco Chocs Doreen, 'thanks to my direction and training in absorption.'

Esmeralda kept a lid on her fury. 'Okay, go ahead. But I can promise you this – it will go badly, very badly.' Then she made an exit any actor would be proud of, marching out of the dressing room with her head held high.

Having spotted Esmeralda coming out of the dressing room, Tolly caught up with her to give her an update on the cue boards. He was shocked and dismayed when she said, 'I'm no longer the director. Go and see that conniving bitch Choco Chocs Doreen.'

He found Choco Chocs Doreen still in Archie's dressing room, along with Isabella fussing over her son. 'Who do I talk to about the cue boards?' asked Tolly.

Choco Chocs Doreen adjusted her paisley silk scarf and proudly pushed her shoulders back. 'Until you are sacked, all communication will be with me, the play's new director.'

Tolly could not believe this news. Choco Chocs Doreen took great pleasure in telling him that, on her watch, he would, 'never appear on stage again!' Just to add to his humiliation, she decided to instruct him in great detail on how to hold the cue boards for Archie, not for him to read the lines, but for him to absorb them.

'Hold the cue boards boldly,' she insisted. 'Archie needs to absorb from a boldly held cue board.'

Tolly held the boards up as instructed.

'I don't see a bold cue board hold,' said Isabella, who was sure that Tolly was jealous of her talented son.

Tolly sighed and held the boards more firmly.

'Better, much better,' said Choco Chocs Doreen. 'Archie, dear,' she said, turning to the spoiled star, 'is he holding the cue boards boldly enough for you?'

Archie glanced over at Tolly. 'Can *it* hold them a bit bolder?'

Tolly wondered how his life had come to this – holding up a board for a moron who had just called him 'it'.

Choco Chocs Doreen demonstrated to Tolly how a cue board should be held boldly. 'Just like this. See how boldly I'm holding the board.'

Tolly held it in exactly the same way as he had done before.

'What about now, Archie?' asked Choco Chocs Doreen.

'*It*'s holding it at the right boldness now,' said Archie with a yawn. 'I can absorb from that.'

'Now, Archie, let's give it try... Absorb for me.'

Archie glanced over at *it* holding the cue board and absorbed the words before projecting their intention by saying a phrase that made no sense. 'More tea, no thank you look fabulous marquee, here comes summers are delightful in trees everywhere.'

Tolly could see a problem. 'Because he's not saying the words on the board, I don't know when to show the next one.'

'Archie's projection of the intention will tell you when to change the cue board,' explained Choco Chocs Doreen, as if she was talking to an idiot, which she was sure she was. 'Try it again.'

Archie re-absorbed the text on the cue board and projected a completely different set of words that made no sense. 'Tweezers do not put food on the table tennis anyone I've got a bat that sees in the dark clouds are coming.'

'He just said a lot of random words,' complained Tolly. 'I still don't know when to show the next cue board.'

Isabella had taken an instant dislike to Tolly in his new role and decided she would have to speak to Choco Chocs Doreen about having him sacked.

Choco Chocs Doreen gave the cue board problem some thought. 'Archie, you could give *it* a slight nod when you've absorbed the board and *it*'ll put up the next one.'

'Fucking amateur,' grumbled Archie, giving Tolly a disapproving stare. 'Okay, I'll give *it* a nod.'

Tolly felt like giving Archie a smack in the mouth. He held the board up for Archie, who absorbed the lines and projected the intention with yet another string of words that made no sense whatsoever. But this time, he gave Tolly a nod to change the board.

Choco Chocs Doreen gave Archie a round of applause for the benefit of his mother. 'What a gifted thespian you are!' she gushed. 'Say no more words, Archie. Save your intentions for tonight's audience.' She pretended to wipe a tear from her eye. 'Oh, Isabella, I apologise for being unprofessional and being mesmerised by your son's ability.'

'I'm so pleased that you see the same star quality as I do in my Archie,' declared Isabella.

'Tonight,' said Choco Chocs Doreen, 'a star will be born. Just you wait and see.'

Tolly took this as his cue to take his cue boards and leave them to it.

The Berwick Theatre was small, only seating three hundred people. Tolly peered out from the wings of the stage and was quite surprised to see all the seats fill up prior to curtain-up. He felt a touch of sympathy for the audience, who had paid good money and had no idea of the fiasco to come. He sorted through the cue boards, ready for Archie to absorb them in the right order, as if that would make any difference. The curtain rose, and Choco Chocs Doreen appeared on stage. As usual, she paused for applause that never came, then began to pace back and forth across the set.

'I hope the wait will not be too long,' she wailed. 'It's lucky I brought some Choco Chocs chocolates with me.' She gave the audience a knowing wink, which left them baffled.

Archie appeared on stage with all the grace of a wooden puppet, stared at the cue board Tolly was holding up in the wings, absorbed the information and projected the intentions to the audience. 'More strawberry jelly dear stalkers are funny hats off to you and me.' In case that line hadn't confused them enough, Archie started shouting about jelly and marmalade sandwiches. It was only two minutes into the play when somebody shouted, 'What a load of old rubbish!' By the five-minute mark, the whole audience were booing and heading for the foyer to get their money back, even Kenny Humble. After ten minutes, the auditorium was empty, and in the queues for refunds, scuffles were breaking out between jostling punters desperate to leave the theatre. Despite there being no audience left, Choco Chocs Doreen insisted the play must go on, so Tolly had to continue holding up cue cards for Archie to absorb. After ten minutes of Archie saying only, 'Blah, blah, blah' because he could not absorb any more, Tolly started skipping three cue cards at a time to speed things up.

At the end of the show, Choco Chocs Doreen led the cast in a bow to empty seats and some staff waiting to lock up.

Later that evening, Choco Chocs Doreen, Isabella and Archie had an urgent meeting and came to two conclusions. The first was that the audience had been too northern to appreciate serious theatre. Their second conclusion was that Tolly had not been holding the cue boards boldly enough, so poor Archie had not been able to absorb as well as he should have.

The next morning, Tolly did some of his best acting after he was summoned to meet Choco Chocs Doreen and Isabella in the hotel breakfast room.

'You ruined last night's performance,' said Choco Chocs Doreen accusingly. 'Poor Archie could hardly absorb because you wouldn't hold the cue boards boldly. It was nothing less than sabotage!'

Isabella got straight to the point. 'You are sacked. I will not have my Archie's career threatened by a jealous understudy.'

Tolly struggled to keep the grin from his face. 'That is a shame. Could you put it in writing, so I can show my agent?'

'Don't worry,' snapped Choco Chocs Doreen. 'I will!' She picked up a white paper napkin from the table, took a pen from her handbag and began writing. 'I'll make sure it mentions your inability to project intentions or even hold cue boards boldly!'

Tolly took the severance napkin and, still suppressing his grin, said, 'Okay, I'll just go and pack my bags. Goodbye and good riddance.'

'Your career is over!' shouted Choco Chocs Doreen, as she watched Tolly walk away with a skip in his step. 'You'll never work in this business again.'

Isabella assembled the rest of the cast and assured them that the performance in Newcastle would be a success because Pipkin had now been dismissed for sabotaging her Archie's formidable talent, and also because Newcastle was a bit further south.

Forty-five minutes after being fired, Tolly was heading for Berwick railway station. He had tried to say goodbye to the cast, but was given the cold shoulder, blamed for the

124

previous night's disastrous performance. He said his farewells to the crew, who he knew he would miss the most, with a promise that he would keep in touch with them. Luckily for him, Berwick was on the Edinburgh to London line, and four hours later, he was staring out at the London suburbs as the train approached King's Cross station.

12

One more time

Malcolm and Bethan, the twenty-something couple Tolly shared a house with, were pleased to see him, and even more pleased when he treated them to a takeaway and drinks down the pub with his wages from the play.

Tolly had received several messages from Michelle over the last couple of days, but as attractive as she was, he could not stop thinking about Zibby. He replied to Michelle's text messages, explaining that the phone signal where he was staying was not very good. He decided not to tell her that he was back in London as she expected him to be away for a month anyway. Later that night, as he lay in bed with his head spinning from too much beer, he decided that acting was not for him and that he would have to join the real world and get a proper paid job. Two days after his return to London, Tolly received a call from Suzanne, saying she needed to see him right away. He had texted her to say that he had been sacked and had had enough of the business. As far as he was concerned, he was no longer an actor and had no need for an agent any more. Besides, he was going to a job interview with a telemarketing firm later that day and was confident enough to believe he would get the job. The interview was not far from Suzanne's office, so he decided to pop in and tell her personally that he had quit showbiz for good.

Tolly entered Suzanne's office at two o'clock that afternoon. She took one look at the green tweed suit he was wearing and said, 'Where are you going, on a shooting party?'

'I've got a job interview at half three. This is the only suit I have.'

'What do you mean, you've got a job interview?'

Tolly produced the paper napkin. 'Here, this is confirmation of my sacking. I think I might be the first actor to lose a job because he couldn't hold a cue board boldly enough.'

Suzanne took the napkin, read it with a faint smile, then tore it up. 'You're not sacked. It was Esmeralda we had the contract with.'

'Esmeralda was replaced by an evil bitch, so I am sacked.'

'Have you read the *Theatre News* today?' asked Suzanne.

Tolly shook his head. 'No, I don't buy it.'

Suzanne handed him the review section of the newspaper. 'Read this.'

Tolly sat down on the armchair close to Suzanne's desk and read the article. It was written by the highly rated north-east critic Sarah Blenkinsopp.

Last night's performance of The Waiting Room *at Newcastle's Queen's Theatre was a record-breaking event. It broke the record for walkouts, refunds and the number of police officers needed to protect the cast from being strung up from the nearest lamp post. I invited several of my friends to see the classic Shaftesbury play. I have seen many versions of the play over thirty years and just happened to have seen a preview of this touring version in London. The minor characters in the play were exaggerated, in stark contrast to the intense minimal delivery of the central character, Sid. I had been raving to my friends and colleagues about that portrayal and was looking forward to them experiencing a rare talent. I was, however, shocked and personally embarrassed when an actress whose character should not appear until near the end of the first act started shouting something about chocolate from the moment the curtain went up. A buffoon appeared playing the part of Sid and began to shout gibberish even though he was obviously reading from cue cards. I apologised to my friends for taking them to this debacle and left the theatre after five minutes. It took another five minutes to get out of the auditorium because all the other theatregoers were heading for the exit at the same time. I confess that I did join in with the booing to show my displeasure. Things began to get ugly at the box office when the theatre refused to give refunds because the play was still being performed. This encouraged a mob to invade the stage and stop the play, so they could get their money back. In all my career, I have never witnessed a play so bad. One of my sources told me that the lead actor who I had originally seen had been sacked, and director Esmeralda Ashdown had been replaced. Theatres struggle as it is to encourage people to attend live shows, and anyone unfortunate enough to witness this abomination would have been put off for life.*

'I call that justice,' said Tolly with a smile. 'It's a shame the mob didn't string Choco Chocs Doreen up, and that moron Archie. I haven't told you, have I? He called me *it*.'

'I've had Esmeralda on the phone. She needs you back to play the lead.'

'I was sacked. I'm not going back. She treated me like shit once Archie was going to play the lead role. I say fuck her! What's the point of doing the play anyway? No one's going to watch it after that review.' Tolly placed the newspaper back on Suzanne's desk.

'It doesn't matter. She received a grant to help put on the play and is committed to perform it in Harrogate or face a six-figure fine. It's for one performance only. After that, the other bookings can be cancelled. If there's no play, they'll sue her, and she'll be bankrupt.'

'Why should I care?'

'Because Esmeralda will sue me, and when she does, I will sue you. I have enough shit going on in my life without being sued because my prima donna client is acting like a little spoiled bitch.' Suzanne reached for her indigestion tablets and chewed on one. 'It's just one fucking day, for Christ's sake!'

Tolly undid the top button of his light blue shirt and loosened his tie. 'I could rearrange the job interview for when I get back, I suppose.'

Suzanne brightened. 'Good, I've bought two tickets for the early train tomorrow morning.' She handed Tolly a printed ticket.

'Two tickets?' asked Tolly.

'I have a brother in Harrogate I haven't seen for ages. I can put the ticket down as a business expense.'

'So you're coming to watch the play as well?'

Suzanne shook her head. 'No, no, no. Have you seen the review?! It's going to be terrible.'

'Thanks for the support,' muttered Tolly as he made his way out of the office.

Tolly read the script again that afternoon and was confident that he still knew all the dialogue. He had a night of untroubled sleep, knowing that he was going to be playing to an empty theatre. He was also secretly pleased that he could do one more performance before retiring from show business for good.

At six forty-five the next morning, Tolly was walking along the platform at King's Cross station to catch the seven o'clock train. Apart from the departure time, he had not bothered to read the information. Now checking the ticket closely, he was pleased to see it was first class. He found the correct carriage and climbed on board. Suzanne spotted him and called out, 'Over here, Tolly!'

He placed his holdall on the shelf above their seats and plonked himself down beside her. 'This is a treat, Suzanne: first-class tickets.'

'Tax-deductible,' she said casually while perusing the breakfast menu.

'I could get used to this,' said Tolly as he wiggled in his seat to get more comfortable.

'Don't get used to it, it's only a one-way ticket. You'll have to make your own way back.'

'Why didn't you buy me a normal return fare? It's probably cheaper.'

'I made a cock-up when I ordered the tickets, and I can only claim so much. Anyway, you won't be my client after you finish the play.' She noticed Tolly's astonished expression. 'What can I say? It's a tough business.'

As the train began to pull out of the station, Tolly stared out of the window. 'I'll be glad when I'm out of it.'

'I had big hopes for you,' confessed Suzanne, 'but sadly, in this business, talent is not enough; you need luck.'

'I'm not lucky, am I?' said Tolly. 'Everything I do goes wrong.'

'You're not lucky, but so what? You're a decent person and in my book that counts for a lot.'

'Am I decent enough for you to pay for my return ticket?'

'No, but that's because you're unlucky,' said Suzanne with a chuckle. 'But I will buy you breakfast.'

Tolly smiled. 'I can't work out if I'll miss you or not.'

With a hearty breakfast inside him and all the tea and coffee he could drink, he relaxed and listened to Suzanne's stories of her own exploits as a young actor struggling to make it. He began to feel slightly ashamed that he was giving up his career after just a few months, when Suzanne had trod the boards for years barely making a living. He wondered whether he should keep trying, but as Suzanne had said, to make it in the business, you needed luck.

The journey took less than three hours, and Tolly was surprised to see Esmeralda waiting outside Harrogate railway station for them. She greeted Suzanne like a long-lost friend before turning to Tolly. 'I'm truly sorry about the way you were treated. I was wrongly advised, and I was influenced by selfish people. You were the best actor in the play, and I regret not telling you that. I know you probably hate me, and I don't blame you, but I do appreciate you coming back for this last performance.' Esmeralda held her hand out for him to shake.

Tolly shrugged and shook her hand. 'It's a tough business, I hold no grudges,' he said grudgingly.

Esmeralda smiled and hugged him tightly. 'Come on, the theatre's not too far away. You can both freshen up there. It's a lovely old building.'

'Suzanne is going to see her brother,' said Tolly, 'so it's just me.'

'I can see him later,' giggled Suzanne. She put her arm through Esmeralda's. 'I want to catch up with my old client.'

Tolly was pleased that Suzanne had joined them, so he would not have to endure any uncomfortable silences. It was just a ten-minute walk to the Palace Theatre. He was greeted warmly by the crew, and even the cast, who had been so frosty towards him before, came over to him and sheepishly said hello. After being shown to his dressing room, he began to wonder where Suzanne had gone. He went in search of her and spotted her sitting in the front row beside Esmeralda. Suzanne noticed him and ushered him over.

'I've discussed the play with Esmeralda as you asked, and she has assured me that the rest of the cast will play it properly.'

Tolly had no idea what she was talking about, but muttered, 'Good.'

'We have time for a rough rehearsal like you requested,' Suzanne informed him, 'so be ready in ten minutes.'

Esmeralda leapt to her feet and rushed off to speak to the rest of the cast.

'What's going on?' asked Tolly.

'It's your last performance in a lead role and I want to see you do it with some decent support.'

'Thank you, Suzanne, it means a great deal to me that you care.' Tolly held his arms out for a hug.

Suzanne held her hand up to stop him coming any closer. 'I don't want to sound cruel, but I haven't done it for you. My brother is an actor, and I made the mistake of telling him you were very good in the role of Sid, so he wants to see the play.'

'You said I was very good? You've never said very before.'

'Don't let it go to your head. I never thought he'd ever see you. Just… just don't fucking embarrass me.'

The rehearsal was full of stops and starts as the cast had to keep strictly to the script and hit their marks, which was unfamiliar territory. Because Choco Chocs Doreen had fled with Isabella and Archie, Pippa was playing her role and still struggling with a few lines. Suzanne had her head in her hands at the end of the play.

'Well done, everyone!' called out Esmeralda. 'I thought that was rather good.'

The cast all seemed pleased with themselves and a lot happier that they no longer felt the need to outact each

132

other. Tolly went over to Suzanne, who was rifling through her handbag and moaning.

'Fuck it! Where is it?'

'What did you think?' he asked.

'I think I need to ring my brother, when I find my fucking phone, and tell him not to bother. They're worse than I remembered.'

'It was only a rough rehearsal,' said Tolly, 'just to iron a few things out.'

'It would take a steamroller to iron that out. Found it! Thank God for that.' Suzanne clasped her phone to her heart before dialling a preset number. 'Jonathon, its Suzanne… Hold on, you're breaking up.' She stood up and made for the exit in search of a clearer signal.

Whatever optimism Tolly had briefly felt about the play turning out to be okay was crushed by Suzanne's reaction to the rehearsal. Nonetheless, he steeled himself to do one last performance where he would give it his best shot, even if no one turned up to see it.

Local councillor Norman Poskin was determined that his home town of Harrogate would be the beacon of culture in God's own county of Yorkshire. This was his first year as the town's arts festival organiser, and he was confident it would not be the last. When he started the job, Norman had known nothing about the arts and thought Picasso's blue period had something to do with painting nude women. To make up for this lack of knowledge, he had been researching culture via the internet for the last three months and had discovered that there were three kinds of culture: popular culture, disliked culture and – the holy grail of them all – 'I don't understand it' culture. Norman's inspired idea was to only put on culture at the festival that no one would understand. The first month had been a big success so far. The artworks on display made no sense whatsoever, the sculptures were unfathomable, and the music concerts even had hardened jazz fans baffled by their absurdity.

The only reason that *The Waiting Room* had made it out on tour was because Norman was on the relevant government arts board, and when he saw an application for a grant to showcase the classic by Shaftesbury, he used all his influence to see that it received its grant. He had also inserted a single extra clause in the contract, requiring the play to be performed at the Harrogate Palace Theatre during the arts festival. His festival programme had been a huge hit with every arts reviewer from every newspaper and TV show in the country. To have so much senseless art in one place had enhanced the town's reputation no end. Culture lovers flocked to see the nonsensical art in all its forms, boosting the town's economy. For the final day, Norman had saved the very best till last. It would be the crowning glory, the icing on the cake, the pièce de résistance. The most highly rated incomprehensible play ever written, *The Waiting Room* by Shaftesbury, was being staged in Harrogate, and it was all thanks to Norman Poskin.

Tolly's confidence took another dip after Suzanne marched back into the theatre, muttering, 'Fuck, fuck, fuck.'

'Bad news?' he asked.

'Yes, it is bad news. He still wants to see it,' she said angrily.

'He's an actor, he's seen bad plays before.'

'It's worse than that. Remember the *Theatre News* review I showed you yesterday? Well, the critic, Sarah Blenkinsopp, has been tipped off that you're playing the lead tonight and has tweeted that she might make the journey down to see you. She has a lot of influence in this business.'

'Should I be flattered or scared?'

'Scared! My brother's seen the tweet and so have his cronies, so that means they'll turn up, and the only audience will be overcritical thespians. Actors love to bad-mouth other actors, especially to critics. What a shit way to end your career.'

Esmeralda, on the other hand, was quite pleased to hear about the possibility that Sarah Blenkinsopp would give the play another chance now that Tolly was back playing the lead. The rest of the cast were grateful to have an opportunity for redemption after fearing for their professional lives because of Choco Chocs Doreen's influence on the play.

'This will be the last performance of *The Waiting Room*, so let's finish on a high,' Esmeralda told the assembled cast. 'I want you all to dial back on the projection. Just this once, try not to be yourselves. Do what Tolly does… Act.'

Watching Tolly apply his stage make-up, Suzanne asked, 'Are you nervous, knowing your performance is going to be pulled to pieces?'

'No,' answered Tolly. For some unknown reason, he had never had nerves before performing in front of people, even as a child. His tutors had urged him to use the adrenaline created by his nervous energy to enhance his performance. When he had told them that he had no nervous energy, they had concluded that it must be his nervous energy causing him to say that.

'I always worried what people would say about me,' confessed Suzanne.

'It doesn't matter what people think anyway. After today, I'm getting a proper job with normal people.'

Suzanne checked to see no one was watching and produced a bottle of pills from her handbag. She placed them on the dressing-room table in front of Tolly. 'I have an idea. Take six of these and you'll pass out. If you're taken away in an ambulance, you can't do the play.'

Tolly gave Suzanne her pills back. 'You're the one who talked me into doing this stupid play, and now you don't want me to do it? I don't understand.'

'My brother's been mocking me for years. Every time I mention an actor on my books I admire, they turn out to be mediocre. He can't wait to see you fail just so he can make my life a bloody misery.'

'Tell him you made a mistake. What does it matter?'

'I wrote on my Facebook page that you had the potential to be one of the greats, and that I would stake my reputation on it.'

Tolly smiled. 'You wrote that about me?'

'I was drunk at the time and didn't know anyone was going to see the fucking play. Maybe we could tell everyone that your parents have just died!'

'My parents are already dead.'

'Faint! Faint at the end of the play! Then I can say you were obviously ill when you were performing.'

Tolly looked askance at Suzanne. 'You want me to faint? Really?'

'Grab your stomach then, just make it obvious you're ill. I'll buy you a first-class ticket back to London!'

Tolly gave it some thought. He could fulfil his obligation to Esmeralda, play his last leading role and have a comfy journey home. 'Okay, I'll collapse after the play. What if there's a curtain call?'

136

'Ha! I've just seen the rehearsal. Believe me, there will be no curtain call.' Happy that Tolly would now collapse, Suzanne went to meet her brother and drop subtle hints about Tolly's poor health.

Esmeralda's hopes of just performing the play as written for the benefit of Sarah Blenkinsopp had changed to dread ten minutes before the curtain was due to go up. She had glanced out from the wings to see the audience taking their seats. She had expected fewer than ten people to turn up. To her horror, she spotted several critics with reputations for ripping plays apart, along with some well-known stage actors who she knew for a fact had played the part of Sid to critical acclaim in their youth. While Esmeralda was in the middle of an anxiety attack, Tolly approached her. 'Esmeralda, I've been thinking about the final soliloquy. I would like to play it a slightly different way.'

Esmeralda struggled to take a deep breath. 'Okay, do what you think is best.'

Suzanne took her seat next to her brother just as the curtain rose for the last touring performance of *The Waiting Room*. To her surprise, the cast delivered their lines, hit their marks and made their entrances and exits perfectly. Tolly, as she had been sure he would all along, commanded the audience's undivided attention. The emotions he conveyed even made her feel something: a tear rolling down her cheek. At the interval, her brother reluctantly conceded that Tolly wasn't bad, but at the same time, he couldn't say that he was good. Suzanne was happy enough with that verdict from her brother, and the comforting thought of Tolly fainting at the end brought a smile to her face. When Tolly appeared on stage after the interval, he received a welcoming round of applause and had to pause before starting. It was something Suzanne had never witnessed in all the versions she had seen over the years. Actors traditionally delivered the final soliloquy as a verbal dirge, spiralling downwards. Tolly had a fresh approach in mind, in keeping with his view of the character of Sid as a person forced to live a life he did not want. He began the soliloquy with quiet anger, his voice subtly rising to a final heartbreaking crescendo of regret. 'A life of lives! A dream of dreams!' Tolly spread his arms wide and screamed to the heavens the final lines of the play, sending a shiver down the spines of everyone in the auditorium. 'The waiting is… OVER!'

For a moment, there was silence. Tolly stood, arms out wide, breathing heavily, and was just about to faint when the audience exploded with roars of approval. The curtain went down, and the roars continued. The rest of the cast were just as moved as the audience. With Esmeralda's urging, they formed a line to take a bow with her in the middle. The curtain rose to show the audience on their feet, expressing their unfettered appreciation for what they had just witnessed. Esmeralda led the bows and was so overcome with joy, she burst out crying. It took five attempts to close the curtain before Esmeralda and the cast could leave the stage.

After congratulations from the rest of the cast and a grateful hug from Esmeralda, Tolly sat on his own in front of the dressing-room mirror. His feeling of elation was subsiding, leaving him tired and melancholy. He checked his phone for train times: there was one in fifteen minutes. Unsure whether Suzanne would pay for a first-class ticket on a later train, he decided to head back to London now. After removing his stage make-up and putting his own clothes back on, he searched for Esmeralda to say goodbye. He popped his head into the large shared dressing room at the rear of the theatre, where the rest of the cast were having a celebratory glass of champagne. 'Is Esmeralda around?' he asked. Stan the corpse smiled and shook his head. 'Goodbye then!' Tolly shouted loudly. Several of the cast turned and gave him a wave.

He searched for the crew, but they were nowhere to be found, so he asked one of the theatre staff at the main desk in the lobby to say goodbye to them for him. He popped his head into the small theatre bar, looking for Suzanne, but it was empty. He did not have her personal phone number to call her, and he suspected she had gone off somewhere with her brother. Taking a last look round the auditorium, he jumped up on stage, turned to the empty seats, gave an elaborate bow and said, 'Now, it really is over!'

As part of the arts festival, a large marquee had been set up behind the theatre, where food and drinks were being served to the audience. Suzanne was being praised by her brother, who was taking great delight in informing his luvvie friends that she was Tolly's agent. Esmeralda was in great demand among the critics, who wanted to praise her bold direction of the final soliloquy.

The crew had taken a break to enjoy the audience's goodwill, instead of hiding from the public like they usually did. Over the next twenty minutes, all the other members of the cast drifted into the marquee, each receiving generous applause. Suzanne kept an eye out for Tolly and when all the cast but him had arrived, she decided to look for him. He was nowhere to be found. She checked inside the theatre and asked a female member of staff if she had seen him.

'If you're one of the crew, he said goodbye,' she said.

Suzanne went back to the marquee and talked to Esmeralda. 'Did you mention the after-show party to Tolly?'

Esmeralda shrugged. 'I thought you did.'

Suzanne reached for her phone in her shoulder bag, knowing very well that she did not have his number on her private phone, but she checked just in case. 'Fuck, fuck, fuck.'

Her brother was horrified when she told him that Tolly knew nothing about any after-show party and, after not being able to find anyone, must have left, presumably back to London. 'There's a taxi rank just around the corner. We should be able to catch up with him.'

Tolly stared out of the train window, feeling pissed off at not even getting a thank you for doing the stupid play. As the train pulled out of Harrogate station, he was unaware that Suzanne and her brother had just dashed on to the platform and were now watching it heading south.

13

Artistic credibility

Tolly's journey from Harrogate to London was not without incident. A points failure had caused a three-hour delay, and when he did eventually arrive at King's Cross station, he found the underground was closed because of a tube drivers' strike. The queues for taxis and buses were hundreds deep, so he opted to walk until he could find some kind of viable transport. The only option that turned up was to hire an e-scooter, which he spotted in a side road. It took him half an hour to download the appropriate app, sign up and give his credit card details before he could use it. After just one mile on the e-scooter in London's busy streets, Tolly had had enough of being terrified and decided to just walk and hope to flag a cab down somewhere en route. It was late in the evening by the time he got back home. Malcolm and Bethan were glued to a late-night horror movie on the TV when he popped his head around the door to tell them he was back and that he was going straight up to bed because of his job interview in the morning. Without taking their eyes off the screen, they both muttered, 'Okay.'

Bethan suddenly screamed, 'HE'S BEHIND YOU!' and covered her eyes in fear of what was about to happen on screen.

'Don't run that way!' shrieked Malcolm. 'That's a dead end!'

'HE'S GOT A FUCKING BIG AXE!' yelled Bethan.

'I'll leave you to your movie,' said Tolly. 'Goodnight.' He had hoped that they would ask him how the play had gone, but they were too busy squirming and hiding their faces behind the sofa cushions.

He woke up later than he had intended the next morning. He hurriedly showered and shaved before dashing out of the house, still grappling with buttons and zips on his green tweed suit. He was ten minutes late, which made no difference because he was made to wait a further twenty minutes in the office foyer before the personnel officer, forty-one-year-old Leia Miles, marched in holding a clipboard and shouted, 'Tolly Pipkin? Which one of you is Tolly Pipkin?!'

Tolly was a bit confused because he was the only one waiting. 'That must be me.'

Leia peered at the green tweed suit Tolly was wearing. 'Have you been shooting?'

'No,' sighed Tolly, 'this is just my suit.'

Leia stared down at her clipboard, produced a pen and ticked his name. 'Follow me,' she said curtly.

She led Tolly down a corridor into a large windowless room.

'Sit,' she ordered, pointing at a plastic chair in front of a big table where two dark-suited, serious-faced middle-aged men were already seated. Leia sat down between them and slapped her clipboard down on the table.

The serious man on Leia's left leant forward and stared coldly at Tolly. 'Why should we employ you at Freedom Services?'

'Because you have jobs that need filling?' said Tolly innocently.

The other serious man added quickly, 'Do you have what it takes to be a Freedom Services employee?'

'I don't know? What does it take?'

'It takes…' said the first serious man. 'It takes… what it takes!'

'I have a lot of what it takes,' Tolly assured his interviewers.

'Can you talk?' demanded Leia. 'Freedom Services employees must be able to talk to customers.'

'I've been talking since I was a child, so, yes, I can talk,' said Tolly.

The serious man on Leia's left pointed his ballpoint pen at Tolly. 'But can you talk and still have what it takes?'

Tolly was getting confused by these questions. 'Do you mean just have what it takes, or take what it takes?'

'He means,' said the other serious man, 'do you have a lot of what it takes to take what it takes?'

'And talk at the same time,' insisted Leia, 'with a lot of what it takes to take what it takes?'

A mobile phone began to trill loudly. The two serious men and Leia all picked up their phones from the table and checked them. Tolly felt his phone vibrating in his jacket pocket; he had forgotten to switch it off. The three interviewers stared at him disapprovingly. By now Tolly had come to the decision that he did not have what it took, and they would not give him a job, so despite their glares, he answered the call.

'Hello, I'm a bit busy being rejected at the moment. I'll call you back.'

'Don't hang up!' screamed Suzanne's voice. 'I need to see you; I have a job for you.'

Tolly gave his interviewers an apologetic smile. 'I'm not interested, Suzanne. Oh, and thanks for clearing off and letting me find my own way back yesterday.'

'Did you get back okay? Because I heard there were problems. I played safe and had a lovely ride back in a taxi with this delightful lady driver called Betty. It was very pleasant.'

'That makes me feel so much better,' sighed Tolly. 'Goodbye, Suzanne. Goodbye forever!' He hung up.

'Sorry about that,' said Tolly, putting his phone back in his pocket. He stood up. 'I can't see the point of wasting any more of my time here.'

'Hold on,' said Leia. 'You can talk.'

The serious man to her right nodded. 'And you might have what it takes.'

'Not what it takes to take what it takes, but after training,' added the other serious man, 'you will have what it takes to take what it takes.'

The other two nodded in agreement.

Tolly shook his head. 'Your company hasn't got what it takes. Why does it take three of you to give a job interview for a minimum-wage employee?'

Tolly received no reply, so he walked out of the room, leaving his three interviewers stunned.

'I don't think he had what it takes,' said Leia. She picked up her clipboard and marked a large cross next to his name. Her serious colleagues nodded their agreement.

When Tolly got home, he found Suzanne in the sitting room with Malcolm and Bethan. She was entertaining them with stories from her past life as a jobbing actor.

'What are you doing here?' asked Tolly.

144

'Waiting for you, stupid,' said Suzanne. She pointed at Tolly's green tweed suit. 'You could say you *shot* off pretty quick yesterday.

Malcolm and Bethan giggled and exaggeratedly tiptoed out of the room.

'Very funny,' dead-panned Tolly. 'Anyway, there was no one around after the play! Well, I'd done what I was asked; job finished.'

'There was a lack of communication yesterday. Someone should have told you about the marquee behind the theatre.'

'Oh, great. There's no point in telling me that now. Anyway, it's in the past. A new normal life is my future.'

'While you're looking forward to your normal life, I'll just let you know that, after your performance last night, I've had several casting agencies calling me. You are, at this very moment, all-out-shit hot.'

'Is that the good all-out shit or bad all-out shit?'

'It's the good of course, and when the reviews have circulated, you'll be in greater demand. Tolly, this is your big break!'

'Maybe I don't want the break,' said Tolly stubbornly.

Suzanne leapt up and slapped his face.

'Will you stop slapping me?!'

'Better actors than you have never got a break, seventy percent are out of work, so stop being a self-deprecating whiney little bitch and thank whatever God you have for your good fortune.'

'We agreed that I'm just too unlucky for this business, so I don't see the point of carrying on.'

'Your luck's just changed! You have an amazing opportunity.'

'I don't care.'

Suzanne slapped his face.

145

'Bloody hell, Suzanne! What was that for?'

'For being stupid.'

Tolly rubbed his cheek. 'If I did decide to carry on, what sort of work would you be able to get me anyway?'

'Come to my office tomorrow morning and we'll discuss all the options you have.'

'Because I respect you, I'll see what's on the table.'

Suzanne smiled to herself. Maybe Tolly would be her pension after all. She knew that for a brief time he would be in high demand because producers wanted names that were getting coverage in the media. They were known in the business as bandwagon producers, and she had thought that perhaps they were just a myth until she began to be inundated with calls and emails.

'Oh, before I go, can I slap you again? I really feel so much better after slapping a man.'

'No!' said Tolly in his most manly voice. 'You enjoy doing it too much, and it's not normal behaviour in any shape or form.' And in a not-quite-so-manly voice, he added, 'Besides, it stings.'

When Tolly turned up at her office the next day, Suzanne went through the offers that had come in. His initial excitement was dampened when he discovered most of them were for game shows or TV adverts. 'No theatre work by any chance?' he asked, desperate to stop his ego deflating further.

Suzanne had to stop herself from getting up and giving him a slap. 'Take it from me, any offer of work is a good offer, even if it's appearing in an advert for haemorrhoid cream.' She held up a printed copy of an email. 'Young men get them apparently; it makes them angry.'

'Please don't tell me that's what you recommend,' sighed Tolly, 'My artistic credibility will be ruined.'

'Not your artistic credibility!' said Suzanne, mocking him. 'Oh, no! We can't have your artistic credibility ruined by a job that pays well and has the potential to keep paying you money every time it's aired on TV. What was I thinking?'

'I have creative standards,' insisted Tolly. 'And doing an ad for pile cream does not meet them.'

'Okay, Laurence Olivier, but I'm holding on to it in case you see sense.'

'I will not lower myself to do it in a thousand years! Are there any other offers apart from game shows?'

'I had an interesting call from a casting director for a live TV drama based on a book by a bestselling author. One of their actors had to drop out at the last minute, and they need someone who can work in a live environment. They're really desperate, so they're willing to give you an audition.'

'Oh, it's great that they're really desperate.'

'If you don't get the part, which you probably won't, I suggest you go for the haemorrhoid cream ad.'

'Let's hope to God it doesn't come to that. Where's the other audition being held?'

Suzanne glanced at down at her desk. 'The auditions are at the Method Hall—'

'I know it,' said Tolly before Suzanne could finish. 'It's where I did the audition and the rehearsal with Esmeralda. When is it?'

'This afternoon at four o'clock.'

Tolly glanced at his phone. The time was four minutes past two. 'That's a bit short notice!'

'Do you want me to call them back and get them to rehire the Method Hall at great expense, just so they can rearrange it for a day that suits you because you're so fucking special, with your artistic credibility?'

Tolly feigned puzzlement. 'Did I just detect a tiny, teeny hint of sarcasm in your voice?'

Suzanne shook her head. 'Just go and fucking meet them.' She handed him a piece of paper with the name of the director. She held up the haemorrhoid cream email. 'And I'll hold on to this just in case.'

14

A psychopathic psychopath

By the time Tolly left Suzanne's office, it was ten past two. In need of something to eat before the four o'clock audition, he headed for the only place he knew close by: the Proper Kaff. On any other day of the week, he would have avoided it in case he bumped into Michelle and Zibby before he had let them know he was back in London, but as it was a Wednesday, he knew it was the girls' day off.

The Proper Kaff had plenty of seats free now the main lunchtime rush was over. Tolly strolled over to the counter where the intimidating figure of Deano was cleaning the coffee machine.

Tolly gently coughed to get his attention.

'You can fucking cough as much as you like,' said Deano over his shoulder. 'I'll serve you when I've finished here. If you don't like it, fuck off, and don't come back.'

'No hurry,' said Tolly nervously. As funny as Deano was, he was still a scary brute of a man as far as Tolly was concerned.

Deano finished his cleaning and turned to face Tolly. 'Well, if it ain't fucking La-di-da. Didn't I ban you? You've got some fucking front coming in here.' Deano pulled his huge shoulders back and clenched his fists.

'No, I wasn't banned,' muttered Tolly nervously. He was about to turn and run when he saw a smile spread across Deano's face. 'You're fucking with me, aren't you?'

Deano roared with laughter, ran round the counter and put Tolly in a headlock. 'I had you fucking going, didn't I?'

Tolly laughed with relief. 'Yep, you fucking had me going.'

'What's it to be then, La-di-da?'

Tolly glanced at the menu on the wall behind Deano. 'Mac and cheese would be great, please, Deano, and an orange juice.'

'Coming right up, La-di-da. Grab a pew and I'll bring it over.'

Tolly sat at the table where he had he first met Zibby and Michelle. A broadsheet newspaper had been left on one of the seats, so he picked it up and struggled with the large pages until he found the culture section.

Two departing builders shouted their goodbye to Deano, only to be told with a roar of laughter to, 'Fuck off, and don't come back.'

Tolly smiled on hearing Deano's now familiar departing words and carried on perusing the latest theatre reviews. Then he heard Deano say, 'Hello, dancer girl.' Tolly looked up from the newspaper; Zibby was standing at the counter.

'I thought Wednesday was your day off,' said Deano, wiping his hands on his black apron.

'It is usually,' said Zibby, 'but I had a meeting with Babs.'

'Make sure she pays you proper,' said Deano. 'Everyone knows you and your mate carry that show. Now, what are you having? The same as La-di-da – mac and cheese and an orange juice?' Deano nodded in the direction of Tolly, who was staring at Zibby with his mouth open like a fish that was surprised to have been caught.

Zibby was just as shocked as Tolly. 'What are you doing here? You're supposed to be on tour.'

'I got sacked,' sighed Tolly, folding up the paper and putting it back where he found it. 'I was replaced by a moronic idiot.'

Zibby turned to Deano, 'Okay, I'll have the same as him, please, Deano.'

'Grab a pew, and I'll bring them both over.'

Zibby sat down opposite Tolly. 'What happened? How did you get the sack?'

Tolly explained what had happened on his brief tour. Zibby found it all very amusing. After Deano had served them their food, she nearly choked on her mac and cheese because she was laughing so much at Tolly's impression of Archie.

Tolly smiled when she smiled and laughed when she laughed; there was something about his friend's little sister that just made the world seem a better place.

'So, what are you going to do for work now?'

'As it happens, I have an audition in about an hour's time at the Method Hall.'

'I've heard of the Method Hall; a lot of musical theatre shows are rehearsed there. I'd love to see it.'

'I suppose you can come along with me if you want to see it,' he said with a shrug.

'I'll give Michelle a call. She'd love to see it, and you, of course. Why didn't you let her know you were back?'

Tolly thought it was best just to be upfront. 'Michelle hangs on to me like I'm a boyfriend or something, and I swear I've done nothing to encourage it, and I don't want to hurt her feelings.'

Zibby smiled. 'Michelle falls for any reasonable-looking man. It's just the way she is. She's already been out with two

151

blokes since you went on your disastrous tour, so don't worry about her feelings.'

Tolly was annoyed at his own vanity for thinking that such a pretty young woman wanted him as a boyfriend. He checked the time on his phone. 'We'd better get a move on if you want to see the Method Hall.'

Paying for both of their meals with his contactless card, Tolly gave Deano a hurried goodbye. Just before the door closed behind him and Zibby, they heard Deano's deep voice shout out, 'Fuck off, and don't come back!'

Tolly hailed a passing black cab on Dean Street, and they jumped in. The middle-aged cab driver knew the Method Hall. He told them he had dropped off an actress there earlier in the year. He couldn't recall her name, but remembered she had one of those funny silk scarves on.

'I forgot about the bloody paisley silk scarves,' moaned Tolly. 'Cabbie, is there somewhere I can buy one en route?'

The cab driver dropped them outside an Oxfam shop that sold snazzy second-hand clothes and was just a few streets away from the Method Hall.

'Why do you need a paisley silk scarf?' asked Zibby once they were on the pavement.

'It's all the fault of poncey thespians,' explained Tolly. 'Because they wear them like a uniform, you don't get taken seriously without one.' He pointed to a display of paisley scarves in the shop window. They were on sale at heavily discounted prices. 'I'll just pop in and get one.'

Zibby followed him in and decided to buy one each for her and Michelle, seeing as they were so cheap.

The Oxfam sales assistant told them that the demand for the scarves had mysteriously dried up, and showed them the different ways you could wear them. So, sporting their matching paisley silk scarves, Tolly and Zibby strolled in the direction of the Method Hall.

When they reached the reception area, Tolly spotted Hugo. He was saying goodbye to a colleague. 'You have an all-out-shit day!'

'Can I help you?' asked Hugo. His smile faltered when he noticed Tolly and Zibby were wearing paisley silk scarves.

'Do you remember me?' said Tolly. 'I auditioned here for *The Waiting Room.*'

'The all-out-shit play by Shaftesbury?'

'Yes, it certainly was an all-out-shit play.'

Hugo recalled the young man's face. He was the person who had told him that all-out shit meant good and that environmentally friendly invisible scarves were all the rage. Thanks to him, Hugo had, over the last few months, become something of a fashion guru for the London set. This was all down to his use of the phrase 'all-out shit' and his second-hand advice on how to wear an environmentally friendly invisible paisley silk scarf. 'Yes, of course. How are you?'

'I'm fine, thanks. I have an audition at four o'clock.'

Hugo put a tick in the reception book before leaning towards Tolly. 'Why aren't you wearing your environmentally friendly invisible scarf?'

At first, Tolly chuckled. He could not believe that the receptionist had swallowed his stupid invisible scarf story. But having been reminded of this, he was slightly annoyed that he had just paid out for a real silk scarf. If he had remembered his earlier ruse, he could have just said he was wearing an invisible one.

'Invisible scarf?!' exclaimed Zibby, not quite believing what she was hearing.

Tolly ushered her away from the desk and whispered, 'Last time I was here, I was the only one not wearing a paisley

153

silk scarf, so I made up a story about wearing an environmentally friendly invisible one. I thought he was just going along with the joke, but he must have believed me.'

Zibby burst out laughing. 'No way!'

'It's the London artsy scene, they'll believe any old bollocks you tell them. I'll try and dig my way out of this, so just go with it.'

Tolly approached Hugo and glanced both ways, as if making sure nobody would overhear him revealing a secret. In a low, confidential voice, he said, 'The word on the street is that invisible paisley silk scarves are no longer all-out shit.'

Hugo was confused by this news but nodded his head.

'Word on the street,' revealed Tolly, 'is that too many people were pretending to wear one.'

Hugo was visibly shocked by the revelation.

'So the kids on the street are wearing visible scarves like ours because they want to be real, and they look real all-out shit wearing them.' Tolly pointed to his own and Zibby's scarves to emphasise his point. Zibby had to turn away to hide her smile.

Hugo still had his real scarf in the reception desk drawer. He opened the drawer and promptly put the scarf on.

Tolly nodded his approval. 'That looks real all-out shit.'

Hugo smiled; he was still up to date and down with the kids. He could not wait to let everyone know that he still had his finger on the pulse of street culture.

'My audition?' prompted Tolly.

'Oh, it's in the main Gielgud Hall. They're expecting you. I'll even take you there myself.'

'Would it be okay for Zibby to come with me?' asked Tolly. 'She's never been in here before.'

'I've heard so much about the Method Hall,' said Zibby, 'I just had to come and see it.'

'I'll give you a tour while Tolly does his audition,' offered Hugo. 'Celia!' he called out loudly. 'Could you take over at the desk, please?'

Celia hurried over as fast as her seven-decade-old legs could carry her and spotted straight away that Hugo was wearing a real paisley silk scarf. 'Oh!' she said.

Hugo was pleased with the reaction to his new look. 'Yes, Celia, it is real, so just deal with it. I'm escorting Tolly and his young lady—'

'She's not my young lady,' interrupted Tolly. He didn't want Zibby to be uncomfortable.

'—and his friend,' Hugo corrected himself, 'to the Gielgud Hall.'

The three strolled along the wide corridor that led to the various rooms of different sizes. Hugo opened large double doors and led them into the Gielgud Hall. Tolly was surprised to see over twenty people there in various discussion groups in front of a small stage.

'Mr Tolly Pipkin's here for his audition!' shouted Hugo. He toyed with his scarf to draw attention to the fact that he was wearing a real one.

A smiling middle-aged woman in a dark suit came over and shook Tolly's hand. 'I'm Mae Allen. I was fortunate enough to see you perform in Harrogate. You were wonderful.'

Tolly was almost lost for words, but he managed to mutter, 'Thanks.'

Hugo said, 'Tolly, I'll take Zibby on a tour while you're showing Mae how real all-out shit you are.'

Zibby gave Tolly a wave goodbye as Hugo put his arm in hers and led her away.

'The audition is for a part that needs to be memorised and performed next week. It's in an episode of a live police drama series,' explained Mae.

'And what's the role?'

'The psychopathic psychopath.'

'A psychopathic psychopath?'

Mae smiled. 'It's a unique twist, isn't it?'

Tolly briefly wondered what it was about him that made Mae think he could be not only a psychopath, but a psychopathic one. 'I have an audition piece that I can perform,' offered Tolly. He had his John Osborne monologue in mind.

Mae shook her head. 'I'm the director, and I know how good an actor you are. But this is television, and the technical team and producers need to know what you look like in front of camera and how your voice sounds. I'm afraid acting tends to take a back seat on TV.'

Mae led Tolly over to the production team, who had no time for pleasantries. They checked over his physical appearance, made him walk, talk and endure various cameras observing his face from every angle. He was told to smile, laugh, be angry and even cry. When they seemed happy that they had shot every part of him they could think of, Mae took him to one side.

'As much as you'd be my top choice to be in the drama, the producers and the writer have to approve you.'

'How many actors have you seen today?' asked Tolly.

'You're the sixteenth,' confessed Mae. 'If you wait around for a couple of hours, you can find out if you've got the part. They need to make the decision today, and time's running out.'

Tolly noticed a number of fairly well-known TV actors chatting to each other on one side of the hall. He had a suspicion that they all would have been Mae's top choice too. Certain that he had no chance of securing the part, Tolly told Mae that he could not wait around because he had an appointment to keep. He found Zibby and Hugo looking at the portraits of the great actors who had rehearsed in the Method Hall over the last thirty years.

'How did you get on?' asked Zibby.

'Not so great. Anyway, I'd rather do theatre work. How was the tour?'

'Hugo is an excellent guide,' said Zibby. 'You could say he was real all-out shit at it.'

Hugo fanned his pretend blushes with his paisley silk scarf. 'It was a pleasure. Now, you must excuse me, I have my duties to attend to.' What he really meant was that he could not wait to let his circle of artsy friends know that environmentally friendly invisible paisley silk scarves were passé and real scarves were real all-out shit again.

'Thank you for inviting me,' said Zibby once they were back on the street. 'It was fun.'

'It was my pleasure. I'm going to get a cab home; I can drop you off on the way.'

'Thanks, it'll save me being squashed on the tube at rush hour.'

It took just a few minutes for Tolly to wave down a black cab, and in just a few minutes more they were sitting in a traffic jam.

Tolly glanced over at Zibby, who was looking straight ahead at the stationary traffic, and noticed how beautiful she was in profile. 'How did your meeting with Babs go?' he asked. 'I overheard you telling Deano.'

'I was letting Babs know that I won't be dancing with Michelle any more. I have a great opportunity to assist a choreographer. It's just a short contract, but it might lead to bigger things, and as a bonus, I won't be too embarrassed to tell my parents about it.'

'What about Michelle? Is she quitting?'

'No, Babs is more than happy for her to headline on her own.'

'Well, I hope it works out for you. Let me know what theatre you're at, and I'll come and see you.'

'It's not theatre work and it's not in London.'

Tolly instantly felt sad. 'So I won't be seeing much of you.'

'A dancer's career is short-lived. I don't want to end up on the London audition merry-go-round for years. Never mind about me. What are you going to do if you don't get this TV job?'

'My agent wants me to do an advert for haemorrhoid cream because it pays piles of cash.'

Zibby laughed. 'Well, if they're going to pay someone to do it, it might as well be you.'

'I never looked at it that way.'

'You're good at what you do; I'm sure you'll get other offers.'

'What are you doing on your night off?' asked Tolly, as the cab moved ten metres and braked sharply. 'Meeting your boyfriend, Pepe?'

'No... he... he's working tonight, in a show thing.'

'What does he think about your new job?'

'Oh, he... he's thrilled.'

'Is he a dancer as well?'

'Um, yes, he is. We worked together in *East Side Story*.'

There was a moment's uncomfortable silence, until Zibby broke it. 'In answer to your first question, I suppose I will be staying in my room tonight, watching TV. Michelle has invited one of her boyfriends round. She must really like this one if she's bringing him home.'

'I have an idea,' said Tolly. 'My housemates have meal-movie night on Wednesdays. Why not join us?'

'And what does meal-movie night involve?'

'We watch a movie while eating a takeaway. It's a lot more fun than it sounds, and it'll save you having to stay in your room on your own.'

Zibby thought about having to watch TV with the sound turned up to drown out the noise of Michelle's love life. 'I would like to come to meal-movie night, thanks.'

Twenty-five minutes later, the black cab dropped Zibby and Tolly off outside his house. Bethan and Malcolm were already slouched on one of the two sofas in front of the TV. Tolly introduced Zibby as his best friend's little sister and informed them that she was going to watch tonight's movie with them.

Bethan gave a big smile and patted the seat next to her. 'Sit with me, Zibby. It's lovely to have another woman in this house for a change.'

'Doesn't Tolly bring lots of girls back?' asked Zibby with a teasing smile.

Malcolm and Bethan glanced at Tolly and laughed.

'Not Tolly,' giggled Bethan. 'He'd rather read some obscure play than have female company.'

'Hey, you're making me sound weird,' protested Tolly. 'I read plays because it might be useful to know them in the future.'

'He is weird though,' said Malcolm out of the side of his mouth.

'I can still bloody hear you, Malcolm,' sighed Tolly in exasperation.

159

Bethan turned to Zibby. 'Seeing as you're our guest on meal-movie night, you can choose what we watch. What type of food do you like?'

'Chinese? Indian?' suggested Malcolm, hopefully.

Zibby shrugged. 'Thai, Italian…'

'Just choose one,' Bethan urged her.

'Italian is my favourite, I suppose,' said Zibby.

'Italian, it is,' said Bethan. 'We haven't had Italian on meal-movie night for ages.'

Malcolm picked up a tablet from the coffee table and began a search. 'Let's see what the movie database recommends.'

'Which restaurant did we use last time?' asked Tolly, opening a takeaway app on his phone.

'Gino's!' exclaimed Bethan. 'Their cannelloni was to die for. Oh, and don't forget to buy some Chianti.'

'So I've chosen the food, rather than the movie,' said Zibby, feeling a bit baffled.

'When we watch a movie,' explained Tolly, 'we eat a dish from that country to make it an immersive experience. It adds another dimension to watching it.'

Bethan nodded in agreement. 'You haven't lived till you've watched *Slumdog Millionaire* while eating a very hot curry.'

'I've found the perfect movie for tonight,' declared Malcolm, '*Cinema Paradiso*, the director's cut. It's got rave reviews and has music by Ennio Morricone.'

'I do love Morricone's music,' said Zibby.

'That's settled then,' declared Tolly. 'Right, the food will be my treat, so what would you all like to eat?' He was distracted from taking orders by the beep of a notification on his phone. 'It's an email from the director I auditioned for.' He read it quickly without showing any emotion. 'I've been offered the part; I'll be playing a psychopathic psychopath. The script will be delivered first thing tomorrow.'

'Typecasting then,' joked Malcolm.

'Well done, Tolly,' said Bethan.

Zibby gave Tolly a quick round of applause. 'I knew you would get it.'

Tolly permitted himself a brief smile before going back to taking the food order.

Just over an hour later, with the room now softly lit by candles, the four cinephiles sat on the sofas, with trays on their laps bearing various Italian dishes; the opening scene of *Cinema Paradiso* began on the large wall-mounted TV.

Zibby was sitting beside Tolly. The Mediterranean sunlight on the screen did seem to enhance the smell and taste of the excellent Italian food, making the experience quite magical. Even the warmth from Tolly's leg beside hers felt reassuring.

As the plates were emptied, the trays piled on to the coffee table, the four movie buffs fell under the spell of *Cinema Paradiso*, and at the climax, with its swooping Morricone music, they all had tears in their eyes. The spell was broken by the insistent ringing of Malcolm's phone in the next room. He jumped up and dashed through to take the call.

Bethan was still crying, but with a smile on her face, when she stood up and took the trays away.

Tolly turned to Zibby, who was also smiling and wet-eyed at the same time. He did not know how it had happened, but at some point Zibby had taken his hand and he had kept hold of it. 'What do you think of meal-movie night then?' he asked, reluctant to let her hand go. He felt a strong urge to kiss her and leant forward slightly.

'I loved it,' said Zibby. She became conscious that she was holding his hand and quickly released it.

Malcolm rushed back in with Bethan one step behind him. 'We've got an urgent pick-up at the airport. They're willing to pay double,' he said excitedly.

He hurriedly grabbed his coat from the hallway and put it on, before sticking his head back through the doorway. 'Bye, Zibby. Italian was a good choice.' He rushed after Bethan, who was already opening the front door while struggling to put her shoes on.

The sitting room door slammed, and there was a moment of silence.

'Don't bother saying goodbye to me,' shouted Tolly.

Zibby chuckled.

Her chuckle made him smile. 'So, this new job, when do you start?'

'In a few weeks.'

'Well, I'll miss seeing you. Maybe I could have your phone number, so we can, you know, keep in touch.'

'I'd like that, said Zibby, 'but my phone's out of action at the moment. I keep meaning to buy a new one.'

Tolly stared into her eyes, consumed by how beautiful they were. 'Pepe's a very lucky man to have you as a girlfriend.'

'About Pepe…' said Zibby, shyly.

Bethan appeared at the sitting room door, breathlessly hopping on one leg, still struggling to put on her left shoe. 'Did you want a lift, Zibby?'

'Oh, yes, thank you.' Zibby nervously stood up, then leant down and kissed Tolly on the cheek. 'Bye,' she whispered, before hurriedly grabbing her things and joining Bethan.

'Sorry to leave you with the washing-up, Tolly,' shouted the departing Bethan. 'See you later.'

Zibby gave Tolly an awkward wave. 'Bye, thanks for a lovely day.' And she hurried after Bethan.

15

Conspiracies-are-true

The last twelve years had been a whirlwind for fifty-two-year-old ex-bus driver and bachelor Colin Champion. As leader of the Conspiracies-are-true group, he had seen membership grow from five people to over three hundred countrywide. The Conspiracies-are-true movement had grown not only because it encompassed all conspiracy factions, from the flat-earthers to the moon-landing deniers, but because Colin had video evidence that alien reptiles were walking among us in human form. Colin had taken it upon himself to give a secret name to these controlling alien reptiles. He referred to them as 'Thems-at-top' and had even thought about trademarking the term after he used it as the title of his explosive book, *Thems-at-top*. This was in fact a one-hundred-page, large-print pamphlet which he had run off on his inkjet printer and sold to his fellow Conspiracies-are-true members for the bargain price of £25.99 plus postage and packing.

Colin Champion saw himself as the saviour of the human race, but he had to keep a low profile because if Thems-at-top found out about his video evidence, his life would be over. The video proof that Thems-at-top were disguised in human form was locked away in a safe-deposit box, and only members of Conspiracies-are-true who were promoted to the level of *bona fide*, and had taken a double secret oath, were allowed to see it.

On this particular evening, two members of Conspiracies-are-true had been granted bona fide status and were taking the double secret oath in Colin's rented house.

Trevor was in his late forties, a nervous type who chewed both his fingernails and the long, dark, greying hair which he tied in a ponytail. He was accompanied by his partner, Jennifer, who was the same age and wore her bottle-blonde hair in a similar ponytail.

'Repeat after me,' said Colin, 'I double promise…'

'I double promise,' they repeated.

'…to never reveal the secrets of…'

'…to never reveal the secrets of…'

'…or talk about…'

'…or talk about…'

'…the secrets of the *Amongst Us* video, on pain of double death.'

Trevor and Jennifer nervously swallowed, before repeating the words, '…the secrets of the *Amongst Us* video, on pain of double death.'

'Please be seated,' said Colin, pointing to the sofa in front of a large flat screen.

Once the initiates were sitting down, Colin puffed on his inhaler and addressed them. 'What you are about to see is not just double secret, but treble secret. No word of what you witness in the *Amongst Us* video here tonight must be mentioned to another living soul outside of this room.'

Trevor put his hand up immediately. 'Does that apply to other bona fide members who's seen it?'

'Trevor, you just took the bloody double secret oath!' groaned Colin. 'You never mention to a living soul what you see outside of this room, bona fide member or not. Thems-at-top have spies everywhere!'

Trevor smiled uneasily and chewed his fingernails. 'I must have missed that bit.'

Colin puffed on his inhaler and stared at him. 'If Thems-at-top find out you've actually seen the evidence, they might well snuff you out, but not before probing you in every orifice to find out where you saw it, which will lead them to me!'

'Oh, I don't think I'd like to be probed,' said Trevor, wriggling in his seat.

'I've forgotten what it's like to be probed,' said Jennifer, glaring at Trevor.

'You can be sure as the earth is flat,' Colin assured them, 'that Thems-at-top do not piss about. Right, I'll start again. What you are about to see is treble secret. No word of what you witness in the *Amongst Us* video here tonight must be mentioned to another living soul outside of this room.' He paused and stared at the new bona fide members, allowing the tension to build. 'I was not prepared for what happened on that fateful day twelve years ago. Thems-at-top tried to silence me because they knew that I knew what they didn't want the world to know, that Thems-at-top are alien reptiles.' Colin paused again, so the tension could build further. 'How do you think they tried to silence me—'

Trevor putting his hand up again stopped Colin in mid-flow. 'I don't know. How did they?'

Colin sighed. 'I was just about to tell you how before you interrupted me!'

'Oh, sorry, it's just that you keep stopping and looking at me like you want me to answer,' explained Trevor.

Jennifer nodded her head in agreement. 'You keep stopping and looking at us.

'I was building up the tension. Okay, I won't keep stopping. Now, if it's okay, I'll continue…'

'You stopped again,' said Jennifer.

'That was a pause, not a stop.' Colin decided just to speak quickly; otherwise it was going to take all night. 'The way the alien reptiles tried to silence me was by sending one of their own kind in human form to manipulate and control my thinking. This happened when I was a bus driver, and after being in its presence for only a short journey, I confess that for one moment I thought the world was round and the moon landings really had happened.'

'You were brainwashed!' suggested Trevor.

'They tried,' said Colin, 'but fortunately, I have natural immunity to alien brainwashing.'

'It's lucky that you do,' said Jennifer.

'Lucky for me, but unlucky for them because I caught them on video. Watch this and you'll see the truth.' He took a remote control from his trouser pocket with a dramatic flourish, pointed it at the TV and pushed a button. Nothing happened. He tried pointing the remote at different angles and then giving it a shake. 'I think the batteries need changing.'

'It could be Thems-at-top sabotaging the remote, so we don't see the truth,' said Jennifer.

Colin took a quick puff on his inhaler. 'I wouldn't put it past them one bit.' With one more shake of the remote and a long press of the button, the TV screen lit up. 'Here we go. Right, be prepared to see the truth.'

After watching the brief video, the new bona fide members sat in silence with their mouths hanging open, unable to quite believe what they had seen.

Jennifer was the first to speak. 'They really are amongst us!'

Colin nodded. 'Thems-at-top have been manipulating the truth for decades, and now they are in human form, they could be anywhere. Even one of you could be a reptile in human form!'

'If one of us is a reptile in human form, it'll be Trevor,' said Jennifer accusingly. 'You should see the way he eats. He treats a knife and fork like they're alien technology.'

Trevor glared back at Jennifer. 'We've been living together for five years, and you never mentioned this before?'

Colin held his hands up. 'I was just using you as an example. You were checked out when you joined Conspiracies-are-true. Do you remember having to wait in the freezing cold reception room? That's where we check to see if people can move in cold temperatures. If they can move about, they're not a reptile in human form.'

Trevor put his hand up yet again. 'How many reptiles in human form have you caught?'

'We thought we'd found one,' confessed Colin, slightly embarrassed, 'but it just turned out to be a bloke who'd died in the cold. He had a dodgy ticker apparently.'

'Or did he?' said Jennifer.

'I think he did,' said Colin. 'He was ninety-six and on his third pacemaker, but then again, you never know. By the way, now you're bona fide members and you've seen the film, you qualify to go on the *Amongst Us* bus tour. As it happens, the next one is in a couple of weeks.'

'Put us down for two tickets,' said Trevor. 'I'm hyperventilating already at the thought of it.' He began breathing deeply.

'He hyperventilates a lot,' said Jennifer. 'When we first had sex, I thought his gasping was passion, until he went blue and passed out.'

'Before you go,' said Colin, ignoring Jennifer's revelation, 'have you bought a copy of my book, *Thems-at-top*, at the bargain price of £25.99 plus postage and packing?'

'Yes, last week,' said Jennifer, 'because you said buying it would help with our bona fide membership application. And we paid the postage and packing even though you handed it to us yourself.'

16

A plan for Tuppence

The TV advert for *Femme Crédule* was received very favourably by the viewing public, and despite the perfume's exorbitant price, it was selling well, especially in the eighteen to twenty-five age group. Tuppence Crow had proved to have selling power and was signed up as the face of *Femme Crédule* for the rest of the year.

Tuppence's initial scepticism about Gus's methods had now been replaced by total confidence in him. When he arranged a meeting with her at her penthouse to discuss the next step in the plan to make her a famous TV celebrity, she was looking forward to another glamorous project. Her confidence took a knock when Gus revealed the next stage of his strategy: she would play the part of a coma patient in a much-heralded live TV drama.

'Tuppence Crow will not be seen dead playing a coma patient!' screamed Tuppence, on hearing this plan.

'Just let me explain—'

'Let me explain,' shrieked Tuppence. 'You're fired!'

Gus chuckled to himself, thinking that she really was one pampered brat. 'Okay, have it your way.'

Tuppence suddenly recalled her father telling her to follow Gus's advice or lose her monthly income. 'Wait. What drama is it?' she mumbled sulkily.

'It's called *Blue Psycho*. It's based on an internationally bestselling book, and I've been told it's going to be a groundbreaking live TV drama event that's also being shown simultaneously worldwide on social media.'

'How does playing a woman in a coma push my celebrity career?'

'A live performance credit on a show seen by millions is good for your credibility, but that's only one part of the plan.'

'One part?' said Tuppence. 'What's the rest? Tell me now!' she demanded.

'All will be revealed,' said Gus calmly. 'You'll be playing the part of the psychopath's girlfriend, and while you're on set, I want you to flirt with the actor playing the boyfriend. I want you to be seen with him in public.'

Tuppence was totally baffled by Gus's plan. 'Why?'

'Publicity,' said Gus firmly. 'Publicity, publicity, publicity.'

Tuppence still looked blank.

'I'll explain; you come from a privileged background, an elite social circle where breeding and wealth are the norm.'

'If you mean we don't mix with commoners, then, yes, I suppose so.'

'Exactly. Now, suppose, for the benefit of gaining media interest, you were seen arm in arm with a blacklisted working-class actor.'

'The shame would be unbearable.'

Gus nodded, his smile growing broader. 'Imagine what the public would say if they saw you in the newspapers and on social media arm in arm with this guy. I can see the headlines – *The face of Femme Crédule dates bad-boy actor.*

It began to dawn on Tuppence that Gus's plan might have its merits.

171

'This way you get talked about in the gossip columns,' continued Gus. 'They'll be saying, "Did you hear about Tuppence Crow going out with that blacklisted actor?" You'll have your picture splashed on every social media page. Glossy magazines will come looking for a scoop on your private life. Your stock goes up, demand for you as a celebrity goes up. It's a win-win.'

'If I go along with it, who is this actor?' asked Tuppence out of curiosity.

Gus had employed a team of researchers to find someone who would be a suitable candidate for his latest plan. He needed to be of a similar age to Tuppence and be controversial, but, and this was the difficult part, also have some artistic credibility. A list of possible contenders who might fit the bill amounted to over thirty. After weeding out those he considered to be too gay, too good-looking or too ugly, Gus had been left looking at a photograph of Tolly Pipkin: a blacklisted actor with rave reviews from snobby theatre critics for a play no one understood. Gus pulled out the photo of Tolly and passed it to Tuppence. There was no record of him working on the advert for *Femme Crédule,* and as Tuppence looked at his picture, she sneered, 'I've never seen him before in my life. Who is he?'

'To the public, he's nobody right now.'

Tuppence gritted her immaculate white teeth and ripped the photograph into pieces. 'I am Tuppence Crow, reality celebrity. I do not want to be seen with a nobody.'

By now, Gus was becoming used to dealing with Tuppence's tantrums. 'The fact that he's a nobody is a good thing; you don't want to be seen with an equal or someone more famous.'

'Why him?'

172

'He ticks all the boxes,' explained Gus. 'He's a rising star in the theatre world with rave reviews, but he must have a dark side because he's been blacklisted. It's a perfect combination.'

'What was he blacklisted for? He's not a pervert or unhinged, is he?'

'No one really knows how he got on the unofficial blacklist. Any director or producer could have added his name. All I could find out is that he's moody and has a forgettable face, which again is perfect. He'll just make you look better. Being seen with him will give you more publicity than you can imagine.'

Tuppence considered the idea. 'Okay, I'll do it, but what if I don't like him?'

'Let's take it one step at a time. You join the cast and I'll sort out the rest.'

17

An unexpected coma patient

Tolly began to read the script as soon as the motorcycle courier had dropped it off. He was pleasantly surprised to see that his part was much bigger than he had expected. He was to play the part of a corrupt police constable who was a psychopathic killer on his days off. As he finished reading the script, he was smiling. The character he was to play was a lead role and a wonderful opportunity to prove himself.

The following week, he attended rehearsals which had already been under way for a month. The cast were friendly and helpful, which was a new experience for him. After his first day, Mae Allen, the director, told him how impressed she was by his ability to memorise lines so quickly. It was not just Mae who was impressed; other cast members with years of experience could feel the intensity he brought to his character and made a big effort to up their game to match him.

Tolly had no idea about who had been cast to play the comatose girlfriend until he turned up at the rehearsal studio on his third day. He was having coffee with the crew and other actors when Mae made an announcement. 'You may have been wondering who will be playing the girlfriend of the psychopathic psychopath police officer played by Tolly.'

None of the cast had given the part any thought. They had just assumed the comatose girlfriend would be played by an extra.

'I can now let you in on the secret,' said Mae with a smile. 'She is the reality celebrity and face of *Femme Crédule* Tuppence Crow!'

Tuppence Crow sashayed into the studio like a catwalk model, carrying a small wicker basket full of bottles of *Femme Crédule* perfume, which she handed out as gifts. Within seconds, Tolly was standing alone as the others crowded round to greet Tuppence. His hands tightened on his coffee cup as he stared at the spoiled brat who had had him sacked. He watched her being fawned over and enthusiastically welcomed by the cast, who were keen to get their hands on the free samples of perfume that were worth a four-figure sum. His heart sank; working with her was going to be a bloody nightmare.

It was another twenty minutes before he was obliged to say hello and shake her hand. She obviously didn't recognise him, and he sure as hell was not going to tell her that she was the reason he was blacklisted. As the day wore on, he could not help noticing that Tuppence kept smiling at him whenever he caught her eye. During breaks, Tolly avoided her like the plague, still pissed off at her for getting him fired from the perfume commercial. At the end of the day of rehearsals and costume fittings, Tolly called out a farewell to the cast and crew and headed for the exit. As he strolled out of the car park past the manned security gate, he heard someone calling his name. He turned to see Tuppence hurrying towards him.

'Hold on, Tolly. I'll walk with you!'

The last thing he wanted was to spend his own time in her company, but he waited for her to catch up out of politeness. 'I thought you'd have a chauffeur waiting for you,' he said with a touch of sarcasm.

'He is waiting,' said Tuppence, 'but I wanted to walk down a street like a common person. I wanted to know what it feels like to be an ordinary person like my character.'

'Your character's in a coma. I think even you could pull that off without going all method.'

'Why are you being so horrible?'

'Why? To put it bluntly, I think—'

'Ouch!' Tuppence winced and rubbed her left eye. 'I think I have something in my eye. Can you look and see if there's anything there? Oh, it feels scratchy.'

Tolly lifted her head back and gently held her eyelid up. 'I can't see anything.'

Tuppence put her hands on his waist, which he thought was odd. Before he knew what was happening, several photographers had surrounded them and were snapping away.

'How long have you been dating?' asked one of the eager paparazzi.

'We're just work colleagues,' giggled Tuppence, whose eye had made a miraculous recovery.

'Tolly, what's it like having a celebrity as a girlfriend?' shouted another voice.

Tolly freed himself from Tuppence's grasp. 'She's not my girlfriend. Now, why don't you lot just push off?'

A crowd had begun to form as passers-by stopped to see who was being photographed.

A black limousine pulled up sharply, and a black-suited chauffeur jumped out and opened the rear kerbside door.

'Tolly, jump in! My chauffeur will give you a lift!' shouted Tuppence, as she climbed into the vehicle. Tolly was being jostled and had one photographer with a camera inches from his face, blinding him with constant flashes. He reluctantly climbed in after Tuppence and sat next to her.

'I'm sorry you were caught up in that,' said Tuppence, as the limousine pulled into traffic. 'I get followed by the press all the time.' She had conveniently forgotten to mention that it was Gus's team that had orchestrated the commotion. Tolly asked the chauffeur to just drop him off at the next corner. Tuppence leant over and kissed him on the cheek before he climbed out. He stood on the pavement, wondering what the hell had just happened.

The next morning at the rehearsal studio, he had just helped himself to a coffee from a drinks machine when another member of the cast, Joy Moore, who played the blind lesbian chief constable, sidled over to him.

'Where's your girlfriend?'

Tolly sipped his coffee. 'Sorry?' He stared blankly back at Joy's curious expression. She was in her late fifties but dressed like a twenty-year-old, probably because her real-life boyfriend was a twenty-year-old.

'You don't hang about, do you?' teased Joy. 'You gave the impression of not being interested in her when all along you and she were an item.'

'What are you on about?' asked Tolly.

Joy held up her phone. On it was a picture of Tolly looking into Tuppence's eyes. Above it, the caption read, *Tuppence Crow gets intimate with blacklisted bad boy*.

Tolly glanced around at the cast and crew; they all seemed to be giving him knowing smiles. 'She had something in her eye!' he explained.

Before he could say any more, Tuppence strode into the room, made a beeline for Tolly and kissed him on the cheek.

'Good morning,' she said teasingly. With a flirty flutter of her eyelashes, she blew him another kiss before swaggering over to Mae.

'I wouldn't have put her down as your type,' said Joy.

'She isn't!' protested Tolly.

It was mid-morning before he had a chance to talk to Tuppence alone in a corner of the studio. 'What the hell are you doing?!' he asked.

'I'm not doing anything,' giggled Tuppence. She put a finger on his lips. 'You are a real Mr Grumpy in the morning.'

'I'm not Mr Grumpy, I'm not mister anything to you. I want you to make it quite clear to everyone that we are not an item, just work colleagues until this job is over.'

'Okay, Mr Grumpy, just for you,' said Tuppence with a sweet smile. 'Excuse me, everyone! I have an announcement.' She paused to give the cast and crew time to start recording her on their phones, knowing very well that the videos would be pushed heavily on social media by Gus. 'I just want to make it clear to everyone that Tolly and I are not an item.' She smiled shyly at him. 'He wanted me to tell you. He's so sweet and considerate.'

There were a few envious sighs from the romantics who could clearly see, or thought they could, that the young couple were in love. Tolly was not satisfied with Tuppence's announcement, so he tried to set the record straight himself.

'I'm not seeing, going out with or dating Tuppence,' he declared. 'She is a work colleague just like the rest of you. As soon as this drama is broadcast at the end of this week, I'll probably never see her again. I hope I've made myself clear.'

Tuppence applauded him and blew him kisses. 'He's so protective,' she said loudly, wiping a non-existent tear from her eye.

Later that morning, Tolly went to see Mae the director. 'I don't understand why she' – he pointed at Tuppence – 'is here for the rehearsals when she's just playing a coma patient. All she has to do is lie down on a bed and keep still!'

'I do what the producers tell me. Anyway, she's your girlfriend, you should know why.'

'She's not anything to me. She's playing some game, and I don't know what it is.'

'All I know is that the execs want her here at the rehearsals. Between you and me, I've heard whispers that they have a massive deal with her father's organisation to provide the main sponsorship.'

'So that's how she got the part. I still don't get why she's flirting with me.'

Mae looked steadily into Tolly's unremarkable face. 'Nor do I.'

Over the next two days, Tolly found himself fighting off paparazzi and social media reporters wherever he went. New pictures of him with Tuppence placing a finger on his lips in the corner of the studio added fuel to the media fire.

When it came to the live performance of *Blue Psycho*, everything was going to plan until Tolly had his scene with Tuppence. It was to be a touching moment when he revealed to his comatose girlfriend that he was a psychopath, but Tuppence, far from being immobilised by her coma, was shaking and fidgeting with nerves. Ad-libbing, Tolly changed his line from, 'If only you could move a muscle' to, 'If only you could move a limb.'

The media's reviews of the drama were generous, with Tolly receiving praise for his convincing portrayal of a psychopathic psychopath. Tuppence had somehow got her picture alongside the newspaper reviews, despite her limited role as the fidgeting coma patient. It was pure coincidence that most of the newspapers were owned by her father's company.

18

A form of persuasion

It was Monday morning, and Suzanne's day had started well with enquiries from some major casting agencies about Tolly following Friday's live broadcast, but by mid-morning, Suzanne was slamming the office phone back down on the desk. So far, she had received four calls from clients telling her that she was no longer their agent because they had been poached by the Big Star agency, a well-respected talent company, with a promise of lucrative work. Her private phone, which was tucked away in her handbag, began to ring. Because the number was only for friends and family, she hurried to answer it. 'Hi!'

'Suzanne Fisher?'

'Who is this?' Suzanne did not recognise the voice.

'My name is Gus Shaver, I'm a representative of Tuppence Crow.'

'I don't care who you are. How did you get this number? It's private.'

'The number was given to me by…' Gus trailed off.

'Fine, don't tell me. If you want to speak to me on a work matter, call me on my business phone.' She hung up. 'Americans, they're so fucking pushy!'

Her office phone began to ring; Suzanne picked it up. 'I'm assuming it's still Mr Shaver.'

'It is. Sorry for using the wrong phone. I didn't realise you Brits were so finicky.'

'We're a lot of things, Mr Shaver. Call me finicky, but I don't like people using my private phone for business. Now, what does a representative of Tuppence Crow want with me?'

'I'm hoping we can meet. I have a proposition that I believe will be extremely beneficial to your client Tolly Pipkin.'

'Tolly?'

'I'm in a coffee shop on the next block; I could be at your office in ten minutes.'

Suzanne was curious as to why someone representing Tuppence Crow wanted to talk about Tolly. 'Okay, Mr Shaver, see you in ten minutes.' It took just a few minutes online to discover that he was known in the States as Glory-Hole Gus because of a widely publicised incident in a public toilet. How come he was now working for Tuppence Crow?

Suzanne was waiting by the office door when Gus Shaver stepped out of the lift into the narrow lobby and swaggered towards her. He was in his late forties, overweight, with thinning hair and dressed like a scruffy FBI agent. The smile on his face was false and his handshake too firm. He introduced himself. 'Gus Shaver, thank you for seeing me at such short notice.'

'Come in and take a seat,' said Suzanne, indicating the upholstered chair facing her desk.

Gus sat down with a grunt of exertion and wiped a bead of sweat from his forehead. 'And please excuse my hasty attempts to arrange this meeting.'

'So, Mr Shaver—'

'Call me Gus.'

'So, Gus, what's your proposition concerning Tolly?'

'You must have seen the photograph of my client Miss Crow together with Mr Pipkin.'

'I've seen it, and Tolly believes he was set up. Why is Tuppence Crow trying to hint at some relationship? You do know he doesn't like her.'

'I'll be frank with you, Suzanne. She doesn't like him very much either.' Gus laughed. 'Young people, they drive you nuts.'

'I'm sorry, Mr Shaver, I still don't understand what you're proposing.'

'Gus, please. Just call me Gus. Let me give you an idea of the benefits that these two people gain from being seen with each other: attention, and lots of it. As you know, Tuppence is a reality TV celebrity—'

'Because her father bankrolled the TV production she was in,' said Suzanne.

Gus gave a reflex chortle. 'That's right, Suzanne, you are right. Let's cut the bullshit.'

'Please do.'

'Your client is blacklisted.'

'Go on.'

'Being blacklisted means he'll never work again.'

'Apparently no one checks or cares about the blacklist now because he's in demand again. In fact, the Blue Psycho production company want Tolly to record several extra scenes for the international TV markets.

Gus smiled. 'That will be the last work he does because I have witnesses who are willing to testify that Tolly is homophobic, misogynist, anti-Semitic, transphobic, and despises Scientologists. Now, that evidence will blacklist him for real.'

Suzanne laughed. 'Is this some sort of joke?'

'I never joke,' said Gus with a smile. 'I want you to persuade Tolly to pretend that he and Tuppence are an item. That's all he has to do. It would be in his interests because of the media coverage he'll receive.'

Suzanne disliked the blackmail element of course, but she could not deny that raising Tolly's profile would create more interest from casting agents. 'Okay, say this does raise Tolly's profile, what's in it for Tuppence Crow?'

'The answer is simple; Tuppence, a rich young woman, publicly shows off her weakness for working-class rebels. We believe the headlines that she'll receive from appearing to have a relationship with your client will raise her own celebrity profile. Is it possible for Tolly to get some tattoos? On his face or neck would be good. You know the type of thing, a skull or a dagger.'

'It seems to be an unorthodox way to raise her celebrity profile. Maybe she should just do another shit reality TV show, but this time without someone whispering what to say in her ear.'

Gus nodded. 'That takes time and has no guarantees. Fortunately, my client is in a position to take shortcuts.'

'I think what you mean is that she has a stinking rich father who can bankroll whatever she does.'

'My client is extremely sensitive. She believes that such rumours about her father using his fortune to help her career would damage her celebrity credibility.'

Suzanne laughed. 'Her credibility as a TV celebrity?! Now, you are fucking joking!'

'It's no joke,' insisted Gus. 'Trust me, I know how to manipulate the media to make her look credible.'

'Anyway, I don't think Tolly regards himself as a working-class rebel, and I'm sure he doesn't want tattoos or anything to do with Tuppence Crow. He won't do it. I think he'd rather quit the business.'

'Even if the arrangement is only for a few weeks?'

'A few weeks, a few minutes, it makes no difference. I know Tolly, and he won't go along with it.'

'I can promise you that he will get more exposure in that short amount of time than he'd get in a lifetime of playing small parts.'

Suzanne had heard of famous acting couples in the distant past who had been seen together purely as a convenient way of stopping speculation about their sexuality and private lives, but she had not heard of anyone doing a similar thing nowadays. 'How is this pretend relationship supposed to work?'

'They'll be seen at the best restaurants, opening nights, that kind of thing, anywhere where it will be reported.'

Suzanne gave it some thought. 'I think you're right that it would benefit both of them, but Tolly is stubborn and independent. He won't do it, I know him.'

'Maybe, in exchange for just a few weeks of Tolly's time, I could help you get your other clients back,' suggested Gus, smirking.

Suzanne's eyes narrowed. 'So, you're the one behind all of them leaving. I should have guessed.'

Gus raised his hands and grinned. 'I deny everything.'

'And this is why you have a reputation for being ruthless, and by the way, I know about the glory-hole incident.'

'Fake news,' stuttered Gus, trying to appear nonchalant.

Suzanne laughed. 'I get it now; you can't get any work back in the States, so you've come over here to peddle your scumbag techniques. Well, glory-hole fucker, you might get away with using blackmail where you come from, but over here, it won't work.'

185

'Blackmail works anywhere. Say, for example, someone promised you that if Tolly refused to go along with this arrangement, they'd ruin your agency for good. Maybe they'd done a little digging and discovered that you struggle to pay your bills as it is, even with all your current clients.'

'I don't know what you're talking about,' she managed to say calmly, hoping that this might all just be a bluff.

'I take no pleasure in resorting to this form of persuasion. No, I tell a lie, I do enjoy using this type of persuasion. Speak to your client and encourage him to do what's best for everyone.'

'If I do as you ask, how will I get my clients back?'

'Don't worry, they'll be back once they've been reassessed and rejected by the Big Star agency.'

'Big Star is one of the top five. How did you manage to get them to poach my clients?'

Gus gave her one of his smug smiles. 'Richard Crow has his fingers in many pies.'

'Why should I trust you? For all I know, you'll ruin me anyway.'

'I may be hardnosed, but I learnt early on that persuasion—'

'Blackmail.'

'Call it what you will. I learnt that persuasion works best when one keeps one's word.'

Early in his career, Gus had used a video of a politician having sex with a young woman who was not his wife to blackmail him. Believing the blackmail material might come in useful in the future, he had gone back on his promise to the man and kept hold of it. Eight months later, the politician, desperate with stress, had forced his way into Gus's office and put a pistol to his blackmailer's head. Gus had been convinced he was going to die. Fortunately, the gun had jammed, and Gus had managed to run like hell to get away. Since then, he had always kept his word.

Gus heaved himself to his feet and gave Suzanne a grin as he placed a business card on her desk.

'As well as ruining you, I'll destroy the career of Tolly Pipkin, and I can assure you that by the time I've finished tarnishing him, it'll feel much worse than being wedged in a glory hole. Call me when he agrees.'

Within ten minutes of Gus leaving, Suzanne had received two more calls from clients who had been poached by the Big Star agency. As she had suspected, they were all going to be working with the same agent who had Tuppence Crow on his books. If she was going to have any business left to lose, she needed to speak to Tolly as soon as possible. The phone rang again, and she picked it up; it was another client leaving.

When Tolly arrived at Suzanne's office later that day and sat himself down in the chair opposite her desk, he was sure she had been replaced with a replicant. The grumpy, surly Suzanne he knew had been turned into a pleasant and smiling version. 'What's wrong? Are you having a stroke or something?'

'There's nothing wrong,' said Suzanne, with a beaming smile. 'It's just nice to see my favourite client.'

'You're always telling me I'm your worst.'

'I don't think I've ever said that.'

'You were dropping me as a client not long ago, and you've slapped my face several times.'

'Only in jest!' protested Suzanne. 'Why would I hurt my favourite client?'

187

Tolly stood up. 'Right, I'm off, you're having a funny turn or you're on drugs or something. I can't tell which.'

'Hold on,' said Suzanne, dropping the false smile. 'I need your help.'

'My help?'

Suzanne nodded. 'I had some American glory-hole wedger visit me,' she fumed.

'Glory-hole wedger?' asked Tolly.

'Yes, he shoved his todger in a public toilet glory hole and got it stuck. It was in all the newspapers in the States. Anyway, he now works for Tuppence Crow's father and is blackmailing me.'

'Let me get this straight, you're being blackmailed by someone who wedged his dick in a hole?'

'Look him up online,' said Suzanne. 'Gus Shaver is his name, and he had to leave the States because of it.'

'How is he blackmailing you?'

'The glory-hole wedger has somehow managed to get the Big Star talent agency to poach my clients.'

'Wow, Big Star is one of the best. I wonder if they'll poach me.'

'Thank you for your loyalty,' she said dryly. 'Don't you see? He's using the Big Star agency to drive me out of business unless I do what he asks. Oh, by the way, guess who owns a big chunk of the agency. I looked it up.'

Before Tolly could guess, Suzanne told him. 'Richard Crow, Tuppence's millionaire daddy.'

'What does he want you to do?'

'He wants me to persuade you to date Tuppence, so she can raise her celebrity profile.'

'Using blackmail to raise her celebrity profile, is he nuts? Let's just go to the police. He can't get away with this, it's crazy.'

188

'It's not just my business he's going to ruin, but your career.'

'Don't worry about my career, Suzanne. I was going to get an ordinary job anyway. Don't let him get away with this.'

Suzanne began to weep. 'I'm not strong enough, Tolly. I'm too old to start again from scratch.'

Tolly had always thought of Suzanne as being tough as nails. 'Look, Suzanne, I'll do what you ask, but if we go along with it, he has to guarantee that you'll get your clients back.'

'I've made some discreet enquiries about him with other media manipulators,' said Suzanne, sniffing. 'They say he does keep his word.'

'An honest blackmailer? Now, that is what I call an oxymoron. Why has he chosen me anyway? It makes no sense.'

Suzanne blew her nose. 'Apparently, having her date a working-class, blacklisted, rebellious actor is going to enhance her celebrity status.'

'Is that the reputation I have? A working-class, rebellious actor? I can't decide whether that's a good thing or bad.'

'Does that matter? I've built this business up by myself over the last twenty years, and that glory-hole wedger wants to ruin me unless I get you on board with this charade for the next few weeks.'

'The next few weeks?!'

'That's how long he thinks it will take.'

Tolly had never seen Suzanne so upset. 'Okay, just for you, I'll go along with it.'

Suzanne wiped her eyes with a tissue. 'I don't think being seen with her will be a bad move for your career. I've already had a couple of enquiries about you just because you were photographed with her.'

'What type of enquiries?'

189

Suzanne looked at the open page of her notebook. 'The haemorrhoid cream people have upped their offer. A morning chat show would like to interview you, and… Hold on, I can't read my writing. An afternoon chat show wants to interview you.'

'Oh, great. Having to answer questions about Tuppence Crow in both the morning and afternoon is my dream career move. Look, I'll do this arrangement for you, but please don't book me in for anything without my knowledge.'

'Okay,' sniffed Suzanne, 'but they all pay very well.'

'I don't care. Please, just let's get this out of the way without me ending up on a celebrity game show. How is this going to work?'

'You and I will agree the terms with the spoiled little bitch and the glory-hole wedger. We have a meeting with them later at her penthouse apartment.'

'You knew I was going to end up agreeing, didn't you?'

'As I said before, you're a decent person.'

'And unlucky, don't forget you said that as well.'

'See? I'm a good judge of character. You're the unluckiest person I know.' Suzanne checked her watch. 'We'll meet them in an hour, so there's time for a coffee before we have to go.'

'Great, I could really do with one too.'

'I'm not going out for them in this state. You can pop to the coffee shop down the road and get them.'

Tolly reluctantly stood up. 'I suppose I'm paying for them as well.'

'Tolly, I know you're too decent to take money from me when I'm distressed.'

'Is that right?!'

'And you're too unlucky for me to give you any money. Now, hurry up; we don't have all day. Oh, get me a Belgian bun while you're there, and one for yourself if you like.'

'I know what I'd like to do with my Belgium bun,' muttered Tolly as he shuffled out of the office.

Suzanne rummaged in her desk drawer and pulled out a compact mirror. She stared at her own sad face and broke into a broad smile. 'You could still tread the boards, Suzi, old girl. You still have it!'

Tolly and Suzanne gazed up at the embodiment of the vast wealth of Tuppence's family that was the Crow Tower, an imposing sixty-storey building overlooking the Thames. Inside the lobby, a smartly dressed security man asked to see their passes.

'We don't have a pass,' Suzanne informed him, 'but we have a meeting with Gus Shaver and Tuppence Crow. My name's Fisher and this is Mr Pipkin.'

The thirty-two-year-old security man, Ralph Goody, was an ex-policeman. He had been asked to leave the force because of his overzealous use of a taser gun on a disabled pensioner who he had believed was going to use her walking stick as a lethal weapon. Ralph stared at Suzanne and Tolly suspiciously. They could be assassins for all he knew. This was his first day in the job and he wanted to make himself indispensable. 'I don't believe you,' he said as he reached for his own illegal taser, which was discreetly hidden in a shoulder holster under his jacket. Ralph thought the woman looked innocent enough, but the man's face looked familiar to him; he had definitely seen it somewhere before, and it couldn't be anywhere good.

'Can't you call his office and check?' asked Suzanne.

Ralph's instinct was to taser them both, but he reluctantly said, 'Wait here.' He marched over to the main lobby desk to talk to the receptionist.

'This is a great start,' muttered Tolly impatiently. 'We can't even get in.'

Suzanne began scrolling through her phone. 'I've got the glory-hole wedger's number, I'll call him.' When she had explained their difficulty to Gus, he instructed her to wait by the lifts, and would come to meet them.

While they waited, Ralph the security man finally recalled that he had seen the man on the TV, and he was a cold-blooded, murderous psychopath.

One second, Tolly was standing by the lifts with Suzanne, waiting for Gus; the next, he was on the floor, shaking with convulsions, after Ralph tasered him with a fifty-thousand-volt charge of electricity.

Suzanne began to scream.

The security supervisor, Bernie, had just returned from a cigarette break when he heard the scream and saw his dopey brother in-law, Ralph, standing over a man jerking uncontrollably on the floor by the lifts. He rushed over. 'Ralph! What the fuck are you doing?!'

'A murdering psychopath,' explained an excited Ralph, loading a new stun cartridge. 'She's going down next,' he said, nodding at Suzanne, who was on her knees, helping her dazed client sit up.

'Give me that fucking thing,' demanded Bernie, snatching the taser from Ralph's hands.

'He's a murdering psychopath!' insisted Ralph, snatching it back. 'She's probably one as well.'

Bernie wrestled the weapon back off Ralph. 'They're not murdering psychopaths! Are you crazy?!'

Tolly had now staggered to his feet and was extracting the electrodes that had pierced his chest.

'Oh!' exclaimed Suzanne. 'I think I know what's happened here. He was a murderous psychopathic psychopath—'

Suzanne's words were enough for Bernie to fire the taser at Tolly, sending him back on to the floor in convulsions.

'It was in a TV drama!' screeched Suzanne. 'He's an actor, he was in *Blue Psycho.*'

All Bernie could do was mutter, 'Oh, sorry,' as he watched Tolly slowly stagger back to his feet.

'See?' said Ralph. 'He was a murdering psychopath. So I was right. Sort of.'

'I'm a fucking actor!' raged Tolly, pulling out the latest electrodes.

'You were very good in *Blue Psycho,*' said Ralph admiringly, 'very convincing.'

'Very chilling,' agreed Bernie.

Gus stepped out of the lift to see a bedraggled Tolly with thin curly wires still protruding from him. 'What's going on?'

'A misunderstanding, sir,' said Bernie. He recognised Gus as one of Mr Crow and Tuppence's advisers.

'Tolly has been tasered by both of your security goons,' complained Suzanne.

'Goons?! That's a bit offensive,' said Ralph, feeling quite hurt by the remark.

Bernie was also sensitive to such criticism. His bottom lip began to tremble. 'It's not nice to call people names.'

'It's not nice to taser people either,' winced Tolly.

'These idiots thought he was a murderous psychopathic psychopath because he played one in a police drama,' explained Suzanne. 'So they shot him with a taser – twice!'

193

Gus nodded. 'A very convincing portrayal, so understandable.'

'Very convincing,' agreed Ralph.

'What are you going to do about it?' demanded Suzanne.

'In a way, it's Tolly's fault for being so good at playing a murderous psychopathic psychopath. They were just doing their job, protecting their colleagues.'

'They're fucking morons!' declared Tolly.

Bernie began to fill up. 'There's no need to be hurtful.'

Ralph gave Bernie a hug. 'We're only doing our job,' he said with a lump in his throat.

'Let's agree that things said and done by both sides were all just a misunderstanding,' said Gus diplomatically.

'They could have killed me!' said Tolly.

'Only a few thousand people have died because of tasers,' Ralph informed him. 'The percentage is quite low considering how many times they've been used.'

'What a fucking comfort that is,' said Tolly as sarcastically as he could.

'Come on,' said Gus, urging Tolly and Suzanne towards the lift. 'Let's have this meeting with Tuppence. You can apologise later.'

'I'm not apologising for being zapped by a couple of morons,' protested Tolly as he followed Suzanne and Gus into the lift.

Ralph and Bernie watched the doors slide shut.

'Some people just don't have any manners,' said Ralph with a disapproving shake of his head.

Bernie sniffed and wiped his eyes. 'I don't know how people like him sleep at night.'

The lift doors opened on to the penthouse suite. Tuppence was waiting in the large reception room with its spectacular views over the city. She looked up as Gus strolled in with Suzanne and the dishevelled Tolly. 'About time,' she said with a scowl. 'I shouldn't be expected to wait, I am the talent here.'

At that moment, Tolly thought it would be a good idea to take the lift back down to the lobby and grab the taser.

'Our guests had a little misunderstanding with security,' explained Gus. 'Take a seat, both of you,' he said to Suzanne and Tolly.

They sat down on one of the two grey leather sofas that faced each other over a wide oak coffee table on which there was a selection of waters and soft drinks.

Tuppence gave a bored sigh and sat on the sofa opposite. Gus sat down on a black leather armchair overlooking them all.

'Help yourself to drinks,' said Gus.

Suzanne declined, but Tolly had a dry mouth after being zapped and grabbed a small bottle of water. He unscrewed the cap and took a slug.

'Can't you use a glass like normal people?' said Tuppence with a look of scorn.

'Can't you mind your own business?' said Tolly, deliberately wiping his mouth with his sleeve.

'Let's just get started,' said Gus. 'The arrangement we agree on today will be a verbal contract. Nothing must be in writing.'

'How do I know you'll keep to the agreement without something being written down?' asked Suzanne.

'You'll just have to trust me,' said Gus with a smile that was unconvincing and scary at the same time, 'because, to be frank, you don't have any choice.'

'What do I have to do?' asked Tolly. Despite his doubts, he wanted to help Suzanne.

195

Gus leant back in the armchair. 'Simple, you and Tuppence pretend to be a couple. Be seen together, pretend to be happy young people in love.'

'I am not kissing him on the lips,' stated Tuppence. 'I draw the line at that. I'd rather throw myself under a bus.'

'A bus?' laughed Tolly. 'You're a spoiled little brat, you don't even know what a bus looks like.'

'I do know what they look like. Daddy has two buses in the estate's transport museum.'

'Your family has a transport museum? Who has a transport museum?!'

'All you have to do,' interrupted Gus, 'is give the appearance of being a loving couple for a few weeks.'

'A few weeks is a bit vague,' said Suzanne. 'We need precise dates.'

Gus tapped his fingers on the arm of his chair as he did a mental calculation. 'Six weeks from tomorrow if Tolly does what we ask.'

'Which is?' demanded Tolly.

'You and Tuppence will go on planned social engagements at celebrity events.'

Tuppence stared at Tolly disapprovingly. 'Do you always look so scruffy?'

Tolly was slightly hurt by the remark. 'I just like to keep it casual. And I like second-hand clothes because they have more character and are more ethical.'

Tuppence gagged involuntarily. 'You're wearing clothes someone else has worn? Is that even legal?!'

'I buy all my clothes from charity shops,' said Tolly defiantly. 'Reusing clothes is good for the planet. I suppose you wear everything once then chuck it away.'

'No, not all the time,' snapped Tuppence. 'Sometimes, I wear clothes twice before I throw them away.'

Tolly's jaw dropped. 'You wear clothes once or twice before dumping them? Who wears—'

'Okay, Tolly,' interrupted Suzanne, 'I think we all know what you're going to say next.' She turned to Gus. 'I can't see these two making it to six weeks.'

'I agree,' said Gus. 'If they can't get on, it has to be Tuppence who calls the whole thing off.'

'I call it off now,' said Tuppence adamantly. 'I will not be in the company of a charity-shop-clothes wearer.'

Gus stood up. 'Tuppence, can I just have a private word with you?'

Tuppence reluctantly followed him out to the corridor, where Gus stood with his arms folded. 'What?!' she asked sharply.

'If you don't want to do it, that's fine, but your father has said that if you refuse my advice, you'll no longer have his financial backing.'

'I'm a celebrity, I can support myself.'

'Okay,' said Gus. 'How many offers of work do you have?'

'I have lots of offers,' lied Tuppence.

'Oh, that's good, because to maintain your current lifestyle, you need at least thirty thousand pounds a week.'

Tuppence smiled. 'But I'm Daddy's favourite. All I have to do is cry on his shoulder and he gives me whatever I want.'

Gus unfolded his arms; in his left hand was a phone. 'You can ask him now, he's on speakerphone.'

'Daddy?'

'Tuppence, just do what Gus asks. I don't want you running to me every five minutes because you're not as famous as you want to be. Do what Gus recommends, or you can kiss goodbye to your penthouse apartment and your credit cards. I mean it this time!'

Tuppence put on the little girl voice that she always used to get round her father. 'Daddy, I wuv you so much. You won't let lickle Tuppy face the kwuel, kwuel world with no pennies.'

'Try me,' said Richard Crow. 'I'm not backing down this time, no matter what you say. Now, listen to Gus; do what he says, and you will get what you want. Gus, I'll speak to you later.'

Gus put the phone back in his pocket. 'Shall we go back in?'

Suzanne and Tolly had been having their own conversation. They had agreed to back Tuppence's judgement by giving her plenty of praise and sympathising with her point of view. They both smiled innocently when their counterparts came back into the room and took their seats.

'Can I just say,' said Suzanne with fake sincerity, 'that Tuppence has a good point? Tolly's charity-shop clothing choices and questionable personal hygiene should not have to be endured by one of our brightest stars.'

Tolly was not happy about the personal hygiene comment, but if it meant getting his life back, he would have to go along with it. 'Nobody would believe for one second that a beauty like Tuppence Crow would be seen dead with a smelly nobody like me.'

Gus applauded them both. 'A good effort.' He stopped clapping and leant menacingly forward. 'But she will be taking part in this arrangement.'

Suzanne and Tolly looked over at Tuppence, who was now sulking.

'I don't have any choice either,' she grumbled.

198

'This is the arrangement,' said Gus, 'Tolly and Tuppence will pretend to be a loving couple for a period of six weeks. By that time, Tuppence will be the number one TV celebrity in the country.'

Tuppence stopped sulking when she heard these words, but then had a thought. 'Hold on. What if he stops going along with it?'

'He won't, because he knows what the consequences are.'

19

The Pepe thing

After the meeting at Crow Tower, Tolly felt the need to let Zibby know what he was obliged to do for the sake of Suzanne's business. He knew she had a boyfriend and saw him as just a family friend, but nonetheless, he did not want her to think that he was really dating Tuppence Crow. He still had Michelle's phone number, so he called her.

'Hello, Tolly. I thought you'd forgotten about little old me.'

'Look, Michelle… I erm...' Tolly could hear her laughing. 'Zibby told you what I said, didn't she?'

'Yes, she did, but if you really wanted to go out with me, I might be willing to drop the others.'

'I honestly don't think I could cope with the pressure of knowing you had reserves in waiting if I didn't come up to expectations. I just wanted to see if Zibby was around today. I need to tell her something.'

'She's out at the moment, but she'll be here this afternoon if you pop round after three. We do need to leave by six though.'

'Great, I'll pop in about half three. It'll only take ten minutes.'

'Ten minutes? I'm sure Zibby would like to see you for a bit longer than ten minutes.'

'I just have some news. It won't take long. I'm sure she'd rather spend her time with Pepe.'

'Pepe?'

'Her boyfriend Pepe.'

'Oh, that Pepe, I thought you meant a different Pepe.'

'How many Pepes do you know?'

'Eight.'

'Really?! Eight people called Pepe?'

'Oh, sorry, someone's at the door. See you later. Bye.'

Two hours later, Zibby opened the front door and stepped into the hallway with a small shopping bag. 'I'm back! Guess who has a new iPhone!'

'Guess who's popping in later to see you,' shouted back Michelle.

Zibby walked into the living area. 'No idea. No one ever pops in to see me.'

'Not even your boyfriend, Pepe?'

'What are you on about?'

'Tolly called to say he wanted to pop in and give you some news, but he said he wouldn't stay long because you'd probably prefer to spend your time with Pepe. Why did you tell him that? When I said you had a boyfriend called Pepe, it was just our code word for lay off, he's mine.'

'It's not our code word, it's yours. I've never had a reason to mention Pepe.'

'It's obvious you like Tolly because you keep mentioning his name every five minutes, so why are you still playing along with having an imaginary boyfriend?'

Zibby went over to the kitchen area and began to unload her shopping bag. 'Because I like him too much.'

'Like him too much? What does that mean?'

'He's my brother's best friend, and my mum's always been very protective of him. She thinks of him as family. It just wouldn't work.'

'You're crazy,' said Michelle. 'He's not you're brother.'

It was twenty to four when Michelle answered the knock on the door. Tolly was standing there, looking shy and awkward. He gave her a smile, said, 'Hi, Michelle,' and gave her an air kiss on the cheek.

'Come in, Tolly.'

He followed Michelle through to the living area, where Zibby was curled up on an armchair, reading a magazine. She made no attempt to stand up. 'Hi, Tolly.'

Tolly felt his heartbeat quicken just from seeing her. 'Hello, Zibby.'

'Would you like a tea or a coffee?' asked Michelle as she went to the kitchen area and filled the kettle. 'I'm just making Zibby a coffee.'

'I'm not staying, but thanks.'

'So, what's this news?' asked Zibby, putting the magazine to one side.

'It's odd news, really. You might be seeing me in gossip columns and on social media a bit. I have a business arrangement to go on dates with Tuppence Crow for the next few weeks.'

'Business arrangement?' said Zibby. 'That's a strange business arrangement.'

'I can't tell you the reason why, but I'm obliged to go through with it.'

'Tuppence is glamorous and beautiful,' commented Michelle, 'and stinking rich with it.'

'And a bit of a bitch, to be quite honest,' said Tolly. 'She hates my guts.'

'There's a thin line between love and hate,' teased Michelle.

'Okay,' muttered Zibby, unable to think of anything more to say. For some reason the thought of Tolly going on dates with Tuppence, even as part of a business arrangement, made her feel oddly jealous.

Tolly suddenly felt awkward. 'Anyway, like I said, if you read about me and Tuppence, it's just, you know, business… show business.' He did jazz hands.

Michelle waited for Zibby to say something to Tolly. The two of them looked as shy as teenagers. 'I have to pop out, Tolly. I've made you a coffee anyway,' she said, pointing to two mugs on the kitchen worktop. 'I'll be a couple of hours. Oh, before I forget, Zibby's not going out with Pepe any more. She hardly ever saw him, so it's not even a big deal.' Michelle blew Zibby a kiss, laughed and left the two of them alone.

Zibby was annoyed with Michelle for putting her in this situation. She stood up and went over to the kitchen.

'Sorry to hear about your boyfriend not working out,' lied Tolly.

'There was no boyfriend,' confessed Zibby. 'When Michelle fancies someone, she tells them I have a boyfriend called Pepe, so she has no competition. He's the choreographer on *East Side Story*, by the way, and happily married.'

Tolly was confused. 'But you said he was working in a show.'

She turned away, unable to look him in the face. 'I don't know why I said that.'

Tolly felt as though a knife had been stuck in his heart. Zibby must have felt so ill at ease with his leering that she had kept up the boyfriend pretence as a defence. 'Well, I'd better go, I have a lot to do.'

'I did try to tell you on the meal-movie night about the Pepe thing…'

'You don't have to explain, I understand everything. I'd better go.'

'What about your coffee?'

'I've had too much caffeine today, but thank Michelle for making it.'

'Oh, Tolly, I'm starting work with my old choreographer next week, so I'll be back living with Mum and Dad for a while.'

Tolly felt another wave of guilt. Had she decided to move away because he had made her feel so uneasy? 'Say hello to your parents. And good luck with your new job. I really hope it works out well for you.' He awkwardly headed for the door.

Zibby was a little taken aback by Tolly's abruptness. 'Thanks for letting me know about the arrangement thing.'

Tolly turned to face her. 'It wasn't that important. I should have just called you, but I didn't have your phone number.'

Zibby picked up her handbag. 'I have the number here somewhere,' she said, searching through a notebook. 'I'm not good at remembering them.'

The last piece of the jigsaw had fallen into place for Tolly. She had deliberately not given him her number before now to make sure he could not pester her. He attempted a smile. 'It's fine. Take care, Zibby.'

Tolly was out of the door before Zibby could say anything else to him. She glanced over at her new iPhone on the kitchen counter, still in its box, now knowing for sure that she was nothing more to Tolly than a friend's little sister.

20

Choco Chocs Doreen

After years of struggling to make a living in the acting world, disappointed that her very brief TV career had not blossomed into something more, Choco Chocs Doreen could barely believe her current good fortune. She was now living at the Billings' townhouse in one of the most sought-after areas of London, receiving a very generous salary as Archie's acting teacher. She and Isabella had become close friends because of their shared admiration for Archie's exceptional talent. The icing on the cake was that Choco Chocs Doreen was not only respected, but revered by Isabella because she was a star in her own right (as Choco Chocs Doreen constantly reminded her) and was sacrificing her own career as a thespian to nurture Archie because she saw in him exactly what she had seen: the finest acting talent of a generation.

One morning, two weeks after she had been attacked on stage in Newcastle, Choco Chocs Doreen was encouraging Archie to promenade up and down the large sitting room when, to her utter amazement, the reality celebrity Tuppence Crow tiptoed into the room, kissed Isabella on the cheek and sat down beside her.

'How are you, my dear Tuppence?' asked Isabella.

'I'm quite well, Auntie Izzy.' She turned to Archie. 'What are you doing?'

'I'm prom… prom…'

'Promenading,' said Choco Chocs Doreen. 'Because Archie has so much charisma, he needs to move; otherwise it builds up too much in one place.'

'That's remarkably interesting,' said Tuppence, who was open to new ideas.

'What do you want, Tuppence?' asked Archie.

'Don't you want to kiss Tuppy, your fiancée?' said Tuppence in her little girl voice. 'I thought I wasn't going to see you for ages because of the play you were in.'

'The play had to be cancelled,' explained Isabella, 'because Archie was sabotaged.'

'Sabotaged? My darling Archie was sabotaged?'

'Sabotaged by jealousy!' declared Choco Chocs Doreen. 'An understudy was jealous of Archie's natural genius and did his utmost to disrupt his absorption.'

'You should have seen Archie on the stage,' said Isabella. 'He oozed charisma from every orifice.'

Choco Chocs Doreen nodded in agreement. 'The audience were so hypnotised by Archie's projection of intentions, they were moved to smash the theatre to pieces.'

'Kiss your fiancée, Archie,' Isabella instructed him. 'When you get married, you'll be kissing all the time.'

'I kissed her last month,' grumbled Archie, 'on the lips.'

'I didn't know Archie was engaged,' said Choco Chocs Doreen.

'Secretly engaged,' explained Isabella. 'Their marriage has been arranged since they were five years old. You can't have wealthy people's blood mixing with a lower social class.'

Archie grudgingly plodded over to Tuppence, kissed her on the cheek, then screwed his face up as though he had just eaten a lemon.

'What a joy it is to see,' said Choco Chocs Doreen, 'two rare talents joined together by true love.' With crocodile tears flowing down her cheeks, Choco Chocs Doreen sobbed, 'I feel my heart is going to burst with happiness when I see such a miracle as this.'

'Choco Chocs Doreen is my Archie's mentor,' explained Isabella.

Choco Chocs Doreen clasped her hands to her heart. 'Oh, Isabella, if the good Lord took me to heaven right now, I could not be any happier. As a humble renowned TV star and acclaimed locum thespian/director, to be mentioned in the same breath as Archie Billings is a joy. Please excuse my tears,' she sniffled, wiping her eyes.

'What do you want, Tuppence?' demanded Archie impatiently. 'I can feel my charisma fidgeting about.'

'Daddy has this horrid adviser who is making me date a working-class actor for the next few weeks,' said Tuppence. 'I wanted to let you know that it's all just pretend. I don't want my Archie to be jealous.'

'Pretend to be dating a working-class oik?' gasped Isabella. 'Is your father raving mad?! I don't like this at all, my Archie's betrothed being seen in public, carrying on with a working-class actor.'

'It's only for six weeks,' said Tuppence. 'Please give me your blessing, Archie. It is just pretend.'

Archie thought for a moment. 'Only if Choco Chocs Doreen approves.'

Choco Chocs Doreen felt all eyes fall on her. 'Can I just ask who this working-class actor would be?'

'Tolly Pipkin,' said Tuppence, 'I played alongside him in that TV police drama.'

'What TV drama?' asked Isabella.

'The one I told you to watch last week.'

Isabella shook her head. 'I'm sorry, Tuppence, but in this house, we do not watch commercial television, so I don't know who you mean.'

Archie shook his head. 'Sounds like an oik's name.'

Choco Chocs Doreen shuddered on hearing Tolly's name. He had been to blame for Archie's lack of absorption, which had led to them fleeing for their lives. 'He was Archie's understudy, Isabella. He was the one that deliberately would not hold the cue cards boldly, trying to sabotage Archie's destiny.'

'*It!*' said Archie. 'I remember him now. He calls himself an actor and he can't even absorb intentions.'

'How do you know him?' asked Tuppence.

'My deluded sister,' said Isabella, 'employed him to cover for Archie while he was…'

'Blossoming into the rare talent that he is,' suggested Choco Chocs Doreen. 'His jealousy of Archie's gift was plain to see.'

Isabella nodded. 'He could not entrance or compel like my Archie. What else was my Archie?' she asked Choco Chocs Doreen.

'Bewitching. He could not bewitch an audience like Archie,' she replied.

'I don't approve of you being with him, Tuppence,' said Isabella. 'What if he tries to take advantage of you?'

'I don't think he will,' said Tuppence.

Choco Chocs Doreen shook her head. 'As a renowned TV actor and acclaimed locum thespian/director, alas, I have come across several working-class actors, and to be frank, they are animals who have no respect for women. They are sex mad.'

'I forbid you to see that oik,' declared Archie.

'Keep moving, Archie,' said Choco Chocs Doreen. 'Your charisma is building up too much.'

Archie did as he was told and paced the room.

'I have no choice. Daddy will take away all my credit cards.'

'Your father's a monster!' declared Isabella. 'There, I've said it. A monster! I shall call him right away and tell him so!'

'There is a solution,' said Choco Chocs Doreen, who had sensed an opportunity. 'If only you had someone with experience of dealing with working-class actors, they could be a chaperone.'

'I can't think of anyone,' said Isabella.

Choco Chocs Doreen tried a subtle hint. 'Someone renowned would be perfect, maybe someone with TV acting experience.'

Isabella clapped her hands. 'Choco Chocs Doreen, you will be ideal as a chaperone!'

Choco Chocs Doreen gave a humble smile. 'To be prised from my student Archie will be an almost unbearable wrench, but if it means that true love will win in the end, then I graciously accept the task.'

Isabella called Richard Crow straight away, accused him of being a beast and remonstrated with him for letting her Archie's betrothed be seen publicly dating a working-class person, even if it was all a sham. Did he have no shame?

Richard tried his best to explain, but after being shouted at by Isabella for several minutes, he agreed to contact Gus Shaver and inform him that the couple must be chaperoned at all times.

To Choco Chocs Doreen's delight, a list of times and dates were emailed over to her, with a message explaining that the Crows' chauffeur would be instructed to pick her up before Tolly Pipkin for each of his dates with Tuppence.

Looking at the list, she noted that there were some very prestigious venues where she could meet important people. Things were looking up for Choco Chocs Doreen.

In contrast, Isabella Billings could not manage a decent night's sleep after Tuppence told her about the dreadful business of her public relationship with a working-class nobody.

Isabella phoned Richard Crow again the very next day and called him an absolute beast. She demanded that the charade cease this very day, because Archie, being the well-born man that he was, should not be forced to watch his betrothed consort with ill-bred scum for the benefit of the media. 'My poor Archie is overwhelmed and distraught,' she said.

'It's only temporary,' Richard assured her. 'Tuppence is obsessed with making it as a TV celebrity. This way, she's guaranteed to get what she wants. It's unconventional, I know, but the media manipulator that has arranged it all is the best in the business.'

'If dear Mary were still alive today, she'd be turning in her grave. I knew her better than anyone, and for her to know that her daughter was being seen in public – in public! – with a working-class actor would have been a torment.'

Isabella had been a bridesmaid at Mary and Richard's wedding. Because of that, she liked to describe herself as Mary's best friend. The arranged marriage between Archie and Tuppence had come about when Isabella had visited Mary in the hospice where she was spending the last days of her life. There had been complications after a heart operation for a genetic condition. Mary had been lying in her bed ashen-faced and hardly in the mood for a visit when

Isabella had turned up. Isabella had always prided herself on being able to fill any silence with ease, so she had done most of the talking while Mary had just politely smiled, wishing this unwelcome visitor would just go away. It had been while she was making sure there was no awkward silence that Isabella had said playfully that her son, Archie, and Mary's daughter, Tuppence, should marry each other when they were adults. Isabella had taken Mary's pained smile as confirmation of a binding contract. Isabella would later embellish the story, saying that Mary had had a premonition of her death, and pleaded with her to link their two families in matrimony, saying that this would make her the happiest angel in heaven.

At the time, Richard Crow had been too grief-stricken to take much notice of the marriage contract that Isabella had drawn up. Over the years, Isabella's constant references to the arranged marriage turned it into an expected future event.

With her adorable son, Archie, so close to marrying into the Crow family, Isabella could not have Tuppence being seen in the company of other young men. She had been young once and knew that desires had no respect for contracts. She herself had had many lovers in the year before her marriage, and the thought that Tuppence might be seduced into matrimony by that oik who had already tried to ruin her Archie's destiny was too much to bear. It was her son Archie who would marry Tuppence, she would make sure of that.

21

Chaperoned

Tolly was at home, struggling to learn his lines for the extra Blue Psycho scenes, when a motorcycle courier turned up at the front door with a large brown envelope. He signed for the letter, guessing it was from Gus Shaver. He was right: it was a list of dates and venues. To his annoyance, he saw that he had a date – if you could call it that – with Tuppence that evening. The two of them would be attending the opening of a new restaurant in the heart of London. He gave a sigh. It was bound to be some pretentious, swanky eatery designed to appeal to the London elite. A limousine would pick him up at six o'clock sharp. He threw the envelope and the list to one side and lounged back on the sofa with his script. After an hour of repeating lines, and close to memorising a lengthy scene, he heard the doorbell ring insistently. He checked the time; it was five forty, too early for the limousine. He opened the front door to the last person he had ever expected to see standing on his doorstep: Choco Chocs Doreen. He just stood staring at her, dumbfounded.

'You're meeting Tuppence soon,' she said, pushing past him. 'You should be ready by now.'

'Hold on, hold on!' said Tolly. 'What the fuck are you doing here?'

'I'm your chaperone,' replied Choco Chocs Doreen, with a smug smile.

Tolly stared at her blankly for twenty seconds while his brain tried to decode what she had just said. He was still confused. 'Chaperone?'

Choco Chocs Doreen held up a typed letter that had been signed by Gus Shaver. 'I'll read it to you. *Due to concerns from Tuppence's betrothed, it has been agreed that Ms Choco Chocs Doreen, renowned TV star and acclaimed locum thespian/director, will chaperone Tolly Pipkin when in the company of Tuppence Crow.*'

'Is this some sort of sick joke?' asked Tolly.

'You don't know, do you?' said Choco Chocs Doreen. 'She's secretly engaged to Archie Billings. Their marriage has been arranged ever since they were childhood sweethearts.'

'That idiot has an arranged marriage with Tuppence?!'

'He is not an idiot! But apart from that, you are correct, so your evil plan to get Tuppence to marry you, so you can get your grubby working-class hands on her fortune, will not work.'

Tolly chuckled. 'That talentless moron is welcome to marry her. I'd rather be poor and single.'

'Don't you dare speak badly of that gifted young man. Archie has the potential to be one of the greatest actors of the age with my guidance as a renowned TV star and acclaimed locum thespian/director.'

'You cannot be serious. He's a rich, spoiled cretin who can't remember his lines.'

Choco Chocs Doreen fumed, 'Archie has something you'll never have – charisma! And magnetism, and the ability to absorb intentions better than anyone. If you insist on insulting Archie, I will inform Mr Shaver that I can no longer tolerate your disrespectful behaviour. And without me as chaperone, this arrangement will have to stop. And as I understand it, you and your agent will be ruined.'

Tolly had thought that pretending to date Tuppence for six weeks was going to be bad enough, but having a chaperone who hated him as much as Choco Chocs Doreen did was going to make his life an absolute nightmare.

'Okay, I won't mention the idiot again.'

Letting this insult go, Choco Chocs Doreen checked her watch. 'Hadn't you better get changed? We leave in ten minutes.'

Tolly was wearing black jeans and a plain, dark red shirt. 'I'm ready.'

'You can't wear those scruffy clothes! You're going to the Grandiose, Kimberly Trollope's new restaurant! The press will be there. It's the only restaurant to get six stars from the *Stellar Guide*, and that was three months before it even opened!'

'You're here to chaperone, not give fashion advice. Anyway, Kimberly whatshername probably gave the restaurant guide a backhander to get six stars. Right, let's get this over with.' Tolly grabbed a denim jacket from a coat hook beside the front door and followed Choco Chocs Doreen to the waiting limousine. The attentive chauffeur opened the car door, and Choco Chocs Doreen climbed into the back seat.

'I'll ride shotgun with the chauffeur,' said Tolly, jumping into the front passenger seat.

'You have to sit in the back with me,' protested Choco Chocs Doreen. 'You should not be mixing with the staff.'

The chauffeur climbed in behind the wheel; he had heard Choco Chocs Doreen's comment and looked over at Tolly.

'Ignore her,' he said. 'She thinks she's royalty.'

After a twenty-minute drive into the city, the chauffeur pulled into a lay-by.

'Why have we stopped here?' asked Tolly.

'You transfer into Tuppence's limousine,' explained Choco Chocs Doreen. 'You must be seen entering the restaurant together. I'll be waiting at the table.'

'Is this really necessary?' asked Tolly. 'I feel like I'm in a cold war drama.'

Another limousine pulled into the lay-by and flashed its headlights.

Tolly's chauffeur leapt out and marched round to open the passenger door. Tolly climbed out and strolled over to the other limousine as if he had all the time in the world, despite the second chauffeur already waiting with the door open. He climbed in and sat next to Tuppence. She was dressed glamorously in a black and white dress with artfully placed gaps in the fabric that showed her bare spray-tanned skin.

'I see you made an effort,' said Tuppence with a scowl, eyeing his clothes disdainfully.

'Have you ever heard the term *done up like a dog's dinner*?' replied Tolly, staring at her dress. 'You should look it up sometime. And another thing, I'm not happy about having Choco Chocs Doreen as a chaperone. It's not necessary. That woman is a pain in the arse; she's only out for herself.'

The limousine pulled into traffic.

'I know that's not true,' shot back Tuppence. 'She has sacrificed her own career to assist Archie. She is after all a renowned—'

'TV star and acclaimed locum thespian/director,' recited Tolly. 'I feel I've heard her say it a thousand times.'

'You're annoyed at her because she has seen greatness in my Archie and not in you.'

215

'Are you really engaged to that idiot?'

'Yes, I am engaged to that idi… How dare you call him that! According to Choco Chocs Doreen, he has more talent in his little finger than you have in your whole working-class body!'

'Six weeks of putting up with you will be bad enough, but adding her as a chaperone just makes me despair.'

'I'm not ecstatic about having to put up with you,' snapped Tuppence. 'The next six weeks can't go quickly enough.'

'I have an idea,' said Tolly. 'If I play up to being the bad-boy working-class actor Gus Shaver wants me to be, it might cut down the number of weeks we have to put up with each other for.'

'Every hour I don't have to be in your company would be a bonus.'

The limousine slowed down as it approached the red-carpeted entrance to the Grandiose restaurant. The media were out in force and had been tipped off that Tuppence Crow was due to arrive very shortly. When her limousine pulled up, there was a frantic rush to get to the best spot. Tolly didn't wait for the chauffeur to open the door; he stepped out as soon as the car stopped. He was immediately shoved out of the way by photographers eager to take snaps of Tuppence. After managing to regain his balance and his dignity, Tolly pushed back the paparazzi who had shoved him, shouting, 'You rude bunch of bastards!'

The Grandiose doormen rushed over and cleared a path along the red carpet to the entrance.

Tuppence climbed out of the limousine and held on to Tolly's arm; she smiled for the cameras before kissing Tolly on the cheek.

'Is he your boyfriend?!' shouted a voice from the paparazzi pack.

'I'm sorry, I don't discuss my private life,' replied Tuppence with a coy smile.

'What's his name?' shouted another voice from the pack.

'Mind your own fucking business,' said Tolly, thinking he might as well make a start on his bad-boy reputation. He led Tuppence into the building.

Gus's team whispered his name in the ears of the paparazzi, who all agreed that he was a thug.

Inside the restaurant, the dining area was decorated in the Bauhaus style, with tubular metal tables and chairs. The staff's black outfits were, as Tolly remarked when he saw them, reminiscent of SS uniforms.

They were led to their table by a sycophantic head waiter. Choco Chocs Doreen was already waiting there.

'Do you have to sit at the same table as us?' moaned Tolly. 'Can't you chaperone from the other side of the room?'

Choco Chocs Doreen ignored him and gave Tuppence a quick glance over. 'Did he try to take advantage?' she asked Tuppence.

'We shared a car for two minutes, so no,' said Tolly, sitting down.

The head waiter, with a whiff of fascism about his uniform, held Tuppence's chair while she sat down.

'If you were a gentleman, you would have done that,' said Choco Chocs Doreen to Tolly.

'If she were a doddery old bat like someone I know, I would've done.'

'I hope you're not referring to me, because I only have to call Mr Shaver,' snapped Choco Chocs Doreen.

'Please just ignore him,' said Tuppence. 'I'm relying on you to assure my beloved Archie that this arrangement is purely business. He trusts you, and so do I.'

'As a renowned TV star and acclaimed locum thespian/director, it lifts my heart to hear those words from the country's leading celebrity.' Crocodile tears once again rolled down Choco Chocs Doreen's cheeks. 'Forgive me if I cry with happiness,' she whispered to Tuppence, 'but just knowing that you and Archie are destined to be life partners brings joy to my humble heart.'

The head waiter handed out menus printed in white on black card. 'What drinks can I get you?' he asked.

'Champagne!' said Choco Chocs Doreen immediately. Her tears had miraculously dried up. 'But it must be French champagne because I'll know if it isn't.'

'I thought all champagne was French,' said Tolly.

Choco Chocs Doreen shook her head and smiled at Tolly as if he was a simpleton. 'As well as being a renowned TV star and acclaimed locum thespian/director, I am somewhat of an expert when it comes to vino. That means wine, by the way.'

'You learn something every day,' marvelled Tolly with a large helping of sarcasm.

'I would like a spring water, please,' said Tuppence. 'I like to keep my toxin intake to a minimum,' she explained to Tolly.

'I'll have a large beer,' said Tolly. 'I'll take my chances with toxins.'

He glanced around at the other tables. They were occupied by a mixture of international celebrities and very smug rich people. His happy reverie of them all choking on their food was interrupted by a woman's scream of delight.

He spotted the celebrity businesswoman Kimberly Trollope making her way to their table with her arms wide open.

'Tuppence, darling, thank you so much for coming. You are looking gorgeous as usual.'

Kimberly Trollope was a ruthless entrepreneur who owned a chain of five-star hotels up and down the country. The Grandiose was her first restaurant, which she had plans to franchise around the world. Inviting Tuppence to her opening evening was nothing more than a business decision. Gus Shaver had offered her outstanding reviews for the restaurant across all of Richard Crow's media outlets.

Tuppence stood up and kissed Kimberly on both cheeks. 'Congratulations on your six *Stellar Guide* stars.'

'I'm blessed to have the world's top chefs working for me.'

'It's a great pleasure to meet you,' gushed Choco Chocs Doreen. 'As a renowned TV star and acclaimed locum thespian/director, I've been an admirer of yours for many years.'

'Bless you,' said Kimberly with false modesty. She peered at Tolly, waiting for another compliment.

'How can you get six *Stellar Guide* stars three months before you even open?' asked Tolly. 'How does that work?'

Kimberley's smile hid her hatred of the young man with Tuppence. 'The reviewer had secret prior knowledge of the menu.'

'Secret prior knowledge of the menu?' scoffed Tolly. 'Does that mean they never actually tasted the food?'

Kimberly felt her face aching from pretending to smile. 'Knowing that we have the world's top chefs working on the menu, the reviewer could subconsciously savour the food.'

Tolly laughed. 'A six-star review of a subconscious tasting? I take my hat off to you.'

219

'I'm sure the food will be delicious,' said Tuppence, who was finding the mounting tension uncomfortable.

Kimberly turned to Tuppence. 'It's an exciting menu.' For the benefit of Tolly, she added, 'As you heard, we are the first ever restaurant to receive a six-star rating.'

'I for one expected nothing less from the country's leading entrepreneur,' declared Choco Chocs Doreen.

Kimberly was now feeling back in control. 'The Grandiose has the honour of being the first omni-vegan restaurant in the world.'

Tolly laughed loudly enough to make the other diners glance over. 'Please tell me you are not combining meat with vegan dishes on the same plate, because that would be absolutely mental!' Tolly had attempted to become a vegan on several occasions, but the smell of a bacon sandwich always tempted him to have one, and once he had done that, he was on a slippery slope that ended with him back on his omnivorous, meat-eating diet.

Kimberly had never hated anyone in her whole life as much as she hated this young man right now. 'What's your name?' she asked Tolly.

'Tolly Pipkin.'

'He's my boyfriend,' added Tuppence, for the benefit of anyone who might be listening in.

Kimberly had come up with the idea of an omnivore and vegan fusion herself. Her chefs had expressed their doubts about serving meat on the same plate as vegan food, and this had forced her to bribe her way to the six-star review just to pacify them. 'Well, Mr Pipkin, the *Stellar Guide* disagrees,' she said angrily. Her raised voice drew the attention of the other diners, who now leant in closer to hear. 'They called it revolutionary; a world first!'

'It will probably also be a world last,' laughed Tolly. 'You can't seriously put meat and vegan food on the same plate. It's a ridiculous idea.'

Kimberly had gambled her own money on the success of the Grandiose restaurant. Potential backers had also voiced reservations about her vision of an omnivore and vegan fusion menu, so she had been forced to front the necessary money herself. She had only done it because she was so confident that her idea was a winner, bolstered by securing the six-star award. Now, on her opening night, this scruffy individual with Tuppence Crow had laughed at her concept and had even guessed that she had paid a bribe. She could not have him attracting any more attention and putting ideas in people's heads. 'I would like everyone on this table to leave.' She waved over the doormen, not only dressed like fascists but ready to act like them, who promptly escorted Tuppence's party out.

The other diners pulled out their phones to film Tolly, Tuppence and Choco Chocs Doreen being ushered from the restaurant.

'The menu's a joke!' shouted Tolly in defiance. 'So are the six stars!' The security staff were now manhandling him and telling him menacingly to shut his big mouth. 'Don't be fooled!' added Tolly as he was frogmarched to the door.

The paparazzi waiting outside around the red carpet were taken by surprise when they witnessed Tuppence Crow being ejected from the Grandiose with her thug boyfriend and an angry-looking middle-aged woman.

'I've never been so insulted,' protested Choco Chocs Doreen. 'Don't you know who I am?'

Cameras began to click away as a doorman helped Tolly on to the street with a firm shove. Tolly turned and shouted, 'Your menu sucks and your waiters dress like fascists!'

221

Tuppence was soon surrounded by jostling reporters who sensed a top story developing.

'Why have you been asked to leave?!' shouted one voice. Tuppence was pissed off with Tolly for getting her thrown out of an upmarket establishment for the first time in her life, but she was astute enough to know that the incident would attract a huge amount of publicity. 'My boyfriend, Tolly, upset Kimberly Trollope,' she explained.

Tolly now found himself being jostled and photographed.

'What did you do to upset her?' asked a female voice with a French accent.

Tolly's adrenaline was still pumping after the manhandling. 'I criticised her menu. I told her that putting meat and vegan food on the same plate was crazy.'

'She has got six *Stellar Guide* stars,' shouted a voice in her defence.

'Really?! Because I think awarding six stars for a subconscious advance taste of the food sounds a bit dodgy.'

Tuppence's chauffeur had been tipped off about her early departure, and her limousine now pulled up outside the restaurant. The driver jumped out and helped her to the vehicle with Choco Chocs Doreen following.

'Tolly!' shouted Tuppence. 'Get in the limousine!'

Tolly fought his way through the paparazzi and ducked into the car. Camera bulbs were still flashing as the limousine pulled away.

Tolly found himself sitting between Tuppence and Choco Chocs Doreen. 'I think that's the quickest I've ever been thrown out of a place,' he said with a chuckle.

'The humiliation,' sighed Choco Chocs Doreen. 'Me, a renowned TV star and acclaimed locum thespian/director, thrown on to the street like a common criminal. Oh, what will my public think?'

'You didn't hang about with your bad-boy act,' said Tuppence with a scowl at Tolly.

'I've worked with him,' said Choco Chocs Doreen. 'That was normal behaviour. Trouble follows him everywhere.'

Tolly checked his watch. 'It's still early. Shall we find somewhere else to eat? I'm feeling quite hungry now.'

Tuppence and Choco Chocs Doreen shook their heads and chorused, 'No!'

There was much more press coverage and social media buzz about Tuppence Crow being ejected from the opening of a new restaurant than Tolly had expected. The next morning, he sat munching his cornflakes in front of a TV news channel. The young entertainment reporter, Caleb, who was camper than the front row at the Eurovision Song Contest, was describing last night's ruckus to the main female anchor, thirty-six-year-old redhead Jenny Martin.

'At the opening night of Kimberly Trollope's new, groundbreaking Grandiose restaurant, who would have believed that squeaky clean Tuppence Crow would be thrown out on the street?'

Pictures flashed up on the screen behind Caleb of Tuppence pushing through the paparazzi, with Tolly snarling at her side.

'Well, that is exactly what happened after she took her new boyfriend, blacklisted bad-boy actor Tolly Pipkin, to the hot-ticket event. Apparently, Pipkin offended entrepreneur Kimberly Trollope by insulting her revolutionary omni-vegan menu. According to witnesses at the restaurant, Pipkin acted like a bully and a thug.'

Tolly choked on his cornflakes. 'What?!'

'What more can you tell us about this Tolly Pipkin?' asked Jenny, for the benefit of the TV audience.

'There's not much to tell. He's a working-class boy who had rave reviews for his performance in the acclaimed play *The Waiting Room*, but is now blacklisted as an actor,' explained Caleb. 'He recently played the part of a murderous psychopathic psychopath in a TV drama alongside Tuppence, which is where their romance apparently began.'

Jenny thanked Caleb, then turned to the camera. Her bottom lip trembled. 'As a person with ginge… red hair, I was the victim of bullying for most of my childhood, and to know that bullies like Pipkin are still swaggering around makes me incandescent with rage.' Jenny began to weep. 'I just hope that Tuppence Crow sees sense and dumps that controlling bully. Now, here's the weather forecast.'

Even Gus Shaver was taken by surprise at the interest in Tuppence and Tolly's fake relationship after just one night. The venue he had chosen for the next public date was the preview of an exhibition by celebrated New York pop artist Rachel Van Gogh. Because Rachel was so revered in the art world, it was obvious that there would be a huge amount of global interest, so what better place for Tuppence and Tolly to be seen next by the media?

On the day that Tolly was going to the Rachel Van Gogh preview, he had been working on one of the extra scenes at the TV studio in which a flash of bright light showed his eyes in close-up. For technical reasons, the shot had to be done several times, and on the last occasion, someone had mistakenly turned the intensity of the light to its highest setting, which left Tolly with sickly coloured bright circles imprinted on his vision. He was promptly taken to an eye specialist who informed him that his eyes where not permanently damaged, but he would need to wear thick-framed sunglasses until the circles faded away and that he should avoid bright lights.

When Choco Chocs Doreen arrived at Tolly's front door, she was a touch more curt than usual. 'Poor Archie was fuming when he found out that Tuppence and I were thrown out of the Grandiose restaurant. He could not absorb intentions for a whole day because he was so incensed. If it were not for my admiration for dear Archie and his family, I would have washed my hands of this whole charade.'

'I dare say the vast amount of money his mother pays you helped with your decision.'

'How dare you! I am sacrificing my own career as a renowned thespian to nurture a true acting talent, and if you make any more ludicrous insinuations, I will have no choice but to inform Archie and his beloved mother that I can no longer engage in this pantomime… Why are you wearing dark glasses?'

'One of the lighting technicians made a mistake and now I have dilated pupils.' Tolly took his glasses off to show her. 'I keep seeing sickly pink circles.'

Choco Chocs Doreen looked into his bloodshot eyes. 'It's like staring into the eyes of Beelzebub himself.' She made the sign of the cross to protect herself.

'Maybe it's better if I don't go tonight. Any bright lights just make me feel sick.'

'You must go,' insisted Choco Chocs Doreen. 'Mr Shaver was quite adamant that you and dear Tuppence should be seen out together tonight.'

225

'I've got a good excuse; I can't see properly. Can't you call him or something?'

Choco Chocs Doreen reluctantly took her phone out of her handbag and returned to the waiting limousine to call Gus Shaver. One minute later, she was back. 'Mr Shaver has some sympathy, but if you fail to attend, he will start the process of ruining you and your agent.' She glanced at Tolly's blue jeans and black tee shirt. 'You're not going dressed like that, are you?'

'I might have been coerced into doing all this stuff, but I'll do it wearing what the hell I like.' Tolly tried to find fault with Choco Chocs Doreen's tasteful outfit, but she looked smart and stylish. Unbeknown to him, she now had a completely new wardrobe for every date she was chaperoning, courtesy of Isabella Billings.

Twenty minutes later, Tolly was climbing out of the car in the same lay-by as before and clambering into Tuppence's limousine. She took one look at his thick-framed dark glasses and said, 'What's with the blind-man glasses?'

'I'm wearing blind-man glasses, as you so offensively call them, because I was nearly blinded by a lighting technician and now I keep seeing sickly pink shapes. I've been advised to wear these until my dilated pupils have gone back to normal.' He lifted the glasses to show her his eyes.

'God, you look even weirder than usual.'

'Thanks for the compliment.' He noticed she was wearing another glamorous outfit that had probably cost a small fortune.

'My Twitter page is getting thousands of tweets thanks to your antics the other night,' simpered Tuppence. 'The horrid things they say about you make me blush.'

'I don't like social media; it's all just hate, flattery and vanity.'

226

'As a celebrity, it would be selfish of me not to let my fans know about my life. Their own lives are so drab, it makes them feel better to know how wonderful mine is.'

Tolly scoffed, 'Really?!'

'It's true. Anyway, everyone knows that to be a global star, you must have an online presence.'

'You can keep your online presence; give me anonymity any day of the week.'

Tuppence's limousine pulled up outside the large Victorian warehouse building that was hosting the Rachel Van Gogh exhibition. As before, the paparazzi had been tipped off and were waiting for Tuppence to make an appearance. There were more photographers this time as the snappers all knew that the right picture of the odd couple together could be worth a month's pay. Tolly climbed out, shielding his dark glasses with his hand to give his eyes extra protection from the incessant flashes. Nonetheless, his eyes started to ache, and the sickly pink circles began to grow brighter. One overzealous photographer pushed a camera right into his face. The blinding flash caused an instant headache.

'Get that fucking thing out of my face,' Tolly growled, pushing the photographer away.

Tuppence managed to hold on to Tolly's arm and beamed a smile for the cameras as he led her through the mass of bodies into the building, muttering, 'Bastards.'

Choco Chocs Doreen was waiting for them in the foyer of the gallery where a row of tables were laid out with finger food and drinks. She was helping herself to a glass of wine and several canapés while informing a smartly dressed young couple that she was a renowned TV star and acclaimed locum thespian/director. When she caught sight of Tuppence, she rushed over.

'I've checked the wine and canapés, Tuppence, and they're safe for you to consume.'

'Are you a food taster as well as a chaperone now?' asked Tolly.

Choco Chocs Doreen checked no one was within earshot. 'It's my duty to protect Archie's betrothed from the dangers of unhygienic catering.'

'I can see why my Archie depends on you, Choco Chocs Doreen,' said Tuppence. 'You are a rock.'

Choco Chocs Doreen batted her eyes and would have put her hands on her heart if they had not been so full of food and drink. 'It fills my heart with joy to hear my name mentioned in the same breath as that talented young man.'

'Can we please get on with looking at this bloody preview?' begged Tolly. 'My eyes are really aching now.'

'You two go ahead,' said Choco Chocs Doreen. 'I'll just check to see if the sandwiches are fit for Tuppence's consumption.'

Tuppence put her arm in Tolly's, faked a smile for any onlookers and whispered to him, 'Please don't embarrass me. Rachel Van Gogh is one of my favourite artists; I have several of her paintings.'

Knowing that the artist's paintings sold for as much as two hundred thousand dollars, Tolly said incredulously, 'You have several?!'

'There she is,' said Tuppence, pointing to a middle-aged woman dressed in a white tailored suit and matching turban. 'She is incredibly talented.'

Tolly would have been the first to hold his hands up and say he knew next to nothing about art, but as he looked at the numerous huge canvases lining the nearest wall, he could not discern any deeper meaning in the stencilled images of an upright vacuum cleaner in various base colours with the word *vagina* scrawled across them in dripping red paint. Where was the artistry in using the same stencil for all of them? Before he could voice his opinion, Tuppence pulled him towards the artist, who was being filmed by a camera crew for a major documentary. She was describing to a group of eager listeners the meaning of the work *Gun Cerise*, which consisted of a large image of an upside down handgun stencilled on to a giant canvas in shades of pink with the word *penis* scrawled across it in dripping red paint.

'…the pink hues represent the flowers on the graves of all those who have been victims of gun crime,' she explained.

The group of admirers nodded avidly at this unique insight.

'The inverted handgun,' she continued, 'represents the demarcation and rebarbative segregation of objectifying dehumanisation.'

The group of admirers nodded their approval, with several opining that this was exactly what they had thought. Rachel Van Gogh had no idea if what she said made any sense; she just picked impressive-sounding words with eleven or twelve syllables and combined them in a more or less random order, but it sold the work, and that was the most important thing.

'What does the word *penis* signify?' asked one thoughtful onlooker.

'There are some elements of one's art that an artist likes to keep as an enigma,' said Rachel. In truth, she found she could double the price of her paintings if they had the word *vagina* or *penis* scrawled across them in dripping red paint. She spotted Tuppence Crow and acknowledged her with a smile. Rachel had been expecting to see her because one of Tuppence's representatives, a Mr Shaver, had contacted her office several days ago to request places on the guest list for

Tuppence and two plus-ones for the first-night preview. Tuppence had bought several of the paintings at her last preview, so Rachel had not hesitated to invite this daughter of a multimillionaire with a taste for expensive art.

Rachel smiled broadly as Tuppence approached her. They double air-kissed for the benefit of the cameras and complimented each other on looking wonderful.

'Oh, Rachel, I love everything I've seen so far,' enthused Tuppence. 'I just want to buy it all. You are a genius.'

'Bless you, Tuppence. All I humbly try to achieve is the truth through art.'

Tolly could not help chuckling at Rachel's remark. She turned and stared at this man wearing dark glasses next to Tuppence.

'Oh, this is my boyfriend, Tolly,' said Tuppence, 'Tolly Pipkin.'

Tolly held out his hand, and Rachel reluctantly shook it.

'Why did you laugh when I said truth through art?' asked Rachel.

'Sorry, it just sounded a bit of a corny cliché,' answered Tolly.

Rachel had battled the art establishment for artistic recognition for years. They had called her pop art Andy Warhol rip-offs. It was only after she had begun selling her work to gullible idiots for vast sums of money that they had started to take her seriously.

'I can assure you,' said Rachel, 'that every piece of art I toil over for weeks on end is speaking the truth!' Rachel raised her voice when she said, 'truth', for the benefit of the camera crew.

'Weeks?' said Tolly looking at the artworks of vacuum cleaners that were identical save for the different shades and the fact that the odd one was upside down. 'The truth is, you

230

probably knocked them all out in one day with the same stencil.'

Tuppence was noticing that Tolly had a way of pissing people off very quickly and tried to pull him away.

Rachel had actually knocked out the canvases in a day, but she was not going to let some shades-wearing fuckhead make insinuations about her work, even if they did happen to be true. 'If you had the decency to remove your sunglasses and see the true hues of the artworks as they are meant to be seen, you would see truth.' She was pleased with that being caught on film and had visions of it being shared on social media. Rachel reached over and pulled Tolly's dark glasses off in an attempt to humiliate him in front of the camera.

Before Tolly knew it, his eyes were subjected to the bright lights of the gallery.

'There,' said Rachel, pointing to her canvas *Gun Cerise*, 'that is what the truth looks like.'

As the pain in Tolly's eyes increased, he grimaced. 'Oh, no! That sickly pink colour is killing me. I feel like I'm going to throw up.'

Tuppence grabbed the glasses from Rachel and began to pull Tolly away. 'It's his eyes,' she explained. 'They're light-sensitive.'

'That unbearable pink hurts like hell,' moaned Tolly. 'If I could pull my eyes out to stop seeing it, I would.'

'You're embarrassing me!' said Tuppence, handing Tolly his sunglasses.

Tolly promptly put them on and let out a sigh of relief. 'I never want to experience that sight again,' he said.

Rachel began to get a bad feeling about how this might look on TV as she watched the camera crew home in on Tolly and Tuppence. She quickly ushered over her personal assistant and whispered in her ear. The assistant immediately sped off to the exit.

Choco Chocs Doreen wandered over with crumbs around her mouth. 'What an interesting picture,' she said, looking at the *Gun Cerise* canvas.

'It's incredibly good,' said Tuppence, hoping that Rachel had accepted her explanation that Tolly's eyes were sensitive.

'Why is the pink so sickly?' asked Tolly, who could still see ghost images of pink shapes even with his protective eyewear back on.

Several security officers rushed in, and Rachel pointed out Tolly. He was then hurriedly bundled out of the gallery, while two female security officers more politely asked Tuppence and Choco Chocs Doreen to leave.

Tuppence was again pissed off about what Tolly had done, but she reminded herself that it would make headlines in the right places. She ran over to Tolly, pushed the security officers out of the way and threw her arms around him. 'Leave my boyfriend alone,' she screamed.

Rachel turned towards her camera crew's director. 'If you show one fucking frame of that asshole dissing my art, I will fucking sue your ass off!'

The paparazzi were once again caught off guard by Tolly's early exit as he was physically escorted from the gallery by the security team. Even the camera crew that Gus had hired to capture footage of the couple were not ready for this. They all rapidly ditched their coffees and cigarettes and grabbed their cameras.

Choco Chocs Doreen could not believe she was being escorted out again. 'You cannot treat us like this!' she protested. 'Tuppence is a reality celebrity, and I myself am a renowned TV star and acclaimed locum thespian/director. This is an outrage!'

232

Tolly had to endure several minutes of flashing cameras and shouted questions before Tuppence's limousine turned up.

'Why have you been thrown out?' asked one voice.

'Tolly never meant to upset Rachel,' said Tuppence in his defence. 'It was a misunderstanding; it had nothing to do with the artwork.'

'Did you like her work?' shouted a female voice. 'She is one of the most popular living artists today.'

'She might well be, but all I could see was sickly pink shapes because—' Before Tolly could finish, Tuppence pulled him towards the limousine that had just pulled up.

Tuppence's chauffeur had parked up a few blocks away, and had been masturbating to a porn movie on his phone in the back of the limousine when he received the call to pick up his passengers as soon as possible. He hastily pulled his pants back up and scrambled into the driver's seat. When he pulled up outside the gallery, Tuppence, Tolly and Choco Chocs Doreen were surrounded by the press. He jumped out of the limousine and instantly felt a draught on his penis. He looked down to see his semi-erect member still protruding from his fly. He pulled the metal zipper up sharply and felt a chunk of his bellend being ripped out. He let out a loud, 'JESUS!' and bent double in extreme pain. Being the professional that he was, despite his inability to stand up straight, he staggered round to the rear door and opened it for Tuppence to climb in.

'Are you okay?' asked Tolly as he went to clamber in after Choco Chocs Doreen. He noticed the chauffeur hunched over and crying in pain.

'Spilled my coffee,' sobbed the chauffeur. After Tolly had climbed in, the driver whimpered all the way back to the driver's seat, feeling the blood dripping down his leg from his butchered penis.

'The humiliation!' said Choco Chocs Doreen. 'To get us thrown out of two establishments in less than a week is hooliganism.'

'Can't you go anywhere without being asked to leave?' grumbled Tuppence. 'It's embarrassing.'

'Dear Archie will not be able to absorb or project intentions for days after hearing about this dreadful episode. You, Pipkin, are a disgrace to the thespian profession.'

Back behind the wheel, the chauffeur felt faint and decided that he should seek urgent medical attention. He radioed the other limousine to meet at the usual lay-by as soon as possible to transfer the passengers, giving the excuse that warning lights were flashing on his dashboard.

Once transferred into the other limousine, Tolly said, 'I'm feeling hungry. Shall we go and get something to eat?'

'No!' said Tuppence and Choco Chocs Doreen in unison.

22

The bus tour

The *Amongst Us* bus tour for bona fide members of Conspiracies-are-true was an annual event that had lost some of its appeal for a number of the longest-standing members because they had done the tour many times and still never seen even one reptile in human form.

The latest bona fide members, Jennifer and Trevor, were eagerly waiting outside their terraced house when a small bus, with the words *The Shirley Children's Charity* hand-painted on it, pulled to a stop in front of them.

The doors hissed open, and Colin waved to them. He read the mystified look on their faces. 'I'm a part-time driver for the charity. They let me use the bus as long as I top up the tank before taking it back.'

Jennifer smiled and climbed on, followed by an excited Trevor. She was surprised to see only three other people on board. 'Oh, I thought we were going to be the last pick-up.'

'You are,' said Colin, 'but it's school holidays, so not everyone could make it, plus there's the Great British Tennis Club tournament on the TV. Right, before we hit the road, I'll introduce you to your fellow passengers. Some, you may know already.'

Colin addressed the three other passengers on the bus. 'Meet Jennifer and Trevor, our latest bona fide members to see the *Amongst Us* video.'

235

'Trevor's so excited about this trip,' said Jennifer, 'he's hyperventilated twice already this morning.'

The first of their fellow passengers to be introduced was a woman in her sixties wearing a pink tee shirt emblazoned with the words, *The moon landings never happened. Get over it!*

'I'm Belinda,' said the large bubbly lady, 'co-founder of Moon-landings-never-happened.'

'Who's the other founder?' asked Jennifer, who was a self-confessed nosey parker.

'We don't talk about Little Terry,' said Colin in hushed tones.

Belinda stoically fought back her emotions. 'Let's just say he was a big disappointment. A co-founder of Moon-landings-never-happened should not be placing bets on the Chinese being the next to walk on the moon.'

'Still,' said Colin, 'a very popular organisation.'

In the seat behind her was a grey-haired, grey-faced man in his sixties, dressed mainly in grey.

'Oh, hello, Derek,' said Jennifer. 'How's your cough?'

'Much better,' coughed Derek.

'I see you know Derek, from of All-medicines-are-poison.'

'We joined him on the anti-medicine protest outside the hospital,' said Trevor.

'It's lucky we were there to take you to A&E when you had that funny turn,' said Jennifer.

'It was only a mild water infection,' coughed Derek.

'Maybe,' said Jennifer, 'but when you started screaming about giant hamsters on bicycles before you passed out, we did worry.'

'I'm going to sue that hospital,' coughed Derek. 'I never gave them permission to use antibiotics.'

'Well, you couldn't, could you?' said Jennifer. 'Not when you were unconscious.'

The next to be introduced was Eddie.

'He's one of our first bona fide members. He was with the flat-earthers, but now runs a splinter group, the Flat-earth-has-flat-bits club,' explained Colin.

Eddie was partially bald. While the top and front of his head were hairless, he had grown the hair on the back of his head down to his shoulders to make up for the lack further forward. He nodded a greeting. 'The flat earth has flatter bits than the flat-earthers think it has.'

'I'm a flat-earth agnostic,' said Trevor, 'only because when you look out from my mum and dad's beach hut, you can just make out the tops of the blades of the giant wind turbines miles out at sea. The rest must be below the horizon.'

Eddie shook his head. 'Classic rookie's mistake. You see, the earth is flatter in some parts than in others. You're just seeing a flatter bit in the distance.'

'Holy fake Bible, that makes sense,' said Jennifer.

Eddie held out a business card to Trevor and Jennifer. 'The club meets once a month if you fancy popping along. We meet up in a back room at the Globe pub.'

Belinda leant over to Jennifer. 'What did you think of the *Amongst Us* video?'

'It's really good, said Jennifer. 'The alien reptile in human form—'

'What on flat earth are you two doing?' said Colin. 'You both took an oath not to talk about the *Amongst Us* video on pain of double death!'

'Oh, I'm a right little chatterbox, aren't I?' giggled Belinda.

'Sorry,' said Jennifer, as she sat down with Trevor on a seat across from Belinda.

'This is a very exciting day for me,' said Trevor, his right leg twitching up and down faster than a jazz drummer's. 'To actually visit alien ground zero is a real thrill.'

'He couldn't sleep last night because he was so excited,' said Jennifer.

Colin climbed back into the driver's seat. 'The first stop on our tour is… the bus stop.'

This information caused a buzz of excitement, and ten minutes later, Colin pulled the bus to a halt outside a large secondary school and turned the engine off. He stood up and addressed his meagre audience. 'This is where the alien reptile was waiting on that fateful day.'

In his usual fashion, Trevor put his hand up. 'Can we get off the bus and look?'

Colin had barely uttered the word, 'Yes' when he was barged out of the way by Trevor, who could not contain his eagerness to see the bus stop up close.

After taking several pictures on his phone, Trevor clambered back aboard, followed by a woman in her seventies.

'You're late again!' she said, holding up a pensioner bus pass to Colin. 'It's not good enough!'

'No, no, no,' said Colin. 'You're on the wrong bus. This is a private bus.'

'Private?'

'It's not a public bus.'

'Well, I want to complain! You shouldn't be waiting at a bus stop with a bus if you're not a proper bus.'

At that moment, a double-decker bus pulled up behind the minibus. 'That's the bus you want,' said Colin, pointing it out to the old lady.

The old lady checked her watch. 'It's bloody late again!' she said, stepping off. 'I'm going to complain.'

Once she was clear of the doors, Colin closed them, started the engine and set off. His bus driver's muscle memory kicked in, and he cut up several cars, resulting in beeps of annoyance.

'Next stop is the drop-off stop!'

Trevor was breathing heavily. 'I'm hyperventilating,' he gasped. 'It's too exciting.'

'Calm down,' pleaded Jennifer. 'If you're like that now, what will you be like when we go to alien ground zero?'

It was a fifteen-minute ride to the drop-off stop, which turned out to be a bus stop on the edge of a village green. Colin switched the engine off.

'This is where the alien reptile in human form got off, thinking that I'd been brainwashed, but little did that alien reptile know that I have a natural immunity to alien brainwashing.'

Eddie had rummaged around in his rucksack and now produced a roll of tin foil. 'I think we should take precautions just in case Thems-at-top know we're coming and try to brainwash us. If we wrap our heads with this foil, it will block the brainwashing signals.'

'Good idea,' said Colin. 'I do have immunity, but why take any chances?'

The group, all with their heads now wrapped in tinfoil bandanas, assembled beside the bus. Colin pointed out a gap between trees on the other side of the village green. 'That is the direction the alien in human form took to meet up with the mothership. And that is where we are going. Follow me, everyone. If for any reason we get split up by alien reptiles, meet up back here.'

Colin led them along a well-worn path across the village green, then off the main path through a wooded area. He stopped and indicated for them to be quiet.

'On that day,' said Colin in a low voice, 'I sensed alien activity and headed that way.' He pointed to a small open area bordered by clipped hedging. 'Let's go silently just in case there's still alien activity taking place.'

Crouching down, he led them towards the hedge and knelt down beside it. He instructed the others to do the same. 'When I reached this point, I knew there was no turning back. Whatever dangers lay beyond this hedge had to be ignored. I had to go on, I had to know the truth even if it meant sacrificing my life!'

Trevor began to hyperventilate again, only this time it was in panic. 'Thems-at-top might be watching! We might get probed!'

'Will you keep quiet?' hissed Colin. 'If aliens are present and hear you, we might all end up getting probed.'

'Let's just leave him here till we get back if he's gone all panicky,' said Belinda, who was cheesed off with Trevor's constant hyperventilating.

'It's just a churchyard and no one's about,' said Eddie. He peered over the hedge and then slipped through a gap in the foliage.

The others stood up and followed him through the gap.

Colin had not been expecting to see any alien activity, but he was nonetheless slightly disappointed that there was nothing out of the ordinary. 'Let me paint you a picture of the events that day. The sky was as black as coal and the light was poor. A weird alien ground mist had begun to form.' He crouched down then began to crawl along a row of headstones.

'I crept my way along here and heard a strange noise. I stopped in fear of my life. I looked up and saw two aliens hovering above the ground near those trees…'

'What happened next?' gasped Trevor, who was now also desperate for a pee because of his nervous excitement.

'I inched forward to get a better look,' continued Colin. 'As I edged closer, I could see two alien figures circling each other, ready to beam aboard the mothership. I heard voices behind me, but when I looked, there was no one there. When I turned back, the aliens had gone.'

'I can sense that aliens have been here,' said Eddie with confidence.

'I feel as though they're watching us,' added Belinda.

'They know we're here,' sniffed Derek. 'They're probably deciding which one of us to probe first.'

Trevor tried to take deep, steady breaths but could not help whimpering. 'I don't want to be probed first.'

'I think the aliens have brought on Trevor's hyperventilating,' said Jennifer, 'in the hope that it would stop us visiting alien ground zero!'

Suddenly, a distant voice barked, 'This way!' They all froze in fear.

'That might just be an innocent person calling to someone else,' whispered Colin. He gazed in the direction of the sound. 'In the worst-case scenario, it's aliens coming to probe or brainwash us. But if we stick together, we'll show Thems-at-top that us humans ain't scared of them one bit!' Colin had some words ready to boost morale. He had tweaked Shakespeare's *Henry V* Battle of Agincourt speech especially for a time like this.

'We shall be remembered – we few, we happy few, we band of Conspiracies-are-true brothers. For those that get probed and brainwashed with me today…' Colin turned to

241

see his fellow Conspiracies-are-true members rushing for the gap in the hedge. 'Bastards! Wait for me!'

23

It's just a stupid game

The incident at Rachel Van Gogh's preview had a bigger impact than even Gus could have expected. The news media were shocked to hear that the acclaimed pop artist's work had been insulted by an actor who was not only blacklisted but working class with it. It pleased Gus to hear of spin-off discussion items where so-called experts explained why good girls were attracted to bad, loutish men. For their next date, Gus arranged for Tolly and Tuppence to be seen at an internationally televised event. They would attend the Great British Tennis Club tournament and not be seated just anywhere, but in the most sought-after seating area there was: the Royal Box. It meant guaranteed media exposure and would without a doubt help to make Tuppence Crow a household name.

Gus had discovered that there were several ways to secure an invitation, and he opted for the one that would be the quickest and involved blackmail, because he knew that always worked. Using his rapidly expanding network of UK shit-diggers, Gus discovered that the sixty-five-year-old vice-chairman of the Great British Tennis Club Society, Wallace Parker-Higgs, had been a long-term customer of a high-class brothel with luxurious premises in Knightsbridge. The Elite Discreet Club, as it was known, catered for politicians, celebrities and anyone who had the extreme wealth necessary to use its services. Gus had obtained video footage of the vice-chairman having sex with a prostitute in the doggy-style position. She was dressed as a ballboy, and he shouted out tennis scores, climaxing with, 'Game, set and match!' closely followed by a satisfied groan of, 'New balls, please…'

The weather forecast for their trip to the Great British Tennis Club had been of a hot and cloudless day, so Tolly was well prepared for the sun in denim shorts, flip-flops, a flowery shirt, his blind-man sunglasses and a straw trilby that looked like it had been nibbled by some hungry animal.

When chaperone Choco Chocs Doreen arrived to pick him up in the chauffeured limousine as usual, she took one look at his beach-bum outfit and let out a loud screech. 'What the hell are you wearing?!'

'What do you mean, what am I wearing? It's going to be a hot day, so I'm dressed in my summer outfit.'

'Didn't you read the timetable? Today is the Great British Tennis Club tournament.'

'I know,' said Tolly defensively. 'I watched it on TV once, and I saw people were dressed casually like this.' Try as he might to like the sport, Tolly could not help feeling that that it seemed to take an awful lot of manpower for two people to play one game of tennis. He had counted over a dozen people and thought that was a lot; then halfway through the game he was watching, they had changed all the line judges and ballboys, which brought the total personnel involved up to more than twenty.

'You and Tuppence are invited to the Royal Box! You must dress smartly and wear a tie.'

'On a scorching day?! A tie!? You must be joking!'

Choco Chocs Doreen was finding her role as chaperone very frustrating. 'You cannot attend dressed like that. Don't you have a nice blazer and trousers?'

'I'm twenty-four, not sixty-four!' Tolly reminded her. 'I've got one suit, and it's tweed.'

'Hurry up and put it on then! Tuppence will be waiting, and if I have to report to Mister Shaver that you are deliberately being difficult, he will no doubt carry out his threats.'

'You're loving this, aren't you?'

Choco Chocs Doreen smiled. 'Yes, I am enjoying it, and after the way you attempted to sabotage Archie's career, you deserve it.'

Tolly pulled his pale blue shirt out of the dirty laundry basket, where it had been since the day of his job interview, and put it on with his green suit.

As soon as Choco Chocs Doreen saw his well-worn tweed suit, she said, 'We're going to the Great British Tennis Club, not a shooting party in a field.'

'It's not a shooting suit. Tweed is very fashionable at the moment. I had to fight three people off in the charity shop to get this.'

'Charity shop?!' gasped Choco Chocs Doreen. 'You cannot be seen with Tuppence Crow in the Royal Box wearing a shabby charity-shop suit.'

'I'm doing my bit to save the planet's resources, so I will be wearing it,' he said defiantly.

'Where's your tie? You have to wear one in the Royal Box.'

'I have one in my pocket; I'm not putting it on till I get there. It's a mad rule, having to wear a tie in the summer.'

'As a renowned TV star and acclaimed locum thespian/director, I frequently have dealings with royalty, and—'

'When have you had dealings with royalty?' asked Tolly, sure that she must be lying.

'In one of my locum thespian roles, I performed in front of the Duke of Cambridge, who, I was told, shed tears of joy at my performance in a play that the locum thespian's Hippocratic oath of secrecy forbids me to mention.'

'That's very convenient,' said Tolly, not believing a word of her story. He stepped outside and found himself getting hot and sweaty just walking to the limousine. Waiting beside the vehicle was a new chauffeur, who opened the rear door. Tolly climbed in after Choco Chocs Doreen. 'What happened to the other chauffeur?'

'No idea,' said Choco Chocs Doreen, bluntly, 'and I don't care.'

Tolly leant forward and called through to the chauffeur, who had just sat down behind the steering wheel, 'Is your colleague okay after spilling his coffee?'

'His er… man bits are a bit delicate,' said the new driver.

'Delicate? He must have really scalded himself badly,' said Tolly. 'He did seem to be in a lot of pain.'

The chauffeur nodded. 'He scalded himself so bad, he had to have three pints of blood and six stitches.'

'Wow, I've never heard of a scalding that bad before.'

Three miles from the Great British Tennis Club, Tolly transferred into Tuppence's limousine. She was dressed in a light pink pastel summer dress that even Tolly thought looked stunning.

He settled himself in the back of her limo. 'That outfit looks new. Oh, hold on, everything you wear is new.'

246

'What the hell are you wearing?' asked Tuppence. 'We're not going grouse shooting.'

'Tweed is extremely popular at the moment,' replied Tolly tetchily. 'I had to fight off three people to get this.' He took a bright red tie out of his jacket pocket. It was already knotted, so he slipped it over his head and tucked it under his shirt collar.

'Please don't tell me you're wearing a charity-shop outfit! We are going into the Royal Box! I'll be humiliated!'

'Tweed's extremely popular. I won't be the only one, you wait and see.'

Tuppence spotted the frayed cuffs of his jacket sleeves and felt like crying.

The limousine pulled up outside the VIP entrance to the famous tennis club. Gus had primed the paparazzi for their arrival, and numerous photographers were waiting eagerly for the pair to step out. The chauffeur opened the rear door and Tolly stepped out from the chill of the car's air-conditioned environment into the stifling air of the hottest day of the year. Due to the gentility of most visitors, the VIP entrance had only two security guards on the gate. Both had worked here for over thirty years, were now in their seventies and harked back to an age when orderly queues were the norm. The two pensioners were swept aside and thrown to the ground by the eager reporters.

'Will you back up?!' shouted Tolly as he found himself being mobbed. His shouts had no effect, so he began to push back at the arms waving cameras in his face.

'Why are you so aggressive?' shouted a reporter after Tolly had pushed him away.

'Because you're all fucking idiots!' answered Tolly, now drenched in sweat.

Several police officers appeared and linked arms to make a corridor, so Tolly and Tuppence could reach the entrance. Tuppence beamed her customary public smile and held on to Tolly's arm in an attempt to cover the frayed edges of his jacket. Once through the throng, Tuppence turned to pose for photographs, loving the attention and noting that her popularity with the news media was definitely on the rise.

To Tolly's relief, the VIP lounge of the Royal Box was air-conditioned. He was not surprised to find that Tuppence knew quite a few of the people there, because they were obviously stinking rich, and the stinking rich social circle was quite small. To his dismay, he saw no other man wearing tweed of any kind; they were all wearing light-coloured, lightweight clothing along with their old school ties. He did spot one other actor, an A-list American who he had read was acquainted with several members of the royal family.

As Tuppence stopped to speak to friends and introduce Tolly as her boyfriend, she became conscious of everyone's eyes on them. She had been in the Royal Box with her father a couple of times in the past, and the guests were always blasé when it came to the rich and famous. The warm and caring smiles she received contrasted with the disapproving looks Tolly was getting. It was the first time that Tuppence realised that Gus Shaver's tactics were really working.

The seating in the VIP lounge was informal. After Tuppence had acknowledged every person she knew, they sat at a table by the large windows that overlooked the hordes of tennis fans excitedly making their way to their seats. A young waiter approached them with drinks on a tray. 'Pimm's?' he said politely.

Tuppence said, 'Yes, please,' and eagerly took a glass.

248

Tolly had heard of Pimm's, but he had never had one before. His first thought was that it looked like a girly drink.

'Sir?' said the waiter, holding the tray in front of him.

'Have one,' said Tuppence. 'It's lovely on a hot day.'

'Why has it got vegetables in it?'

Tuppence giggled. 'It's cucumber, it's traditional.'

Tolly reluctantly took a glass. 'I'd rather have a lager.'

'I'll bring you a lager, sir,' said the waiter, promptly walking towards the bar area, where two bar staff were pouring out various other drinks.

'What do you think?' asked Tuppence after Tolly had taken a sip.

'It's a thirst quencher, I suppose,' he said before taking out the straw and swigging the rest in one go.

The waiter returned with a half pint of lager. 'That was quick,' said Tolly, picking it up and placing the empty Pimm's glass on the tray.

'Would you like another Pimm's?' asked the waiter.

'I better had, seeing as it's so hot,' said Tolly. The waiter headed back over to the bar.

'They are surprisingly strong,' warned Tuppence. 'I wouldn't drink them too quickly.'

'It's got vegetables in it; how strong can it be?'

'It's a long day, just pace yourself.'

Tolly liked to think that he could hold his liquor and had a reputation for it among some of his friends. He took several gulps of lager. 'I'm a grown-up, I know my limits.'

A waitress appeared with glasses of champagne on a tray. Tolly took one. 'I never get to drink champagne.' Just as he said that, the waiter appeared with another Pimm's and noticed Tolly's lager was now half empty. 'Would sir like another lager?'

'Sir would love another lager,' answered Tolly. He noticed Tuppence's disapproving look. 'I drink lager all the time. This one makes it a pint. I'm still legally under the limit to drive a car.' After polishing off the champagne, finishing his lager and swigging back another Pimm's, Tolly sipped his fresh glass of lager and began to relax.

'The royal princesses have arrived,' said Tuppence excitedly. 'Stand up when royalty enter the room.'

As he stood up, Tolly kicked the table leg, causing his empty champagne glass to topple and smash loudly on the tabletop. As the princesses turned briefly to looked in their direction, they spotted Tuppence and gave her a friendly wave.

'How do you know them?' asked Tolly, as a member of the waiting staff rushed over to clear up the broken glass.

'We were at school together. They are lovely girls, but between me and you, they're a bit spoiled.'

'Really?' laughed Tolly.

'What's so funny?'

'They're not the only spoiled princesses here. You're the most spoiled brat I've ever come across.'

'How dare you insult me! If I were a spoiled brat, I wouldn't have to put up with the humiliation of being made to be seen with a ruffian like you as my boyfriend, which by the way would never really happen in a million years.'

'Don't flatter yourself, you're not the catch you think you are.'

Word had begun to go around the VIP lounge that Tuppence's boyfriend was a thug and had been thrown out of the Grandiose and the Rachel Van Gogh preview. Eyes were beginning to glance disapprovingly in his direction.

Tuppence noticed the looks, so for the spectators' benefit, she brushed a hair from Tolly's forehead.

250

'What are you doing?'

'Pretending we're a loving couple, which is difficult because I hate you.'

Tolly noticed that they were getting a lot of attention, so he put on a big smile and kissed Tuppence on the cheek. 'It feels like I'm kissing a warm corpse,' he whispered in her ear.

'I wish you were a corpse,' she shot back.

The guests began to wander out of the VIP lounge to their seats overlooking the centre court as the two top male tennis players walked out on to the grass below.

'Let's take our seats,' said Tuppence. 'We're here to be seen after all.'

Tolly swigged back the rest of his lager and followed Tuppence out to the arena. It was nudging thirty degrees as the hot sun beat down on the Royal Box. He was already sweating again by the time they sat down on green padded seats in the row behind the two princesses. Tolly was sure there were more cameras pointing at him and Tuppence than at the tennis players. Tuppence had spotted them as well, so she grabbed hold of Tolly's hand and gazed avidly into his eyes.

'What are you doing?' he asked.

'I'm pretending you're interesting,' she whispered.

Tolly smiled and whispered back, 'I'm pretending you're pretty.'

Tuppence laughed for the cameras and muttered through her fixed smile, 'I really do despise you.'

Tolly was now perspiring profusely as the players began their warm-up routines. He overheard a middle-aged couple sitting behind him say they hoped it was going to be a five setter. He leant over to Tuppence. 'What does "five setter" mean?'

Tuppence's face lit up. 'It means playing the full five sets, so the match would take three or four hours. Wouldn't that be brilliant?'

The umpire had just called for, 'Quiet, please,' which produced an instant hush. Tolly reckoned that he would probably end up dead if he sat in this blazing sun for three to four hours in his tweed suit. 'You must be fucking joking!' he said, more loudly than he had intended.

All the people sitting in the Royal Box turned their heads to give Tolly a collective disapproving glare. In fact, he realised that every face around the centre court, including the players, line judges and ballboys, had turned to glower at the source of the voice.

'Quiet, please!' repeated the umpire, looking directly at Tolly.

Tolly felt his face turning red, not just from the heat, but also from embarrassment.

After twenty minutes of the first set, with the scores level at three games all, Tolly whispered to Tuppence, 'I feel nauseous. I think I might faint if I sit in the sun any longer.'

She glanced at his face: it was drenched in perspiration, with sweat droplets running down his nose like a waterfall. 'You'll have to wait for the players to take a drinks break before you get up.'

'I can't wait,' said Tolly. 'I need a piss as well.'

'You can't just get up and leave when the match is in play. It's bad tennis etiquette. Just wait.'

Two minutes later, during a crucial break-of-serve point, Tolly burst out in a voice louder than he had intended, 'Bollocks to tennis etiquette, I don't think I can wait.'

By this point, Tolly was oblivious to the fact that it was the two princesses sitting in the seats directly in front of him, so when they turned their heads to glare at him, he glared right back. 'Never heard anyone say bollocks before?! You should get out of your ivory towers and try mixing with normal people! Oh, and tennis etiquette is bollocks! At the end of the day, it's just a stupid game.' He stood up and scrambled along the row of seats, receiving grumbles of disapproval from all those having to move their legs out of his way.

The player about to break serve only had to hit the ball back over the net after his opponent had slipped and fallen over. Catching sight of Tolly moving from the corner of his eye, he mishit the ball, sending it into the net.

The knowledgeable tennis crowd understood the reason for the mishit and began to boo Tolly as he stumbled over the A-list actor's foot and fell on top him. He was now hot, angry, sweaty, dying for a piss and being booed. He clambered to his feet and addressed the jeering crowd. 'It's just a stupid game for the upper and middle classes!' he shouted. 'Do you really need all those people' – he gestured at the line judges and umpire – 'to play one game?!'

The crowd booed him again, and Tolly stumbled a bit further before stopping to address them again. 'And the scoring makes no sense! Fifteen-thirty-forty?! That's just three points! And why does some of it have to be in French?! That's just bloody pretentious. Look!' he hollered, pointing at the ballboys. 'They use children to pick the ball up. That's child slave labour! You should be booing the organisers, not me!'

He was relieved to finally stagger into the air-conditioned VIP lounge where he immediately took his jacket off. His light blue shirt was now dark blue and sticking to him like a second skin. He found the toilets, relieved himself, then put his head under one of the sink's cold taps until he had cooled down. When he went back into the VIP lounge, Tuppence was standing waiting for him with a scowl on her face.

'I've been asked to leave the Royal Box,' snapped Tuppence. 'This arrangement is off! You have humiliated me once too often.'

'Good,' said Tolly, 'because I can't face going to any more must-be-seen places.'

Choco Chocs Doreen was waiting outside the exit. She rushed to Tuppence's side and put an arm around her. 'I saw what he did to you,' she said with sympathy. 'He humiliated you in front of millions of people. I just hope dear Archie was walking off his charisma and did not see what this… this heathen has done to you.'

'I didn't do anything to her,' protested Tolly. 'Anyway, I'm sure plenty of people have to get up during a match. It's no big deal.'

Choco Chocs Doreen could only glare at him before turning her attention back to Tuppence. 'The limousine is on its way.'

Word had got out that Tolly and Tuppence were leaving, and within thirty seconds, they were surrounded by paparazzi, angry members of the public and several police officers.

The chauffeur was not surprised to get a call to pick them up; he had been warned that this might well happen. He drove to the VIP pick-up point just as a mass of people emerged. He jumped out, opened the rear door and quickly delivered his passengers to safety from the clamouring mob. Ten minutes later, as they headed towards the city, Tuppence was still fuming and Choco Chocs Doreen just shook her head every time she glanced at Tolly, but he had started to feel a lot better in the cool of the air-conditioned car.

'I'm feeling a bit peckish,' said Tolly. 'Shall we go and get something to eat?'

'No,' said Tuppence and Choco Chocs Doreen together.

'In that case,' said Tolly, 'can you drop me off by the Chinese takeaway at the top of my road?'

Tolly was feeling quite upbeat by the time he was dropped off outside the Oriental Garden takeaway, so he phoned his housemates to see if they wanted to join him. Laden down with food, Tolly was greeted like a life-saving hero as he entered their shared home. They all tucked into the variety of dishes, and Malcolm and Bethan promised to take him to the local pub as a thank you, so the meal was soon followed by a long, boozy night.

24

The Morning Show

The Morning Show was hosted by the casually dressed husband and wife couple Cary and Loretta Bennett. Cary, whose real name was Cyril, was in his late fifties, had dyed black, thinning hair and a permanently serious expression on his spray-tanned face because his latest facelift prevented him from smiling. Loretta was of a similar age, but her facelifts had taken away any signs of ageing. She had just one expression – smiling broadly – due to the Botox injections she had been given in a two-for-one deal at the same time as she had had her teeth whitened. It was ten twenty, and after two hours of live television, the pair were wishing away the last ten minutes of the show. All morning, they had been teasing their audience that some startling revelations were coming up, and now was the moment for the reveal.

As Tina the weathergirl finished her segment, Cary heard the director's cue in his ear and looked into the camera as he read the teleprompter.

'Those who witnessed the shocking behaviour of blacklisted actor Tolly Pipkin at the Great British Tennis Club tournament yesterday have been letting off steam this morning, and our cameras were there to capture their understandable fury and rage. We asked the public, what do you think of Tolly Pipkin? Here are some of the answers.

The VT package started with a female couple in their sixties wearing Billy Jean King tee shirts. They were both very angry.

'Ee's a bleedin' disgrace to the country,' said the taller of the two in an East End accent. 'Cause ee's got a [BEEP], ee finks ee can act like a [BEEP]!'

Her partner nodded. 'Ee insulted the bleedin' royal family, insulted this bleedin' country, insulted everyone in the bleedin' centre court and I bet he 'ates lesbians. Ee's a bleedin' git!'

'Ee's a [BEEP] and I'd cut his [BEEP] right off!' added her partner.

Next, a very old man dressed in a Chelsea pensioner uniform shakily saluted the camera. 'I'm ashamed to be British because of him,' he said with a tremble in his voice. 'He's a disgrace. I didn't get shot in the [BEEP]s by the Argie-bargies to have the Great British Tennis Club abused, and members of the gracious royal family insulted by the likes of that traitor. He should be put against the wall and shot in the [BEEP]s to see how he likes it!'

Next, a mature, smartly dressed woman representing the tennis club appeared, visibly agitated. 'The club strongly denies the accusation that the sport is for the upper and middle classes. Anyone from any walk of life is welcome to play tennis here at the Great British Tennis Club, providing of course that they become a member after putting their name on the waiting list, supplying references and paying the monthly subscription. As for Tolly Pipkin, his behaviour was repulsive! He has been officially banned from the Great British Tennis Club for life, plus an extra twenty years, for his troublesome conduct.'

As the show cut back to the studio, Loretta shook her head in dismay before turning to camera. 'Here on *The*

Morning Show, we can now bring you an exclusive about Tuppence Crow and the truth about her blacklisted actor boyfriend.'

The camera pulled back to reveal Loretta was now seated on a sixties-style armchair beside a large orange sofa where Isabella, Archie and Choco Chocs Doreen were sitting.

Loretta put on the serious face she used when presenting investigative items, but the Botox meant nobody watching could tell the difference as her smile did not move. 'My three guests this morning have experienced first-hand what this blacklisted actor is really like. In the studio with us this morning we have Isabella.'

Isabella smiled at the camera and said, 'Good morning, Loretta.'

'Seated next to her is her son, Archie.'

Archie just looked confused. Isabella gave him a nudge with her elbow. 'I'm a brilliant actor!' he blurted.

'And,' continued Loretta, 'they're joined by—'

'Yes, it is me, Loretta, Choco Chocs Doreen, the renowned TV star and acclaimed locum thespian/director. Your viewers will know me, of course, as the face of Choco Chocs chocolates. I alone was responsible for a seven percent increase in Choco Chocs chocolates sales, which is very humbling.'

Loretta had no idea what she was on about. 'Can I start with you, Isabella? What can you tell us about the scoundrel Tolly Pipkin?'

Isabella's bottom lip trembled. 'He is a liar and a deceiver! I had the misfortune of employing him as Archie's understudy—'

'Archie is one of the most talented theatre actors of his generation,' interrupted Choco Chocs Doreen. 'He exudes charisma and mesmerises the audience.'

258

Isabella nodded in agreement. 'And he absorbs intentions like no other actor. Pipkin was jealous of his genius and did everything he could to ruin Archie's stage performances.'

'Archie has the potential to be – no, I must be honest – is the greatest theatre actor of his generation,' said Choco Chocs Doreen. 'Please forgive me if I shed a tear. It's just the thought that I, a humble renowned TV star and acclaimed locum thespian/director, have had the privilege of guiding his genius. It's overwhelming.'

'You are the wind beneath his winds!' declared Isabella.

Choco Chocs Doreen pretended to burst into tears. 'Oh, Isabella, let the good Lord take me now, because I could never again experience such joy as this.'

'Does Archie have any acting roles coming up that the public could see?' asked Loretta.

'Until Archie learns to control his charisma,' said Choco Chocs Doreen deadly seriously, 'it would be unfair to let the public see him perform.'

'Some members of audiences that have seen him on stage were so bewitched and mesmerised by his acting,' said Isabella, 'they have promised to burn down the next theatre where he appears.'

'I understand that it was not just Archie's acting skills that Pipkin was jealous of,' Loretta prompted.

Isabella hugged her son. 'When Pipkin discovered my Archie was secretly engaged to Tuppence Crow, he grew even more jealous and did his utmost to seduce her. Yes, seduce her!'

Archie raised his fists. 'He's a ruddy oik who deserves a good thrashing.'

Loretta turned to Choco Chocs Doreen. 'Is it true that, at the request of Isabella and Archie, you chaperoned

Tuppence because her management had forced her to be seen in Tolly Pipkin's company?'

Choco Chocs Doreen took a deep sobbing breath and nodded. 'It is true, Loretta. I felt it was my solemn duty to protect her. Archie is so dear to me that I could not let that monster Pipkin come between him and his true love.'

'I understand that you knew right away what Pipkin was planning to do.'

Choco Chocs Doreen nodded. 'I certainly knew what was on his depraved working-class mind. It was fortunate that I was there because he had lust in his eyes and a bulge in his trouser department. Yes, Loretta, a bulge! It was perfectly clear that he wanted to seduce Tuppence and deflower her! I can tell you, Loretta, that as a renowned TV star and acclaimed locum thespian/director, I have never seen lechery like it!'

Archie stood up and began to stamp his feet on the studio floor. 'Pipkin's a ruddy oik!'

'Don't lose your temper,' pleaded Isabella. 'You know what happens to your charisma.'

'His charisma is building to dangerous levels,' explained Choco Chocs Doreen. 'He could mesmerise us at any moment. Oh, no! He's going into a charisma trance!'

Isabella jumped to her feet and took it in turns with Choco Chocs Doreen to clap their hands in front of Archie's face.

He quickly snapped out of his charisma trance and was persuaded to sit back down on the sofa.

'Is Archie okay?' asked Loretta, suspecting that excessive charisma might be the least of his problems.

'Oh, yes,' said Choco Chocs Doreen. 'When you have a natural talent like Archie, any upset can unbalance your charisma, but with the skills I've developed as a humble renowned TV star and acclaimed locum thespian/director, I'm helping Archie learn to handle his precious gift.'

'It's all Pipkin's fault,' added Isabella. 'He should not only be blacklisted from acting, but blacklisted from humanity!'

'He is evil personified,' declared Choco Chocs Doreen, 'and a disgrace to the thespian profession!'

Loretta turned to the camera. 'While we've been on the air, we've received an unprecedented number of messages about Pipkin's abhorrent behaviour and will of course keep you updated.'

Gus was behind the cameras in the *Morning Show* studio, watching his new plan in action. Tolly Pipkin's latest antics had turned out to be too much for the public, and their dislike of him was beginning to have a negative effect on Tuppence's popularity as a celebrity. It was time to change tack.

'We do have one last surprise guest,' announced Loretta, 'a special guest who would like to say a few words to her beloved Archie.'

Tuppence appeared and walked over to the orange sofa. With obviously faked emotion, she held out her arms in front of her as though begging and said, 'Have no fear, Archie, darling. You are my true love, and I will never be in the company of that horrid Tolly Pipkin ever again!'

Isabella burst into tears. 'Go to your beloved,' she urged Archie. 'Take her in your arms.'

With a few helpful shoves and pushes from Isabella and Choco Chocs Doreen, Archie stood up and held his hand out as though to shake Tuppence's hand, and said, 'How do you do.'

Tuppence pushed his hand aside and hugged his rigid body. 'Archie, you are my true love, and I want the world to know it!'

261

Overcome with phoney emotion, Choco Chocs Doreen stood up, clasped her hands to her heart and declared, 'I feel as though I will die with pure joy!'

Isabella, with tears welling in her eyes, hugged Archie and Tuppence. 'True love can never be separated!'

Loretta smiled at the camera. 'A scoundrel with a bulge and thoughts of lechery has been' – Lorretta waited until the close-up was just right to capture how moved she was pretending to be – 'defeated by true love.' She sniffled. 'Thank you for watching.'

Gus smiled as the live transmission ended. His next plan was so brilliant and foolproof, it had put him in the mood to go cruising public toilets in search of a glory hole.

*

It was a struggle for Tolly to get up that morning. After taking a shower and swallowing two tablets for his raging headache, he switched his phone on. There were twenty-three missed calls and several texts from Suzanne which all contained the words, *Meet me at my office. It's urgent!* He tried to call her, but the line was busy and so was her desk phone.

With his head pounding, he sat in silence at the kitchen table and forced himself to eat some muesli and drink a glass of milk before heading off to meet Suzanne. He took a bus and walked the last mile to her office, hoping it would make him feel better. He was surprised to see her outside her building, puffing away on a cigarette with a few other nicotine addicts. She spotted Tolly, took a last puff and threw the stub into the gutter, or meant to, but it hit a chunky man riding an electric scooter, and she had to endure a barrage of expletives as he sped away.

'Try walking, you fat bastard!' shouted Suzanne after him.

'Making friends?' said Tolly.

Suzanne stared at his face, a deathly pallor somehow evident beneath his sunburn. 'You look like shit.'

'I have a little bit of a hangover. I had a couple of celebratory beers last night after Tuppence called the arrangement off.'

'So, you're not up to date on the ruckus you caused yesterday?'

'There was no ruckus. I had to save myself from pissing my pants and dying of heat stroke during the stupid tennis, but I'd hardly call it a ruckus.'

Suzanne took her phone out of her shoulder bag. 'It's a slow news day, so it made a few front pages in the newspapers. I'll read you a bit of one… *Cultural treason! Blacklisted actor Tolly Pipkin brought shame upon the nation by insulting the royal princesses and offending the people's treasured sport of lawn tennis.* It goes on to say that you're basically a yob and that you must really hate this country.'

Tolly smiled. 'They said that?'

'You desecrated the country's favourite summer event. The upper and middle classes are so angry, they've started several petitions. One is to strip you of your British nationality, another one just wants you locked up, and for some reason, there's one calling for you to be castrated.'

'No one's stupid enough to sign any of those.'

'They're online, so they've already racked up half a million clicks. I think castration is winning at the moment. Fuck with middle England and that's what you get. I liked your parting shot, by the way, *They use children to pick the ball up. That's child slave labour.*

'Did I say that? It must have been the heat.'

'You think that was the worst of it? Well, you're in for a shock.'

263

Tolly followed Suzanne up to her office. The desk phone was incessantly ringing.

'The fucking thing's been going all morning,' sighed Suzanne. She unplugged the phone line. 'I've had to switch off the ringtone on my mobile because it's been driving me nuts, and I think my computer is about to explode, trying to cope with all the emails. It's all your bloody fault.'

'My fault?'

'Because I'm your agent, all my contacts in the business have told me in no uncertain terms that if I keep you as a client, they'll never use me again.'

'Because of what I did yesterday?'

'Oh, if it were only that! But, no, it's not just that. It's because of what happened on breakfast TV this morning. Look on any social media site and you'll find it trending.' Suzanne went over to her desk and tapped at her keyboard. 'Sit down and watch this.'

Tolly sat down behind her desk and peered at her computer screen. He watched the segment from *The Morning Show* with amusement.

'What do you think of that?' asked Suzanne after it had finished.

Tolly laughed. 'It's hilarious!'

'I'm glad you think it's funny, because you'll have plenty of time to laugh about it, now you're out of work. I'm dropping you. Goodbye. Shut the door on the way out.'

'Dropping me?! Hold on, I never wanted this arrangement. I did it for you because you begged me to.'

'Tolly, your career is definitely over this time. You're about as popular as chlamydia in a nunnery.'

'So that's it, is it? You're saying I'm now unemployable because I did a couple of trivial things.'

'Insulting members of the royal family and disrespecting tennis are not trivial to the majority of people in this country.'

'And are you really dropping me?'

'Of course I am. What do you expect? Having said that, I still have one offer on the table.'

'It's the haemorrhoid cream advert, isn't it?'

Suzanne nodded. 'It'll pay every time it's aired.'

Tolly recalled what Zibby had said, 'If they're going to pay someone to do it, it might as well be you.'

'Fine. I'll do it,' said Tolly.

'What about your artistic credibility?' said Suzanne with a touch of sarcasm.

Tolly felt embarrassed. 'I must have come across as a vain, pompous prima donna when I said that.'

Suzanne nodded. 'Yes, you bloody did. I'll get you the details.' After a few clicks of her mouse, a nearby printer spat out an A4 sheet. 'Take that with you, the audition's in a couple of days' time. Don't forget to wear a paisley scarf.'

'Audition?! You never said anything about an audition! I thought they wanted me.'

'You know what, Tolly?! You somehow think that because you happen to be good at acting, everything is going to fall in your lap for you like you're in a movie. Well, fucking grow up! Do the audition, smile, be nice, laugh at their shit jokes, and once they've signed the contract, you can go back to being the jumped-up little prick that you are now.'

'You're not very supportive, are you?'

'No, because I'm fed up with your whingeing.' She looked Tolly in the face. 'It's just work. It's all just fucking work.'

25

Zibby's new workplace

It was Zibby's first day as Pepe's assistant for a gig that he had insisted was unique and completely unlike anything else. When she had tried to push him for more information, he had laughed, asked her to trust him and insisted he would explain it all on her first day. Pepe had texted her the postcode, so she had fired up her satnav for a forty-five-minute drive that ended with her pulling up outside a village hall built of green corrugated tin. Zibby thought that there must have been some mistake, but then she noticed Pepe's red sports car in the car park, so she parked up next to it. She stepped out of her small hatchback and spotted him hurrying towards her with his arms open wide and a huge grin on his face. He was in his early forties, tall, mixed race and ruggedly handsome. 'You found this backwater then!'

She rushed over and hugged him. 'I missed you.'

'I missed you too.' He air-kissed her on the cheek.

'I thought you'd given me the wrong postcode. I had dance lessons in this old village hall when I was little.'

'I take it that you haven't been here for a while, but all will become clear.' Pepe stood back and looked at her. 'My God, girl, you look fit and well. I'm going to have to start doing exotic dancing instead of the gym.'

'What sort of dance will I be teaching?' asked Zibby, having only been given a brief job description.

Pepe smiled mischievously. 'First, let's get a coffee, then I'll fill you in.'

'Can you buy a coffee here?' said Zibby, looking around and only seeing a row of rundown houses and some sad-looking hedges.

'Looks are deceiving,' laughed Pepe. 'Come with me, Dorothy, to the wonderful Land of Oz.'

Pepe led her down a wide alleyway that had been hidden by trees. Moments later, they stepped out into a bustling market square.

'Welcome to the ghost lovers' village,' laughed Pepe.

'Ghost lovers?' asked Zibby, puzzled.

'I'll explain.' He pointed across the square. 'The coffee shop's just over here.'

She followed him past the busy market stalls, which only seemed to be selling touristy souvenirs, to a coffee shop with outside seating. They sat down overlooking the busy square. Pepe smiled at her confused expression. 'It's mad, isn't it?'

'What's happened to this place?' said Zibby, noticing that the numerous gift shops were doing as brisk a trade as the market stalls. 'The village wasn't like this when I was a girl.'

A young waiter approached and took their order for two cappuccinos.

'Well,' said Pepe, as if he was about to reveal a big secret, 'the churchyard here now has famous ghosts.'

'Ghosts?'

Pepe nodded. 'A few years ago, a ghostly couple were seen by witnesses dancing on one of the graves.'

Zibby felt goosebumps on her arms. 'The ghost lovers?' she said.

'The story goes that hundreds of years ago they both tragically died in a stagecoach accident the week before their wedding. Guess what happened on the day they were due to be married.'

'Their ghosts appeared,' guessed Zibby.

'Yes!' said Pepe. 'They were seen dancing together in the churchyard again by reliable witnesses just over a decade ago. Since then, couples have been coming to the churchyard to dance with them, hoping their love will last as long as the ghost lovers'.'

Their coffees arrived. Zibby took a sip. 'It's a lovely story, very romantic.'

'I know,' agreed Pepe. 'Even death wasn't able to part the dancing ghost lovers.' He took a gulp of coffee.

Zibby smiled. 'I gather my role has something to do with that.'

Pepe nodded. 'Ever since the sighting, the numbers of couples wanting to dance with the ghost lovers, hoping that they will reappear, keeps increasing. Last year, the church had to start restricting the numbers.'

Zibby finished her coffee and wiped the froth from her mouth with a napkin. 'It's odd that I've never heard of it.'

'Up until a year ago, it was just a local event, but photographs appeared in *National Geographic* of the strange English village ritual and that opened the floodgates. Anyway, a TV executive heard about it and bought the rights from the church to broadcast it. It will be shown live around the world. People will watch in the hope that the ghost lovers do reappear.'

'And I take it that it's your job to choregraph the dance.'

Pepe nodded smugly. 'Audrey the director wants the couples to dance with lots of skirt swishing because she wants to take thermal-imaging shots from above with a drone. She thinks it will look ethereal, whatever that is.

268

Anyway, the most important thing is that it will look good on both our résumés.'

Zibby felt excitement welling inside her. 'I love it! I love the whole concept.'

After their coffee, Pepe suggested that she have a look around the village on her own, and meet him back at the village hall later. The first thing she did was to buy a guidebook. It gave a more detailed history of the ghost lovers' dance and had old photographs of couples dancing in the churchyard. After a stroll through the busy streets, she spotted a sign for the church and followed it. A path led her across a wide village green where a few outside broadcasting trucks were already parked up. The path joined the main drive up to the church, which appeared to be just as busy as the market square. A sign on the drive said, *The ghost lovers tour*, with the face of a clock indicating the time of the next tour. It was due to start in just five minutes, so Zibby bought a ticket from the female guide whose name tag on her high-visibility tabard said *Brenda*. She was in her sixties, a thin, wiry, no-nonsense woman who liked to wear a yellow beret because she thought it was functional and someone in a supermarket queue, who had happened to be colour blind, had once mentioned that it suited her.

One minute before the tour was due to start, she held up a small red flag. 'One minute before the tour starts. One minute!'

A couple in their eighties had not quite heard what she had said and asked her to repeat it.

Brenda raised her eyes to the heavens. 'I said the tour starts in one minute!' she checked her watch. 'It's in thirty seconds now! No, hold on, twenty… Forget it, forget it.' She held up her red flag. 'The tour starts now, follow me!'

269

Without waiting for the dozen ticket holders to assemble. Brenda marched the short distance to the church entrance, where she impatiently waited for the stragglers to catch up. 'We usually start the tour with a look inside the church, but my fellow guide Maureen is still in there with another group.'

She was used to having to work around Maureen, who was always behind schedule. Brenda had always thought that Maureen being in a wheelchair should speed things up, what with the floor of nice, even flagstones.

'So…' sighed Brenda, 'we'll get straight on with the tour of the churchyard. THIS WAY!'

Brenda marched ahead of her group, leading them further into the churchyard and stopping in an open area where they could gather around her. Once again, Brenda reluctantly waited for the stragglers, tapping her foot impatiently until the couple in their eighties caught up. 'Take your time, we don't want any accidents!' Brenda had an unfortunate way of speaking that made her sound extremely sarcastic, but she was completely unaware of this. 'Don't worry about holding the rest of the group up. I'm sure they have all the time in the world.'

The elderly couple apologised to the group, who all insisted that no apology was necessary.

Brenda held one arm out to indicate the churchyard. 'The ghost lovers have been seen in this churchyard on numerous occasions over the last two centuries—'

'On how many occasions?' asked a dark-haired, spotty-faced teenage boy, standing with his proud parents. All three were wearing identical turquoise hiking jackets.

'He's very inquisitive,' said his mother proudly.

The father nodded and addressed the group. 'Our Rodney is a borderline genius!'

Brenda stared down at the borderline genius. 'Numerous means many times.' For a moment, she lost her thread. 'Let's see… according to folklore—'

'Folklore isn't fact,' said the borderline genius. His mother proudly ruffled his hair.

His father gave an exaggerated roll of his eyes to the group. 'That's the problem with having a child who's a borderline genius like our Rodney: they just know everything.' He smugly patted his smiling son's head.

Brenda once more stared down at the borderline genius. 'Folklore, in this case, is the oral tradition of passing down information through the generations because, Rodney, in those days not all people could read or write. Didn't they teach you that at school?'

The rest of the group, who had at first been intimidated at the thought of having a borderline genius among them, were now starting to regard Rodney as borderline stupid.

'According to folklore,' continued Brenda, 'the ghost lovers were a young couple who were engaged…' She stared down at the borderline genius. 'That is the term used when two people commit themselves to a future marriage.'

Rodney nodded meekly. 'I knew that.'

Brenda continued, 'They were tragically killed in a stagecoach accident in 1849 en route to York just days before they were to be married. The road at the time ran alongside the churchyard perimeter.' Brenda could not help but peer over at the borderline genius. 'That means boundary or border, in case they didn't teach you that at school.'

'I did know that,' said Rodney sheepishly.

'I'm sure you did… I'm sure you did.' Turning back to the rest of the group, Brenda said, 'According to legend, the couple had met at a ball, which I'm sure most of you will know is a dance party.' She momentarily glanced at the borderline genius. 'And while dancing a waltz, they fell in love.'

There was a collective, 'Ah,' from a number of the women.

'The last official sighting was made by the vicar and two ground staff. It was the fifteenth of July and like most English summer's days, it was miserable and overcast day.'

The group chuckled.

Brenda was always pleased to get a laugh there. 'It was late afternoon, and a knee-high ground mist covered the churchyard. The birds in the trees were unusually silent. The vicar, Nancy Dickens, who had been having a team talk with her grounds staff in the church hall, sensed something was wrong and went outside. As she stared out over the gravestones, she heard someone humming a tune... the tune of a waltz!'

Brenda waited for the 'Oohs' to stop before continuing. 'The vicar focused her eyes in the direction of the strange noise and saw a blurry figure floating on the mist. Meanwhile, her colleagues had also sensed something was amiss and joined her outside. With her eyes transfixed on the apparition, the vicar pointed in its direction and whispered, "Look." As her colleagues stared in bewilderment, it became obvious that the blurry figure was in fact two figures dancing a waltz. Something interrupted the ghosts and they just disappeared. As you can imagine, the sighting attracted a great deal of local press attention.'

'When did ordinary couples start dancing in the churchyard?' asked Zibby.

'On the first anniversary of that sighting,' replied Brenda. She glanced briefly at the borderline genius. 'A year later.'

'I knew that,' grumbled Rodney.

'The first couple to dance lived in the village,' explained Brenda. 'They were moved by the story, so they decided to dance here on the anniversary, hoping the ghost lovers would reappear. Their dancing attracted more and more attention, and year on year since that first anniversary, the number of couples has kept on increasing, so much so that the church has had to limit the numbers. This year, the event is to be televised for the first time, which is very exciting.'

This information encouraged the group members to take pictures with their phones and cameras.

Brenda's red flag went up. 'This way!'

She marched over to two large yew trees a short distance away, hurriedly followed by the borderline genius and his parents. Zibby and the other group members walked with the elderly couple, assuring them that there was no need to rush. Brenda glanced at her watch and, in her usual unintentionally sarcastic tone, said, 'Take your time, I have all day!'

When the group had finally assembled again, Brenda said, 'The ghost lovers were spotted by the vicar and her ground staff in this area between the two yew trees,'

This vital piece of information resulted in phones and camera shooting pictures of the immediate area.

'Where is the exact spot?' asked Rodney.

'The witnesses could only say the area where they saw the ghost lovers, not the precise spot.'

'That was my deduction,' said Rodney. 'It was logical.' He gave a smug, self-assured smile.

'That's why he's a borderline genius,' remarked his mother.

Confident that he had now shown he was more intelligent than everyone else, Rodney said, 'Anyway, I don't

273

believe in ghosts. There's no actual scientific proof they exist. I am, even at this young age, a man of science.'

Rodney's father beamed proudly. 'He's far too intelligent for his own good.'

'Yet…' said Brenda, 'he is on the ghost lovers tour. Which is about a sighting of ghosts. Now, tell me, how intelligent is that?'

The group stared at Rodney, all now thinking what a stupid boy he was.

Zibby noticed the graves in this part of the churchyard were more elaborate and showier than those elsewhere. All the carvings and marble must have been expensive. 'Why are the graves different here?' she asked Brenda.

'It's just a coincidence,' shrugged Brenda. She had been instructed to avoid talking about the difference in the gravestones. The truth was that this section of the churchyard had been set aside for the upper classes and the wealthy who did not want to be buried next to common scum and working-class people.

Before anyone else could ask about the difference, Brenda raised her red flag. 'Follow me and we'll go into the church.'

Zibby let the group walk on. She had all the information she wanted about the ghost lovers' dance and had seen where it had happened. She spotted a nearby bench and sat down overlooking the spot between the two yew trees. Somehow, she instinctively knew that the ghost lovers' dance was going to shape her life in some way. After a few minutes of contemplation, she checked the time on her phone and headed back to the village hall where she found Pepe in discussion with a group of people from the TV company. The hall had not changed at all since she had a dancing lesson there twelve years ago. It still had cream

274

coloured walls and the same musky odour. While she waited for Pepe, she went over to a large map of the churchyard which had marks to show where each couple would dance. She smiled when she noticed that the marks made the shape of a heart for the benefit of the thermal-imaging drone shots.

'How did you get on?' asked Pepe, appearing next to her with a clipboard in his hand.

'It's really interesting and surreal at the same time. I did buy a guidebook and took the ghost lovers tour; well, most of it.'

'I did tell you it was a unique opportunity.'

'Unique, it certainly is.'

'They've given me the finalised schedule,' said Pepe, looking at the clipboard. 'We have five days to get the couples up to speed with the dance, do a dress rehearsal and have them spot-on for the live broadcast. I take it you noticed the positions of the dancers.'

'I like the heart shape, it's a nice touch. Right, what do you want me to do?'

'Easy day to start,' laughed Pepe. 'I teach you the steps, and then for health and safety reasons, we go and do the dance in every marked spot to make sure there are no obstacles or anything that might injure the couples.'

'So, I learn the dance and do it another twenty-five times?'

Pepe nodded. 'And dressed in a ball gown.'

'In a ball gown?!'

'Twirling dresses, they could get caught up on something—' He was interrupted by a female voice.

'How are things going with the dance, Pepe?'

Zibby turned to see a woman in her sixties dressed in a black cassock with a white collar.

275

'Fine, Reverend, it's all going to plan at the moment. Let me introduce you to Zibby, she's helping me teach the couples the dance. Zibby, this is the Reverend Nancy Dickens, who you could say is responsible for the ghost lovers event.'

Zibby gave the vicar a big smile. 'It's a pleasure to meet you. I've just been on the ghost lovers tour, and heard about your first-hand experience. It must have been wonderful to have seen them.'

Nancy still had to remind herself that it was twelve years since she had first sighted the ghost lovers. The story of the sighting would have just been forgotten if it had not been for her fellow witnesses, the gravediggers Stanley and Cynthia, exaggerating the story in the local pub. On that night, a reporter for the local free newspaper had happened to be there and overhear their tale. The story had appeared the following week in the local paper, which in turn had been read by someone who worked for the local BBC news. The story had been broadcast locally before eventually appearing nationwide.

To her complete surprise, Saint Mary's suddenly became a centre of interest and attention. With very few parishioners, the church had been in need of vital maintenance, with no hope of raising the necessary funds. The donations from members of the public who were keen to see the churchyard where the ghost lovers danced began to swell the church's coffers. Reverend Nancy had believed it was all just a one-off thing and that interest would soon wane, but as the anniversary of the sighting drew near, there had been renewed interest from the media. They had wanted to be present at the same time as the ghosts had been seen the previous year. Some members of the public had had a similar desire to see if the dancing ghost lovers would reappear. On that first anniversary, one camera crew and a small crowd had gathered to see if the ghost lovers would return. No dancing ghost lovers showed up, or any other ghosts for that matter, and Reverend Nancy had been conscious of the general feeling of disappointment among the public and the media. The story would have ended there and then if it had not been for a young local couple, Emma and Liam, who had been brought up with the story of the ghost lovers, and who were due to be married in Saint Mary's the following week. Emma had been inspired by the thought of a couple whose love for each other had endured beyond death, and she had hoped her own love would last just as long. She had taken Liam by the hand and, in tribute to the ghost lovers, danced between the yew trees where they had last been seen. The camera crew had been quick to turn their lens on the dancing couple. Then Emma's explanation that she wanted her love to be as strong as that of the dancing ghost lovers had struck a chord with romantics up and down the country.

The following year, a dozen onlookers had turned up to see if the dancing ghost lovers would come again, and this time, three young couples had danced, to the delight of the onlookers.

For the fifth anniversary, Little Takeham Parish Council, seeing an opportunity to boost the local economy, had had new signs made, declaring this to be the ghost lovers' village.

Reverend Nancy's tiny congregation had started to swell with younger people happy to be associated with the church of the ghost lovers. The local builder was always the first to buy her a drink when she walked into the pub, because he now could not build houses fast enough to cope with demand from those wanting to live in the ghost lovers' village.

Last year's eleventh anniversary had seen fourteen couples dancing in the footsteps of the ghost lovers and had attracted the attention of *National Geographic* magazine. This year, on the twelfth anniversary, the church hierarchy had sensed an opportunity to make some real money from the ghost lovers dance. At first, some church officials had expressed reservations about sightings of dancing ghosts in one of their churchyards because this did not entirely fit with the Bible's teachings. However, the church accountants' predictions of vast amounts of income had been enough to persuade even the most reluctant to sell the TV rights to the highest bidder.

Reverend Nancy gave Zibby a gentle smile. 'God definitely moved in a mysterious way on that particular day.'

26

Ouch-Heaps

Tolly had taken a cab to Shepard's Bush studios for his haemorrhoid cream audition, and followed the signs for studio three. Inside the large studio was a set dressed as a bathroom, complete with fake shower and toilet. Tolly was spotted by an intense young man in his early twenties wearing a paisley silk scarf. 'Can I help you?'

'I have an audition,' said Tolly.

The intense young man now looked confused as well as intense. 'You're not wearing a paisley silk scarf. How do I know you're a real actor?'

Tolly cursed himself for forgetting to wear the bloody thing again. 'I lost it on the way here. I'm Tolly Pipkin, I'm here for the audition for the haemorrhoid cream.'

A full-figured woman in a business suit standing beside the camera rig looked up on hearing the words haemorrhoid cream. She rushed over. 'No, no, no! We do not use the word *haemorrhoid*, we prefer the term *heap*!'

'Oh, okay,' said Tolly, with a shrug.

'You're that blacklisted actor, aren't you?' asked the intense young man.

Tolly sighed. 'Unofficially blacklisted, but yes, I am.'

'I'm Geoffrey, the director and visionary for this project. This is Patti Cornish,' he said, indicating the business-suited woman. 'Patti is head of marketing.'

Tolly chuckled. 'Patti Cornish… If that's the name you had at school, I bet all the kids called you Cornish Pasty,' said Tolly, ribbing her.

'No, they did not!' lied Patti. Hearing the words, 'Cornish Pasty' again gave her a touch of anxiety. It had taken years to get people to stop calling her that name. For some reason, once the words were in someone's head, they could not help saying it. 'Can we get on with the audition? Geoffrey, tell Mr Pipkin what is required.'

'Of course,' said Geoffrey. 'Now Tolly, the scene involves you sitting on the toilet.' He gestured for Tolly to sit on the waiting toilet.

Tolly reluctantly went and sat on it.

'Good,' mused Geoffrey. 'Now, pretend you're doing your normal business when, suddenly, your face contorts with the intense pain from your haemorrhoids—'

'Heaps!' Patti corrected him.

'I meant intense pain from your heaps,' said Geoffrey. 'Can you have a go at that expression for me? Can you?'

Tolly gave a half-hearted look of pain and discomfort.

'Bigger!' said Geoffrey, all his attention concentrated on Tolly's face.

Tolly tried to look like he was in more pain.

'Be vocal,' urged Geoffrey.

'Jesus fucking Christ!' screamed Tolly, with an expression suggesting pure agony.

'No religious references,' said Patti.

Tolly tried again. 'Aargh! I've never known pain like it!' he screamed, hamming it up.

'Not bad,' said Geoffrey, nodding his head. 'In the next scene, you apply the Ouch-Heaps ointment—'

'Ouch-Heaps?' said Tolly. 'Is that what it's called?'

'Ouch-Heaps will capture the heap market,' said Patti confidently. 'Our research shows there is a huge demand for heaps products among men under thirty.'

'It's probably all the junk food they eat,' joked Tolly. 'Hey, Cornish Pasty, I mean Patti, maybe you should make an advert telling young men that they'll get heaps if they keep eating rubbish.'

'Just do as you are asked,' said Patti dismissively. 'We don't need your opinion.'

'Now, Tolly, go from extreme pain to joy,' Geoffrey instructed him, 'as the Ouch-Heaps ointment takes effect.'

Tolly slowly changed his expression from pain to pleasure.

'Good!' said Geoffrey, nodding. 'What do you think Cornish Pasty, I mean Patti?'

She shook her head. 'No, I don't see him as the face of Ouch-Heaps.' Patti was fucked if she was going to give the job to him now he had let the Cornish Pasty out of the bag. No wonder the fucker was blacklisted.

*

'I don't know how you managed to fuck up that audition,' moaned Suzanne. 'It was a sure thing!'

Tolly sat in the chair beside her desk and shrugged. 'I don't think Cornish Pasty, I mean Patti liked me.'

'That's easy to understand. I don't like you.' Suzanne threw her hands up in the air. 'Well, that's it. I give up being your agent. I'm not prepared to waste any more time on you.'

'So that's it? After all I did to help you?!'

'I'm done with you. My other clients are back, so I can drop you now. Goodbye, have a good life and don't come back.'

'Can I just say you are the worst agent I've ever had?! Okay, you've been the only one, but you're a selfish person who couldn't give a fuck about anyone but yourself.' Tolly stared at her, hoping that his words had hit home.

Suzanne smiled at him and put a hand to her heart. 'That's the nicest thing you can say to an agent. Thank you, Tolly!'

Later on, Malcolm and Bethan were less than sympathetic when Tolly told them he'd failed to get the job for the haemorrhoid cream and now Suzanne had taken him off her books because no one would give him a job.

'How are you going to pay your share of next month's bills?' asked Bethan.

'You've only just caught up,' added Malcolm. 'You can't expect us to keep making up the difference, we're both on benefits!'

'That's not quite true, is it, because of the airport runs with the minibus? I'll pay you back, I always do.'

'The thing is,' said Malcolm, 'we… You tell him, Bethan.'

'I'm pregnant' stated Bethan baldly. 'We like you, Tolly, but we're going to have a family, and we'll need every penny from now on. I'm sorry.'

'I'm the one who's sorry. Don't worry, I'll make sure I have the money.' He opened his arms wide. 'Congratulations, the two of you! Let me hug you both. It's joyous news! I'm genuinely happy for you.'

Bethan gave Tolly a hug. 'We'll miss you when you move out.'

'Move out?'

'We'll need to decorate your bedroom for the baby,' explained Malcolm.

'There's three bedrooms!'

282

'We'll need the other bedroom for when our parents come and stay,' said Bethan. 'My parents will be travelling from Wales; they'll want to stay with us and the baby.'

'Did you know you have to let the paint smell go away before you let a baby anywhere newly painted surfaces?' asked Malcolm. 'It gives off fumes.'

'When do you want me out by?'

'We thought by the end of next month,' said Bethan.

Tolly did a mental calculation. 'That's five weeks!'

'Plenty of time to find a new place to live and get a job that pays regular money,' Malcolm reassured him.

Tolly had a dreadful feeling that his life was over before it had even started. He was now in his mid-twenties with no prospects, nowhere to live and on his own. Wasting no time, he went to search for work online and found that he was not qualified to do anything but minimum-wage jobs. His next search – for rooms to rent – confirmed that, without his aunt's help, he could not afford to live anywhere in London. The uncertainty about his future sent his mind into a storm of anxiety, and it was the early hours of the morning before he fell into an uneasy sleep. At twenty past three, after just an hour's unsatisfying rest, his phone's relentless ringing jerked him fully awake again. He checked the caller's number: it was his aunt Wendy. He sat bolt upright.

'What is it, Wendy?' He had called her Wendy even when he was a child. 'Are you okay?' She would only ever contact him at this time in the morning if something was seriously wrong.

Despite the thousands of miles separating them, the sound of Tolly's voice made Wendy instantly feel close to him. She could still picture him as a frightened five-year-old boy with guarded eyes. Weeks before that first meeting, she had been happily living in Australia without ever knowing he existed at all; it was only by pure luck that she had found him. She had been 60 years old at the time, divorced, with two daughters of her own in their late thirties who she hardly saw any more. They had their own families, and now lived on the other side of the vast country. Having immigrated to Sydney with her parents when she was a teenager, Wendy still occasionally felt the strong pull of the country of her birth. With no ties to bind her, she had decided to spend six months in the UK and trace her family tree. She had known her family was small, but when she had eventually started researching, she had been disappointed to find out that she apparently had no living relatives. The disappointment had turned to shock when she had found out that her last living relation, a second cousin called Joseph, had died only a year earlier. Not only that, but he had been also a widower. The next discovery had been the bombshell; at the time of his death, the widower had had a baby son. With the help of a lady called Pearl, who had lived next door to the cottage she was renting, Wendy had managed to track down this young boy and discovered his name was Tolly.

Her neighbour Pearl Drake had been a retired spinster who had worked behind a desk for the Metropolitan Police for over thirty years and had specialised in following paper trails. With her formidable skills and the contacts that she had made over the years, she discovered that Joseph's wife had been brought up in an orphanage and had had no family. It had taken Pearl two long, solid days to track down the boy. He had been living with foster parents who had applied to adopt him.

Not being one to beat about the bush, Wendy immediately hired a car and, on a sweltering summer's day, driven the ninety miles to see him. She had pulled up outside a house that was in the middle of a rundown estate, close to a small park where children had been playing, and she had wondered if Tolly was one of them.

The green front door of the house had been in desperate need of a coat of paint, and the doorbell button had been broken so she had knocked on the door. There had been no answer, even after several harder knocks, and Wendy had cursed her luck that no one had been home. She had been about to give up when she had heard a gruff voice shout, 'Get on with it!' from somewhere behind the house. She had followed the sound of the voice to a side gate and found it was open. With calls of 'Hello, anyone home?' she had made her way along the side of the building. When she had reached the backyard, she had spotted a young boy dressed in old clothes that were too big for him pushing an ancient and rusty mechanical lawnmower.

An unshaven man in his fifties, wearing trackie bottoms and a dirty white sleeveless vest, had been sitting on a deckchair with a can of beer in one hand, glaring at the child. 'Push harder, you little bastard,' he had ordered.

A large woman had appeared from the house, humming along to an old song that had been wafting out of the door. With a large tub of ice cream in her hand, she had sat down in a deckchair next to the man. As she had scooped a spoonful of chocolate ice cream into her mouth, she had finally spotted Wendy.

'Who are you?' she had said, spitting chocolate ice cream out of her churning mouth along with the words.

'Hi, my name's Wendy. I found out I'm related to young Tolly here. I'm his second cousin or something like that.'

'You could be anybody!' the man had snarled, obviously drunk.

'You're not allowed to be here,' the woman had said through another mouthful of chocolate ice cream. 'The boy's our responsibility. You can't turn up and talk to a child in our care without making an appointment with social services. You could be anybody!'

'You could be anybody!' the man had slurred, before swigging his beer. 'We got responsibility!'

Wendy had rushed over to Tolly and cupped his face in her hands. She had noticed bruises and felt her heart melt as his big eyes stared into hers. She had whispered in his ear, 'I'm your family. Would you like to come and live with me?' Up until that moment, she had had no long-term plans, but now, seeing him like this, she had instantly known that she would do everything in her power to look after him.

Tolly had nodded his head. By this point, the woman and drunken man had been on their feet.

'This is private property, and the boy belongs to us,' the woman had said.

'Why does he have bruises?' Wendy had demanded.

'Because he's clumsy,' the woman had sneered. 'He won the lottery when we fostered him,' she had said with a sniff. 'We spoil him rotten. You tell her, Tolly. We spoil you, don't we?'

Shaking with fear, Tolly had nodded his head.

'See? We love him like ee's flesh and blood.'

'Flesh and blood!' the drunken man had repeated. 'You could be anybody!'

Even though she had been crying inside, Wendy had said with a big smile, 'Okay, I'll get an appointment next time.'

She had left with one last glance back at the tiny figure of Tolly. The drunk man had slurred, 'We'll get the police if you come back without a thingy-bob! You could be anybody!'

She had cried all the way back home and had gone straight to see Pearl, telling her all about what she had discovered and pleading for her help.

286

After assuring Wendy that everything would be fine, Pearl had made several phone calls. The following afternoon, Pearl had accompanied her to the foster home, where a social worker, a lawyer and two police officers had been waiting.

When the woman had opened the door, the lawyer had thrust papers into her hand, and the social worker had insisted on entering the house. Wendy had not waited for permission, but pushed past her, calling out Tolly's name.

She had found him standing on a box at the kitchen sink, scrubbing a frying pan. She had suppressed a sob of heartache. 'You can put that stuff down, sweetheart. You're coming home with me.'

She had held his small hand. He had held hers tightly in return, as if he had been afraid she would leave without him. 'I promise I'll never let go of you.'

'Stop! You could be anybody!' the woman's partner had shouted, staggering in from another room. 'We'll get the police!'

The lawyer, who had thought Wendy might have exaggerated her story about Tolly, had been quick to shield them. 'My client is not anybody; she's his legal guardian.'

'Are you okay?' repeated Tolly down the phone line.

'Oh, I'm fine, sweetheart,' said Wendy. 'I have some news for you.'

'News?'

'News,' she said excitedly. 'You won't believe this, but they were talking about you on the TV this morning!'

Tolly rubbed his sleepy eyes. 'I bet it was about the tennis thing.'

'Yes, it was! My God, sweetheart, you certainly seem to have pissed a lot of people off over there. Hey, why didn't you tell me you were blacklisted? And what did you do to get blacklisted? It's not drugs, is it?'

'It's not drugs. Can I tell you about it when I'm awake? It's just after three a.m., and I'm exhausted.'

'Don't you want to hear what they're saying about you on TV over here?'

Tolly knew from experience that British news was reported abroad quite often. 'Let me guess, he's a disgrace and something along the lines of ban him from everything.'

'Oh, God, no. The Aussies love what you did and what you said.'

'Really?'

'Not only that, but someone also found out that I brought you up and contacted me about a work offer for you!'

'A work offer? I don't understand?'

'They found out about the reviews you received for that play you did, *The Waiting Room*, and they want you to play the lead over here. I said I'll talk to you first. Now, isn't that news worth waking up for?'

'It's an all-out-shit play! Why would they want to watch that?'

'All-out shit means good, I heard that last week.'

Tolly had been giving serous thought to going to live with his aunt; she had a big house and was always begging him to come and stay with her. He had dual nationality, thanks to her adopting him, so it would be easy to do.

'As it happens, Wendy, I was going to call you anyway. I've decided that living here in Britain doesn't suit me—'

'You're coming here to live!' screamed Wendy excitedly.

'If you can put me up until I find my feet, I will.'

'Sweetheart, you're family. You can stay as long as you like. Now, tell me why you were blacklisted. I have to know!'

It was five in the morning by the time Tolly finished explaining and hung up. With his mind made up, he started thinking about making plans to leave the country of his birth, promising himself that he would never set foot on its snobby, celebrity-obsessed, self-righteous soil ever again. Then he promptly fell asleep.

27

The dance lessons

Over the next two days, Zibby and Pepe were introduced to the lucky twenty-five couples who had been picked at random to take part in the ghost lovers dance, and began the process of teaching them the moves. Pepe had kept the steps for the dance simple; it was the combination of posture and arm movements that would elevate the overall effect when all the dancers were synchronised. On the afternoon of the second day, during a break, Pepe and Zibby were joined by the director, Audrey Cutter, who told them she had exciting news. A celebrity couple would be joining the ghost lovers dance. When Pepe asked who they were and when they should expect the new additions, he was told that the names would be announced in the next few days, but he would have to travel to them at a secret location the following day to start teaching them the steps. That was a rest day for the other couples, so Pepe asked Zibby if she would like to go along and help teach the celebrities the dance, and she eagerly agreed.

The next day, Zibby arrived at the village hall to find a limousine waiting to take her, Pepe and Audrey to the secret location. Once they were on the road to London, Audrey revealed that the celebrity couple were none other than Tuppence Crow and her fiancé, Archie Billings. Audrey read his biography off an email that had been sent to her. 'Archie

Billings is, according to this, the greatest stage actor of his generation.' Audrey shrugged. 'Never heard of him.'

Pepe was confused. 'They're the celebrity couple?'

'It's business,' explained Audrey. 'The TV production company's goal is to make money, and from what I understand, the sponsor offered a six-figure sum on the condition that Tuppence Crow and Archie Billings would take part.'

An hour later, the limousine pulled up outside a large Georgian townhouse in a leafy street close to Regent's Park. A small, dark-haired woman opened the big blue door of the house and watched the three visitors climb the entrance steps.

'Welcome to the Billings residence,' said Choco Chocs Doreen. 'Yes, it is I, Choco Chocs Doreen, renowned TV star and acclaimed locum thespian/director, but please do not be intimidated.'

Audrey held out her hand. 'Audrey Cutter, director. This is Pepe, the choreographer, and Zibby, our dance teacher.'

'It's a joy to meet you all, especially a fellow director. I of course am a director of theatre.'

'I direct in the theatre as well,' said Audrey. 'What have you done?'

'Alas,' sighed Choco Chocs Doreen, 'as a locum director, I am sworn to secrecy.' She motioned closing a zip across her mouth. 'Please follow me. Tuppence and Archie are raring to go.'

Choco Chocs Doreen led them into a spacious, ornately decorated and white-walled room with red marble flooring where all the chairs and furniture had been pushed back against the walls. 'Isabella has... Sorry, I mean Mrs Billings has made this room available.'

Pepe looked around, nodding his head. 'Yes, this will be just fine.'

Choco Chocs Doreen pointed to a sash hanging beside the huge white marble fireplace. 'When you want drinks, just call for the maid and she'll get what you want. The lavatory is in the hallway. Right, I'll just go get our talented celebrities.' Choco Chocs Doreen tottered off.

Pepe delved into his small holdall and produced a Bluetooth speaker. Within seconds, he had the *Blue Danube* waltz playing.

Zibby took her dance shoes from her own holdall, sat on one of the armchairs, and proceeded to put them on.

'How long do you think it will take to teach them?' asked Audrey.

'It depends on their dance experience,' said Pepe. 'But the dance isn't that complicated. Once we teach them the basic steps, they can practise on their own.'

Choco Chocs Doreen appeared at the door. 'It is my pleasure, and if I can be selfish and say my great honour, to introduce you to Isabella.'

Isabella made a grand entrance. 'Please, just call me Mrs Billings.' She smiled at Choco Chocs Doreen. 'I am the one honoured to have you guide my Archie.'

'Forgive me if I cry,' said Choco Chocs Doreen, choked. 'My heart is filled with pure bliss.'

'I'm Audrey Cutter, the director, and this is Pepe and Zibby—'

'I don't need to know who they are, do I?' said Isabella, looking back towards Choco Chocs Doreen. 'They are here to teach a dance, and teachers are tradespeople, aren't they?'

'That's right,' agreed Choco Chocs Doreen.

'Well, get them to start teaching,' said Isabella.

Pepe gritted his teeth and stared at Audrey as if to say, 'What the fuck?!' She took him to one side and whispered, 'If they pull out, the sponsorship money goes with them. I'll make it up to you, I promise.'

Pepe nodded to Zibby that they were having to put up with this.

'Archie! Tuppence!' shouted Choco Chocs Doreen. 'They are ready for you now!'

Archie sulkily trudged in wearing black tracksuit bottoms and a white tailored shirt, followed by Tuppence, who was wearing pink tights and a tutu.

'I know how to bloody dance,' moaned Archie. 'I don't need teaching.'

'I did ballet,' said Tuppence, 'so I have had training.' She forgot to mention that she had only done ballet for a year when she was eight.

Pepe gritted his teeth and decided not to bother wasting time on small talk. 'Okay, to start, my colleague Zibby and I will—'

'Bibby?' laughed Archie. 'Did you say Bibby? What a stupid name.'

'It's Zibby,' said Zibby.

'That sounds just as stupid,' tittered Archie. 'Well, come on then, whatever your name is! Let's get on with it!'

'Zibby and I will show you the dance,' said Pepe, touching the screen on his phone. The *Blue Danube* began to play again. 'The piece of music has been edited down to four minutes. Notice how we take our starting positions; we wait for the intro to end and then we… dance.' Pepe and Zibby began to waltz. Their twirls were restrained at first, before building to a climactic finish.

'Was that it?' sneered Tuppence. 'Huh, it's not very impressive.'

'There will be twenty-five other couples doing the same dance, so it will be a spectacle,' explained Audrey.

'Gus wants us to do that silly dance?' asked Tuppence. 'Why?'

'He believes it will help you and Archie become global celebrities,' explained Isabella.

'It's being shown in twenty different countries,' added Audrey.

'When they sees Archie's charisma and bewitching presence,' exclaimed Choco Chocs Doreen, 'he will be a shining star across the whole world!'

'You, teacher woman, show me the steps then,' demanded Tuppence.

Zibby now wished she was still doing exotic dancing. She took her starting position. 'It's a basic waltz time.' She began to twirl while counting, 'One two three, one two three…'

Tuppence watched her and tried to copy her moves. It became obvious to Pepe and Zibby very quickly that she was so absolutely useless that it was possible she had three left feet.

Choco Chocs Doreen clapped her hands. 'I do believe Tuppence has learnt it already!'

Pepe turned to Archie. 'Watch my steps and copy them.' Pepe performed steps that mirrored Zibby's. 'One two three, one two three.'

If Pepe had thought Tuppence had no rhythm, her moves made her look like a professional ballerina in comparison to Archie's stomping around out of time like Frankenstein's monster.

Isabella and Choco Chocs Doreen began to applaud enthusiastically.

'My Archie has so much talent,' declared Isabella proudly.

294

'I can honestly say I was mesmerised,' said Choco Chocs Doreen. 'He can even project dance intentions.'

Pepe stared angrily at Audrey, who shook her head, warning him not to say anything.

'Let's try getting the two of you to dance together,' said Pepe. 'Zibby and I will do the dance slowly, and you try and copy us.' Pepe and Zibby moved through the dance in slow motion.

Tuppence and Archie shuffled clumsily, both out of step, out of time and treading on each other's feet.

Pepe whispered to Zibby through a fixed smile, 'They are hopeless.'

After a minute, Pepe put the slow dance out of its misery, so that Archie could get his breath back.

Isabella and Choc Chocs Doreen simultaneously burst into tears and applauded Archie and Tuppence.

'They are an enchanting couple!' proclaimed Isabella.

'I was spellbound!' cried Choco Chocs Doreen. 'To see two people in love and with so much talent brings tears to my eyes. If I hadn't known this was your first time, I would've believed you were the professionals!'

Isabella and Choco Chocs Doreen turned to Audrey to have these opinions confirmed.

'A very good start,' said Audrey tactfully. 'But as they say, practice makes perfect.'

'Archie keeps treading on me,' winced Tuppence.

'I'm not treading on you,' said Archie. 'You keep putting your feet under mine.'

'I propose,' said Pepe, 'that I dance with Tuppence, and Archie dances with Zibby,'

The swapped partners and Pepe counted the steps for Tuppence. 'And one two three, one two three, one two three…'

295

'Count with me,' urged Zibby, as she struggled to wring any rhythm from Archie. 'One two three, one two three…'

After twenty minutes, a dispirited Pepe said, 'Let's take five.' He beckoned Audrey and Zibby over to a corner of the room. 'There is no way those two are going to be ready. I've never come across two more inept dancers in my life. Any suggestions?'

'They have to dance,' insisted Audrey.

'What do you think, Zibby?' asked Pepe.

'If all else fails, we could maybe get them to just turn in a circle?'

Pepe nodded. 'We'll keep going and hope that something might click. If not, we'll get them to hold hands and just turn in a circle.'

'It's going to fuck up my thermal-imaging drone shots,' groaned Audrey.

'How much longer will you be teaching?' asked Choco Chocs Doreen after they had returned from their huddle.

'We're here for the day,' said Pepe.

'A whole day?! But Archie needs his charisma training,' protested Choco Chocs Doreen.

'You may need a whole day to teach ordinary common people,' added Isabella, 'but you are dealing with high breeding and natural talent when it comes to my Archie and Tuppence.'

'Even so,' said Audrey, 'practice makes perfect and—'

'Yes, you've already said that once,' interrupted Choco Chocs Doreen. 'But when you have a couple with so much natural dance ability, you hardly need a whole day.'

'It's best to have as much practice as possible. The dress rehearsal on the morning of the dance is in just three days' time,' explained Pepe.

'I have an appointment with a personal shopper in Selfridges at two o'clock!' said Tuppence dismissively. 'I don't have all day! I'm terribly busy.'

'And if Archie's charisma isn't kept under control with my training, he'll become too mesmerising,' added Choco Chocs Doreen.

'Why don't we keep going till lunchtime and see how we're getting on then?' said Audrey as diplomatically as possible.

For three more painful hours, Pepe and Zibby tried their hardest to coax Tuppence and Archie into doing the simplest of steps, but in the end, they had to admit defeat and tell the golden couple to hold hands and turn in a circle. Even that turned out to be a problem because Archie became dizzy after only one turn and had to have a sit-down. The lesson finally came to an end when Archie suddenly stomped out of the room.

'I feared this would happen,' said Choco Chocs Doreen. 'Archie's pent-up charisma is starting to leak. I could feel myself being mesmerised by him. Did you all feel it too?'

'We certainly did,' answered Isabella, on behalf of everyone.

'Will Archie be coming back?' asked Audrey, completely confused by the talk of his charisma.

'No, I believe it would not be wise for Archie to continue while his charisma is in full flow,' explained Choco Chocs Doreen. 'There's too much risk of him bewitching you and you ending up in a trance.'

Zibby, Pepe and Audrey glanced at each other, all of their faces asking, 'What the hell is going on?'

'Well, I thought that lesson went very well,' said Isabella. 'My Archie and Tuppence will shine like the stars they are on the big night. And, Tuppence, dear, you were wonderful; your dance training really showed.'

'Bless you, mother-in-law-to-be,' beamed Tuppence.

Isabella's eyes reddened. 'If only your mother could look down and see you and Archie dancing together, she would surely be the happiest angel in heaven.'

'Sorry,' said Audrey, 'but Tuppence and Archie still need to learn the dance.'

'Did you not see the dance intentions that Tuppence and Archie were projecting?' said Choco Chocs Doreen. 'Their performance was captivating, enthralling—'

'It might have been captivating and enthralling,' interrupted Audrey, 'but it was not the dance they were contracted to do. It has to be the same waltz as the other couples.'

'The same?!' exclaimed Isabella. 'The same as ordinary people?!'

Choco Chocs Doreen shook her head. 'As an experienced, renowned and acclaimed locum thespian/director, I can assure you that when Archie and Tuppence dance, all eyes will be on them.'

'I'm sure you're right about that,' said Audrey ruefully. 'Nevertheless, they still need to learn to do the waltz.'

'We could come back tomorrow,' suggested Pepe tactfully. 'I'm sure it won't take long to make sure that Tuppence and Archie are one hundred percent happy with their moves. We don't want to be accused of not doing our best for the star celebrities.'

Isabella reluctantly said, 'If you insist on wasting your time, come back tomorrow then.'

Audrey, Pepe and Zibby had only just sat down in the limousine when Zibby giggled uncontrollably.

Pepe smiled. 'What is it?'

'I had an idea that they were going to be a bloody nightmare,' chuckled Zibby. 'My friend – well, my brother's friend – told me about his experience with Tuppence and Archie, and I thought he was exaggerating, but he was right, they are horrible people.'

'I think the mother and the so-called locum thespian/director are ten times worse than those two,' said Audrey with a smile.

'Oh, Zibby,' said Pepe, 'Audrey and I had a little chat while you were taking off your dancing shoes, and… Audrey's better with words than I am,' said Pepe, chickening out.

Audrey gave Pepe a glare for backing out of a job that was supposed to be his. 'We want you to take one for the team, Zibby.'

'What does that mean?'

'Come back tomorrow on your own and spend another day teaching them,' said Audrey with a sympathetic smile.

'On my own?!'

'It's only one day,' said Pepe. 'If it wasn't for all my other responsibilities, I would have done it… I'll make it up to you, I promise.'

Zibby felt like she was caught between a rock and a hard place. 'Okay, but you'll owe me for this!'

A car was arranged to pick Zibby up the next morning and drive her to the Billings' house. The chauffeur, a man in his sixties, gave her a card with his phone number on it. 'I'm to wait until you call me, so I'll stay within a ten-minute drive.'

299

Zibby thanked him, grabbed her holdall and walked up to the Billings' front door. It was answered by Isabella, who looked her up and down before saying, 'I believe you require the tradesmen's entrance at the rear.' Then she promptly closed the door.

Zibby gritted her teeth and followed the path round the side of the building. Choco Chocs Doreen was waiting for her at the back door. 'Follow me, your gifted pupils are raring to go.' Zibby followed through the hallways to the same room they had used the day before. Tuppence and Archie were already waiting, and there was the surprise addition of a man in a dark suit standing beside them.

'I'm sorry I missed you yesterday,' he said in an American accent. 'I'm Gus, Gus Shaver.'

Zibby recalled Pepe mentioning Gus Shaver. He was a media manipulator. Pepe had told her that he was known in his native New York as Glory-Hole Gus because he had got his knob wedged in a toilet cubicle wall.

'Hello, Glory… be to God on high.' Zibby quickly made the sign of the cross over her chest. 'There is always time to praise the big man.' She pointed heavenward to reinforce her point. 'My name is Zibby.'

Gus gazed at her suspiciously before dismissing her slip as an innocent remark from a religious fanatic. 'How did our two celebrities get on yesterday?'

Zibby was desperate to say that they were both useless, but she just mumbled, 'Very well.' Then she rushed away to put on her dance shoes.

'They were magical!' said Choco Chocs Doreen. 'Archie can project dance intentions better than a professional dancer.'

Isabella agreed. 'From a distance, it was impossible to say who were the experts.'

'I did ballet,' said Tuppence, 'so dancing comes naturally to me.'

'I'm just brilliant at dancing,' boasted Archie.

'Great,' said Gus. 'Let's see what we have.' He nodded for Zibby to begin the lesson.

'I'll do the dance first and then we'll carry on from where we left off yesterday.' Zibby set up her Bluetooth speaker and started the music on her phone. For the demonstration, she danced the waltz on her own. Then she said to Tuppence and Archie, 'If you'll take your positions…'

They held each other awkwardly, with Zibby adjusting their hand positions till they were just right.

'They look like the perfect couple,' said Gus approvingly.

Zibby played the music again and waved to cue them to start dancing.

Gus stood with arms folded and watched Archie and Tuppence's latest attempt at dancing the waltz. He had seen two-year-old toddlers hearing a song for the first time who could dance better than this pair. He waited for the music to stop.

Choco Chocs Doreen and Isabella applauded enthusiastically.

'Bravo!' said Choco Chocs Doreen.

'I was entranced!' exclaimed Isabella.

Not to be outdone, Choco Chocs Doreen said, 'It was so moving! To see two talents who are so much in love dance together so wonderfully is a thing of real beauty.'

Gus took Zibby to one side. 'They are fucking terrible, aren't they?'

'There has been improvement since yesterday—'

'You can cut the bullshit with me. I can see that they're probably the worst students you've ever had. What can you do to make them look even half presentable?'

301

'There are only a few days to go, so they really do need to practise solidly for the rest of the day at least.'

Gus nodded. He went over to Isabella, who was now wiping Archie's brow with a damp cloth. 'They need to go again.'

'Again, so soon?' said Isabella. 'Archie and Tuppence haven't had their after-dance tea and biscuits yet.'

Choco Chocs Doreen held a small battery-powered fan close to Tuppence's face. 'Talents like Archie and Tuppence exude so many dance intentions that they need to recharge their mesmerism glands!'

'How long was the dance?' Gus asked Zibby.

'Not quite four minutes.'

'It took a lot of work and cost a lot of money to get Tuppence and Archie on to this show, and if they really want the celebrity status that they say they desire, they should be practising the dance at least ten times an hour for the next eight hours!'

'That's impossible,' said Tuppence. 'I'm booked in for a wax at one o'clock.'

'And Archie has his absorbing lessons this afternoon!' said Choco Chocs Doreen.

'Cancel them. This dance is more important,' insisted Gus. 'I have to go and finalise the arrangements, so keep practising for the rest of the day.'

Once he had left, Isabella said, 'What a rude, horrible man.'

'Americans!' said Choco Chocs Doreen, as if that explained everything. 'They're so unsophisticated and prone to jealousy. I could tell that he was envious that two young talented Britons like Archie and Tuppence could outdance Fred Astaire and Ginger Rodgers after just one day of lessons.'

Zibby was not surprised to be told later that day that her services were no longer required because Tuppence and Archie had reached perfection. She gladly packed her things and left the house before calling for her lift home. Spending time with Tuppence inevitably made her think of Tolly, and she briefly considered calling him to see if he wanted to meet up, but she decided that it would just be awkward. As promised, the chauffeur arrived within ten minutes of the call, and Zibby steeled herself to update Pepe and Audrey on the celebrities' progress, or lack of it.

28

A farewell visit

'Come on in!' said Anton. 'Let me take your bag.'

Tolly was out of breath after walking up five flights of stairs with his overnight bag because the lift was out of action. It always felt strange to visit Sam and Anton in the town where he had been brought up. He still remembered these apartment blocks being built. 'Does that lift ever work?' panted Tolly.

Anton shrugged. 'Sometimes, but we always use the stairs because it's good for you.'

Tolly followed Anton into the hallway and slipped his shoes off.

'I'll put your bag in your room, Tolly.'

Tolly followed him into the tastefully decorated bedroom. He had stayed in it on several occasions and, as usual, Anton had laid the room out better than a five-star hotel. 'Thanks for putting me up for the night.'

Anton placed Tolly's bag on the bed and gave him a hug. 'It's always lovely to see you. Sam and I will miss you when you're on the other side of the world.'

'You can always video call, or better still come out and see me once I've settled in.'

'We'd love that.' For a moment, Anton looked like he was going to cry. 'Right, I'll get the coffee on while you settle in.'

A coffee was waiting when Tolly went to the kitchen after quickly freshening up. 'Where's Jenks?' asked Tolly, using the nickname Sam had been given at school.

'He's out playing tennis, but he'll be back soon.'

'Tennis?! When did he start playing tennis?'

'He's been playing for months now. He wanted to do something that didn't involve as many injuries as playing football.'

'Did either of you hear about my tennis episode?'

'No!' said Anton, trying not to laugh. 'Why?'

'Oh, nothing.'

Anton burst out laughing. 'It's all they talk about at the tennis club, according to Sam. You really pissed a lot of people off. He's had to deny knowing you in case he loses his membership.'

Tolly smiled. 'I have a habit of pissing people off, a lot of people.'

Later that evening, after a Chinese takeaway, the three of them sat in the sitting room, drinking wine and enjoying the simple pleasure of chatting. When the conversation wound its way to Tolly and Sam's school days, Anton stood up.

'I'll leave you two old codgers reminiscing about the good old days.' He smiled at them both, pleased to see Sam happy and relaxed. 'I'm off to bed. See you in the morning.'

'Goodnight, Anton,' said Tolly.

Anton shut the door behind him.

'I envy you and Anton. You're both happy.'

Sam nodded. 'I'm very lucky.' He turned to Tolly. 'I hope you'll be happy on the other side of the world. Are you sure you want to go?'

'I'm sure as I can be. I've got nothing here. I had a dream about making it as an actor, but I'm too unlucky according to my ex-agent. Look at me, I'm unemployable, no family…'

'You have friends!'

'I do have friends,' said Tolly, raising his glass to Sam. 'But I need to think about my future, and it's not here.'

'My sister will miss you. Yes, she told me about meeting you in Soho.'

'What did she tell you?'

'I saw her at Mum and Dad's a couple of days ago. She told me everything.'

'Everything?'

'She told me about the exotic dancing, if that's what you're trying to avoid talking about.'

'I met her when I was rehearsing near to where she and Michelle were…'

'Exotic dancing.'

'That's right. They were in the local café. To cut a long story short, I vainly told her I was playing the lead, and she saw Archie Billings' name on the theatre poster, so she assumed that was me. When I saw her at your birthday party, she made me promise not to tell you or your parents, and you know when I make a promise, I never break it.'

Sam knew this was true; he had confided in Tolly when he was barely a teenager that he liked boys more than girls, and Tolly had kept his promise not to tell anyone.

'How is Zibby?'

'Busy with her new gig; she's working with Pepe, her old choreographer.'

'I remember her mentioning him,' said Tolly, also remembering that she had pretended that Pepe was her boyfriend to stop him pestering her. He sipped his wine. 'Did Zibby say anything about me at all?'

306

'That she joined you and your housemates for a meal-movie night, which by the way I think will catch on, but that was all she said.'

'Oh, good!' said Tolly.

'What does that mean? You're holding something back. What is it? Tell me.'

'Okay then. Well, since I've known Zibby, the grown-up Zibby, not the little girl that…'

'I get you, carry on.'

'Since getting to know the—'

'Grown-up Zibby, you've said that already.'

'Let me finish! Since getting to know Zibby, I've grown very fond of her, and I think my fondness for her has made her feel uncomfortable in my presence.'

'What do you mean? Have you been trying to touch up my sister?!'

'No, I have not! I did hold her hand briefly when we were watching the movie, but that was innocent on my part.'

'Really? It sounds creepy. No wonder she was uncomfortable. Did she tell you that?'

'No, she just didn't want to give me her phone number and invented a boyfriend to put me off.'

'You really must have made her uneasy.'

'I genuinely like her so much, it hurts to think that I've made her feel like that.'

'If it's troubling you that much, just tell her what you told me.'

'I think I will speak to her, you know, get it off my chest before I go. When do you think would be the best time?'

'Not any time soon. She's working hard on this creepy dance job that's being shown on TV.'

'Creepy dance job?'

'I think it's weird; she's training couples to dance in a churchyard, something about dancing ghosts.'

Tolly was puzzled. 'Is it for a Halloween special or something?'

'No, it's some weird village ritual. Zibby reckons it'll be spectacular.' Sam laughed. 'I ask you, how can a local village ritual be spectacular?'

'Where is this village then?'

'It's a spot not far from here, Little Takeham.'

'If it's not far, I might just drop in on her tomorrow.'

'You'll be lucky to see her. The actual ghost dance is tomorrow, so she'll probably be tied up all day.'

'From my limited experience of TV production, she'll be sitting around, twiddling her thumbs for most of the time.'

'In that case, go and see her.'

29

Dance day

It was the day of the ghost lovers dance, and Zibby had excitedly arrived at Little Takeham's village hall at six thirty that morning, looking forward to the day ahead. She joined Pepe for a coffee in the catering bus to go over their timetable for the day. After a brief meeting with Audrey, they grabbed a lift in one of the numerous golf buggies that were constantly toing and froing to Saint Mary's and went to inspect the unusual stage setting.

The churchyard had changed a lot in the last twenty-four hours. There was now a tier of seating on the boundary for an audience and VIPs to watch the event. Cameras and lighting rigs were being set up to capture every moment in the odd arena.

Zibby and Pepe had a list of the couples, along with their dancing ability level. The weaker dancers were to be kept away from the edges, so they could keep time with the dancers around them. Zibby jotted down where Pepe wanted each couple to dance. Once they were happy it should all work out fine, Pepe said, 'Now, what about the celebrities? Or FMs, as we will call them today, which stands for fucking morons.'

Zibby had just taken her last sip of coffee, and Pepe's remark made her involuntarily snort it out of her nose as she laughed.

Pepe smiled as Zibby mopped her face with a tissue. 'Audrey had a good idea; we'll get them to dance under the yew trees. That way, they won't fuck up the drone shots.' He strolled over to the ancient trees with Zibby following him. 'They'll be shielded by the trees either side. Behind them will be the church, so no camera angle. Just a view from the front, and I'm sure Audrey can position the cameras so that they'll be partially hidden by the gravestones.'

Zibby nodded. 'That'll work. It's such a shame that two horrible people will be at the spot where the ghost lovers were last seen. It should be a couple who are truly in love.'

'I agree,' said Pepe, 'but because our celebs are fucking morons, we don't have a great deal of choice about where we put them.'

By the time they got back to the village hall, the couples had already begun to arrive, having been coached in from a country hotel close by. The production assistants were well organised and sent the couples to the appropriate marquees and trailers for costumes and make-up. While Pepe went to greet the FMs, who were due any minute, Zibby went around chatting to all the nervous couples, assuring them that they would enjoy both the rehearsal and then the ghost dance itself.

A production assistant interrupted her while she was sharing a joke with some of the couples on the double-decker dining bus.

'Zibby, Pepe wanted me to tell you that the FMs have just arrived.'

Zibby checked the time on her phone: it was now getting on for ten. They should have turned up an hour ago. Zibby glanced out of the bus window. A black stretch limousine was parked outside the village hall. Audrey, Pepe and two assistants were waiting for the FMs to climb out.

Inside the car, the chauffeur – now recovering from the unfortunate meeting of his penis and his zip – was awaiting instructions from Mrs Billings.

'Driver, can't you get any closer to the kerb?' she asked.

'There is no kerb, ma'am.'

'Don't be flippant with me! If there is no kerb, then park closer to the door. I do not want my son and his fiancée wasting energy on unnecessary steps.'

The chauffeur put on his seat belt, started the engine, put the car in gear, checked his mirrors, released the hand brake… and drove the limo forward two centimetres.

'That's better,' said Isabella. 'Why you couldn't have done that in the first place is beyond me. Now you may open the door.'

The chauffeur slowly struggled out of the driver's seat. He still had stitches in his penis, so movement was painful. He limped to the rear door and opened it. Isabella and Choco Chocs Doreen climbed out, dressed in shimmering silver outfits that were more suited to a red-carpet event. They were closely followed by Archie, dressed in a gold suit, and Tuppence, wearing a gold cocktail dress.

Audrey skipped the pleasantries and came straight to the point with Archie and Tuppence. 'What happened to the white outfits that you were fitted for?'

Isabella stepped forward and with a condescending smile said, 'The chauffeur has put them in the boot of the car. You see, white does not suit my Archie, and Tuppence only wants to wear white on the day she marries my precious boy.'

'They are supposed to represent the ghost dancers,' said Audrey as patiently as she could. 'Who's ever heard of a gold ghost?'

'Archie and Tuppence do not need to wear white,' said Choco Chocs Doreen, weighing in. 'They have the talent to

311

project a white ghostliness while wearing clothing more suited to their celebrity status. They are, after all, the stars of this amateur production. Now, if you would kindly lead the way to their dressing rooms, Archie needs to have a rest before his performance.'

Audrey reluctantly led the entourage to a large Winnebago, still insisting that they should wear the white outfits that had been specially prepared.

Pepe asked the chauffeur for the outfits from the limousine's boot. He spotted Zibby and ushered her over. 'Audrey's not happy. The FMs are refusing to wear white. They're fucking up the whole thing before it's even started.'

'Is this the biggest one they do?' asked Isabella, glancing disdainfully around the spacious interior of the Winnebago.

'It's the biggest and best they have. Two bedrooms, two bathrooms. Along with the seating area, it has a dressing room and a make-up area,' said Audrey.

'The one I used on my *Femme Crédule* shoot was much bigger,' sneered Tuppence.

'I'd be surprised if it was,' said Audrey, 'because this is the biggest one in the business.'

'When I did my Choco Chocs chocolates advert,' said Choco Chocs Doreen, 'they joined two of these together for me.'

Audrey had sussed out that the self-proclaimed thespian/director was a jumped-up parasite.

'Why can't we have two joined together?!' demanded Isabella.

'Because I'm one hundred percent positive that they don't join up,' said Audrey firmly.

'What do you think, Archie, darling?' said Isabella. 'Is it good enough for you?'

'I don't like the cream on the walls,' said Archie. 'It reminds me of horrid rice pudding.'

Before Isabella could insist on a colour change, Audrey said, 'This is the only Winnebago available, and it's going to have to do for the next few hours.' She then walked straight out of the vehicle before the stars and their entourage could reel off any more complaints.

30

Motherlode

Colin Champion, ex-bus driver and founder member of Conspiracies-are-true, made a point of never watching the main TV news because it was fake alien news. He also made a point of not reading any of the daily newspapers because they were run by Thems-at-top. He preferred instead to delve into the Dark Web in search of the truth, no matter how long it took. But when it came to eating his cooked breakfast, his self-prescribed vaccine against alien brainwashing, on a Saturday morning, he liked to read the weekly local newspaper. This was just to keep abreast of the lies being pumped out by Thems-at-top, he would explain if anyone asked. He skipped the fake local alien news and went straight to the personal ads in search of ladies who earned their living by selling sex. He searched through the ads, reading them carefully because some were genuine lonely-hearts ads. He'd found that out the hard way when he had replied to an ad for a *sin cure gentleman*. He had thought that meant spanking, so he had called the number and told the woman he would like to spank her and then fuck her arse off. He soon discovered she was a retired magistrate and victim of a printing error who was looking for a *sincere, gentle man*. The police had been quite understanding under the circumstances, but the experience meant he now double-checked the classifieds to make sure they were genuine sex ads. One caught his attention:

Claudia, voluptuous twenty-five-year-old virgin would like to meet a real gentleman who knows how to give an innocent girl a good time in every possible way, front or rear. Without rubber negotiable, no time-wasters, cash only.

Colin was convinced that the ad might have a double meaning and jotted down the number.

He was munching on a sausage, fantasising about the positions he would fuck voluptuous Claudia in, when he turned the page and saw a small black and white photograph of a schoolboy. Colin immediately began to choke. He gasped for breath until he managed to cough out the chunk of sausage. There, underneath the half-chewed piece of processed meat, was the alien reptile in human form that had set Colin on the path to his destiny. He quickly read the article. The boy had attended the local school years ago, and now the headmaster had written an open letter, distancing the establishment from his ex-pupil's atrocious behaviour and assuring parents that it was not a breeding ground for communist rebels who hated tennis and the royal family. The alien boy's name was Tolly Pipkin.

Colin did a quick online search. Pipkin was now a 24-year-old actor who had been blacklisted. He nearly choked again when he read that the alien in human form had until recently been dating Tuppence Crow, the daughter of tycoon Richard Crow, who was definitely one of Thems-at-top because he was filthy rich. As Colin read more, the extent of the alien web was revealed in front of his very eyes. Tuppence Crow was secretly engaged to Archie Billings, heir to the Billings empire: another link to Thems-at-top. The next item he read was the motherlode. Crow and Billings were to be the celebrity couple in the ghost lovers dance, which was taking place in the churchyard in Little Takeham, alien ground zero, this evening.

Colin smiled to himself. This time, the world would have concrete evidence that Thems-at-top were alien reptiles in human form. He immediately called an extra emergency meeting with Conspiracies-are-true's bona fide members and revealed to them that Tolly Pipkin had been the boy alien in the *Amongst Us* video and was now, in his adult human form, not only a controversial actor, but one of Thems-at-top.

'I knew there was something odd about him,' said Belinda. 'I was watching the Great British Tennis Club tournament on the telly. He turned up, insulting the royal princesses and slagging off the game. I must confess, though, that he did make me wonder why they do some of the scoring in French.'

'I saw that,' coughed Derek. 'Did you see the way he pointed towards the umpire? His arm was very strong. He was subtly telling the world that Armstrong stepped on to the moon.'

'He made a point about mentioning ballboys,' said Eddie. 'He was saying balls are round and so is the earth!'

The heads of all the bona fide members nodded. Now they knew the truth, it was obvious.

'That's what they do,' explained Colin. 'They subtly brainwash the public. As leader of Conspiracies-are-true, I say we move fast and plan to show the world the truth that Thems-at-top are alien reptiles controlling everything. No matter what the danger, it's time to release the *Amongst Us* video online.

It took three hours for Colin to get the video uploaded to a popular social media video platform. He nervously clicked the play button, and hoped that Thems-at-top had not somehow got wind of what he was doing.

The image flickered, revealing Colin's younger face staring down into the camera lens. The picture spun and showed the blurry figure of a young man in a school uniform retreating. Colin's gasping voice whispered over the top of the images. 'Wait till the Conspiracies-are-true members see this! Thems-at-top are among us in human disguise!' The image then went black before showing a close-up of Colin's face again. 'I've just got back from dropping a passenger off at the bus depot. It's been forty-five minutes since the alien in human form left the bus, and I'm going to see where he went.' The camera pointed towards a steeple protruding over the tree line, then it tracked shakily along a path leading into some trees and bushes. The camera continued shaking as it scanned around this area. The light was poor, but as the camera automatically adjusted to the light level, the scene that emerged was of a churchyard with mist at ground level. 'This is where the alien reptile in human form went,' panted Colin. 'I'm now investigating the area for any alien reptile in human form activity…'

The shot moved to a low-level view of the churchyard. 'It's really misty now… Hold on, I hear something… I'm going to have a look.'

The screen showed wobbly images of headstones poking out of the mist, as Colin had crawled through the churchyard with the camera in his hand. The shuddering images remained out of focus as the camera zoomed in and out. Now, there was fear in Colin's whispered voice. 'I see two of the aliens in human form!'

Figures began to come into focus on the screen. It showed what appeared to be an old woman in the arms of the schoolboy. Astonishingly, they appeared to be floating on the mist, spinning in a circle. 'There's two of them,' said Colin's frightened whisper. 'There's a humming noise, and they're orbiting one another. It must be their way of communicating to the mothership.' Colin could be heard desperately taking several puffs of his inhaler before croaking, 'I heard noises!' The camera shakily spun around to reveal only mist and bushes. The shaking lens whirled back in search of the aliens in human form, but the figures were no longer there, just swirling mist. 'They've disappeared,' gasped Colin. The camera pointed upward, revealing a church steeple and darkening skies, before the screen turned completely black.

Colin had texted every conspiracy theorist he knew, telling them about his plan. He stared at the number of views that his video had notched up in just a short space of time. At this rate, it would be double figures by tomorrow.

31

An apology

Sam and Anton both had work the next day, so after arranging to meet up in London before Tolly left the country, they left him to finish his breakfast and let himself out. Tolly checked the local bus times on his phone and noticed that the stop for Little Takeham was just outside his old school. The timetable said half past the hour, from eight a.m. to eight p.m. on weekdays. It had been a long time since he had walked the streets of his childhood, so he decided to stroll past his old house.

Things had changed very little in the town since he had moved. He ambled into Laurel Crescent and stood outside the nineteen-thirties terraced house where he had lived with Wendy until he was twelve years old. She had nursed him and cared for him after his ordeals with the foster family and given him a childhood that was happy. It was a house that had fond memories, and no doubt Wendy would have still been living there if it had not been for her daughter's diagnosis and the hurried return to Australia, taking Tolly with her.

Tolly had opted to catch the eleven thirty a.m. bus, and when he reached the stop at twenty-eight minutes past, a woman in her seventies was already waiting.

Tolly gave her a smile and said, 'I haven't missed the bus then!'

The woman shook her head. 'It'll be late as usual, it's always late. I've complained so many times about it being late.'

'It must get held up in traffic, I suppose,' said Tolly.

The woman shook her head. 'No, it's because the drivers are bloody useless. They spend more time chatting and drinking tea than they do driving.'

Tolly waited alongside the old woman, who tapped her feet and constantly checked her watch.

It was not long before a small bus turned the corner and pulled up at the stop.

'About bleedin' time,' moaned the woman. The bus door hissed opened, and she clambered on.

'What bleedin' time do you call this?' she said to the middle-aged female bus driver, while showing her pensioner bus pass.

The bus driver, who had been on the receiving end of quite a few complaints from this passenger, gave a big sigh. 'Good morning, Mrs Todd. I'd say about half past.'

'About?! About?! Well, about's just not good enough! I'm going to complain to your superiors!' grumbled Mrs Todd. 'Me and this gentleman have had to wait. It could have been pouring down with rain! We could have got soaked to the skin and gotten pneumonia because you think *about* is good enough. For your information it is now' – Mrs Todd checked her watch – 'half past!'

'Oh!' said the bus driver. 'That's good then. Must have been a bit early today.'

'Early's no good!' moaned Mrs Todd without missing a beat. 'Someone could have been running for the bus, and missed it because you were too early! I'm going to complain to your superiors!' Mrs Todd tottered to a seat close behind the driver, so she could shout additional criticisms en route.

Tolly stepped up on to the bus. 'Little Takeham, please.'

'We can't drop you off at the village green today,' said the driver, whose name tag said *Fiona*. 'There's an event on, but there is a temporary bus stop by the village car park, which is just a few minutes' walk from the village centre.'

'That's fine.'

'Three pounds forty, please.'

Tolly handed over the money in change. 'Thanks very much.' He took his ticket and sat down a few rows behind Mrs Todd, who was already complaining to the driver again.

'If you can't drop people off where they want to go, you should offer a refund! I'm going to complain to your superiors!'

The bus made only one other stop on the journey, to let an old lady who was a friend of Mrs Todd's get on.

'I've saved you a seat, Betty!' shouted Mrs Todd, even though it was still just her and Tolly on the bus. Betty showed her pensioner pass and sat down next to her vociferous friend.

'Did you notice the bus was early? It's because the driver' – she pointed at Fiona to avoid any possible confusion – 'thinks she's Nigel bleedin' Mansell. No regard for timetables, that one. She shouldn't be putting our lives at risk by driving at high speed! I'm going to complain to her superiors! There was no way we were doing thirty miles an hour over that last zebra crossing. It was more like a hundred and thirty!'

'Actually, I think the bus was a minute late,' said Betty.

'That does not surprise me one bit,' groused Mrs Todd without even pausing for breath. 'She' – pointing at Fiona again – 'drives like she's on her bleedin' summer holidays and has all the time in the world. I'm going to complain about her!'

321

Tolly had to endure ten more minutes of Mrs Todd's constant complaining before Fiona pulled up at a stop and called out to Tolly. 'This is the stop for Little Takeham!'

Tolly grabbed his bag, thanked Fiona and stepped off the bus. Before the doors had even hissed shut, he could hear Mrs Todd's voice. 'No respect for age, that one! I had to literally fight him to get on the bus first…'

The bus sped off, leaving Tolly wondering if Mrs Todd had a good word for anybody she had shared a bus with, apart from Betty. Looking around, he was surprised how busy the village car park was. Adjacent fields were being used as overflow car parks. He checked the time on his phone: it was eleven fifty-two a.m. He thought it would be a nice gesture to buy Zibby some flowers as an apology. He spotted a sign that pointed towards the village centre and followed it in search of the village shop. He knew that sleepy little village stores often surprised you with the range of goods they stocked. He followed the footpath and thought for a moment that he had stepped into another world. Far from being a quaint English village, it appeared to be a major tourist attraction. A large arch-shaped sign read, *Welcome to Little Takeham, home of the ghost dancers,* with a painted scene of a ghostly couple dancing.

Bemused, Tolly followed the stream of tourists and found himself in the centre of the village, where the shops and market stalls were bustling. The pub-cum-hotel off the square was busy, with people sitting at tables outside, and the plentiful gift shops along the main street all seemed to be doing a healthy trade.

Tolly spotted a gift shop that had a rack of guidebooks outside the door and went over to look at one.

He flicked through the pages. There were photographs of couples dressed in their finery, dancing beside graves. The back cover of the guide gave a brief explanation.

The ghost lovers dance is a ritual that takes place in the grounds of Saint Mary's church, in the village of Little Takeham. It celebrates the village legend that two ghost lovers haunt the churchyard. Each year on the fifteenth of July, couples confirm their eternal love by dancing a waltz among the graves. Over the years, the event has increased in popularity and now attracts attention from around the world.

Tolly was puzzled about why he had never heard of this tradition, but he assumed it must be a quirky village custom that had only become popular over recent years. He found a florist that specialised in making wreaths for the ghost lovers. Tourists enjoyed laying flowers to honour the lovers' timeless devotion, and the florist enjoyed picking them up when everyone had gone home and selling them again the next day. Tolly bought a dozen red roses, despite thinking they were overpriced to take advantage of the tourists.

'The ghost lovers will adore that tribute,' said the middle-aged florist, already looking forward to getting them back later, so she could resell them.

'Oh, they're not for the ghost lovers. They're for a friend.'

'Is she buried in the churchyard?' asked the florist with her fingers crossed.

'No, alive and well.'

The florist's face fell faster than dirt being thrown on to a coffin. 'Thank you for your custom,' she said begrudgingly, and thrust the flowers at him. As she watched him walk away, she toyed with the idea of putting up a notice that said, *Flowers for dead people only.*

Roses in hand, Tolly set off in search of Zibby. He spotted the church steeple poking out above the village roofs and headed in that direction. He followed a busy path towards Saint Mary's and soon found himself on the church's shingle drive, which was now edged with thick electrical cables.

A temporary waist-high fence surrounded the church, cutting off the rest of the churchyard and blocking the way ahead. Several bored people, clutching two-way radios and wearing white tabards with the word *Security* written on them, stood guarding the single entry point. A noticeboard zip-tied to the fence said, *Closed due to filming*. A young couple with a small wreath that, unknown to them, was on its third journey to the churchyard, approached a security man to ask where they could lay their tribute. He pointed to a spot further along the fence where wreaths were already piling up, and assured them that all of these offerings would be moved to the famous part of the churchyard once filming had finished.

Tolly peered past the security people and could make out dozens of crew members setting up lights while a team of gardeners trimmed the grass and clipped the trees and hedging.

'You can leave those roses for the ghost lovers by the fence,' said a security man whose tabard read, *Head of security*. 'They'll be laid out after filming.'

'They're not for the ghost lovers,' said Tolly. He was wise enough to know that the security would not let him in without a pass, even just to see a friend. 'These flowers are for my mother's grave.'

'Oh,' said the security man. 'You can tell me where her grave is, and I'll put them on for you.'

Mrs Todd's earlier complaining suddenly gave Tolly inspiration. 'Are you saying I can't visit my own mother's grave?!' he stormed. 'Are we living under Nazi rule where a son cannot lay flowers on his own mother's grave?!'

'Please, sir,' said the security man, 'it's just that a TV production company has permission to close the churchyard for filming. It's only temporary.'

'This is a disgrace! I want to complain!'

Tolly's raised voice drew people over to see what the fuss was about.

'If you'll just wait for a moment, I'll see if I can get permission to give you a pass,' the security man reassured him.

'Oh, I need permission now, do I?! We all know who gave permission – Hitler! It's outrageous that I'm not allowed to lay flowers on my mother's grave because of Hitler!'

A man in his late seventies came to Tolly's aid. 'Let him lay his flowers! My old mum and dad didn't get bombed by the Luftwaffe night after night so British people would have to get permission to put flowers on their mother's grave!'

The old man's wife chipped in. 'My great aunt Jeannie didn't join the land girls and dig up potatoes to have thugs like you push innocent young men around and tell them they need permission to lay flowers on their dear old mum's grave!'

The crowd had built up considerably by now, and the story that spread among them was exaggerated on every telling, so the people at the back believed that a young man had just been beaten up for wanting to visit his mother's grave.

The old man, who had boxed a bit as an amateur fifty-five years ago, took off his jacket and rolled his sleeves up. 'Come on then, Fritz. Let's see how you like this permission.' The old man put his dukes up and shuffled unsteadily on his feet.

325

The security man wondered how the fuck this had all kicked off.

The old man threw some air punches and began to gasp. 'Come on, Fritz, put 'em up!'

The security man had dealt with extremely violent groups in the past, but this was a hundred times worse. He promptly gave Tolly a clip-on visitor pass.

'Please go in, sir. Sorry for the misunderstanding.'

Tolly went over to the old man and raised his arm in the air. 'The champion of people's rights!'

A big cheer went up, as if the old man and his wife really had saved the crowd from Nazi tyranny.

Tolly walked on into the churchyard and was impressed by the way the TV company had set it up for filming. All the camera angles were covered without other crew or cameras being in view. He spotted Zibby talking to a young couple who were obviously going to be in the dance. The young woman looked beautiful in her pastel green ball gown, and her partner correspondingly handsome in his matching tailed suit. Tolly watched Zibby for a while, struck by her natural beauty and ease.

She was laughing when she spotted him. Tolly felt guilty for suddenly ending her moment of happiness. She hurried over to him, looking concerned.

'Tolly? What are you doing here?'

'I wanted to see you before I—'

'Take five!' said Audrey's voice through a megaphone.

'Good timing at least,' said Zibby.

'Oh, I brought you these,' he said, presenting her with the dozen roses, 'as an apology.'

People had begun to congregate around the spot where they were standing. 'Let's go over here,' said Zibby.

326

She led him over to a bench close to two yew trees. They sat down.

'What are you apologising for?'

'For being inappropriate.'

Zibby laughed. 'Have you turned into a Victorian all of a sudden? What are you on about?'

'I made you uncomfortable in my presence; so much so that you pretended to have a boyfriend. I just want to clear the air and tell you that the last thing I would ever want to do is make you feel uneasy. I'm sorry.'

Zibby shook her head. 'I'm not uncomfortable when I'm with you. If anything, I feel sad because you see me as just your friend's little sister. I don't want you to see me as just that.'

'I don't see you that way. I see you as a beautiful, independent woman.'

Zibby smiled. 'I see you as a talented, caring man.'

Tolly gave a loud sigh of relief. 'Does that mean we're still friends?'

Zibby smiled. 'We're still friends… good friends.'

Tolly felt the urge to kiss her, but thought that would probably be a perfect way to make her feel uncomfortable. 'Zibby,' he said, glancing around at the odd location for a TV dance show, 'what is this ghost lovers dance thing? I saw some photographs of couples dancing in a guidebook, but that's all I know.'

'Oh, it's a village tradition. Apparently, back in the eighteen hundreds, a couple died in a tragic accident nearby. It's such a sad story. It happened only days before they were due to be married. It's said that they've haunted the churchyard ever since, and they were actually seen by witnesses not that many years ago. On the anniversary of the sighting, couples come and dance with them, hoping their love will last just as long.'

Tolly smiled. 'I can see why it attracts couples to dance. It's a great story.' He gazed at Zibby, thinking her face was even more beautiful than he remembered.

'I'll tell you what,' said Zibby, 'these flowers you gave me, let's leave them on the spot where they were last seen as a tribute to the ghost lovers.' Zibby stood up and led Tolly to the famous spot between the two yew trees. She placed the flowers beside a gravestone there. 'I always get a tingle when I stand here, like I'm standing next to them.'

Tolly looked at the gravestone – an old slab of flat sandstone with a shallow bowl shape worn into it over the centuries – and had an odd feeling of déjà vu.

Audrey's voice through the megaphone interrupted them. 'Let's go again, please!'

'Sorry, Tolly,' said Zibby. 'I have to help the dancers with this rehearsal. Oh, before I go, guess who the celebrity dancers are.'

Tolly shrugged. 'Someone sad and desperate for publicity?'

Zibby chuckled. 'Well, they are that; it's Tuppence Crow and Archie Billings.'

'No fucking way!' blurted Tolly.

'All those things you said about them were true. They are horrible people.'

'Take your positions!' said Audrey's amplified voice.

'Promise you won't disappear,' said Zibby.

Tolly pointed to his visitor badge. 'I'll pop back later. I'll go and grab a coffee and get something to eat in the village. The last thing I want to do is bump into Tuppence Crow and Archie Billings again.'

32

The dress rehearsal

So far, everything was going to plan with the dress rehearsal. The couples had been taken up to the churchyard where Pepe and Zibby showed each couple their position for the dance. The technicians had the sound and lighting all set up for the rehearsal. Unfortunately, the only thing missing was the celebrity couple.

Audrey had sent a runner to find out where they were. Ten minutes later, the young woman was back and looking anxious. She hurried over to Audrey and nervously said, 'They say they're not ready.'

'Not ready? What the hell are they playing at?' fumed Audrey.

'I noted down what the Choco Chocs lady told me,' said the runner. She read from her notebook, 'Archie's charisma is too compelling, and it needs to subside before we can risk letting him loose on the public.'

Audrey had hoped that this live event would help boost her TV career, but having to deal with such egotistical and talentless twats was putting that at risk. 'Let's make a start!' she ordered.

Cameras were made ready; the drone took off and hovered high above with its thermal-imaging camera pointing down at the church grounds.

Audrey gave the cue for the couples to enter the churchyard in their pairs and take up their positions. Pepe and Zibby walked alongside them, encouraging good posture and reminding them to smile. Audrey peered at the monitors showing multiple angles of the couples and the ghostly thermal images from the drone camera. It was going to look fabulous.

'Cue music,' said Audrey.

The *Blue Danube* began to play over the speakers situated around the perimeter. Pepe and Zibby walked among the couples like a pair of conductors, counting them through the first twenty seconds of music, so that they would all start to dance the waltz at exactly the same time. However, the beautifully synchronised dancing was disrupted when Choco Chocs Doreen swept into the churchyard followed by Archie, Tuppence and Isabella.

'Make way for the talent!' shouted Choco Chocs Doreen, pushing past several couples and making them lose their place in the routine.

'Stop, stop, stop!' shouted Audrey, putting her head in her hands in frustration.

The music stopped abruptly, and a general air of confusion spread throughout the group.

Audrey climbed down from her position on a raised platform overlooking the churchyard, angrily marched towards the four latecomers and was immediately confronted by Isabella Billings.

'How disrespectful! My Archie and Tuppence are the stars of this silly ghost dance, and you should not be rehearsing without them! It's… it's outrageous!'

'I can't have dozens of people waiting around,' Audrey informed her. 'A lot of technical issues may need to be addressed, and time to wait around is something I do not have.'

'This amateurish freak show would be treated as a joke if it did not have the A-list talent of Tuppence and my Archie taking part!'

Audrey bit her tongue, knowing that she could easily get pulled into an argument which she did not have time for. 'Okay, people,' shouted Audrey. 'Let's start again.'

Isabella smirked. 'That's more like it! Oh, and one more thing, Tuppence and Archie don't want anyone making eye contact. Communicate that to your people, will you?'

Choco Chocs Doreen nodded her head in agreement. 'A-listers like Archie and Tuppence find the jealous stares of those with no talent off-putting. I myself had the same experience after my TV success.'

Audrey gritted her teeth. 'Zibby, show our celebrity couple to their place and we'll go again in five.'

Zibby led Tuppence and Archie over to their position by the two yew trees. 'This is your spot here, the pathway between these two gravestones. The other dancers will enter and take their places. The music will start, and I'll cue you to begin dancing.'

Tuppence was not happy. 'I don't know what Gus was thinking, having me dance among gravestones. I'm a celebrity! I should not be here among dead people!'

'What dead people?' asked Archie.

'It's a churchyard,' moaned Tuppence. She pointed to the nearest gravestone. 'There's a dead person under every one of them!'

Archie was confused. 'People don't die, they go and live on a lovely farm like Grandpa and Grandma.'

Tuppence had spent more time with Archie in the last week than she had in her whole life before. Even though

331

they were destined to be married, she was fed up with his stupidity already. 'No, they don't! People die, and the people left alive dig a hole, stick them in the ground, and put a gravestone on top!'

'But, but the lovely farm?' stuttered Archie.

'There is no lovely farm!' snapped Tuppence.

Archie stood motionless, his eyes glazed and staring.

Tuppence prodded him. 'Archie?'

Archie remained unmoving and unblinking.

'You should be in your positions; the rehearsal's about to begin,' pleaded Zibby.

Tuppence tried giving Archie a shove, but he still stood motionless with a vacant expression. 'Archie! Answer me this minute!' she demanded.

Archie's lips moved. 'But the lovely farm…' he mumbled.

Zibby heard Audrey shout, 'Cue music!' She frantically waved her arms in the air to catch Audrey's attention. 'We're not ready, sorry!'

Audrey looked to the heavens. 'Jesus, what now?'

Choco Chocs Doreen and Isabella had been watching Archie and Tuppence from close by. They rushed over.

Isabella had not seen that expression on Archie's face since he had accidentally seen her naked in the shower with a banana. 'What is it, my angel?!' she asked.

'Lovely farm…' muttered Archie.

'What have you done to Archie?!' said Choco Chocs Doreen, glaring accusingly at Zibby.

'I haven't done anything!' she protested.

'She told Archie that dead people don't go to the lovely farm,' explained Tuppence.

'In the ground…' whispered Archie. 'Dead people in the ground… No lovely farm.'

Isabella glared at Zibby. 'How dare you tell my precious angel that there is no lovely farm!'

Choco Chocs Doreen was confused. 'What lovely farm?'

Isabella took Choco Chocs Doreen to one side and whispered to her, 'Archie was such a delicate boy, when his grandparents died, we told him they had gone to live on a lovely farm before going to heaven. You know how sensitive and special he is! Now, thanks to that stupid girl, he's having a tizzy fit.'

Choco Chocs Doreen clasped Isabella's hands. 'The gifted ones like Archie need to be protected from mortality. We just have to make sure this tizzy fit doesn't affect his ability to project intentions.'

Audrey stomped over with a face like thunder. 'What's the hold-up now?!'

'Sabotage!' Choco Chocs Doreen informed her. 'This girl' – she pointed at Zibby – 'has sabotaged Archie's artistic composure and given him a tizzy fit!'

'I want her fired this minute,' demanded Tuppence, hoping that Zibby being sacked would put her in the clear by leaving nobody to dispute her version of events.

'I didn't say anything,' insisted Zibby.

'Go and see Pepe,' said Audrey. 'I'm sure this can be sorted out.'

'No lovely farm, no lovely farm, no lovely farm,' chanted Archie.

'There is a lovely farm!' Isabella said reassuringly. 'Choco Chocs Doreen will tell you the same.'

'Archie, look at me,' coaxed Choco Chocs Doreen. 'I can promise you that dead people go to the lovely farm.' She drew on her acting talents to give him a reassuring smile. 'We'll all go to the lovely farm one day.'

'Lovely farm…' muttered Archie. 'Not ground.'

Isabella stared at Audrey. 'One of your people has given Archie a tizzy fit deliberately!'

Audrey had had enough of the celebrities, the arrogant mother and the so-called locum director, and now what the fuck was this about tizzy fits?

Archie began to sway and chant, 'No lovely farm… In the ground… No lovely farm.'

Choco Chocs Doreen and Isabella hurried back towards the Winnebago.

'We might need to call an ambulance,' said Isabella.

Choco Chocs Doreen agreed. 'If we do, ask for two in case some of the paramedics become mesmerised by Archie's charisma.'

'What about the rehearsal?' shouted Audrey.

Isabella turned to face her. 'The rehearsal for Archie and Tuppence is over! And if that girl' – Isabella levelled an accusing finger at Zibby, who was talking to Pepe – 'is not dismissed immediately, you will have no major celebrities dancing tonight in this amateur production!'

33

Goodbye

Tolly was sipping a coffee while people-watching through the coffeeshop window when he spotted Zibby walking quickly towards the building. He looked over as she opened the shop door, glanced around, marched over to where he was sitting and sat down opposite him with a growl.

'Are you okay?' he asked.

'No! I am not okay. Guess what. Go on, guess!' Before Tolly could give a complete random guess, Zibby continued, 'I've been told by Audrey—'

'Who's Audrey?'

'The director. I've been told by Audrey that the celebrities and their entourage want me fired!'

'What for?'

'According to that stuck-up bitch Tuppence, I told Archie that when people die, they're buried in the ground.'

Tolly shrugged. 'What's wrong with saying that?' He picked up his coffee to drink the last quarter of a cup.

'Archie's been told that when people die, they go and live on a lovely farm.'

Tolly was in mid-swig and spluttered the coffce out of his mouth and nose simultaneously, spattering the window with brown splotches.

Zibby burst out laughing and helped him clean up with paper napkins from the table. 'He's now having a tizzy fit, according to his mother.'

'Live on a lovely farm? Isn't that what they tell children when a pet dies?'

'In Archie's case, it's people,' explained Zibby. 'Thankfully, I didn't get fired, so I can still help with all the other couples. I just have to keep out of the celebrities' way. On the plus side, I can spend some time with you.'

'Great!' Tolly caught the eye of the waiter. 'I'll buy you lunch.'

For the next hour, they sat and chatted easily over a light meal, then went for a stroll around the village.

'What was it you were going to say to me earlier, before you had to go back to work?' asked Tolly as they ambled towards the church.

'You go first,' said Zibby. 'What did you want to tell me?'

'I came to tell you that I'm going to stay with my auntie Wendy.'

'How long for?'

'No idea. Because of being blacklisted and the Great British Tennis Club business, I can't get any work. My housemates need my room, and I can't see a way of surviving without an income. So, I might see if I can make a living down under. My aunt reckons there's interest in me playing the part of Sid in *The Waiting Room* again.'

'But don't you hate that play?'

'I'm going to have to learn to like it. What did you want to tell me?'

Zibby felt her heart sink. She would probably never see him again once he had started his new life. 'It doesn't matter,' she said, forcing a smile.

The conversation that had been easy between them had now turned difficult and awkward. With the village hall in sight across the packed village green, Zibby said, 'I'd better go and see how our couples are doing. They must be getting nervous.'

'Can I meet up with you later?' said Tolly.

Zibby shook her head. 'I'm going to be so busy from now on, I might not get a chance to stop at all.' She kissed him on the cheek. 'Goodbye, Tolly. Good luck in your new life.'

Before Tolly could utter another word, Zibby had run away in the direction of the village green.

Tolly flashed his visitor's badge to gain access to the churchyard in the vain hope that he would see Zibby again. He watched the crew go through the final technical checks for the live transmission. He recognised some of the camera operators from his live shoot of *Blue Psycho*, so he spent a while chatting to them, hoping that Zibby would find time to talk to him again. He managed to catch sight of her late in the afternoon with Pepe as they went through another dance rehearsal with the couples. She also spotted him, gave a sad smile and went back to work.

With just over an hour to go before the live broadcast, Tolly felt he could not fight the inevitable any longer: he was going to remain nothing more to Zibby than her brother's friend.

He gave back his visitor pass to the security guard as he left the fenced-off area, then retraced his footsteps back to the temporary bus stop and hoped the buses to Brenford were still running.

Pepe had been looking for Zibby, but no one had seen her for the last half hour. He stood outside the village hall, wondering where she could be. He had tried calling her phone, but she had not answered. He tried her number again and heard a faint ringing from the car park. He followed the noise to Zibby's car and spotted her hunched down in the driver's seat. He opened the passenger door and climbed in next to her. Her eyes were red, and she was not her usual cheerful self.

'Are you okay, Zibby?'

'Oh, sorry, Pepe, I just needed a minute. I was just about to come and find you,' she sniffed.

'What's wrong? It's not the FMs upsetting you, is it, because—'

'No, no, it's a personal thing.'

'Has it got something to do with that young man I saw you sitting with on the bench earlier?'

Zibby nodded. 'His name's Tolly, Tolly Pipkin.'

'Ah! The blacklisted actor, I've heard about him.'

Zibby told Pepe the story of how she and Tolly had met and the strong feelings she had for him, and that he had chosen today of all days to tell her he was leaving the country, probably for good.

Pepe put his arm around her. 'I saw the way he looks at you. Believe me, your feelings are not unrequited. I recognise the look of a man in love.'

'You think so?'

'Zibby, I know so! So don't give up hope just yet.'

Zibby kissed him on the cheek and smiled. 'Thank you, Pepe. Thank you for listening to a stupid girl.'

'I'm here whenever you need me, okay? Now, let's check on the couples and make sure this ghost lovers dance is a success.'

338

34

Tizzy fit

'I don't know what that… that American fool was thinking of!' said Isabella, holding a wet towel to Archie's forehead as he reclined on a sofa. 'To suggest that Archie and Tuppence work with amateurs is a disgrace. This is what happens! My Archie has a tizzy fit.'

Choco Chocs Doreen sat on the sofa beside Archie, massaging his neck. 'Archie is so tense, I fear his charisma is clogging up.'

'How are you, Archie?' said Tuppence, still feeling secretly guilty for causing his tizzy fit.

'Lovely farm,' muttered the delirious Archie.

'Yes, my darling,' said Isabella. 'Everyone goes to the lovely farm.'

'Do you think I should try the emergency services again, Isabella?' asked Choco Chocs Doreen. 'I still can't believe they wouldn't send an ambulance to attend Archie's tizzy fit!'

'I even told them we go private, and they still refused.'

Tuppence's phone beeped. She checked it and for the next thirty seconds repeatedly groaned the words, 'Oh, no!' while staring at its screen.

'What is it?' asked Isabella.

'A friend has sent me a link to a video. It shows Gus Shaver with his penis wedged in a toilet cubicle wall!'

Isabella and Choco Chocs Doreen rushed to peer over Tuppence's shoulder as she played the video clip. It clearly showed Gus Shaver on a stretcher, with his engorged penis wedged in a cut-out section of a toilet cubicle partition.

'I knew there was something deviant about him the moment I saw him,' said Choco Chocs Doreen. 'When you are a renowned TV star and acclaimed locum thespian/director, you pick up on these things.'

Isabella was incensed. 'I shall have words with your father, Tuppence! How could he let a depraved man like that guide your career?!' She immediately called Richard Crow on his private number, which she had insisted he should give her because they were to be family.

When he answered, Richard Crow sounded depressed. 'Hello, Isabella.'

'Did you know that the man you employed to guide your daughter is a wicked pervert who shoves his penis in a… What was it called again, Tuppence?'

'A glory hole.'

'That man put his penis in a glory hole and got it wedged! Now, that, Richard, is disgusting and the work of the devil. I just hope Mary is not looking down.'

'I knew about that,' sighed Richard.

'Do my ears deceive me?! You knew that this Satan worshipper was thrusting his manhood into glory holes?! They should call them gory holes because it is disgusting, against nature and depraved!'

'But Gus is good at what he does—'

'Good at what he does?! That cubicle sodomite recommended your daughter and my son take part in an amateurish TV production in a churchyard, yes, a CHURCHYARD! And now, thanks to that disciple of the devil, my precious Archie is having a tizzy fit!'

340

'Gus assured me that this TV event would thrust Tuppence and Archie on to the front pages.'

'The only thrusting that heathen knows about involves a hole in a public toilet cubicle. I demand you fire the degenerate immediately. If Mary were alive, she would have died of shock!'

'Okay, I'll call him, but Tuppence can't then come running to me, complaining about not being a big enough celebrity.'

'Make sure you do fire him immediately, because if I come face to face with that pervert, I might well succumb to a tizzy fit of my own.' Isabella hung up. 'Sorry if I was short with your father, Tuppence, but it had to be said.'

On another day, Gus would have been disappointed to be fired, but now he could not care less. He had a new job offer, an offer that would take him back to the States and the sleazy world of politics which had always been his dream. A Republican presidential nominee with a reputation for infidelity, bullying and bullshitting wanted Gus as his press secretary. His work clearing the name of a politician caught sniffing coke off two naked rent boys had been hailed as genius, and he was now back in big demand. The sooner he could leave this stupid country with its dumb-ass class system, the better.

'Can I see the video of the glory hole?' asked Archie.

'Not while you're having a tizzy fit,' said Isabella. 'Seeing that obscene filth would be too traumatic for your delicate nature.'

'Why did he put his willy in a hole in the wall?' said Archie.

'Because he's a disgusting, depraved, wicked, perverted man,' replied Isabella. 'And because of his sinful behaviour, he will not be allowed to go to the lovely farm.'

'In light of this new information,' said Choco Chocs Doreen, 'it may be wise to reconsider letting Tuppence and Archie take part in this ghost lovers dance, because it could well be a satanic ritual for perverts. I'm sorry, Isabella, but I cannot stand by and let these two talents be used to open up the gates of hell, so deviants can indulge in depraved sexual activities!'

'I agree with Choc Chocs Doreen,' said Tuppence. 'This ghost lovers dance is the most stupidest idea anyone has come up with. Dancing in a churchyard? My social media fans don't want to see me dancing with my beloved Archie among dead people.'

Archie heard the phrase, 'dead people' and fell back into his tizzy fit. 'Lovely farm, not ground… Lovely farm, not ground.'

'I'm going to see that director right now,' declared Isabella. 'I'll tell her that Tuppence and my Archie will not be taking part in this sinful witchery!'

'I'll come with you,' insisted Choco Chocs Doreen. 'As a renowned TV star and acclaimed locum thespian/director, I know how to deal with these people.'

Before she left, Isabella put her hand on Archie's forehead. 'His temperature's all in a tizzy as well. Tuppence, dear, call the chauffeur to come and collect us, and on the way back, we'll take Archie to a private hospital for a check-up.'

Audrey the director was talking to Pepe when she spotted Mrs Billings and the thespian parasite striding towards her.

She gave a sigh; no doubt there was going to be another problem to deal with.

Just as Isabella opened her mouth, Audrey said in a tired voice, 'What is it this time?'

'I wish to inform you that Tuppence and my Archie will take no further part in this pagan ghost lovers dance,' sneered Isabella.

Choco Chocs Doreen nodded her head in agreement. 'As a renowned TV star and acclaimed locum thespian/director, I have never come across such an amateurish production as this! No renowned thespian like myself would lower themselves to take part in such satanic perversion! No wonder Archie had a tizzy fit; his charisma was fluctuating wildly in the face of all the depravity!'

'They have a contract,' said Audrey. 'They can't just drop out at the last minute. We go live in just over an hour.'

'When the contract is with the devil, you certainly can drop out at the last minute!' snapped Isabella.

'I have contacts in the world of theatre because of my work as a renowned TV star and acclaimed locum thespian/director,' added Choco Chocs Doreen, 'and I can assure you that you will never work with top talent like Archie and Tuppence ever again!'

Isabella nodded in agreement. 'Come on, Choco Chocs Doreen. Let's leave this pagan festival of debauchery. The sooner we get Tuppence and my delicate Archie away from this place, the better.'

Audrey watched them arrogantly strut away. 'Fuck! Where am I going to find replacements now?'

'I think I might have a celebrity for the dance,' said Pepe. 'He's a friend of Zibby's. He visited her earlier today. There's a chance he might still be here.'

'Who are you talking about?' asked Audrey.

'Tolly Pipkin.'

Audrey had read all the tabloid headlines about how Tolly Pipkin had upset the middle classes, but what interested her more was the talk of the blacklisted actor's performance in *The Waiting Room*. In fact, she had heard about it everywhere she went in showbiz circles, and several people she knew claimed to have witnessed it first-hand. The opportunity to say that she had directed Tolly Pipkin could well be a feather in her cap. 'Let's find Zibby.'

After forty minutes of waiting, Tolly was about to give up and call a cab when a bus finally came trundling round the corner. As he put his arm out to request it to stop, he heard Zibby's voice calling him.

'Tolly, wait!'

He turned around and saw Zibby in the passenger seat of a golf buggy, which was being driven by a woman wearing a paisley silk scarf.

The bus pulled up and opened its doors. The bored male bus driver gave Tolly a blank stare and said, 'Are you getting on or what?'

'One moment, please,' said Tolly.

Zibby jumped out of the golf buggy and dashed over to him. 'Tolly, we need your help.'

'My help?'

'Audrey will explain,' said Zibby.

Tolly then saw Audrey clambering out of the driver's seat of the golf buggy and hurrying over.

'Tolly, I hate to drop this on you at such short notice, but I need a celebrity to fill in for Tuppence Crow. She's pulled out at the last minute, and all our advertising has mentioned a surprise celebrity guest dancer.'

'I'm not a celebrity,' said Tolly. 'I'm a nobody.'

'Are you getting on or what?' demanded the driver, checking his watch.

'One second,' said Tolly. He turned back to Audrey. 'If I was introduced as a celebrity, people would feel short-changed.'

'That may be true, but you're the closest thing I have to one.'

'Please do it, Tolly,' begged Zibby. 'The dance is going to be really special. I feel a real connection with the ghost lovers and so will many others. It has heart.'

'I recognise you!' said the bus driver, pointing at Tolly. 'You played that psycho nutter and pissed off people who like tennis. My wife was bloody furious with you; she loves watching the Great British Tennis Club tournament.'

'See, Tolly?' said Audrey, with a smile. 'You are a sort of celebrity.'

'Say I did say yes,' said Tolly, 'who would I be dancing with?'

'We'll find someone,' said Audrey.

Tolly looked into Zibby's pleading eyes. He could see that she was truly passionate about the project. 'I'll do it if you do it with me, Zibby.'

'Me? No, no, no.'

'She'll do it,' said Audrey brusquely. 'Driver, you can close the doors and go. Now, for fuck's sake, let's hurry!' Audrey rushed back to the golf buggy.

'I can see why she's a director,' said Tolly.

With Tolly and Zibby on board and Audrey at the wheel, the golf buggy hurtled towards the village green.

'Don't you want to know if I can dance?' asked Tolly, hanging on for dear life.

'It doesn't matter,' shouted Audrey. 'I don't care if you just stand there and let Zibby dance.'

They skidded to a halt beside the broadcasting trucks, and Audrey immediately began barking out orders to her waiting assistants. Zibby was whisked away in one direction and Tolly was rushed away to the costume truck where he was rapidly dressed in Archie's white suit with tails. Next, he was hurried over to the make-up truck where two young women worked simultaneously to give his face and hands a ghostly pallor. Once his new look was complete, he was pushed back into the golf buggy and whizzed up to Saint Mary's church.

Pepe was waiting for him at the access point in the temporary fencing, and smiled with relief when he saw Tolly dressed in his ghostly attire. 'Come with me. We go live in ten minutes.'

Tolly followed Pepe into a broadcasting truck on the shingle drive. Inside, Audrey sat with several colleagues in front of a dozen monitors, all showing different camera angles.

'He's ready,' said Pepe, moving to one side, so the director could see Tolly in his outfit.

'You look the part,' said Audrey approvingly. 'Just let Zibby do the dancing, and with any luck we'll get away with it.'

'How does it all play out?' asked Tolly.

'It's a forty-minute programme. There'll be presenters in a London studio who will introduce and explain the ghost lovers dance. Ten minutes before the dance begins, they'll cut live to us here. Zibby will fill you in on what to do.'

'I know it's all last minute,' said Pepe, 'but you'll be fine. Zibby's with you, she'll guide you.'

'Okay,' said Audrey. 'Go break a leg, Tolly, but please don't do it for real until after the dance.'

346

Pepe led Tolly past the couples waiting to enter the churchyard and along the side of the church until they came to the two yew trees. Zibby was already waiting there, catching her breath after her own rushed makeover.

Tolly stopped in his tracks when he saw Zibby. She was dressed in a stunning, off-the-shoulder, white satin ballgown with white elbow-length gloves. The gown was full skirted and nearly touched the ground. Her make-up gave her the same ghostly pallor as him and highlighted her beautiful cheekbones.

'Are you okay, Zibby?' asked Pepe urgently.

Zibby took a deep breath. 'If I can do exotic dancing in Soho on a nightly basis, I can do this.'

Pepe smiled. 'You'll be wonderful, Zibby. There's no other dancer I'd rather have doing it. Tolly, best of luck, just be guided by Zibby and you'll be great.'

Zibby appraised her dance partner in his white tailed suit and spectral make-up. He looked truly dashing in the outfit.

'I'll leave you two to it,' said Pepe. 'I need to get back to the other couples.' He headed off behind the two yew trees, leaving them alone.

'You look amazing,' said Tolly. He wanted to say she was the most beautiful thing he had ever seen.

'You make a good ghost yourself,' replied Zibby, thinking that he looked so handsome. 'Did Audrey explain how things go?'

'Yes, we pretty much wait for the spotlight to hit us.'

'That's right. The music will start, and I'll dance in front of you. The cameras won't be focusing on us long. The dancing couples will be lit up and start dancing together. When the music stops, we go into darkness.'

'Got it,' said Tolly. He noticed Zibby's hand was shaking and held it. 'Don't worry, I won't cock it up for you.'

'I just want it to be as wonderful as the version in my head.'

'You really have a thing about these ghost lovers, don't you?'

A voice on a loudspeaker counted down the final seconds to the start of the live transmission from the church. It was to be hosted by one of the witnesses of the ghost dancers, Reverend Nancy Dickens.

For the occasion, Reverend Nancy had opted to wear her smart civilian clothes: a long black dress, a white shawl and a pearl necklace. From a distance, they looked very much like her work clothes.

Tolly and Zibby could see a large screen a short distance away showing Nancy's introduction.

'Welcome to Saint Mary's church, the home of the ghost dancers. I have had the good fortune of being the vicar in this parish for the last fourteen years, and along with two colleagues, I witnessed the ghost lovers dancing here, in this very churchyard, on this very night twelve years ago. I can't promise that the ghost lovers will turn up tonight. All I can say is that if they do, they will not be dancing alone.'

Tolly turned away from the screen to look at Zibby. She noticed him staring.

'Is my hair okay?' she said checking for loose curls.

'I… I just want to remember this moment with you.'

Zibby turned away. 'Strange thing to say to a friend.'

'You're not just a friend.'

'What am I then?'

'You're a beautiful, wonderful person.'

'You forgot to say your friend's sister.'

'I wish you weren't my friend's sister,' sighed Tolly.

Zibby turned to look at Tolly. 'You wish I wasn't?'

'If I wasn't your brother's friend, then you… you might see me differently, not just as… another brother.'

'Hold on,' said Zibby. 'You're the one who sees me as a sister.'

'No, no. You're the one who sees me as a brother.'

In the dim light, they peered at each other's dumbfounded expressions.

'I've been worrying about making you feel uncomfortable because I thought my feelings for you were too obvious,' confessed Tolly.

Zibby smiled. 'I thought you were being aloof because I was just a sister to you.'

Tolly smiled back and held her hand. 'We're not blood relatives. We're free spirits, and we can do as we please.'

'Just two people.'

'Just two people,' agreed Tolly. 'Just us, here, alone.'

Zibby squeezed his hand and smiled. 'We're not exactly alone; we have company.'

Tolly glanced around, expecting to see someone. 'Where?'

Zibby looked at the names on the closest gravestones. 'We have the company of loving husband Shirley Winston Heep – an odd name for a man, but there you go – and the Honourable Alfred Islington-Hughes.'

Tolly stared at the names as though in a trance and whispered, 'It can't be.'

'Tolly, are you okay?' Zibby watched him kneel down and wipe away years of fine dirt from one headstone to reveal the inscription, *He was gifted by God to be richer and better than his fellow men.*

Zibby leant down and read it over Tolly's shoulder. She chuckled. 'My God, he must've thought a lot of himself.'

Tolly spun round and stared at the name on the other gravestone; it definitely belonged to loving husband Shirley Winston Heep. 'No, no, no.'

'Tolly, what is it?'

He felt as though his head was about to implode. 'Zibby, I've been here before.'

35

Twelve years ago

It was a Saturday afternoon when Tolly first found out that the woman who had briefly fostered him was dead. He had been invited to his friend Sam's house to keep him company because his little sister was having a sleepover, and the house would be full of screaming ten-year-old girls.

He and Sam took refuge in the sitting room, along with Sam's grandfather, Charlie, whose tinnitus was struggling to cope with the girls screaming and giggling in the other rooms.

As Tolly and his friend played video games on the TV, Charlie sat down in the armchair and leisurely browsed the death notices page in the local paper.

'Well, I never! Guess who's dead!' said Charlie, pointing to a section of the page he was reading.

Sam shrugged. 'Who?'

'Bobby Allen!'

'Who's Bobby Allen?' asked Sam, not taking his eyes off the TV screen.

'I worked with him for ten years at the paint factory. He had a funny eye. Always cycled everywhere, fit as a fiddle, he was. Well, before that bus drove into him, he was.'

Tolly and Sam glanced at each other and chuckled.

'Oh! Well, I never! Guess who else is dead!' said Charlie. 'Go on, guess!'

351

'I don't know, Grandpa,' sighed Sam.

'Tommy Burns! I used to go to school with his sister. Always had nits, she did.'

Charlie enthusiastically searched for more names he recognised. He found it uplifting to discover someone he knew had popped their clogs before him. 'Well, I never! Guess who's dead!'

'Grandpa, I don't know!' groaned Sam.

'I'll tell you then. Beryl Buckler! God, she was a nasty one at school. A right bully.'

'Grandpa!' pleaded Sam. 'We're trying to play a game!'

Charlie chuckled. 'I saw her once years ago, butchering an Elvis song down the pub when they had a karaoke night. What a racket she made!'

'Oh, Grandpa, I just lost because you put me off,' complained Sam.

'All right,' sniffed Charlie. 'I won't say another word.' He went back to perusing the deaths with a smile on his face. 'Well, I never! Guess who's dead!'

Hearing the name of Beryl Buckler had given Tolly a shock. Later in the evening, he managed to get hold of Charlie's paper and found out the time and place of the funeral. On the day it was due to take place, he made a decision to go, and found the church on a local map.

His aunt Wendy often used the phrase, 'I'll dance on their grave' when someone died who she did not like. With that in mind, he decided to go and dance on Beryl Buckler's grave. He did not mention his plan to his aunt because he knew she would talk him out of going, and urge him to forget about the past. On the day of the funeral, he skipped school in the afternoon and, still wearing his uniform, waited at the bus stop by the entrance, which he knew was on the bus route to the village where the memorial service was taking place.

When the small bus eventually turned up, Tolly found he was the only passenger and felt obliged to reply to the asthmatic bus driver's constant chat.

'Funeral, you say?' wheezed the driver, whose name badge said *Colin*.

'Yes, at the church in the next village.'

'Religion! Ha, it's all bollocks,' said Colin, puffing on his inhaler as the bus took a sharp turn. 'Thems-at-top want the human race to be religious, so they can control us!'

Tolly had no answer to that because he did not know what the bus driver was going on about.

'Thems-at-top don't want you to know the world is flat either!' Colin the bus driver said it as though revealing an obvious truth. 'It can't be round, can it? I mean you take water,' – he pronounced it as *wort-er* – 'it always lays flat, don't it?'

Tolly felt the driver's eyes on him in the rear-view mirror. 'I suppose so.'

'Well, there you go then! How can it go round corners if it's flat?! See?! It's all a lie by Thems-at-top, and it's being taught in schools! Luckily, I was expelled from mine, so I never got brainwashed with their lies.'

The driver puffed on his inhaler again. 'You take them moon landings, they was all false,' he added, 'knocked up in a film studio by Thems-at-top.'

Tolly was quite sure even at his young age that the world was round, and the moon landings had happened. 'Really?'

'That's why I ended up being a bus driver,' said Colin defiantly, puffing on his inhaler again. 'Thems-at-top know that I knew what they want everyone else not to know.'

Tolly felt Colin's eyes staring at him again.

'I could've been a bus inspector,' he wheezed, 'but once Thems-at-top found out that I knew what they didn't want me to know, the door to promotion was slammed in my face!'

Tolly felt a bit scared of the driver now and opted not to say anything.

'Alien reptiles!' exclaimed Colin. 'Thems-at-top are alien reptiles controlling the human race with lies.'

Tolly thought about everything the lunatic driver had said so far. 'What do the alien reptiles get out of it?' he asked out of curiosity. 'What if the world is flat and there were no moon landings, how do alien reptiles benefit from not revealing all that? What do they get out of it?

'Well, er, well…'

Thankfully for Tolly, the bus pulled up at a stop by the village green.

Colin was still stammering, 'Er, well…' when he opened the bus doors out of habit.

Tolly stepped down on to the road and said, 'Thank you,' to the bus driver, who was still desperately trying to think of a reason why the alien reptiles would do all this.

The funeral service had already started by the time Tolly reached the church. One of the pall-bearers near the entrance, who was rubbing his back and wincing, assured Tolly it was okay for him to go in. He crept into the ancient building and received a disapproving stare from a large woman dressed in a long-skirted black suit who was standing just inside the door. He sat down in the nearest pew and noticed the female vicar also giving him a brief glance before she continued with the service.

After Beryl Buckler was eventually put in the ground, with the help of firefighters, Tolly watched from a distance as two gravediggers hurriedly began to fill the hole up with dirt.

The weather had changed by the time the grave had been filled, turning overcast and gloomy. A ground mist began to form. Once Tolly was sure he was alone in the churchyard, he went over to the pile of flowers that now covered the fresh grave. He stared down as if trying to see through the blooms and the dirt. Then, after another glance around to make sure that he really was alone, he moved some of the wreaths and stepped on to Beryl's grave. He stood there, satisfied that she was six feet under him, then slowly began to dance. The imaginary tune in his head played faster and faster, so he matched it with quicker and quicker steps. He started to cry, remembering the cruel way she had treated him when he had just wanted to be loved. 'I'm glad you're dead! Dead! Dead!'

His dancing was interrupted by a voice. 'What are you doing?'

Tolly froze. He turned to see a little old lady in a cream coat, holding a watering can.

'She was cruel to me when I was five years old,' explained Tolly, wiping the tears from his eyes. 'So, in revenge, I'm dancing on her grave.'

The woman thought for a moment about what the boy had said and nodded as though it made perfect sense. She smiled. 'Good for you.'

Tolly grinned sheepishly.

'How does it feel?' she asked out of curiosity. 'Does it make you feel happier?'

'It does,' sniffled Tolly, wiping his nose on his blazer sleeve. 'It feels like… like something that was hurting me has gone away.'

The lady nodded her head thoughtfully. 'It must feel wonderful to be rid of that pain. Hurt eats away at you like a disease.' She gave Tolly a sad smile. 'You carry on. Don't let me stop you dancing.' Clasping the heavy watering can with both hands, she shuffled away.

'Let me help you,' offered Tolly, stepping off Beryl's grave. He took the heavy watering can from the woman, using both hands to carry it.

The little old lady led him to a section of the churchyard that had herringbone brick paving on the paths. 'My husband was buried here sixteen years ago.' She spoke the words without emotion.

The graves in this area were showy and ornate. Tolly noticed a small metal sign with the words, *VIP sacred ground.*

'What does that mean?'

The little old lady sighed. 'VIP means very important person, but believe me, no one's more important than anyone else. Everyone buried in this section was arrogant and selfish,' she explained. 'They had been giving money to the church to guarantee their place in heaven and threatened to stop the funds unless they had their own section in the churchyard where they didn't have to lie for eternity next to common people.'

Tolly could not help giggling.

'I know,' said the little old lady, with a smile. 'It's ridiculous, isn't it?' She stopped by a raised black granite slab with a matching headstone. Tolly read the inscription.

The Honourable Alfred Islington-Hughes. He was gifted by God to be richer and better than his fellow men.

'He was a vain man,' said the little old lady, reading Tolly's thoughts.

Tolly noticed there were no flowers or plants on the grave. 'What's this water for?'

The little old lady pointed to an ancient slab of flat sandstone nearby where the name of the occupant had long since worn away. Over the centuries, a large, shallow bowl shape had appeared. 'The birds and animals drink from there, so I just top it up with fresh water and give it a clean every now and then.'

Tolly spotted a smile of pride on her face when she stared at the old sandstone slab.

'He was cruel to me,' said the little old lady, the smile dropping from her face as she turned back to her husband's grave. 'Alfred used to hit me. He was a controlling, unkind, heartless man.'

Tolly was taken by surprise. He felt too young to know how to respond to something like this.

'We were happy at the beginning,' she said, 'but as the years passed, he began to hate me for not giving him a son, not a living one anyway. You know, I never shed a tear when he died. I was pleased.'

'Oh, dear,' was all Tolly could think to say.

'I wish I could get rid of the hurt inside of me. It blackens my soul.' She turned to Tolly. 'Do you think dancing on his grave would make my hurt go away?'

Tolly shrugged his shoulders. 'You could give it a try.'

The old lady hesitated for a moment, then stepped over to Alfred's grave. Putting one hand on the headstone to steady herself, she carefully stepped on to the black granite slab.

Tolly spotted her wobble, so he put down the watering can and rushed over to offer her his hand. 'I think it might be safer if I get on with you.' He stepped on to the black granite slab and held both her hands.

The lady smiled. 'He hated the waltz,' she said, before humming the *Blue Danube*. She began to sway. Tolly knew the music, it was used in the film *2001*, which he had watched numerous times because it was a favourite of Wendy's. He started to hum along with the little old lady and nervously chuckled at how ridiculous it must look. The old lady was smiling and breathing heavily. She held on tightly to Tolly's arms to steady herself. 'I do feel better for doing this,' she said, with a smile. 'It's as though a dark weight is being lifted off me.'

'That's good,' said Tolly. He noticed that her face now looked younger.

'What's your name?' she asked.

Tolly hesitated. If his auntie Wendy found out that he had skipped school, he would be in trouble. 'It's er…' Panicking that he was taking too long to answer, Tolly glanced around and caught sight of a gravestone close by that had the words *Beloved husband* carved on it. He read the engraved name that followed. 'It's Shirley.' Tolly cursed his luck. Out of all the headstones, he had chosen the one with the weird name.

'Shirley? That's an unusual name for a boy.'

'I know,' was all he could think to say.

'My name is Dorcas. It's a pleasure to meet you, Shirley. I just wish I'd thought of dancing on his grave before.'

She stumbled, held Tolly closer for support, and continued humming the *Blue Danube*, as they danced in a slow circle.

A noise from the rear of the churchyard ended their moment. 'Someone's coming,' whispered Tolly. He stepped off the black granite slab stone carefully because the thickening mist now hid the ground below. He then helped the little old lady step down.

They heard several whispered voices. 'This way, Shirley,' said the little old lady. 'There's bound to be some rule against dancing on graves.'

Tolly was surprised at how quickly she now walked compared to earlier. She led him through the graves to a shingle car park beside the church. Through the trees, in the distance, he could just make out a bus approaching the village green. 'I have to go now,' he said, ready to dash away.

Dorcas clasped his hands. 'Thank you, Shirley. I don't think you realise how much you've helped me today.' For months, she had done nothing but contemplate how miserable and pointless her existence was, but now, because this boy had helped release the years of pent-up hate inside her, she could see a future.

The sound of nearby voices made Dorcas let go of Tolly's hand as she turned towards them.

Now free, Tolly sprinted away towards the bus stop, running between the trees as fast as his legs would carry him, praying he would catch the bus and not have to explain to Wendy what he had done.

As the voices faded, Dorcas turned to speak to the boy, but he had mysteriously disappeared.

36

The ghost dancers

Tolly stared at the name on the gravestone under the words *Beloved husband*. He felt as though his head was about to implode. 'Zibby, I've danced in this very spot once before.'

Zibby stared at Tolly, wondering if he had gone crazy. 'What are you talking about?'

He briefly told her the tale of how he had gone to his foster mother's funeral service when he was twelve years old with the idea of dancing on her grave because of the way she had treated him, the little old lady who had caught him, and her desire to dance on her husband's grave.

He pointed to the black granite slab for the Honourable Alfred Islington-Hughes. '…and when she stepped up to dance her hate away, she nearly fell over, so I stepped up and danced with her. She would have fallen over otherwise.'

'Did anyone see you?'

'We heard voices, but I don't think so.'

'You say you were twelve?'

Tolly nodded. 'I'm sure I was. That was the year I went to Australia with Wendy.'

'You're twenty-four now and we are about to celebrate the twelfth anniversary of the ghost dancers being sighted.' Zibby sighed. 'You and the old lady must have been spotted. My God, Tolly, you are one of the ghost dancers!'

Tolly could not miss her look of disappointment even through her ghostly make-up. 'I can't be! It's just a coincidence.'

Zibby felt disheartened. Something that she had believed proved true love could continue over the mists of time was just a silly romantic fantasy. 'It's a shame really. I wanted to believe in the ghost lovers.'

'The ghost lovers were around long before I was born,' said Tolly, hoping to make amends for shattering her dream. 'If they exist, they're still here.'

The couples were introduced by Reverend Nancy. Looking elegant and impressive in their outfits, they slowly began to enter the churchyard. Once in their designated places, each couple took their dance positions. Thick dry ice started to flow between the gravestones, spreading its misty tendrils among the dancers and setting an eerie mood.

Zibby peered into Tolly's apologetic eyes and smiled. 'I would never have thought in a million years that I would end up waltzing with a real ghost dancer.'

There was a moment of silence before Reverend Nancy Dickens said, in a loud, commanding voice, 'Let the ghost dance begin!'

The lights slowly dimmed, as though a shadow was falling over the churchyard and its swirling ground mist.

The first notes of the *Blue Danube* began to play.

'When the spotlight hits us, look as ghostlike as you can,' Zibby instructed Tolly, 'and I'll dance in front of you.'

Tolly clasped her hand.

'What are you doing?'

'I want to make it up to you. I can dance the waltz. I've been watching the rehearsals, so I know what to do.' He could not help but notice Zibby's doubtful look. 'I did ballroom dancing when I was in Australia, and my agent

361

made me take dance lessons to increase my chances of work. Trust me, I can do it.'

'Because you're a real ghost dancer?' laughed Zibby.

'Yes, so let's do it properly.' He quickly stepped on to the black granite slab and helped her up to join him. He held her right hand with his left, and placed his right hand on the small of her back. The music was coming to the end of its twenty-second introduction. A bright spotlight picked them out in their white outfits. Their new elevated position gave the illusion that they really were floating on the swirling mist. The sudden surprise of seeing these two ghostly figures poised and ready to dance caused a number of gasps from the watching audience.

Zibby counted Tolly in to the start of the waltz. 'We go in three… two… one.'

They began to waltz in time with the music. Zibby was amazed at how wonderful Tolly's dancing was, and felt goosebumps on her skin as she gazed into his pale face, almost glowing in the light.

The twenty-five other dancing couples, in their pastel colours, were now synchronised with the ghostly figures in white, and lights on the ground lit up the dry ice from below, adding to the churchyard's unworldly feel.

Audrey directed the camera shots from the monitors in the broadcasting truck, delighted with what she was seeing.

Zibby had never felt as close to Tolly as she did at that moment. They waltzed in a tight circle, and she wished it would last more than just four minutes.

The music soared to a crescendo.

'Get ready to stop,' said Zibby. 'We freeze in three… two… one.'

The music stopped abruptly. Tolly and Zibby hit the finish perfectly. They stood gazing into each other's eyes.

Tolly leant forward and kissed Zibby on the lips; she kissed him back, pulling him close. Taking their cue from the ghost dancers, the other couples did the same as the lights went out.

'Give me a thermal shot from the drone,' barked Audrey. On screen, the ghostly figures of the couples began to break from their embraces. The two ghost dancers were still kissing. 'Let's finish with the thermal image of them kissing. Zoom in… What the fuck?'

Three figures were crawling towards the ghost dancers from different directions. 'Who the fuck is ruining my thermal drone shot?!' demanded Audrey.

Tolly reluctantly stopped kissing Zibby. 'Why don't you come with me to Australia?'

Zibby had had a crush on Tolly when she was just a little girl, always showing off in front of him and being loud. Now, as a grown woman, she had fallen in love with him. 'I'd like that.'

They stepped down from the stone slab. Tolly smiled shyly, and as he leant forward to kiss her again, he caught a glimpse out of the corner of his eye of figures rushing towards him.

Zibby screamed as Tolly was tackled to the ground by three men wearing tinfoil bandanas.

'You're not beaming anywhere!' said Colin Chapman.

'What's going on?' demanded Zibby. 'Who are you?'

Colin stood up, leaving Eddie and Derek to keep hold of Tolly. He clambered up on to the black stone slab of the Honourable Alfred Islington-Hughes, stood in a defiant pose that he had practised in the mirror over the years and raised a revolutionary fist. Knowing that the cameras were

363

on him, he launched into the speech that he had also practised in front of the bedroom mirror at the same time as the defiant pose.

'We are the bona fide members of Conspiracies-are-true,' wheezed Colin. 'And we now have evidence that the world is run by alien reptiles in human form!'

He pointed at Tolly struggling to free himself. 'I have posted online video evidence of this alien reptile beaming up to a mothership!'

'Are you fucking nuts?' said Tolly, still struggling to get free.

'The human race will never be slaves to alien reptiles,' continued Colin, 'because we have something those cold-blooded creatures don't have – human intelligence! And that's why the flat world will never be dominated by them.' He puffed on his inhaler. 'To find out more, buy my book, *Thems-at-top*, only available through the Conspiracies-are-true website, at the bargain price of £25.99 plus postage and packaging!'

Now, it was Colin's turn to be wrestled to the ground – by two large security men. He managed to wriggle free and ran towards the nearest camera, grasping its lens and staring into it.

'The world is flat, men never went to the moon, and the lies are all coordinated by alien reptiles in human form!'

The security men soon had Colin in their grasp again, straining to release the camera from his grip, but he kept ranting down the lens.

Two more security personnel turned up and finally helped their colleagues prise Colin's fingers from the camera.

'The alien reptiles will never win!' shouted Colin, as he was put in an armlock. 'Because humans like us want to know the truth, even if it isn't there to find out.' As one final protest as he was dragged away, Colin hollered, 'The truth is a lie, the lies are a lie, and that is the truth!'

Five months later

Zibby stood in the wings of the theatre, watching Tolly recite the final soliloquy from *The Waiting Room*. She had watched every performance since the very first night in Sydney and still felt the hairs go up on the back of her neck. From the start of the tour of the vast country, *The Waiting Room* had played to packed houses wherever it was performed. Despite no one having a clue what the play was about, the audiences were generous and held Tolly in high regard, not just because of the Australian connection, but because he was talented, blacklisted, despised by the English middle classes and possibly an alien reptile in human form, although the jury was still out on that one.

Since the day of the ghost dance, Tolly and Zibby had been inseparable. With two months left of the tour, Tolly was already certain that he never wanted to play Sid in the all-out-shit play ever again. Zibby's own plans to teach dance were on hold for a while, but she would definitely be heading back to Little Takeham in July to help at the next ghost lovers dance.

The ghost lovers experience had made Zibby wonder whether true love really could endure through the mists of time. Now that she and Tolly were a couple there was no longer any doubt in her mind: it would last forever.

Epilogue

By a cruel twist of coincidence and his own stupidity, Gus Shaver revisited the public toilet that had been the scene of his original humiliation and found the freshly bored glory hole in the cubicle wall too much of a temptation. Once again, he inserted himself up to the hilt, unaware that it had been drilled by the same DIY enthusiast as the first one. Gus now resides in Canada under a different name.

Colin Champion found himself in great demand in America as a speaker on the conspiracy theories circuit. His talks to the flat-earthers, the moon-landing deniers and the reptilian elite believers have made him a conspiracist superstar. After every talk, Colin sells signed copies of his book *Thems-at-top* for the bargain price of $29.99.

Tuppence Crow and Archie Billings went on to become a popular celebrity couple after a TV company made a show about the build-up to their wedding. They appear regularly on TV celebrity shows and are now in talks about starring in a follow-up reality series called *Extremely Rich and Married*.

Choco Chocs Doreen now runs an acting academy, thanks to the very generous support of her best friend, Isabella. The Choco Chocs Doreen thespian technique involves teaching students the art of absorbing and projecting intentions. So far, none of her pupils have found any acting work.

Suzanne Fisher's hopes of finding a client who would be her pension were given a boost when Tolly called her out of the blue and asked her to be his agent again. She has received offers from numerous casting directors and is looking forward to finally representing an A-list client.

Dorcas Islington-Hughes moved away from Little Takeham six months after dancing on her husband's grave and pledged the rest of her life and vast wealth to good causes. She started the Shirley Children's Charity which over the years has raised millions of pounds for deprived children around the world. Over the years, she had suspected that Shirley might be an actual ghost, sent to help her in her hour of need. Now nearing her ninetieth birthday, Dorcas caught the end of the ghost lovers dance on TV. As the camera zoomed in on the two central figures, something about the man reminded her of Shirley, her own ghost dancer.

The end

Printed in Great Britain
by Amazon